Select praise for author Sophia Singh Sasson

"This is the first book in Sophia Singh Sasson's *Nights at the Mahal* series, and I just fell in love with her world. There is deep research and there is innate knowledge, and Sasson skillfully blends the two in her memorable worldbuilding."

—*Frolic* on *Marriage by Arrangement*

"How [the author] created a multicultural and interracial romance is fantastic. The book is well written and balanced with solid arguments, well described settings and powerful scenes."

—*Harlequin Junkie* on *Boyfriend Lessons*

"*Marriage by Arrangement* by Sophia Singh Sasson is an...enjoyable romance from an author to watch."

—*Fresh Fiction*

"*Marriage by Arrangement* is a fun tale that sizzles with intensity, drama and pathos and it's one which will have contemporary romance fans adding Sophia Singh Sasson's name to their auto-buy list."

—*Bookish Jottings*

An excerpt from *The Texan's Secrets* by Barbara Dunlop

Nick squeezed her hand. "I think you're secretly a wild rose."

Emilia's heart skipped because it came close to the truth. She had an untamed streak, something deep inside her that liked to shake things up. She was trying to tamp it down, but she still loved the thrill of going rogue.

"What about you?" she asked.

"What about me?" He turned to face her.

"Wild or tame?"

He gazed into her eyes, rose-colored light on the planes of his face. "I wish I could say tame."

"Why?"

"It's safer than wild."

Her heartbeat deepened and her skin warmed with an undeniable sexual attraction.

"If I was tame..." He slowly lifted a hand to her cheek, then slid spread fingers into her hair. "I'd behave myself right now."

"Where's the fun in that?" she whispered, tipping her chin to a better angle.

He gave another low chuckle and brought his mouth to hers.

SOPHIA SINGH SASSON

&

NEW YORK TIMES BESTSELLING AUTHOR

BARBARA DUNLOP

PATERNITY PAYBACK
&
THE TEXAN'S SECRETS

DESIRE

Special thanks and acknowledgment are given to Sophia Singh Sasson and Barbara Dunlop for their contributions to the Texas Cattleman's Club: Diamonds & Dating Apps miniseries.

Recycling programs for this product may not exist in your area.

ISBN-13: 978-1-335-45790-5

Paternity Payback & The Texan's Secrets

Copyright © 2023 by Harlequin Enterprises ULC

Paternity Payback
Copyright © 2023 by Harlequin Enterprises ULC

The Texan's Secrets
Copyright © 2023 by Harlequin Enterprises ULC

For questions and comments about the quality of this book, please contact us at CustomerService@Harlequin.com.

Harlequin Enterprises ULC
22 Adelaide St. West, 41st Floor
Toronto, Ontario M5H 4E3, Canada
www.Harlequin.com

Printed in U.S.A.

CONTENTS

Sophia Singh Sasson puts her childhood habit of daydreaming to good use by writing stories she wishes will give you hope and make you laugh, cry and possibly snort tea from your nose. She was born in Mumbai, India, has lived in Spain and Canada, and currently resides in Washington, DC. She loves to read, travel, bake, scuba dive, make candles and hear from readers. Visit her at sophiasasson.com.

Books by Sophia Singh Sasson

Harlequin Desire

Tempted by the Bollywood Star

Texas Cattleman's Club: Diamonds & Dating Apps

Paternity Payback

Nights at the Mahal

Marriage by Arrangement
Running Away with the Bride
Last Chance Reunion
Making a Marriage Deal

Visit the Author Profile page
at Harlequin.com for more titles.

You can also find Sophia Singh Sasson on Facebook,
along with other Harlequin Desire authors,
at Facebook.com/HarlequinDesireAuthors!

Dear Reader,

I am thrilled to share book seven in the Texas Cattleman's Club series. Jack and Willa's story is about two people who have been hurt in the past but find themselves given a second chance at love.

Jack and Willa have pasts that have left them feeling jaded and cautious. But as they're thrown together once again, they must learn to let go of their fears and trust in each other. As the story unfolds, I hope you will be swept away by the ups and downs of their journey, laugh and cry with them, and root for them as they navigate the challenges that love throws their way.

At its core, this is a story about the power of forgiveness, the importance of communication and the beauty of second chances.

Thank you for taking the time to read my book. I hope you enjoy it as much as I enjoyed writing it.

Hearing from readers makes my day, so please email me at Sophia@SophiaSasson.com, tag me on Twitter @sophiasasson, Instagram @sophia_singh_sasson or Facebook.com/authorsophiasasson, or find me on Goodreads, BookBub @sophiasinghsasson or my website, sophiasasson.com.

Love,

Sophia

PATERNITY PAYBACK

Sophia Singh Sasson

This book is dedicated to all those who need a second chance to make things right.

Acknowledgments

Thank you to the awesome Harlequin Desire editorial team.

It's lonely being an author but the amazing community of South Asian romance writers always keeps me going.

Last and most important, I wouldn't be an author without the love and support of my family.

One

"He's pimping you out, darling."

Willa tossed the empty Coke can in frustration, barely missing Rogerio's head. He caught it with ease and attempted to toss it into the nearby trash can, but it bounced off the rim and rolled across the floor.

Willa let out a heavy sigh, stood up from her rickety chair and picked up the can. She looked around the cramped office, shared by three other beat reporters. The gray walls and brownish carpet reflected her dark mood.

"David is not pimping me out. He's asked me to get close to Jack Chowdhry to get dirt on him. It's no different than getting close to a source to get information."

Are you trying to convince Rogerio or yourself? She didn't want to discuss this with Rogerio. It required her to think about what it would mean to see Jack again. The only way she was going to get through this assignment was to pretend that Jack was just another story.

Rogerio raised his brows. He was only slightly taller than her at five feet four, with black hair, brown eyes and one of those stocky builds that came from too much time spent on the weight machines in the gym. "He's your ex and your baby daddy. It's a lot more than working a source."

"Shhhh." Willa stood and quickly went to the office door to make sure no one was in listening range.

"Relax, everyone on this side is gone for the day. There's no one here to hear your deep, dark secret."

She rounded on Rogerio. "Listen to me. Only you and my sister know who Priya's father is. Jack Chowdhry doesn't even know I have a daughter, let alone that he's the father. I want to keep it that way. Understood?"

Rogerio stood and placed his hands on her shoulders. "Don't worry, your secret is safe with me." He dropped his voice. "Seriously, Willa, I don't think going to Royal is a good idea. David only cares about one thing—ratings. And he doesn't care who he uses to get them."

So what's new? It was her lot in life to have bosses who took advantage of her. At least David wasn't stabbing her in the back like Jack had; his slimy intentions were perfectly clear. "I don't have a choice. If I want to get out of the gossip beat, I need to get this story. I made a deal with David."

"You're a talented journalist. If it weren't for Jack, you'd be David's boss today. Give it time—the right story will come along."

She retook her seat behind the desk. She didn't need to be reminded of what Jack had done. Her last piece was on the best Christmas craft markets in the city. She'd gone from exposing dirty politicians to writing fluff pieces about New York socialites.

"I can't keep waiting for that. I'm thirty-seven years old. I've got to get my career on the right track. How hard can it be? A man like Jack has to have plenty of skeletons in his closet. I just need to find one good one and get out of there."

"That might be true, but I'm afraid that while you're looking in his closet, you'll end up in his bed."

A knot formed in her stomach. "That's something that will never happen." While she wouldn't have chosen to do a story on Jack, revealing his underhanded ways wasn't such a bad idea. The media loved him; he was the shrewd businessman who had built a media empire and had now turned into a philanthropic rancher. She didn't believe it for a second. If he was in Royal, it was to work on a scheme that would make him richer and more powerful. She couldn't wait to pull the curtain from the show he was putting on for everyone.

"Are you sure? Have you seen the guy?" Rogerio tapped on her laptop and held it up for her to see. Jack Chowdhry's face filled the screen. *Damn him.* She'd been following the Diamond Gate story but had avoided looking at Jack's images from the latest stories. He'd been instrumental in brokering peace in the infamous feud between the Del Rio and Winters families. The Del Rios had accused the Winters family of stealing their family's heirloom necklace—an accusation that had ig-

nited national attention when the impressive diamonds
were found on the ancestral Winters estate. Jack had
orchestrated a deal between the families that included
the return of the glittering necklace and compensation
for the theft. The necklace would be going on display at
the Texas Cattleman's Club soon and a sneak peek press
conference was happening tomorrow for the public to
not only see the famous necklace, but to also show the
feud was officially over. Jack was expected to be there
and it was Willa's job to use the ruse of the diamond
story to get close to Jack.

Get close but not too close, she reminded herself.
The goal was to reestablish herself as a serious journalist by exposing his farce. Destroying him was a side
benefit. She stared at the screen. How was it possible
that he'd gotten more handsome in the last five years?
He still had that cocky half smile that showed off his
dimples, the stubble that she could still feel on her skin
if she closed her eyes, and the slight curl in his hair that
twisted perfectly around her finger.

"I mean, look at that perfectly bronzed skin, those
bedroom eyes, that..."

"You're worried about me jumping his bones? I think
I'm going to keep my eye on you," she quipped. She
didn't need Rogerio pointing out how devastatingly
handsome Jack was.

"That's what I'm saying. A man as delicious as that,
you'd have to be made of stone not to get all hot and
bothered in his presence."

"The only thing his face reminds me of is how he
ruined my career. He knew how hard I'd worked on that

story—I risked my life for it and he gave all the credit to another reporter." She blew out a breath. "Jessica Danan is now a prime-time news anchor on CMG—her career took off after Jack handed her that story."

Rogerio stepped toward her and gave her a hug. "Oh, honey, you've got to stop thinking about what might've been. You are going to get back on top."

She nodded. Jack had tanked her career, and he would be the one to rocket it back to the top. "Let's get back to the business at hand. All the hotels in Royal are booked. I'll work on finding us a place to stay, you work on the air tickets. I need to get out of here and home to Priya."

"How are you going to keep her away from Jack?"

"I'm not taking her. Kylie agreed to watch her for me." Willa shared a brownstone with her sister, Kylie. Priya loved her aunt but she wouldn't be happy with Willa leaving her for days. More importantly, Willa hated being away from Priya. The little girl was her whole world and she didn't know how she was going to get through the next few days without her. She'd debated taking Priya with her. She had a babysitter who was always willing to travel with her, but there was no way Willa was letting Priya anywhere near Jack. He'd already taken too much from her.

Jack Chowdhry took a breath. *This is going to suck.* He handed his keys to the valet and looked toward the stables where the press conference was being held. The number of reporters with microphones and cameras was staggering.

"Are you ready to go into the fray?"

Jack turned to find Misha Law smiling at him. She leaned forward and he returned her hug. "Where's your other half?" Misha had recently started dating Trey Winters from the infamous Winters family. "He's already inside, I had a meeting about k!smet's upcoming IPO." Jack smiled down at Misha. She was an attractive woman with auburn hair that she wore in a wavy bob, hazel eyes and a kind smile. What Jack admired most about her was that she was a self-made woman. She had recently launched a social app with a successful dating platform that had taken Royal, and the whole country, by storm. There had been some hiccups along the way but Jack was glad to hear that Misha was ready to make the initial public offering—IPO. It would allow her company to raise some serious capital to take the app to the next level.

"You really should sign up for k!smet. Wouldn't it be great for the stock price if the great Jack Chowdhry met his love match through the app?"

Maybe I should think about it. The app's Surprise Me! feature had made some interesting matches that had worked out well. He hadn't been serious about another woman since Willa St Germaine. It was time to settle down, start a family. He was forty-four years old. How much longer could he wait? The running joke in the family was that by the time Jack had children, he'd be mistaken for the children's grandfather. "I don't know if I'm ready for the app yet."

Misha stopped and grabbed his arm. "C'mon, you are

one of the most eligible bachelors in Royal. Plus, as I said, having you on there will really help with the IPO."

"I'm not that great," he said, somewhat embarrassed by the effusive praise. There was a time when he'd ridden high on such accolades but he'd learned that they didn't mean much.

"Don't be modest. The way you negotiated between the Del Rio and Winters families was masterful."

Jack waved his hand dismissively. If he'd known that he would become the story, he'd never have agreed to play peacemaker for the Texas Cattleman's Club. He had debated skipping the press conference but remembered that hiding made him all the more interesting. There were already reporters camped outside the gates to his ranch. He had a statement prepared for the night, and hopefully he could throw the limelight back onto the Del Rios and Winterses. There was a wedding and a baby in the near future. Surely that made for a more interesting story than him?

"You should take advantage of the media presence here to promote k!smet," he said, changing the subject.

Misha looked thoughtful. "I try to promote it every chance I get. Could I remind everyone it's tomorrow night?"

"I'll get you some mike time."

"Thanks! You look great, by the way."

He'd opted for cowboy boots, boot-cut jeans and an untucked collared shirt with the first two buttons open for the night. *Not many men can pull off an untucked shirt but you have the ass for it.* He smiled as he thought of Willa, wondering how she was doing in New York.

He had looked at the list of networks who were here to cover the party. Her network, NYEN—the New York Entertainment Network—had called his office for a comment but they hadn't requested a media pass for the event tonight. Willa's talents were wasted at that tabloid-like network but there was nothing he could do. He'd tried to get her a job after the debacle five years ago but she had disappeared from his life, refused to take his calls, emails, text messages or social media DMs. He'd even left paper messages at her building. How could he blame her after what he'd done? It had been five years and his guilt over Willa still burned deep in his heart.

"Hey, now, is my woman complimenting another man." Trey Winters met them on their way to the sta-bles and bent down and kissed Misha. At six foot one, Trey towered over Misha but was just a little taller than Jack. He stuck out his hand and Jack shook it.

"Jack's going to join the app," Misha said excitedly.

Jack held up his hand. "I will think about it."

Trey placed a hand on his shoulder. "I've invested a lot of money because I believe in it. I certainly had my doubts about the Surprise Me! Function, too, especially after it matched Jericho and Maggie but—" he looked lovingly at Misha "—love is found in unexpected ways."

Jack's heart squeezed. Could he have what Misha and Trey had? Did he even deserve it, especially after what he'd done to Willa?

"Y'all better get inside. The press is getting restless to see the man of the hour."

Jack turned as Preston Del Rio slapped him from be-hind. Preston had recently found out that he was about to become a father and since then Jack had only seen him smiling. He was engaged to Tiffany Winters, yet another Del Rio and Winters match that had worked out well.

"They want to see the diamond necklace." Jack was scheduled to unveil the necklace to show everyone in attendance and for the press at large. As soon as proper security was in place, the necklace would be going on display at the club for the public to get a closer look. The TCC was expecting large numbers and wanted every precaution taken before allowing the necklace to be viewed. This was just a sneak peek.

Preston greeted Trey and Misha and they all chatted as they made their way to the stables entrance. Jack fell behind, letting Trey and Preston talk. Trey's sister was having Preston's baby; the two men were about to become family and it was nice to see them getting along. Not that long ago, the two would've crossed the street to avoid running into each other.

As he neared the entrance to the stables, he stopped. *It can't be.* He closed his eyes. Not every five-foot-three woman with silky blond hair was Willa. He was seeing things because he'd just been thinking about her. He opened his eyes just as the woman turned.

His heart stopped. *Willa!* Their eyes met for just a second and her gaze seared him from the inside out. Then she turned and he wondered whether she'd seen him at all. He quickly walked toward her. She was in a heated conversation with Jared, the TCC staff member who was checking the guest list.

"I don't understand why you can't call the network

and check our credentials," Willa was saying. He looked at her. She was wearing a turquoise dress with knee-high boots. His heart beat wildly as he took in her blazing blue eyes and slim figure.

"What's the problem, Jared?" He stepped forward. He was talking to Jared but his eyes were on Willa. He couldn't believe she was really here. She met his gaze with a hard look and he flinched. It was the same way she'd looked at him the last time he'd seen her. When she'd walked out of his life.

"Sir, they aren't on the guest list. I can't give them a press pass."

Willa was still glaring at him.

"How many people?" Jared asked.

"Just the two of us. Willa St Germaine and Rogerio Silva with NYEN." A man stepped forward and stuck out his hand. Jack shook it, barely noticing him.

"It's okay, I'll vouch for them." Jack said.

Rogerio nudged Willa, who finally seemed to find her voice. "Thank you."

"It's nice to see you again," Jack said, his throat tight.

"Mr. Chowdhry, it's a pleasure to meet you. Might we get an interview?" Rogerio chimed in.

Jack forced himself to look at Rogerio. He wasn't planning to give any individual interviews. The whole idea of coming tonight was to turn the attention away from him.

"Jack, we're ready for your statement," one of the TCC staff called out to him.

He turned to Willa. "I'm making a statement for

the press. After that I'd love to catch up with you. It's been a while."

Willa narrowed her eyes. "Mr. Chowdhry, are you willing to give us an interview?" Her voice was as icy as the cold look in her eyes.

"Two old friends can't just talk?"

"We're not friends," she said. "If you want to talk to me, it'll be through an interview."

She hadn't changed one bit—the same old cutthroat journalist that he'd first met. He smiled. "I'll make you a deal. For every question of yours that I answer, I get to ask you a question."

She narrowed her eyes. "You've got a deal."

Finally, he was going to get some answers.

Two

"What is wrong with you?" Rogerio whispered as soon as Jack had walked away.

Willa couldn't bring herself to look at him. What was wrong with her? She thought she was prepared to see Jack, had even practiced the nonchalant lines she would deliver when she first saw him. Instead, she'd frozen when she turned and saw him staring right at her. It was as if no time had passed between them. Their last meeting came rushing back at her, the pain of betrayal, the heartache, the anger—it all threatened to drown her.

Over the years she'd thought about forgiving him; despite what he'd done, she wouldn't have Priya without him. But seeing Jack again reminded her that the wounds he had inflicted were deep and her anger still burned strong. How was she going to interview him?

How was she going to sit across from him and pretend that she was just a reporter and he was just a story? At least she had Rogerio.

"Willa, are you going to be able to interview him?"

No.

"Of course. I'm a professional." Her throat was dry. She grabbed a drink from the tray of a passing waiter. It was only after she'd downed half the glass that she realized it was a cocktail. Rogerio handed her a bottle of water.

The media were gathered on the lawn where a stage had been set up. Jack had just been introduced and was making a statement. She should pay attention but all she could do was focus on settling her churning stomach. Rogerio taped Jack's statement and dutifully took pictures of the grand necklace at the heart of the Diamond Gate story. At least he had the wherewithal to maintain their cover.

"I'll be back," she whispered to Rogerio.

"Where are you going? The media are asking questions."

She ignored Rogerio and made her way out of the crowd. She asked a passing staff member where the bathroom was and made her way there. Thankfully, it was a single bathroom set up in a trailer. It was the nicest portable bathroom she'd ever been in. There were flowers on the marble sink and a basket full of single rolled towels. She splashed cold water on her face, ruining her mascara. She looked at the dark splotches on her face. *I'm not going to let him do this to me. Not again.*

It had taken months for her to get herself together

after the last time she'd seen him. In one night she had gone from breaking the story of a lifetime to quitting her job. The next week she'd discovered she was pregnant with Priya. She had been on her way to tell Jack when Jessica Danan appeared on TV. Willa had been working for over a year on finding proof that the mayor of New York City was deeply embedded in the Mafia. She'd risked her life working informants in the darkest parts of the city and when she was finally ready to publish the story, Jack had pulled her off saying that it was too dangerous and the network wasn't going to air it. Willa had quit in protest. Then he'd gone and given the story to Jessica. She'd been so stupid—there had been plenty of rumors of Jack and Jessica sleeping together but Willa had ignored them as idle gossip. Losing her story was something she could've gotten over, but Jack's betrayal had put her in a tailspin. The stress and heartbreak had jeopardized the pregnancy and she had to go on bedrest until Priya was born. The doctors had called it pregnancy related depression but it was a broken heart. It had taken Priya's sweetness and her sister's support to pull her out of that dark place. She'd only gotten back to work two years ago, and this was her first chance at her real story. She wasn't going to screw it up.

She used the rolled washcloths to wipe her face, then reapplied her makeup. Willa St Germaine was going to get back on top, and this time she'd do to Jack what he'd done to her—trample him along the way.

Rogerio was standing toward the back of the crowd when she found him. "What'd I miss?"

He looked at her. "You look better. Gave yourself a pep talk?"

She nodded. "I'm ready."

"Good, because he's done up there. He just handed the mike to some woman who's announcing a party for her social app."

"K!smet! Turn on the camera, we should get this."

He raised his brow but complied. Willa did a quick search on her phone. She remembered reading about the app. There had been some attention on it, especially when the diamond story broke, because the dating section of the app had matched a couple from the Winters and Del Rio families.

"We should ask Jack if he can introduce us to the CEO." She nodded toward the woman who was announcing a prelaunch IPO party for all members as a thank-you.

"We should go to that party. It's tomorrow night."

As soon as Jack stepped off stage, he was surrounded by reporters. Willa gestured to Rogerio and they made their way through the crowd. When Jack saw them, he waved and made his way toward them.

"Sorry, folks, but I'm only giving one interview tonight and it's to Willa St Germaine."

For just a second, Willa enjoyed the envious looks thrown by the other reporters. She felt confident and in control, but as Jack stepped toward them, a shiver ran down her spine. Suddenly, she was acutely aware of his presence, the heat radiating from his body, and the scent of his woodsy cologne. She glanced over at him, her heart racing, and found herself caught in his intense gaze. Willa's breath stuck in her throat as Jack leaned in closer, his body inches away from hers. "Let's get out of here."

He means for the interview. He led the way and she and Rogerio followed. They walked to the main clubhouse. "There's a small room the restaurant uses for private dining. We can go there."

They were soon in a room decorated like an old-world saloon with wood paneling, a thick wooden table and rich leather chairs. The walls were adorned with paintings of rolling hills and horses while the scent of aged whiskey and cigar smoke clung to the air. Tall windows and high ceilings offered a stunning view of the sprawling greenery and setting sun outside.

The table could comfortably seat ten. Jack took a seat at the head of the table. It would've been childish to take the seat on the opposite end, so she took the one next to him, even though it meant they were a little too close for comfort. She would've preferred to have the table between them.

Jack smiled and her heart stopped for a beat. *Damn those dimples.* Rogerio cleared his throat. "I'm all ready."

Willa straightened. "Thank you for giving us this interview."

"It's great to see you. How have you been?"

"Very well, thank you." She smiled a little too widely. *How dare you ask me how I've been.*

"Great speech… I'd like to ask you—"

"You missed most of it."

He'd noticed she was gone?

"Rogerio heard it," she said without missing a beat.

"So why did the Winterses and Del Rios select you to negotiate the return of the heirloom necklace?"

"I'm on the board of the Texas Cattleman's Club. As a pillar of the community, TCC felt we could be helpful in bringing the issue to a resolution. I was asked because of my experience negotiating in the corporate world."

It was the canned answer he'd been giving everyone, as she knew he would, but she had to start with the soft balls to warm him up, get him to drop his guard.

"Now I get to ask you a question."

Wait, what? She mentally slapped her head. It was the price he'd asked to give the interview. Jack Chowdhry didn't give anything away for free.

"After CMG, you disappeared for more than two years. Where were you?"

Clearly, he wasn't going to start with soft balls for her. *Wait, he kept track of me?*

"I took some personal time."

He stared at her and she felt her insides wilting, but she met his gaze. He wasn't the only one good at giving nonanswers.

"What do you mean—"

"One question at a time," she said firmly.

His lips twitched and she was momentarily distracted by the little dimples in his cheeks. He knew she could never resist his cocky half smile. Involuntarily she found her eyes focused on his lips, remembering what it was like to kiss him, to have him kiss her. She took a breath to refocus on the interview. It was dangerous being so close to Jack, to smell him, see him, feel his heat.

"What did you get from negotiating the deal?"

"I don't understand the question."

"You didn't take any compensation from the families to be the negotiator and the TCC didn't pay you. So what did you get out of being the negotiator?"

He frowned. "If you're asking about monetary compensation, I didn't get any. I did this because Royal is my home and I wanted to help. Plus Jericho is a close friend, and he knows being a TCC board member, I'd be neutral."

"So you did this out of the goodness of your heart? The last deal you negotiated for CMG included a six-figure bonus for you." She'd meant to sound neutral but couldn't keep the distrust out of her voice.

He leaned forward. "Five years is a long time, Willa. I don't do things like I used to."

As he leaned forward, his scent wafted over her and her nerves pinged.

"People don't change that much," she said caustically. Rogerio sucked in a sharp breath behind her. She'd almost forgotten he was there.

Jack leaned back and laughed. "You certainly haven't changed."

"You don't know anything about me," she spat, her voice dripping with venom. Jack always thought he could size people up with one look, get the upper hand within seconds of any meeting.

Rogerio put his hand on her shoulder but she shrugged it off. Jack's smile faltered but stayed on his face, making her clench her fists. *Still the same arrogant ass he's always been.*

"My turn to ask—"

She braced herself for the inevitable question about whether she was still angry at him. Jack loved to ask rhetorical questions so he could take the floor and wax poetic about his philosophy or approach. He had tried to contact her after the day in the newsroom when she'd thrown her badge and walked off but she'd blocked him on social media, email, cell. When he somehow found a way to get her a paper note, she'd turned on her stove and thrown it into the gas range without reading it. She'd nearly set off the smoke alarm in the building but it had been worth it. She knew what he was going to say; he always had an explanation for his decisions, a smooth way to paint him in the right light.

"Where are you staying in Royal?"

The question caught her off guard. "Why does it matter?"

He wagged his finger. "That's not an answer."

She was about to tell him that her answer was that it was none of his business when Rogerio spoke up. "The hotels were all booked so we've got a rental on Paso Street a few miles outside of town." Willa shot him a look.

Jack shook his head. "The area around Royal is relatively safe but the buildings on Paso Street are pretty run-down. The accommodations can't be that great."

"They're fine…" Willa began to answer.

"They're horrible. I'm pretty sure I saw a mouse in my bathtub."

Willa turned. "Rogerio!" Clearly her silent warnings weren't having an effect.

He gave her an innocent-looking smile and shrugged.

"Well, I can't have you guys staying there. Why don't you come stay at my ranch? We can finish the interview there tomorrow."

"No!" Willa hated the high pitch of her voice.

"We would love to." Rogerio spoke over her.

Jack stood, took out a card from his jeans pocket. *Since when does he wear jeans?* Why had she just noticed that now? He motioned to Rogerio for a pen and Rogerio handed him one.

"Here's my personal cell. Just ask any taxi or Uber driver to take you to the Chowdhry ranch. I'll let the gate know to expect you."

"Thank you for the hospitality but I'd rather just finish the interview now." Did she sound as desperate as she was feeling?

He held out the card but she stood frozen. Rogerio reached out and plucked it from Jack's hand.

"My phone has been buzzing like crazy. Let's talk tomorrow when we have more time. Besides, I'd love to show you my house and catch up properly."

"Thank you, we'll head over in about an hour," Rogerio said.

Jack smiled at her, then left before she could formulate the words to tell him to go to hell.

As soon as he was gone, she turned. "What the hell are you thinking?"

Rogerio put his hands out in surrender. "Darling, this interview was on a bridge to nowhere. He just gave us a gift. Think about it. If we're staying at his house, we can talk to the staff, whoever else is living there. What better way to get some gossip on him?"

She hated that Rogerio was right. "Damn it."

He put his hands on her shoulders. "I'm sorry. I can see you're having a hard time with this."

"No, I'm…"

He raised his brows and she blew out a breath. Rogerio wasn't just her cameraman, he was also her friend and neighbor. They'd met at the local convenience store when she was still at home with Priya. He'd helped her get the job at NYEN.

"This story is a bad idea."

He nodded sagely. "I'm not a big enough person not to say I told you so, but now that we're here, let's make the best of it. That man is too suave to spill his secrets during an interview. Staying with him is the only chance we have to get close to him. I'll help."

Even as she nodded, she had a sinking feeling that this was not going to end well for her.

Three

As Jack stared at his watch, the ticking seconds felt like an eternity. His pulse raced with anticipation, the weight of five long years of guilt bearing down on him. He'd finally get the chance to explain everything to her. He paced the room. Had she changed her mind? She'd clearly been reluctant to begin with but he'd correctly read Rogerio. The man was smart enough to know that he'd get a better story staying with Jack. Maybe he should've talked to her at the TCC. He mentally shook his head. It was not a conversation to rush through. He'd made that mistake five years ago and had waited this long for a second chance. He didn't want to take a chance of letting her leave without hearing his side of things.

As he paced around the room, his mind drifted back

to that night at CMG when he'd made the call to take Willa off the story. Her leaving had been a defining moment in his life, when he'd finally decided that he didn't want to be that guy—the one who only thought about his company and business. He'd spent the next two years transitioning the leadership of his business empire, giving up his board seats and figuring out where to settle down. He'd come to Royal by chance. Dev, the son of his parents' friends, the Malliks, lived in Royal part-time and had invited them to come stay at his ranch. He'd come along with his parents, curious as to how a jet-setter like Dev had come to settle in Texas. Once he'd seen the town, he'd fallen in love with it. The scenery, the sense of community, the importance of family had all drawn him to the town. Dev and his wife, Caitlyn, had shown him the property that now made up his ranch. At the time a large plot of land had become available, and he'd spent a year building his home.

He looked at his watch again and resumed pacing the spacious foyer of his house. The soaring ceiling was two stories high and held a glittering chandelier that cast a warm glow throughout the space. Towering columns flanked the entrance to the living room and dining room, both rooms visible through the open doorways.

His phone rang. "Sir, the guests you were expecting just came through the front gate."

He thanked the estate night manager and opened the front door just as a rental car pulled into the covered brick driveway.

Willa was driving. Rogerio hopped out of the car. "This place is something else."

Jack smiled. He'd personally worked with the architect on every last detail.

"Where should we park?"

"You can leave the car here with the keys in the ignition. My night manager will park it in one of the garages."

"Still living the high life," Willa said with more than a touch of disdain as she exited the car. She was still wearing the turquoise dress that curved around her in all the right places and he couldn't help but notice that she'd put on a new coat of lip gloss.

"I work hard and enjoy living well," he said, keeping his voice light. *She has every right to be mad at me,* he reminded himself. "Let me give you a tour."

"We've had a long day. Do you mind if we turn in for the night?"

Jack's assistant had called all the rentals on Paso Street and found out that Willa and Rogerio had booked a place for three nights. There was plenty of time for a heart-to-heart. He'd waited five years—he could wait another night.

He led them into the house. There were six guest cottages scattered across the vast property. His family had relatives in India and Europe who had open invitations to visit whenever they wanted. Each guesthouse was decorated with antiques and art and included a mini-kitchen, bedroom, living room and bathroom. A couple of the cottages had two bedrooms to accommodate families traveling with kids. Rogerio and Willa would've been more comfortable in those cottages but they were designed to offer the guests, and him, privacy. He wanted Willa close.

"Wow, this is amazing." Rogerio filled in the silence with questions about the house and decor. Jack was happy to answer his questions, proud to show off what he'd built. Willa was quiet as Jack grabbed her duffel bag and led them up the grand staircase to the second floor where the bedrooms were located.

He walked Rogerio to the east wing. Rogerio's mouth hung open as he walked into the room. "This room is bigger than my apartment. It's Italian, isn't it?"

Jack nodded. "Each of the rooms here is decorated in a different style."

The room included a queen-size bed covered with plush blue and silver linens and a large tufted headboard. A pair of antique bedside tables flanked the bed with ornate lamps that threw soft shadows into the room. The room's focal point was a large, hand-painted fresco depicting a serene Italian vineyard.

"I'm in heaven. I don't think I'll ever leave."

Jack smiled. "Then we'll leave you to it." He was more than happy to close the door on Rogerio. He led Willa down the hallway. He was giving her the bedroom closest to his. As if sensing his intensions, she stopped halfway down the hall leading to the west wing. "There are plenty of rooms here. I'd like to be close to Rogerio."

"Does he have night terrors?" Jack asked facetiously.

Willa rolled her eyes. "You'll like the bedroom I've picked out for you," he said quietly and walked down the hall.

She paused, then followed him. He opened the door to his favorite guest room. It was spacious and airy, with floor-to-ceiling windows that opened out onto a balcony overlooking the lush gardens below. The walls were painted a soft shade of lavender, accented by gold and white trim. A crystal chandelier hung from the center of the ceiling, casting a warm glow across the room.

Willa stepped into the room, and while her body remained stiff, a small smile played on her lips. Jack could tell she was enchanted even though she didn't want to be. The bed was the centerpiece of the room, a plush four-poster with a delicate lace canopy. The bedding was a mix of silk and satin, in shades of gold and cream, and piled high with fluffy pillows.

He could picture Willa jumping onto the bed, letting her body sink into the soft pillows, her gold and brown hair splayed across the cream bedspread.

"This reminds me of that room we stayed in Paris, the one…" She stopped.

"…the one where we made love for the first time," he finished.

"I was going to say had sex."

She walked to the vanity table and set down her purse. "It's a very nice room. Now I'd like to turn in for the night."

"Willa, we need to talk about the George Wright story." He had intended to wait, but the way she stared at him with cold, unyielding eyes and a taut, rigid posture made him uneasy. Her face was a mask of composure, but he could sense the simmering tension emanating from her like a palpable force, ready to boil over at any moment.

Willa's lips thinned into a tight smile. She took a step closer to him. "Okay, then," she said, her voice low and controlled. "Why don't you start by explaining how you took one year of my work and gave it to the woman you were sleeping with?"

What!

"What're you talking about?"

"Jessica Danan." Her voice shook with palpable anger.

She couldn't possibly think he was sleeping with Jessica. Then he looked at her face and the ice in her eyes spoke volumes. *Shit, that's what she thinks?* "Is that why you didn't take my calls? You thought I gave the story to Jessica because I was sleeping with her?"

She put her hands on her hips. "You told me you were killing the story because it was too dangerous." Willa closed the distance between them and stuck a finger into his chest. He caught a whiff of her perfume. She still used the rose and vanilla scent. "You said the network couldn't run the story. It was too volatile. Legal said it created too much liability. Security was concerned about how the Mafia might retaliate against me personally. Then you go and run the story anyway."

He grabbed her finger, unable to resist touching her. She glared at him but didn't move her finger. "If you'd taken a single phone call or read any of my emails, you'd know what happened after I talked to you in the newsroom. I learned that CNTZ had caught wind of the story.

One of your informants decided he was going to double-sell the information. They were going to scoop it."

"So instead of calling me to come do the story you gave it to Jessica Danan?"

"The threat of violence was still very real. Security and the network executives thought it would be safest not to attribute the story to a single reporter. We didn't want to give the Mafia a target. Jessica was just supposed to anchor the story."

"Why didn't you call me to anchor the story?"

"Because I was afraid for your life." He grabbed her hand, pulling her one step closer to him. Her eyes were blazing but she didn't make a move to step away from him. "Do you have any idea how dangerous that story was? The Mafia doesn't think twice about dumping a body into the East River or through the trash compactor. Security said there was no way to protect you. Jessica wasn't supposed to take credit for the story. We were going to say 'unnamed reporter' but she decided to change the script on air. Do you have any idea what happened to Jessica after she aired that story? She got attacked right outside our building. Her assigned bodyguard barely got her to safety. She was in the hospital for three days. Then we flew her to a remote village in Nova Scotia to hide her. It wasn't until George Wright resigned as mayor and the police rounded up the major players that she could return. By then you had disappeared."

Willa's expression softened slightly. "You could've issued a correction, let it be known that it was my story."

"I brought it up but the story was really hot by then.

If we issued a retraction on any portion of the story, it could've jeopardized the case the FBI was putting together."

"Do you think I'm that stupid?" She pulled her hand away from him. "When has the network ever cared about police procedure. You didn't want to issue a retraction because it would've embarrassed the network." She stepped back, pinning him with a look so cold it sent shivers down his spine. "The network didn't care about me, but neither did you. You could've made it right, but you chose not to."

His chest tightened. How did he explain to her that he'd been in love with her. He'd bought a ring and was going to propose. Jack had even paid for private security to supplement what the network had but everyone kept telling him that there was no way to ensure her safety. He couldn't risk her life, not for a story. "The threat wasn't completely gone and I didn't want to risk your life"

"It wasn't your call to make. It was my life, my story, my risk, my decision."

"Look, I feel horrible about the way things ended between us. I'm sorry. But you also didn't give me a chance to explain." He'd lost track of how many times he'd tried to contact her. Then she'd moved out of her apartment and disappeared. He had hired a private investigator to track her down but then called the guy off. If she didn't want to be with him, he wasn't going to chase after her. Had he made the right decision? Maybe he should've gone after her. It was not as if he'd been able to forget about her.

"Wow, if that was your apology, it really sucked." She walked to the doorway and gestured for him to leave.

Four

Despite the cloudlike bed, Willa slept fitfully. Priya was an early riser and usually woke Willa by six thirty. Royal was two hours behind New York time but it was already seven by the time she got out of bed. She video-called Priya, who spent five minutes describing the hard poop she'd had the day before, then ran off to make breakfast for her stuffed unicorn. Her sister gave her a rundown of the day's plans. Willa didn't tell Kylie that the story she was chasing included Jack. She and her sister had always disagreed on how to deal with Jack.

Last night Jack had taken some of the wind out of her sails but the anger that had simmered and brewed inside her for five years hadn't gone cold. Even if he hadn't been sleeping with Jessica Danan. Even if he hadn't purposely given her the story, he had no right to decide that the story had been too risky for her. At that time, they'd only been together six months. There was no permanent commitment between them. She hadn't even gotten up the nerve to tell him she loved him. How dare he take such liberties with her career?

He knew that she knew the risks when she started to pursue the story. She'd been the one to get security involved early because she was afraid for one of her sources. Security had given her a bodyguard for when she went to meet her informants, and to walk her home when she worked late. Jack knew all of this; he'd seen how hard she worked on the story, the risks she'd taken to double-check her facts. Willa had put together a solid story and he'd just handed it to Jessica out of some sense of old-fashioned machismo. How dare he? Not only that, he'd had every opportunity to put things right. She didn't blame Jessica for taking credit for the story. Why wouldn't she? She saw an opportunity and took it. The woman had always been cutthroat, but where was Jack's protective instinct then? Why hadn't he made sure she didn't get shafted?

She sighed and used the decadent bathroom to take a long shower. She texted Rogerio but he didn't answer. She rummaged through her duffel and came up with jeans, a tank top and a light jean jacket. Despite it being December, Royal was warm. It was snowing when she'd left New York. She blow-dried her hair and left it loose. *Just a tiny swipe of mascara and gloss.* There was no harm in looking good.

Dressed, she looked at her phone. Rogerio hadn't texted her back but it was well after eight thirty. It was a Saturday but Jack would be at work by now. He always worked Saturdays. She could find some breakfast, then figure out the plan.

The house was even more beautiful in the daylight. The sweeping staircase leading down to the foyer had a wrought iron balustrade. Large windows let in natural light and made the crystal chandelier sparkle. Everywhere she looked, the house screamed of Jack. The traditional details with modern touches and the understated elegance was all him. The fact that this house was in Royal still didn't compute for her. Jack had owned a four-bedroom penthouse in the city. He'd converted the bedrooms into an office, game room and closet. *I don't want to encourage guests. That's what hotels are for.* What was he doing with a house like this?

She had no idea where the kitchen was but it didn't take long for her to hear Rogerio's laugh. She followed the sound to a spacious, well-equipped kitchen that any professional chef would be envious of. The breakfast nook was a solarium-like space with a circular table that sat twelve.

"Good morning,"

Her eyes connected with Jack's and her heart skipped a beat. Why did he have to look so handsome in the mornings? He liked to air-dry his hair, so it was always slightly damp in the mornings and had that irresistible messy look. Jack flashed her a smile and her heart skipped another beat. He was dressed in a cream polo shirt with the top two buttons open, a tuft of chest hair poking out. The shirt showed off his beautiful brown skin. Why wasn't he dressed for work? She was used to seeing him at the breakfast table dressed in a business suit, busily clicking on his phone. The only thing in front of him was a cup of coffee.

A spread of fresh fruit, pancakes, muesli, scrambled eggs and bacon was artfully laid out on the table. She took a seat next to Rogerio and loaded her plate.

"You have to try the toasted pecan caramel topping on your pancakes, I swear it tastes like heaven."

"It all looks delicious," she said.

"Let me know if you need anything else." Willa nearly jumped as a man wearing a chef's hat came up behind her. He was carrying a pot of coffee.

"This is Steve. He's the morning chef."

Willa smiled at Steve. "The food looks amazing." She held out the cup from her place setting and Steve filled it for her. The aroma was intoxicating. She added some cream and took several sips, letting the hot brew fortify her enough to face Jack.

"When's a good time for us to complete the interview?" After last night's conversation, one thing was clear. It was foolish to think she was going to be able to spend any significant time with Jack and stay neutral. The best thing she could do was get a story and get out of there. She would do an interview with him and ask Rogerio to go around and make friends with the staff. With any luck, they'd be on their way home tomorrow.

"Actually, Jack and I made plans." Rogerio said nonchalantly.

Willa nearly spat out the fresh-squeezed orange juice she'd just sipped. She glared at Rogerio and he smiled at her.

"I proposed that we do a profile on Jack and he agreed." Rogerio gave her a pointed look. "He suggested you shadow him today and I'll get some footage of the staff and grounds. His ranch manager is going to show me around."

Bad, bad idea. Hadn't she and Rogerio talked about this? On the way to the ranch, she and Rogerio had come up with a plan. They'd ask Jack to do a profile on him as a pretense to follow him around for a day and talk to his staff. But she'd made Rogerio promise that he wouldn't leave her alone with Jack. What was he thinking?

"I have a pretty light day today, so it should give us plenty of time to talk."

She stared at Jack. She'd already said everything she needed to say to him. She ate her delicious breakfast in silence while Rogerio kept up a steady stream of small talk. As soon as Jack excused himself to take a phone call, she turned on Rogerio.

"What the hell were you thinking? You know I don't want to be alone with him."

"I know, but listen to why I had to do it. All the staff are here right now but they only work half days on Saturdays and have Sunday off. This is our only chance to talk to them alone. C'mon, it's the candid camera."

She sighed. The candid camera was named after the idea of distracting people or making them think no one was watching and getting them in a candid moment. They'd used it several times to get people to give up their secrets. Her favorite one was when she'd excused herself to go to the bathroom after a sleep-inducing interview with a minor celebrity. The target had taken a phone call where she openly talked about skimming money from the charity gala she was throwing. Rogerio had captured it all on camera while pretending to admire the table setting.

"Look at it this way. If we work hard today, we'll be able to leave tomorrow." He grinned at her.

"You're lucky you're smart," she said. As good as the breakfast tasted, she pushed her plate away. The knot in her stomach was twisting. She didn't want to spend the day being next to Jack, smelling him, listening to his voice, and pretending that she was just on another story.

"So what's on the agenda today?" Her voice was a little too bright as Jack walked back into the room.

He gave her a dimpled smile. "How about a tour of my home, then we can go into town. I have to make a quick stop, then I have a surprise for you."

It's not a date.

"Sounds great. I'll join you on the house tour and I'll take some footage," Rogerio broke in before she could open her mouth to protest.

"You don't have meetings?" How was she going to get dirt on him if she didn't see what he was working on? She'd searched online and every database she could think of. He still held shares in all the old companies he used to have in his portfolio but he seemed to have resigned from all boards except the TCC. His LinkedIn page listed his profession as "rancher." Unless he was digging for oil on this property, what was he doing? She refused to believe that the media mogul who ran multiple companies, didn't blink twice before deciding to fire people, and had a reputation for hostile takeovers, was raising cattle. She needed to find out what he was really up to. Maybe the property tour would reveal some answers.

They started in the house, which had seven guest bedrooms, each decorated in a different motif. Jack left his room to last. His room was a lavish retreat in vibrant shades of deep maroon, gold and silver. Rich textiles hung in the wall and a silk duvet draped the large carved wooden bed. Willa didn't let her eyes linger too long on the king-size bed. She didn't want to imagine Jack in that bed.

Rogerio had no such filters. He ran his hand over the rich linens. "This is the most decadent fabric I've ever seen."

Jack smiled. "I had it imported from Rajasthan."

He walked to the French doors and opened them to an expansive terrace. They stepped onto the terrace and she gasped. The landscape stretched out as far as the eye could see. Rolling hills undulated in the distance, carpeted in a sea of tall grass and wildflowers. A family of deer grazed lazily in the distance, their white tails flashing in the sunlight. Beyond them, a small herd of cattle wandered in the fields. On the near side of the property, nestled near the edge of the tree line, stood the stables, their wooden walls gleaming in the sunlight. Horses of all colors and sizes milled about, nuzzling each other and grazing on the fresh grass.

The scene was so breathtaking that even Rogerio couldn't find words.

They visited the stables, which was an impressive

structure with enough room for more than a dozen horses. There were several staff tending to the animals. There was also a large pond stocked with fish, a pool complete with pool house and hot tub, and a greenhouse where Jack proudly showed off his hydroponic tomatoes.

"What're all those buildings?" Rogerio asked.

"Cottages. Staff use some of them. One of them is my parents' apartment." He pointed to the larger of the buildings that reminded Willa of an upscale hunting lodge.

"Your parents live here?" Jack was full of surprises. When his parents came to visit in New York, Jack put them up in a hotel, barely carved out enough time to have dinner with them and complained if they stayed more than two nights.

"They're getting on in age, so I thought it was best they stay close to me. Hey, how are your parents doing?"

Willa smiled. "They're well. They decided to do the retirement thing and move to Arizona." Her parents had been a godsend during her pregnancy and after she gave birth. They owned the townhouse that she and Kylie lived in now. She had moved in with them and they'd helped take care of her and Priya. Willa never would've gotten through the last few years without her family.

"Are your parents home now?" Willa had met Jack's parents exactly once right before the incident with the Mafia story. It had been over dinner at Per Se, one of the most exclusive restaurants in New York City. She'd immediately liked them. They were immigrants who had moved from Delhi and right after they'd gotten married.

As young twentysomethings, they'd started off working at a relative's grocery store, then bought one of their own. By the time Jack was a teenager, they had a chain of Indian grocery stores. Jack didn't just take over the family business after he did his MBA; he took it to the next level by building an empire. His parents were obviously proud of him, yet Willa had clearly seen regret in their eyes when they talked about India. His mother had cutely asked if Jack planned to make and honest woman out of Willa and he had let out a monologue in Hindi that she didn't need the language to understand.

"They're in India now. They'll be back in a few days."

"Too bad I'll miss them. Tell them I said hello." He looked at her strangely and she immediately regretted her words. They sounded too familiar. His parents probably didn't even remember her. Who knows how many women Jack had introduced them to in the last five years.

"What're they doing in India?" Rogerio asked.

"They're there to do some traditional prayers for Priya's death anniversary." Jack replied, his voice breaking ever so slightly.

Rogerio's eyes looked like they would pop out of their sockets. "Priya is…was… Jack's sister." Willa explained to him, giving him a pointed look. "She died ten years ago." To Rogerio's credit, he recomposed his face pretty quickly.

Jack had turned away from them and was walking back toward the house. Rogerio pulled her aside. "You named your daughter after his sister," he whispered furiously. Willa knew Jack was out of hearing range but she shushed Rogerio. "She meant a lot to Jack and I thought Priya should have something of him." The name had popped into her mind the moment the sonogram showed she was having a girl and she hadn't been able to let it go.

They left Rogerio at the main house. One of the many ranch staff brought out a red Porsche Carrera. Jack opened the passenger door for her and Willa let herself sink into the leather bucket seats. He got behind the wheel and eased the car out down the ranch driveway.

"Are you still angry at me?"

"Why would I be angry at you? For ruining my career and giving the biggest story of my life to another reporter?"

"How can I make it up to you?"

She snuck a look at him and was sorry that she did. He had that cocky half smile that showed off his dimples and made him irresistibly handsome. *Why do I still find him attractive?* Maybe it had been too long since she'd dated. Being a single mother didn't make it easy to be on the dating scene. Between her job and how expensive childcare was, she didn't get the opportunity to get out much. At her sister's insistence, she had signed up for some online dating sites. She'd actually had some decent dates with men who were intelligent, handsome, successful and sorted out with their lives. But for all of them, her daughter was a deal breaker, and Willa couldn't blame them. In a city where there were more people than square feet of livable housing, the thought of raising a child was daunting.

"Do you have a time machine where you can go back and not be a macho pig who thinks he knows best?"

"My time machine is broken right now."

He turned briefly toward her as they hit a red light. "Look, I can't get you a story about a major city mayor who's really an embedded Mafia boss—but I can get you out of the rut you're in at NYEN."

Her blood boiled. *How dare he?* It was one thing for her to feel that way but he didn't need to rub salt in the wounds he'd given her to begin with.

"I'm perfectly happy at NYEN."

"You are not. I've seen the stories they have you on. They clearly don't know the talent they have." *Wait.* He had seen her stories? Did he know that she was going to be in Royal? There was no way he'd known that she was coming to the press conference yesterday. David had purposely kept their names off the guest list to surprise Jack. That meant Jack had been keeping tabs on her. The thought pleased her more than she cared to admit.

"You know the k!smet app? They are about to launch an IPO. I can get you an exclusive interview with the CEO, Misha."

"You're right. It's nowhere close to making up for the Mafia story."

"C'mon, hear me out. There's been a lot of media attention on the app. The IPO is going to be huge and you can have the inside track. In fact, Misha is having a prelaunch party tonight to thank members and I'll get you an invitation."

The offer wasn't bad. She herself had thought about doing the story in addition to the one on Jack. But she wasn't going to say yes and have Jack think that she was on her way to forgiving him.

"So, aside from brokering deals between the Capulets and Montagues, what do you do with your days?" This was a good time to ask him questions. While he was driving, she could study his expressions without being distracted with how he was looking at her.

He smiled. "I think the Del Rios and Winterses put Romeo and Juliet's parents to shame. But to answer your question, I run the ranch."

"And…."

"And that's really it. I get involved in Royal events but I've divested as many of my business holdings as I could, and have given up my corporate board positions."

"Why the sudden change from being a media mogul to rancher?" She tried to keep her voice neutral.

"It wasn't sudden. We haven't been in touch for five years—a lot can change in that time. I bet your life isn't the same anymore."

She involuntarily flinched. *Did he know about Priya?* It would be just like him to hire a private detective to find out about her. That was why she had used the name of a dead soldier on Priya's birth certificate and given her the St Germaine last name. New York wasn't that big a city when it came to hiding from powerful men.

"Don't you miss the excitement?"

He shrugged. "No shortage of excitement in Royal. You're here from the city chasing a story."

He had a point but there was a little too much nonchalance and amusement in his voice. Her reporter senses were tingling. "What made you pick ranching? It's not something you ever talked about." She was trying to ask the same question in different ways to see if he would slip up, give her a little thread that she could pull on and unravel the real story. He was hiding something. The reason he'd moved to Royal might be the key to her story. There was something not quite on the up-and-up and she would find out what it was.

"I came out to Royal to visit a family friend and fell in love with this place. It has all the fine things I enjoy, restaurants, good whiskey…" He gave her a dimpled smile and color rose in her cheeks. Whiskey was their special drink, the one they drank together on the cold New York nights when they were naked and in the mood to celebrate. "…and I like the pace of life here, the focus on family, enjoying the outdoors. It's a more healthy way of living, physically and mentally."

"It sounds like something out of a brochure." She purposely didn't keep the skepticism out of her voice.

"I questioned it too when my friend Dev described it this way, but then I spent a week here and was sold."

He parked the car in a street spot. Willa and Rogerio had driven through this part of town yesterday. It looked like the quintessential small-town Main Street with brick sidewalks, cute stories and lamppost streetlights. Jack turned to her. "How about this? Stay here for the week and follow me around. There's no way to explain how this town makes you feel. You have to experience it yourself. You can attend the k!smet party, then at the end of week, return home."

No way. She couldn't be without Priya for that long.

While Priya was more than happy with her aunt, Willa had never been without her for more than two days. Just the thought of going a whole week without seeing her made her chest hurt.

"It's a very generous offer but I'm afraid I have to return to the city. I have to file the story on the Winters diamond necklace."

"Didn't you already do that? I saw the article that posted on the network website this morning."

Busted. She knew for a fact that he didn't watch or read NY.EN. What had he said about the network back when they were both at CMG? *It's the network equivalent of a cheap, greasy diner where the food might taste good in the moment but it's going to make you sick.* He was checking up on her.

"That was coverage of last night's event. I'm doing a broader story on the necklace." She unbuckled her belt and opened the car door to stop him from asking any more questions about her supposed story. The missing necklace has been pretty well publicized. If that was her real story, she'd be hard-pressed to find an angle that hadn't already been covered ad nauseam.

"So what're we doing here?"

He smiled. "We're here to go to the rodeo."

Five

Jack enjoyed the look on Willa's face. She'd never been to a rodeo. He hadn't missed her expression of incredulity when he said he was just a rancher. Nor had he missed her less than subtle questions trying to drive at what he was *really* doing in Royal. He couldn't blame her. The Jack she knew had been obsessed with just two things: power and money. Ironically, when he decided that he'd made enough money and moved to Royal, he'd made even more. The stocks he hadn't divested were doing well, and the startups he'd chosen to invest in had exploded.

"Are we watching the rodeo in a bar or something?" she asked. They were walking down Main Street.

"We're watching the real thing. But before we do, I need to get you something."

He didn't need to see her face to know that she was probably narrowing her eyes at him. Willa liked to be in control. They were almost to the shop he wanted to go to when he spotted Maggie Del Rio down the street entering Natalie Valentine's bridal shop. He crossed the street and walked over to the shop, Willa following him.

"You getting married?" Willa asked as they entered the store.

"Would it bother you if I was?" he asked her.

"Jack!" Maggie exclaimed as soon as she saw him. She was dressed in jeans, a plaid shirt tied at the waist, and cowboy boots. She gave him a quick hug, then turned to Willa with interest. "You're a face I haven't seen around here."

Willa smiled and stuck out her hand. "Willa St Germaine."

"This is Maggie Del Rio," Jack said though he suspected Willa already knew from the look of recognition in her eyes.

"What brings you to Royal, Willa?"

"Your family, actually. I'm here covering the necklace story."

Maggie's smile faltered. "There's really nothing left to cover."

Jack knew that Maggie was sick of all the attention and drama surrounding the two families. "Willa's also an old friend. We worked together at CMG. I'm trying to convince her to stay in Royal and cover the k!smet party." That got Maggie's attention. Misha was Maggie's best friend and also a client of Maggie's graphic design business so she was invested in k!smet being successful.

"You should try the app. It's how I met my fiancé." Maggie was talking to Willa but he didn't miss the pointed look she gave him.

"Ah, Jack, I'm glad you're here. Maybe you can talk some sense into Maggie."

Jack turned to see Natalie Valentine emerge holding a sparkly cream dress. She was a slight woman with wispy blond hair and bright blue eyes.

Maggie sighed.

"Maggie wants to buy a dress off the rack. Can you imagine? Such a momentous wedding and she'd going to wear some mass-produced dress. Look at this beautiful Vera Wang that just came in."

She gestured to Jack, who had no idea what she wanted him to do until she handed him the dress and mimed him holding it up in front of him.

He caught Willa's smirky smile and held the dress in front of her body. "It is a nice dress." Willa rolled her eyes at him but he held the dress in front of her for a few more seconds. He still had the engagement ring he'd bought for her: a two-carat sapphire with two small diamonds on each side. The plan had been to propose the night she aired the Mafia story. Over the years he'd thought about his decision and wondered whether he should've let her go forward with the story. Ultimately Jessica Danan had been fine, the threat had abated and she'd gone on to have a nice career. Even knowing how things had turned out, he couldn't imagine making a different decision based on what he knew back then.

The threat to Willa's life had been real, and while she didn't care, he loved her too much to have risked her safety. *Had loved.* Past tense. He had to remind himself of that. *This is about making it up to her, not falling back in love with her.*

He set the dress down on a nearby couch. He did not need a mental image of Willa in a wedding dress. She had broken his heart when she disappeared. He'd made the decision to pull her off the story as her boss's boss. It was business. She quit her job, that was her right, but she'd also chosen to throw away their personal relationship.

"Listen, Jack, Jericho and I wanted to do this together but time is getting away, so I'm going to ask." Maggie paused and Jack tensed. He hoped that they didn't want him to negotiate some other issue between the two families. He was done with all the media attention. "We'd like you to officiate our wedding."

Jack stared at her. Why would anyone want him to participate in their wedding? He hadn't dated anyone seriously his entire time in Royal. He was the epitome of a man who couldn't find love. "Why would you want me to officiate? I'm not a minister. Don't you need a license or something?"

"It's a simple application with the town hall and they'll deputize you to officiate. Please, Jack. Jericho and I are very grateful for what you've done to bring our families together. We want that spirit of harmony reflected in our wedding. It would mean a lot."

He eyed Willa and she was staring at him, an inscrutable expression on her face. There was a time when he could tell what she was thinking, when they had a telepathic way of communicating. *That was a long time ago.*

"Please, Jack. I'll even fill out the paperwork and bring it to you for signature."

He waved her off. "It's not the paperwork. This is such a big moment for you and Jericho, and I'm touched that you want me to play such an important part."

Maggie smiled. "Then say yes."

"Yes."

Maggie gave him a quick hug. "Jericho will be so pleased."

Natalie restarted her bid to have Maggie pick a designer dress, so he waved goodbye to Maggie and Natalie and ushered Willa outside.

"So rancher, peace negotiator and now wedding officiator?" Willa said. Jack felt her incredulity and shared it.

"I wasn't expecting that. But that's what so special about Royal—the people here have Texas-sized hearts. The Del Rios and Winterses treat me like family now."

"Maggie seems really down-to-earth," Willa commented they walked.

"She is. That's why I wanted you to meet her. If you ask nicely, she might let you cover their wedding."

"That still wouldn't make up for the Mafia story."

He sighed and stopped on the sidewalk. He needed to look her in the eyes for what he wanted to say. "Willa, you can hate me all you want. I admit I shouldn't have let Jessica take credit for the story but I don't think pulling you off it was a bad decision. Your life was in danger and I chose to protect you."

"But you didn't make that choice for Jessica."

"I didn't want her taking credit for the story. She did that on her own."

"But you didn't issue a retraction."

"It was too late."

"So you say."

He held up his hands. "You believe what you want. Look, I'm happy to help you out here but just remember that I'm not responsible for the decisions you made. You quit your job and disappeared. Maybe if you'd stuck around, Jessica wouldn't have felt so emboldened to take credit, maybe we would've issued a retraction. You are just as responsible for what ultimately happened as I am."

The murderous look on her face told him that she felt differently. So be it. He might not have been the best boss, but he'd been a good boyfriend and didn't deserve to be walked out on.

He strode to the store and opened the door. She stepped through without looking at him.

"Jack Chowdhry, what can I do for you?"

Jack smiled at Pete Ludwig, the owner of the *Hattery*. Pete made and sold all the hats in the store. Jack introduced Willa. "We're on the way to the rodeo, and I need a hat for her."

"A hat?" Willa looked genuinely amused.

"I think you'll find the rodeo is more enjoyable if you wear a cowgirl hat," Jack said and Willa smiled.

One of the first genuine smiles she had given him and his heart warmed.

"I've never owned a cowgirl hat before," she said to Pete who beamed at her, then proceeded to pull off a number of hats from the shelf. There was nothing pink or made of straw in his store. He only used premium materials and specialized in dress hats.

"Let's start with this 40x hat." Pete handed her a soft brown hat.

"What does 40x mean?"

"You know how diamonds are measured in carats? Well, quality hats are measured by the amount of beaver fur in them. A 200x hat is going to be a hundred percent beaver fur." He retrieved a cream-colored hat and handed it to Willa.

"Beaver fur?" Jack didn't miss the skepticism in her voice.

Pete patted the hat. "Don't worry, these hats are cruelty free. My vendors are in Canada where there are strict rules for fur farming. They make sure those animals are treated so nice, it actually makes me wanna be one of them."

She smiled and put on the hat. His heart pinged; she looked good in a cowboy hat, like she belonged in Royal.

"Why don't we get her a 1000x hat," Jack said. It was what he had and he wanted to get Willa the best.

"Wait, if 200x is a hundred percent beaver then what's a thousand?"

Pete pulled a dark brown hat and handed it to Willa, encouraging her to feel it. "A 1000x is beaver fur mixed with mink. It's one of the finest hats made. This one has a buckle made with eighteen karat gold."

Willa gasped and handed the hat back to Pete. "I think I'm good with the first one. I don't need something so fancy."

"If Jack's buyin', young lady, I think you should get the best. It'll look good on you." He placed the hat on her head and damn if Pete wasn't right. The hat fit perfectly on her head.

"Shall we crease it for her, then?" Pete said.

Jack nodded.

"Wait, I'd like to pay for it myself."

Jack waved her off. "Pete, I'll settle up with you," he said as he nudged Willa out of the store. If she found out that the hat cost as much as her monthly paycheck, she'd have a fit.

They returned to the car and drove to the rodeo. Country music blared from the speakers and mixed with the excited chatter of the crowd as they approached the small arena. The air was thick with the smell of hay, dust and fried food. The sun was warm but a slight cool breeze made for a perfect day.

As they made their way to their seats, Jack saw contestants warming up in the arena, practicing their skills with ropes. The crowd was a mix of families with young children and rowdy groups of college students, all dressed in their best cowboy boots and hats.

"I see why I needed the hat." Willa quipped and Jack returned her smile. When he lived in the city, he'd never have dreamed of coming to an event like this but one thing he'd learned in Texas was there was nothing more entertaining than a good rodeo. He hoped the event would bring some levity between him and Willa. The tension was thick between them and he wanted to make peace. They might disagree on who was right or wrong five years ago but it was important for him to have closure with Willa. He wanted to move on with his life, find a wife, have children and raise a family. It wasn't as if there was a shortage of women. He was one of the most eligible bachelors in town, and everyone from the board of the Texas Cattleman's Club to old Pete had set him up with highly desirable women. He had been the one who couldn't close the deal and he knew why. He needed Willa to forgive him, and this was his chance.

As the rodeo began, the announcer's voice boomed over the loudspeakers, introducing the different events.

"Hey, Jack." Jack recognized his friend's voice and turned to find Nico in his typical baggy T-shirt and jeans, his messy auburn hair capped with a beanie. Nico had become a master of invisibility. Despite not being guilty, he'd done a stint in prison and now avoided attention in case someone recognized him.

"Willa, this is Nico."

Nico eyed Willa as he shook her hand, then gave Jack a raised-eyebrow look. "Nico, Willa St Germaine is a former colleague of mine from CMG."

Nico grinned. "Ah, so you are indeed *that* Willa."

Willa looked at him, then at Nico. "What has Jack said about me?"

Jack put a heavy hand on Nico's shoulder. Bro code for *Shut your mouth, what I shared stays between us*.

But Nico had that evil glint in his hazel eyes. "Oh,

he's had plenty to say about you but if I say anything more right now, he might just dislocate my shoulder. So how about we catch up another time?"

"Nico…" Jack didn't bother hiding the warning in his tone.

"Why don't you come to my sister's party tonight? Misha is about to take her app, k!smet, public and has an event tonight for members."

"Misha Law is your sister?" Jack could almost see Willa's mind connect the dots and realize that Nico was the brother with the unsavory past. He made a mental note to tell her not to exploit Nico's past in whatever story she wrote about k!smet.

"Nico has his own company…"

"AlgoXcell, the app development company."

Willa never ceased to amaze Jack. Nico's ownership in AlgoXcell was not public knowledge. Her talents were being wasted at NYEN. While he had her attention, he had to convince her to let him help get her a job. He'd sold CMG, which had been renamed from Chowdhry Media Group to Consumer Media Group, but he still had a lot of influence at the network. Every year they begged him to take a board seat that he turned down.

Nico went quiet. Jack knew he was uncomfortable with being recognized. "I'd love to chat some more but I'm meeting a new client before the show starts. Why we couldn't meet in my office, I'll never know." He turned to Willa. "I do hope you'll come tonight, and if you haven't already, sign up for the app. There are a lot of eligible bachelors in Royal." He nodded at Willa, then left.

She turned to Jack. "Did you sign up for the app?"

Busted.

"It's to help Misha with the publicity for the upcoming IPO. The app has a lot of potential but she needs the IPO to bring in some more serious cash as soon as the stock is opened to the public. The company valuation has come in high but ultimately the success of an IPO rests on people being excited about investing in the company."

"That's why you want me to do a story on k!smet, to help your friends."

Jack sighed. "I see it as a win-win. K!smet has been getting a lot of media attention, so Misha won't have any trouble attracting the media to her IPO launch. But I don't believe most journalists can produce as good a story as you can, which is why I'm willing to vouch for you with my friends and get you exclusive access."

"I suppose the price of that exclusive access will be some quid pro quo on what the story can and cannot say."

"Have I asked that of you?"

She looked away. The announcer's voice boomed over the loudspeaker once again, introducing the first event—bull riding. Jack and Willa took their seats. Jack surreptitiously looked at Willa as she was mesmerized by the sight of the first bull entering the starting gate. The bull was massive, his muscles rippling as he bucked and snorted, angry at being caged in the gate where a rider was climbing onto its back, gripping the rope tightly. At the rider's nod, the starting gate that had caged the bull swung open. The bull exploded out of the chute, its hooves kicking up dust as it bucked and twisted, doing everything in its power to dislodge the rider. The cowboy hung on for dear life, his body slamming against the bull's back with each buck. The tension in the arena was palpable as the rider fought to stay on, the bull bucking with even more intensity. Willa's eyes were wide, and her hands gripped the edge of her seat as the cowboy finally tumbled to the ground.

"Is he okay?"

Jack nodded. "This is expected. The sport is to see who can stay on the bull the longest. That guy made it 8.3 seconds, a pretty decent score." He pointed to the electronic scoreboard.

The next one was even more hair-raising. The rider was bucked off the back of the bull but he managed to somehow hold on to the rope and attempted several times to reclimb onto the back. Willa gripped his hand in earnest as the whole crowd sat on the edge of their seats. Jack smiled. Willa was the kind of reporter who would go into a tornado to report on the danger faced by a community but a horror movie got her every time. She couldn't take the suspense. He squeezed her hand reassuringly as the rider finally gave up and let himself fall to the ground.

"I can't believe those riders. That takes serious guts."

"Yeah," he said. "They're pretty amazing, aren't they?"

That was when Willa noticed she was holding his

hand and pulled her arm with such force that she nearly fell out of her seat.

"We have a past, Willa. I think it's okay if we try to be friends."

Willa looked at him with such sadness in her eyes that it pinched his heart.

"There are some things you can't come back from, Jack."

Six

It was late afternoon by the time they returned to Jack's house. While Willa had fun at the rodeo, she hadn't managed to get a single piece of information that would make for a good story. She hoped Rogerio had done better. If there was one thing she had learned during the day, it was that spending time with Jack was dangerous. There had been too many moments in the day when it felt like old times, when she'd forgotten about what he'd done, when she hadn't remembered the secret she was keeping from him: the big one about Priya, and the small one about why she was really in Royal. The newly reformed Jack seemed to have all the things she loved about the old one, and none of the parts that she hadn't liked. It was all a recipe for disaster. This time she wasn't just playing with her own emotions, she had Priya she needed to consider.

"I have some emails to return. Steve said he left sandwiches and some sides in the fridge for us if you're hungry."

Willa thanked him and escaped to her room. She texted Rogerio. They had to get out of Royal. As she waited for Rogerio, she sat in one of the armchairs in her Paris-themed room and looked for flights. If they left in two hours, they could make it to Atlanta by midnight. Then they either had to wait overnight at the airport or drive to New York. She was okay with either.

Rogerio burst through the door without knocking. Even before he said a word, Willa's heart sank. It was clear from the excitement in his eyes that he'd found out something.

"There is definitely a story here," he burst out. "It has to do with Priya."

Willa's heart stopped, her breath caught in her chest and she couldn't breathe. Had Jack somehow found out about Priya? She thought she'd been careful but what if she hadn't?

"Not your Priya, Jack's Priya," Rogerio said softly, taking a seat in the armchair across from her.

Willa took a deep breath.

"Priya died ten years ago."

Rogerio nodded. "Yes, but Jack uncovered something about her death. Apparently, it wasn't an accident like he thought."

Willa leaned forward. As far as she knew, Priya had been hit by a drunk driver in New York City when she was returning home from a party late one night. The driver had been caught and jailed to the maximum sentence of life in prison.

"How did you find this out?"

"Steve, the chef. We've been um…getting to know each other. By the way, he made this pasta salad for lunch that is to die for. You have to go down and try some. It has arugula and…"

"Rogerio! The story about Priya."

"Right. Steve was one of the first people Jack hired for this estate. Steve was friendly with the contractor who was building this house. Anyhow, the contractor told Steve that Nico Law came to visit the property with Jack. The contractor was all up in arms about it because this Nico had just got out of prison and he thought the guy might be trying to con Jack. So he eavesdropped on their conversation and discovered that Nico and Jack were friends and that the driver who hit Priya was in the same prison as Nico. He found out something about Priya's death and whatever it was made Jack give up CMG and leave New York City."

Willa's nerves were tingling. Jack had been very close to his sister and her death had devastated him.

"Did Steve have any more details?"

Rogerio shook his head. "He heard this story second-hand. The contractor is no longer in Royal but I have his name. We can try and track him down."

Willa nodded. "We also need to talk to Nico. I met him today at the rodeo…"

"The rodeo?"

"I'll tell you about it later. Let me see if I can get a number for Nico."

"Good luck with that. Apparently, the guy is super secretive, near invisible. You aren't going to find him in the phone book."

"But I can ask Jack for his number, maybe under the guise of wanting to do a story on k!smet. Nico is Misha Law's brother."

Her mind was going a mile a minute. What could possibly have happened that made Jack give up everything? Was someone blackmailing him? Was he somehow responsible for Priya's death? She shook off the last thought. When she started dating Jack, only five years had passed since Priya's death and he was still very affected by it. If he had something to do with her death, it was not on purpose. In any scenario, there was a story there that could be good.

"So what's the plan?" Willa asked.

Rogerio smirked. "You have steam coming out your ears, darling. Or as they say here, darlin'."

Willa rolled her eyes at his fake Texas twang. "Misha Law is having a party for k!smet tonight. Jack said he'll get me an invitation. Nico will be there. He mentioned the party to me today. I'll have to talk to him there, catch him off guard. Then we can leave tomorrow. No reason to stay here longer than necessary."

"Um, how about the fact that this is better than any dude ranch you could pay for, not to mention the fact that the food is amazing."

"This is not a vacation, Rogerio."

"Look, just one day here and we've found a murder mystery. Let's stay a few more days and see what we find."

"We can't stay."

"Why not? We don't have any other stories we're covering and Jack's invitation seems pretty open-ended. Aside from a story on him, we can work on that k!smet story."

Willa didn't like it. She didn't want to be away from Priya and she didn't like the idea of spending any more time with Jack.

"Let's stay a few more days at least. I have a date with Steve tonight. We're having dinner in Royal. He's been here a long time and knows all the restauranteurs. Maybe he can give me some more leads.

She slumped into the chair. "Tonight, and tomorrow night. That's it."

Rogerio bit his lip and Willa could almost see his mind coming up with additional arguments to stay longer. Then another thought struck Willa. "If you're going to dinner with Steve, that means I'm alone with Jack for the party."

"Steve said he's not dating anyone and usually spends nights alone at home."

Great. Jack and her all alone at home was not an image she needed.

"Didn't we discuss this? I don't want to be alone with Jack."

Rogerio leaned forward and put his hand on her knee. "I say this with love—you two have unresolved romantic issues. The tension between you last night and this morning was as thick as a frozen milkshake."

"Well, you know why that is."

"Yeah, but he's not just some ex. He's your baby daddy and there might come a day when you need a kidney or something from him. You need to make nice. And—" Rogerio bit his lip "—I think you need to tell him about Priya."

"Rogerio, no!"

"Look, I was talking with Steve and he said that Jack's parents have been bugging him to get married. Every morning at breakfast they show him potential women they can set him up with and it's clear that Jack is seriously considering it. Think about it. Someday he will have children. Priya will have half brothers and sisters and one of them will take a 23andMe DNA test and realize that they are related. Then your daughter is going to hate you for not telling her of the existence of her father."

Willa looked away. Rogerio was right. She'd thought about the fact that Priya would one day want more of an explanation than *some children have mommies and daddies and some only have mommies*. When Priya was mature enough to ask her the tough questions, she wanted to have answers.

Suddenly she was exhausted. Nothing made sense anymore. She'd come to Royal to get dirt on Jack and get her career back but all of a sudden, she was wondering whether or not to tell him about Priya.

"Willa, one day there is going to be a father-daughter dance at Priya's school and she's going to want to ask whether her father knows she exists. If the answer is no, then Jack won't be the bad guy."

She buried her face in her hands. Rogerio was right. She'd grown up with two parents and hadn't really thought about what it might be like for a little girl to grow up without knowing who her father was. At some point Willa assumed she would marry, settle down with someone, and whoever it was would adopt Priya. But that was such a naive plan. No decent man would want to lie to his daughter about her paternity.

"You need to establish a relationship with Jack, find a way to tell him about Priya."

"What if he wants to take her away from me?" Her voice cracked. It was the worst fear of her life; she would rather stay on the gossip beat at NYEN for the rest of her life than have Priya taken away from her.

"That's why it has to be done right. You have to make nice with Jack. If he wants to be part of Priya's life, you have to let him. He doesn't strike me as the kind of guy who would take a daughter away from her mother, but from what Steve's said about him, he probably will want to have a role in her life."

Willa closed her eyes, willing for an easy answer to present itself.

"Let's see how it goes tonight. If I get the opportunity, maybe I'll tell him tonight."

Seven

Willa didn't know what one wore to an IPO pre-launch party for a dating app. But she didn't have a lot of choices since she'd packed light, so she wore the same dress that she had the night before. She blew out her hair so it hung in shiny waves down her back, and took her time doing her makeup.

It was all worth it to see Jack's appreciative glance when she walked down the stairs. He'd offered to give her a ride since Rogerio took the rental car for his date with Steve. Jack looked and smelled amazing. He was wearing jeans with an untucked white shirt, open at the collar.

"Your match tonight will be one lucky guy."

"My match?"

He led her to the red Porsche and opened the door for

her. "Up until the stock goes public Misha is planning events, contests and giveaways to highlight all aspects of the k!smet app. Tonight the party is going to show-case the Surprise Me! feature for the dating section of the app, so if you show up to the party single, you're going to get roped into trying your luck."

"Is participation mandatory?"

"No, but Misha can be very persuasive. She already got me to agree to do it. You should too—it might be fun. Have you created an account on the app?"

Willa sighed. She had created an account because she knew only members were invited but she hadn't activated it. There was enough going on with her life right now without inserting a love interest.

When they got to the Texas Cattleman's Club, the party was just starting. It was indoors in the clubhouse common area, which was a large open space with soar-ing ceilings, comfortable couches and armchairs, a brick fireplace, and a wood bar in the corner. Waiters were passing out hors d'oeuvres and champagne. Jack grabbed a glass and handed it to Willa.

"So, are you two going to play?" Willa turned to find Misha smiling at them.

"Exactly what are we playing for?"

"Love." She looked between Jack and Willa, then winked at them. "The Surprise Me! feature tonight matches you with someone that the app thinks is per-fect for you based on our algorithm. The first ten cou-ples to get a match tonight get an all-expense paid date and a ticket to the IPO launch party. You don't have to be here in order to win, but any couple in attendance will also receive a bottle of Cristal."

"I don't know. I'm planning on going back to New York tomorrow, it's not like I have time to see if my match works."

"Plans change. You never know…" Misha said playfully. "C'mon, try it out. Don't you want to see how it works for your story?"

Willa sighed. "Okay, but can I get a few minutes with you to ask a few questions."

"For a friend of Jack's, how can I say no."

It took Willa a few seconds to activate her profile on k!smet and enter the contest. Maybe the app would match her with Nico and she could use the opportunity to interview him.

By the time the party got underway, there were more than a hundred people gathered in the common room. Jack introduced her around the room. Willa found herself enjoying the company of the Royal residents. They all seemed to love Jack, and for a little while Willa forgot that time had passed between them. It seemed so familiar to be at a party together. Jack always managed to stop the waiters who had the quiche that she loved; he knew when to steer away when the conversation died down. She found herself having a good time. It wasn't until she saw Nico standing alone in a corner that she remembered why she had come to the party in the first place.

She made an excuse to go to the bathroom and approached him.

"The party seems to be a success. Are you having a good time?" she asked.

Nico smiled at her. "Don't tell my sister, but no. These public parties are not really my thing. I'm here to support Misha."

"You're a good brother. So do you think the IPO will go well after the rough patches that started at ByteCon?"

"Ah, always the reporter."

"Guilty." She figured she would soften him up with some easy questions about the app before getting into the Priya story.

"I think k!smet's success speaks for itself. It's a good product and investors see that. Misha has a lot of interest in the IPO."

"Will you invest in the company, other than the fact that Misha is your sister?"

"I have invested in it despite the fact that she's my sister." He grinned to let her know he was joking. "And I plan to increase my investment. In all seriousness, I would've invested even if she wasn't my sister. Like I said, it's a good product with a lot of potential customers in all areas—lifestyle, business and especially dating. There's a lot of people out there looking for love."

"Are you one of them?"

"Me, looking for love? No, thank you. What about you? Are you and Jack getting back together?"

She bristled at the question but was glad that they'd gotten to Jack. "Jack and my time has passed. I understand you two know each other pretty well. Even back when you were in prison."

She knew she'd gone too far as soon as she saw him straighten. "Yes." From the look on his face, Willa knew that he was about to end their conversation.

"Listen, cards on the table. I care about Jack and I heard a rumor that you gave him information about the death of his sister. What was it?"

Nico shook his head. "That's something you're going to have to ask Jack about."

Willa sighed in frustration. She hadn't gotten as much as she wanted but Nico's tone and face clearly conveyed that there was something to tell there. He did have some information about Priya's death.

She returned to find Jack and the others gathered around Misha, who was directing everyone into a nearby barn for dinner and dancing.

A country music band was playing on stage and a wooden dance floor dominated the center of the barn. The ceiling was covered with string lights. The smell of hay and barbecue mixed with the festive chatter of the crowd. The band was good and it didn't take long for people to gravitate to the floor.

"Want to dance?" Jack asked, holding out his hand.

Willa hesitated for a moment, feeling nervous and self-conscious. She wasn't much of a dancer. But then he smiled at her, a warm and reassuring expression that made her feel braver. She took his hand, feeling the rough calluses of his palm against hers, and let him lead her onto the dance floor.

The music was slow and sweet, a classic country ballad that Willa had heard before. She felt Jack's arm wrap around her waist, pulling her close, and she instinctively placed her hand on his shoulder. They moved together in a simple two-step, their bodies swaying in time with the music. Willa felt a thrill run through her as she realized how good it felt to be held by Jack, to feel his strength and his warmth against her. For a while, they danced in silence, lost in the rhythm of the music and the intimacy of the moment. Then Jack leaned down and whispered in her ear.

"You look beautiful tonight," he said.

Willa's cheeks grew warm as she looked up at him, meeting his gaze.

"Thank you," she said softly.

Willa felt a pang of disappointment when the song ended and Jack pulled away from her, but then he took her hand and led her off the dance floor.

"Want to go for a walk?" he asked, gesturing toward the open barn doors.

Willa nodded, her heart fluttering. They stepped outside into the cool night air, the stars twinkling above them.

"Do you ever wonder what would've happened if we'd stayed together?" Willa surprised herself by asking the question.

Jack gave her a dimpled smile. "More often than I'd like to admit." He held out his hand, palm up. She looked at his upturned hand and placed her hand in his. He squeezed it lightly.

As they held hands, Willa couldn't help but feel overwhelmed by the wave of emotions that rushed over her. Memories of their time together flooded her mind, both the good and the bad. She had tried so hard to forget him, to move on with her life, but seeing him again made it clear that she had never truly let go.

Jack's thumb stroked the back of her hand, and she felt a shiver run through her body. His touch was electric, sending a jolt of desire through her that she had thought was long-buried.

"I've missed you, Willa," he said softly, his voice laced with longing.

She looked up at him, meeting his gaze. She could see the sincerity in his eyes, and she knew that he meant every word. But could she trust him? Could she risk her heart again? A part of her still loved him but a bigger part was still angry, still hurt.

"We had our chance five years ago," she said, her voice barely above a whisper.

He let go of her hand, then stepped close, so close that she could feel his breath. "Are you saying there's nothing left between us?"

His mouth was right there. All she had to do was stand on her tiptoes, and her lips could touch his. A slight breeze caressed her hair and she shivered. Jack ran his hands down her goose-bumped arms. Her nerves were on fire.

"I don't want to make the same mistake twice," she whispered, her heart racing.

He leaned in, his lips hovering just inches from hers. "What if it wasn't a mistake?" he murmured, his eyes locked onto hers.

Her resolve crumbled as his warm breath brushed against her skin. She closed her eyes and tilted her head up, inviting him in. Their lips met in a soft, gentle kiss.

It wasn't enough. She wanted so much more from him. As their kiss deepened, Willa's fingers tangled in Jack's hair, pulling him closer. His arms wrapped around her waist, holding her tight against him. The kiss grew more intense, their tongues tangled, their bodies pressed together.

When they finally pulled away, they were both breathless, their eyes locked onto each other's. Willa's heart was racing, her mind reeling from the intensity of the kiss. She couldn't believe how much she still wanted him after all these years.

"We can't do this" she whispered. It was too dangerous, getting this close to Jack.

"There's something here, Willa."

She couldn't deny that there was.

"We're not a good match, Jack," she said, her voice barely above a whisper. "We never were."

Willa's heart lurched as she looked into Jack's eyes and wished things could be different. But they weren't. They had always been from different worlds, and now those worlds seemed farther apart than ever. "You have your entire life here in Royal," she continued, "and I'm still trying to make it as a national reporter. You're ready to settle down with a wife and kids and I…." *already have a daughter.* She swallowed. "I need to focus on my career."

She wasn't going to pick up and move to Royal. This was her time to make it as a journalist. She'd already lost her career once because of Jack; she couldn't give up her dreams again for him.

He stepped back and was about to say something when they were interrupted.

"All guests inside, please. The Surprise Me! matches are being announced." One of the TCC staff came around with a bell.

Jack touched her arm but she pulled away. They went back inside where a crowd was gathered around Misha. Willa's lips tingled from the lingering touch of Jack's mouth.

"All right everyone, check the app. I have the results here of our surprise matches. Here they are." She began to read off the names. Willa looked at her phone and nearly dropped it.

"And for our last match, no surprise here. If you've talked to them tonight, you know they are perfect for each other. Jack Chowdhry and Willa St Germaine." Misha walked over and shook Jack's hand. Willa was stunned. Of all the people in the room, the app matched her with Jack?

Jack leaned down. "I guess we are a match after all."

Eight

Willa and Jack left the party early. They drove back to the ranch in silence, each lost in their own thoughts. *Why did I kiss him?* All the old feelings were flooding her heart. She had loved Jack, which was why he could hurt her as badly as he had. The doctors might have thought the depression was related to pregnancy horomones but she knew that those two years were about how much she missed Jack. How could she risk going back to that place? There was no way things could end well with Jack. He'd never felt the same for her as she had for him. Not once had he told her he loved her.

She also had Priya to consider. What would Priya say if Willa introduced her to Jack? Priya was just small enough that she would probably embrace her daddy. A few more years and that same conversation would be filled with hurt and recriminations. Rogerio was right, Willa had to find a way to tell Jack. Which was all the more reason to stay away from him. If she and Jack rekindled their relationship and it didn't work out, what would it mean for Priya?

When they returned to the ranch, she excused herself and went to her bedroom to change out of her dress. She called her sister and told her all about Jack.

"Willa, why didn't you tell me?" Kylie's face filled the phone screen and her blue eyes were wide with worry.

Her eyes stung with tears. "I know how you feel about Jack. If I told you I was going to see him, you would've talked me out of coming here."

"So why tell me now?"

"Because I want you to talk me into coming home."

Kylie frowned. "When you come home, can you forget about him?"

"How can I? Priya…." She couldn't even finish the sentence. As young as she was, her daughter was so much like her father. She had the same soft brown eyes, dimples in her cheeks, and dark hair. Even beyond looks, she had Jack's charm and take-charge attitude.

"You'll always wonder, Willa. Now that you've opened the door, you need to walk through it and make sure you can close it for good." Willa squeezed her eyes shut. That was not what she wanted to hear. Her sister had always been anti-Jack, even when they were just dating, before Priya. She'd been afraid that Willa was too invested in the relationship and that Jack didn't return her feelings. Kylie was the one who had advised

Willa not to contact Jack all these years to tell him about Priya.

"Mama?"

Willa opened her eyes to see Priya's face fill the screen. Her daughter stared at her with big brown eyes. Priya's wavy hair hung in loose pigtails, and her cheeks were as pink as the unicorn pajamas she wore. Priya climbed onto her sister's lap.

"Now what are you doing out of bed so late?" Willa said admonishingly though she was glad to see her daughter.

"I had a bad dream and came to look for Aunt Kylie."

"Aww sweetheart, do you need mama to sing you the bad dreams song?"

Priya nodded and Willa sang the silly words she had made up to the tune of twinkle twinkle little star. "Bad dreams, bad dreams go away, don't come back another day...."

Priya's eyes welled up with tears and she sniffed softly. "I miss you mama. I want you here with me."

Willa's heart ached for her daughter. She fought back her own tears and mustered all the brightness she could in her voice. "I'll be home soon. Why don't you tell me who you saw on the playground today."

Despite the tears that still hung on Priya's cheeks, her eyes brightened. Kylie had already filled Willa in on the fact that they'd seen Priya's best friend from pre-school at the neighborhood playground. Priya excitedly chatted about her playground adventures.

Willa listened and soaked in the sight and sound of her daughter. There was so much more of Jack in her than Willa had appreciated before. The way she widened her eyes when she was excited, the way her mouth twitched when she was trying to control her amusement.

When she finally yawned, Willa told her to go back to bed. "I love you sweetheart."

"Come home soon, Mama."

She blew Priya a kiss and the little girl jumped off her aunt's lap and headed back towards her room. Kylie appeared back on screen. "Be careful."

Willa ended the video call. Her sister was right. She needed to sort out her feelings for Jack. She couldn't go through life wondering whether something could have been between them.

She made her way to the kitchen and was greeted with the delicious aroma of peppers, onions and seasoned meat. Her heart leaped into her chest as she saw Jack with his back turned to her at the stove. He was wearing an apron and had something sizzling on the gas.

The kitchen was starting to feel like home to Willa. She loved the warm, creamy color of the walls that complemented the rich wood cabinets.

As she approached, he turned and gave her a dimpled smile that made her toes curl.

She leaned against the edge of the island, watching as Jack deftly flipped a piece of meat and tossed in a handful of chopped peppers and onions. She hadn't eaten at the party and her stomach rumbled.

"You cook now?"

"Some basic things."

"What're you making?"

"Steak fajitas."

My favorite. "I thought you had a full-time chef."

"Steve is half-time. He does breakfast and lunch for me and the staff who come to work here but then he goes home for the afternoon. I try to make dinner. Ma still likes to cook. Usually, it's just us for dinner. Aside from the night manager, and a few ranch hands who stay to do the evening feed and make sure the animals are good, everyone goes home."

"Smells amazing," she said, her eyes on the sizzling pan. "Can I help?"

He gestured to the bar stools on the island. "Take a seat. Want a drink?"

"Sure, what're you serving?"

He grinned and her stomach flipped. "Margaritas of course."

Of course. They'd met at a Mexican bar that was a popular Friday night hangout of those who worked at CMG. Everyone knew of Jack Chowdhry, the owner, but no one had really interacted with him. One night, he'd walked into the bar, bought pitchers of margarita and became friends with the entire crew. They hadn't officially started dating for six months but Jack came to the bar every Friday night and asked her out until she finally said yes.

Jack lowered the flame on the gas, then removed a pitcher from the fridge. He handed her a salt-rimmed glass and poured a margarita on the rocks. Just the way she liked it.

She took a sip and savored the salty, tangy taste. It

was probably the best margarita she'd ever had. "Wow, what did you put in here?"

"The key is good tequila. The one I use is one hundred percent agave añejo."

As Jack finished up the fajitas, he turned off the stove and slid the sizzling pan onto a nearby trivet. He grabbed a couple of plates from the cabinet and began to assemble the fajitas with care, layering the tender meat, the sautéed vegetables, and a generous dollop of guacamole onto each plate.

Willa's mouth watered as she watched him work, taking in the savory scents of the fajitas and the colorful array of ingredients.

"I wasn't even hungry but I'm starving now," she said as he slid her plate forward, then took a seat next to her at the island.

They chatted about Royal while they ate, Jack filling her in on the local restaurants, festivals and the operations of his ranch. For a while she forgot about the fact that Jack was the man who broke her heart. The conversation between them was easy; it always had been. They could talk about everything from whether Coke was better than Pepsi all the way to geo politics.

Dinner was so delicious that Willa finished her generous plate. "Is there an exercise room in this palace? I feel like I need to run a few miles."

Jack smiled. "I do have a gym but how about some fresh air. It's a beautiful night. I have a trail that goes around the property."

Just like everything else on the property, the walking trail was perfectly designed to fit into the surroundings.

Willa hadn't realized that they'd spent hours talking over dinner. The night sky was an inky blue and studded with stars. The trail was a lighted footpath that provided just enough illumination to walk safely without interfering with the beauty of the night.

"Wow, I don't think I've seen this many stars."

"Yeah, that's the beauty of not being in a city." There was a waxing gibbous moon and Willa imagined Priya there with them. The little girl loved the *Goodnight Moon* book but they rarely got a clear enough view of the moon in the city.

"This will be a great place to raise children."

She stopped short. Had he read her mind?

"Excuse me?"

He stepped close to her and she became a little too aware of the closeness of his body, the heat emanating from him. "Sorry, didn't mean to startle you."

"Since when do you want kids?"

He shrugged, "Since I turned forty and realized what's important in life."

Her chest hurt. They'd celebrated his thirty-ninth birthday together. That was four months before they broke up. Priya was born around the time he turned forty.

He touched her cheek. "Willa…"

She didn't let him finish the sentence. Suddenly, his scent, the way a lock of his hair fell onto his forehead, the dimpled smile. It was all too much. She went on her tiptoes and touched her lips to his. He was fast on the uptake and wrapped his arm around her, pulling her close.

It was a gentle kiss at first, filled with a longing and a tenderness that had been building between them. Willa's hands found their way to Jack's face, tracing the lines of his jaw, feeling the stubble on his cheeks. He deepened the kiss, his arms wrapping tightly around her waist, pulling her against his body.

Willa's tongue traced the seam of Jack's lips, inviting him to open up to her, and he eagerly obliged, their tongues dancing together with the familiarity of the past, and hunger of the last five years. Somewhere in the back of her mind, Willa knew she should stop, that it shouldn't go further than the kiss. but it was like a dam had opened up inside her. Her body was pressed against his as her hands skimmed the hard muscles of his broad chest. Jack's hands were in the small of her back and the feel of his hard body pushed her over the edge. She wanted him with the kind of smoldering pressure that made volcanoes erupt.

She slipped her hand under his shirt, feeling the rough hair on his chest and the smooth skin of his back. He moaned as she ran her fingernails down his back, knowing it would drive him crazy.

"Willa." He broke the kiss long enough to say her name with a thick, throaty voice that made her grind her body against his, eager to feel him hard against her core.

He looked down at her with dark eyes. *No turning back now.*

"Are we really doing this?"

She nodded. In a flash, he stepped away from her. A sound of protest escaped her lips before he grabbed her hand. "There's a guest cottage not too far."

In the last five years, she'd been with one other guy: a sweet man whom her sister had set her up with. They'd dated for several months. Arnie had been attentive, down-to-earth and ready to settle down. The perfect man. She had really liked him but he'd never lit her up after a whole night together the way Jack was igniting her right now.

They nearly ran to the cottage. Jack threw open the door, dragged her inside, then kicked the door close. His mouth was on her, his hands under her shirt. He cupped her breasts, rubbed her nipples with his thumbs. She broke the kiss to take off her T-shirt. He unhooked her bra and she lifted the hem of his shirt. Her hands moved to his belt, working ferociously to unbutton his jeans and slide them down.

"Slow down," he teased but she wasn't going to listen. His erection told her that he was just as desperate to be with her as she was with him. Somewhere in the tumble of getting their clothes off, Jack had maneuvered them to the bedroom. Willa didn't register anything about her surroundings; all she could think about was Jack, how good he felt, how much she wanted and needed him, how much she'd missed him.

Her legs pushed up against the edge of the bed and Jack put his hands on her butt and lifted her onto the bed. He started with trailing kisses down her neck, his core hot against her own. She arched her back as his mouth found her breasts and his fingers pressed on her core then slid inside her.

"I've missed you," he whispered, before bending down to take one of her nipples in his mouth, swirling his tongue around it until it was so hard that Willa couldn't stand it. She moaned and lifted her hips, urging him to give her what she wanted. Jack teased her some more with his mouth and fingers until she grabbed his erection and stroked him, enjoying the way he groaned and rasped her name. Finally, he lifted himself, went and found a condom from somewhere and slid it on.

When he entered her, the pleasure was so intense that Willa screamed and dug her nails into his back. He pushed in and out slowly at first, increasing his tempo to match the thrusts of her hips. It didn't take Willa long to give in to the orgasm that had been smoldering inside her. She clenched around Jack, enjoying the feel of her body clinging onto him. Her pleasure was so intense that she didn't even notice when Jack finished.

Her body was spent. Jack moved her under the soft blankets and held her under the sheets, his body spooning her the way she liked. It didn't take long for her to feel him hard against her back. She moved against him and he trailed kisses down the back of her neck, cupped her breasts and they began all over again.

The rest of the night was a blur of pleasure and passion as they explored each other's bodies, rediscovering the love that had brought them together in the first place. Willa didn't know when night turned into morning but when she woke, Jack was gone.

Nine

Jack hoped Willa didn't wake in the time it took him to go to the main house and return with breakfast. He hadn't expected last night to happen but was glad it had. He'd been kidding himself to think that he was over Willa. Last night had proven to him that he clearly wasn't over her. In the last five years, he'd been with exactly two women. Both were extraordinary people he would've been lucky to be with. But he hadn't experienced the passion and intensity that he had with Willa, not even close. The relationships had been entirely mundane and inconsequential.

He figured he just hadn't found the right woman but he was wrong. It was Willa. It had always been Willa. For the last five years, he'd been angry and hurt at the way she'd walked out. So what if she disagreed with him for taking a story. That didn't mean that she could walk out on their relationship and disappear for five years. She'd hurt him more than he cared to admit.

Jack stared at the breakfast tray. He'd spent a long time trying to forget her. He had trusted her with his heart, and she had walked away without so much as a goodbye. Could he trust her not to leave him again? Was he willing to risk his heart again?

Sighing, he picked up the tray. He could hold on to that anger but if there was anything he'd learned, it was that life was uncertain. Willa was the love of his life and he still had feelings for her. The way she'd reacted to him last night, she clearly still felt something for him. This time he had to make sure that he didn't lose her.

He returned to the cottage carrying a tray of juice, coffee, and waffles with strawberries and whipped cream. Her favorite breakfast. It was funny how he hadn't been able to remember whether his last girlfriend liked tea or coffee but Willa's every like and dislike was seared into his memory.

As soon as he stepped into the cottage, he sensed it. Willa was gone.

Where the hell is Rogerio?

They needed to leave right away to make the next flight out of Houston back to New York City. What had she been thinking last night? She'd given in to her desire for Jack without fully thinking through the consequences. Part of her wanted closure. They'd never really broken up or said goodbye to their relationship. That night when she'd left him, they'd fought about her story.

He'd talked about all the reasons he couldn't air the story but not once had he said he loved her, that he was trying to protect her because he couldn't lose her. Their relationship hadn't mattered to Jack; she'd been just one more in the endless stream of girlfriends he'd had before her. Not that she could blame him. When they started dating, he'd made it perfectly clear to her that he was not the type of man to settle down and marry. That was what had ultimately stopped her from telling him about Priya. She didn't want him to stay with her out of some sense of obligation, and Priya was better off without a father than one who saw her as a mistake.

For years, Willa had clung to the memory of Jack like a drowning woman to a life raft. He had been her panacea of passion, the one person who had ever made her feel truly alive. No one else had ever come close to connecting with her, emotionally or physically, the way Jack had. She wanted those memories to be flawed. She was sure that she had built Jack up in her mind, romanticized their time together until it was more than it ever really was. Last night was supposed to have been goodbye, a way to get him out of her system, to realize that Jack was not so extraordinary, that whatever they had between them was far in the past.

Except, last night had been better than she remembered. They had been so in sync, so perfectly matched in every way. The feel of his lips still made hers tingle. Her body was still alive with the feel of his hands. That was not how it was supposed to go. How was she going to think objectively about whether or not to bring Jack into Priya's life when she was so conflicted about whether or not she wanted him in hers? She needed to get away from him so she could think more clearly.

She was frantically throwing things into her duffel bag when she heard the knock on the door. Her heart caught in her throat as she turned to see Jack standing there, wearing the same clothes from last night, and looking way too delectable.

"Willa." His voice was hoarse.

"I can't do this Jack."

"Why not?"

Because I have a daughter with you. I can't fall in love with you; it's not just me that'll get hurt this time. I have to put Priya first.

"We've done this before, Jack. It didn't work out so well."

"And whose fault is that?"

You can't be serious. She turned to him and put her hands on her hips. "Do we need to replay how you took away the biggest story of my life and ruined my career?"

"I took away the story for your safety. You ruined your career by quitting your job and disappearing."

I disappeared because I was pregnant with your daughter. There was no way to explain why she left without revealing Priya's presence.

Jack stepped toward her and she wanted to back away but there was some unseen force that kept her rooted in place so she could catch his scent, feel the heat of his body, soak up the warmth of his eyes.

"We had a disagreement at work. Fine. You quit your job in protest, that was your right. But you didn't just walk out on your job, you also walked out on me. Without so much as goodbye. You just threw away our relationship."

She sucked in a breath. Might as well say it all. "Were we even that serious? It's not as if you had declared your love for me."

He stared at her for several beats, "I had a ring for you."

Her heart stopped in her chest. *What did he say?* "What ring?" She managed to choke out when several moments of silence had passed and he hadn't elaborated.

"An engagement ring. I had it all planned out. I was going to take you out after the story aired and propose."

Her throat closed. She wanted to say something but her mouth was glued shut. He was going to ask her to marry him? How had she not known? She had spent months after their breakup analyzing every part of their relationship, trying to determine how he might feel about a baby.

He took another step forward and put his hands lightly on her arms. Tears stung her eyes but she blinked them back. Jack went on. "That night when I canceled the story, security had come to me with their threat assessment. They clearly told me they couldn't protect you and I was not going to take a chance with your life. You're right, I wouldn't have treated Jessica that way but that's because I wasn't in love with her."

You stupid fool, why didn't you just say all these things five years ago. Our lives would've been so different!

"Why didn't you….why didn't you tell me all this that night?"

"Because I didn't think you would walk out of my life. I thought what we had was more than just work. If you'd bothered to return any of my calls, maybe we could've worked through things."

How could I have taken your calls? By the time her anger had cooled, the pregnancy overshadowed everything else in her life. What if she hadn't acted so emotionally and talked to Jack after their fight five years ago? He would've proposed and she would've known that he was already planning a future for them. She still wouldn't have forgiven him for taking away the story but maybe he could've found a way to make it right after the network decided to air the story. Jessica wouldn't have taken credit for the story with Willa standing right in front of her. She and Jack would've married and Priya would know her father.

Then again, would she have married Jack? After what he'd done, would she have forgiven him? Probably not. But she would've told him about Priya. The main reason she hadn't told him was because she didn't want him to think that he owed her something.

Jack leaned in, his face close to hers, their noses touching. "Let's try this again, Willa. We owe it to each other to see if what we felt last night is real."

That's the whole problem. What if it isn't? If things didn't work out between them, it would be even harder to tell him about Priya.

"What have we got to lose, Willa? If it doesn't work

out, nothing changes, but if it does, just think about what that means for us."

It would mean a family for Priya. She wasn't sure if she actually nodded but Jack bent his head and kissed her with such sweetness that all she could think about what how right it felt to be in his arms. How much she wanted him, wanted the love that he was offering.

The kiss was long and slow and it melted her heart.

"Should we move that bag into my room?"

She smiled. "Let's take things one day at a time. I'll stay here for now."

"I guess I'll have to live with that." He dropped a kiss on her forehead. "There is one other thing I need to talk to you about."

He stepped back from her. "It's about Priya."

Ten

Willa's heart leaped in her throat. Jack knew about Priya. Why had she thought she could keep it from him? What if he wanted to be part of her life? What if he didn't?

"Priya's death wasn't an accident."

Willa nearly choked with relief. He was talking about his sister. Then the look on his face made her freeze. "What do you mean?"

"At the time she died, CMG was GMG, Gagan Media Group, and I was a senior producer for the prime-time news. You remember that I was personally involved in a story about George Wright."

Willa nodded. George Wright was the mayor whose Mafia ties she had uncovered. Jack had turned her on to the story.

"He was then running for mayor. I had him on bribing a judge to get a ruling his way when he was a prosecutor. When I broke that story, his political aspirations would've been over. He paid the driver to hit Priya on purpose. He was just supposed to injure her but…" His voice cracked and she grabbed his hand and squeezed it.

"He wanted to send me a message. However, I never got the message. That night, GMG decided we didn't have enough proof to run the story." He rubbed the back of his neck. "I had no idea that Priya's accident was more than what it seemed until your story was about to air. That's when George Wright decided I needed a message. He sent me an anonymous note about what really happened to Priya. I had no choice but to stop your story. I didn't want to risk what happened to Priya to happen to you."

"Oh, Jack, I'm so sorry. I wish you'd told me."

"There was so much going on at that time. I didn't know what to believe. It could've just as easily been a scare tactic but that's why I had to take the threat seriously. Later on, I found out that the driver who hit Priya was in prison with Nico. I had met Nico years ago at a conference. Brilliant computer programmer. He was about to start his own company when fate kicked him in the nuts and sent him to prison instead. Nico remembered me when I reached out. I got Nico to find out from the taxi driver what the real story was and it turns out that ol' George wasn't bluffing."

Willa was sick to her stomach. Jack had gone through a lot by himself. He'd been so close to his sister. To know that she'd died because of a story he was working on had to be devastating.

"That's why I sold CMG and changed my life. It was a wake-up call about what's really important in life."

"Jack…" She put her arms around him and he returned her hug, holding her tight.

"It's okay. I've had five years to process this. The worst part was having to tell my parents. In an odd way, this was what brought us closer together. They never blamed me."

"That's because you're not to blame."

"It was my story. I put a target on her back."

"He is a corrupt politician who deserves to rot in prison. Why didn't you publish the story about Priya?"

"Because jailhouse gossip is not proof. By publishing the story without adequate proof to get the guy arrested, I would be putting my parents, my brother at risk. I've already lost Priya, I can't risk anyone else. Thanks to your story, the guy has been punished. He's no longer the mayor and his political career is over."

"He should be in prison."

Jack stepped back from her. "Willa. This is not a story." His voice had more than a hint of warning.

"But…"

"No, Willa, listen to me. George Wright may not be the mayor anymore but he's a dangerous man. I told you about Priya because I needed you to understand why I was so afraid for your life, but this is not a story for you to write about. It can put you and my family in danger and…"

Rogerio knocked on the door, interrupting them.

Jack shot her another look, his message clear.

"What did I miss?" Rogerio raised his brows as he caught the expression on their faces.

So much had happened in the last few minutes. What should she tell Rogerio? The story they had come to find was right in front of her, but so was the father of her child and an opportunity for her to find love.

"Jack has kindly offered us his house for the next few days so we can interview Misha Law for the story on the k!smet IPO."

A big smile broke out on Rogerio's face and Jack smiled at her.

"Rogerio and I will need to talk about what we tell our boss."

Jack didn't look pleased at the not-so-subtle dismissal but he left.

Rogerio closed the door behind him.

"You slept with him, didn't you?"

Her eyes widened. "How did you know?"

"Are you kidding? The way you two were standing, so familiar, and the energy in the room. The past couple of days there's been this simmering sexual tension. Today you two seemed more at peace."

"You saw us together, didn't you?"

He grinned. "Steve told me. Jack came into the kitchen and asked for a breakfast tray for you."

She sank into an armchair. "What am I doing, Rogerio? I didn't mean to sleep with him but now that I have, I can't just leave and pretend it didn't happen."

"No, you can't. For your sake, and Priya's, you have to see if there is still something between you."

"But what happens when it doesn't work out between us."

"If…*if* it doesn't work out then you're no worse off than you are now."

"Yes, I am. Because before it was just about me and him. Now Priya is in the mix. No matter what happens, he and I are connected because of her. If it doesn't work out this time…." She buried her face in her hands.

"If five years hasn't put out the fire between you two then no amount of time will. This was bound to happen whenever you two reconnected. Better it happen now, before you tell him about Priya, so you can see what's really there between you."

He was right. If she'd told him about Priya and then they rekindled their relationship, she would forever be left wondering whether he was with her out of obligation.

"All right, we're staying for a few days. We need to figure out what to tell David."

"Yeah, I don't have any more leads on the story about Jack's sister. I talked to some of the Royal locals while Steve and I were out last night but they all think Jack walks on water. Nothing more on how Jack's sister died."

Willa's stomach churned. She wanted to tell Rogerio, but not without first talking to Jack. He could be stubborn but maybe she could talk to Nico again now that she knew more of the story and see if she could get some more details. There had to be a way to punish George Wright for what he did. *That man is responsible for so many deaths. He should be in prison.*

"I'm going to tell David we're tracking down some leads, but until then, we can file a story on how Jack is going to officiate the first Winters-Del Rio wedding. He should like that fluff piece."

"Can I ask the obvious question?"

"Like I can stop you."

"What will you do if you find some explosive story on Jack and you two are still hot and heavy?"

"I'm a journalist first."

"No, you're a mother first. And he's your baby daddy."

You don't need to remind me. He was right. Except, she knew what the story was, and it wasn't about Jack being a bad guy.

"Why don't you go down to breakfast? I need to call and check on Priya."

Rogerio stood but then stopped at the door. "Just one more thing." He shifted on this feet. "Steve was talking about how much Jack wants a family. It got me thinking, what if he wants custody of Priya?"

Willa's heart stopped in her chest. She couldn't even contemplate the thought. Jack would never do that to her. Would he?

Once Rogerio was gone, Willa collapsed on the bed and video-called her sister. Kylie and Priya were having eggs and toast for breakfast. Priya was making a convincing argument that she should be allowed to take a jam sandwich for lunch. Kylie was trying to negotiate for cheese and tomato with a side of strawberries.

Willa missed the routine of their little family. They had a two-bedroom apartment in her parents' brownstone. Kylie had one bedroom and Willa and Priya shared the other. There was no yard and no playroom for Priya. Her toys were scattered in the living room and her bedroom; her coloring pencils and papers littered the dining room table. Willa looked out the window at the expanse of green. Priya would love it on the ranch with space to run around, horses, and a room of her own. Didn't she deserve to know her dad and experience this life too? Was Willa being selfish by keeping this from her?

Once Priya got distracted with something else, Willa asked Kylie if she could watch Priya for a few more days. Kylie readily agreed.

By the time she showered, put on a T-shirt and jeans and got downstairs to breakfast, Jack and Rogerio had already eaten and Steve had cleared the table. Jack had also showered; he was wearing a crewneck T-shirt and jeans, his hair slightly damp. He pointed to a plate. "Fruit, yogurt and a waffle."

My favorites.

"What should we do today?" Willa asked a little too brightly. Now that she'd decided to stay a few days, she was a little nervous about what to do or how to behave. She was used to a hectic schedule of chasing down multiple stories, pickup and drop-offs for Priya, packing lunches, figuring out what her picky toddler was willing to eat that day for dinner. Weekends were for park play dates, frantically figuring out childcare if she had to work, and family movie nights.

Eating a leisurely breakfast with nothing planned for the day was making her itchy.

"I've got plans with Steve. We're going to the farmers market."

Willa looked at Rogerio. Since when did he go to a farmers market? Rogerio's idea of a perfect Sunday was shopping, a football game and a pub crawl. His idea of cooking was putting a frozen meal in the microwave.

"How would you like a horseback riding lesson?" Willa turned to Jack with equal surprise. "Since when do you ride horses?"

"Since I became a Texas rancher."

She couldn't picture it, Jack with his perfectly cut designer business suits riding a horse. As if he'd read her mind, he grinned. "I know, if you'd asked me five years ago if this is where I'd end up, I wouldn't have believed it either."

"I don't think I have horse riding clothes."

Jack smirked. "City girl. Don't worry, jeans and a T-shirt are fine. You can wear sneakers for today's lesson. Once you get a little advanced, we'll get you riding boots."

Jack led Willa to the stables. As they walked down the aisle, the sound of whinnies and neighs filled the air. Jack stopped in front of a muscular quarter horse with a shiny coat and a white blaze on its forehead. "This is Thunder." Willa looked at the horse with a mix of excitement and nervousness. She had never ridden a horse before and his size was a little intimidating.

"First things first, let's introduce you two," Jack said patting the horse's neck. "He's a gentle soul but he can be skittish around new people. Let's have you make friends with him."

"How do we do that?"

"Come on, I'll show you."

He opened the stall door and walked inside, motioning for Willa to follow. "Just stand beside him and let him sniff your hand," Jack said. "Then, start petting him gently, like this."

Jack demonstrated by running his hand down Thunder's neck and back, making soft circles. The horse nickered and leaned into Jack's touch, his eyes half-closed. Willa felt oddly jealous of the tenderness with which Jack was handling Thunder. Would he be just as caring with their daughter?

"Your turn," Jack said, stepping back and gesturing for Willa to take his place.

Tentatively, Willa approached the horse and held out her hand. Thunder sniffed it, then nuzzled her palm with his velvety nose. Willa giggled in delight and started petting him, copying Jack's gentle movements.

"See? He likes you already," Jack said with a grin. "Let's saddle him up."

One of the ranch hands helped them get Thunder ready. "I'm going to have you get comfortable on Thunder in the ring, then we can go on a trail ride."

Willa stood nervously in front of Thunder, her heart racing with excitement and fear, unsure if she could trust herself to control such a powerful animal. Jack stood beside her, his strong hands resting reassuringly on her shoulders.

"Ready?" he asked, his deep voice sending shivers down her spine.

"As I'll ever be," she said, her voice barely above a whisper.

"Good. First things first. We need to make sure you're comfortable in the saddle." Jack helped her up onto the horse and adjusted the stirrups to the right length for her legs. "Now place your feet in the stirrups and hold the reins like this," he instructed, demonstrating how to hold the reins properly.

Willa copied his movements, feeling a sense of exhilaration and pride as she sat tall in the saddle. Thunder shifted beneath her, snorting softly as if sensing her apprehension.

"Good job," Jack said, placing his hand on her thigh. "Now let's take things slowly. I'll lead Thunder around the arena so you can get a feel for him."

As Jack led the horse forward, Willa concentrated on keeping her balance and following his movements. With each step, she felt more confident, her body relaxing into the rhythm of the horse's gait.

"You're a natural, Willa," Jack said, a smile playing on his lips. "I knew you'd be a great rider."

Willa blushed at his compliment, feeling a warm sense of pride fill her chest. She looked up at Jack, meeting his gaze, and for a moment they locked eyes. She could see it so clearly, Jack teaching Priya how to ride a horse like this. Her daughter would eat it up.

As they continued to ride, Jack offered her guidance and encouragement, teaching her how to steer the horse and adjust her speed. Willa soaked up every word, feeling more confident with each passing moment. She'd never seen Jack like this. Willa had seen him as a boss, ordering people around, as a master negotiator getting what he wanted, as a charming and passionate man who melted her heart. But she'd never seen him as a teacher, as an outdoor man who could teach someone how to ride a horse. A man who could be a father, a good one.

After a while, Jack suggested they try something a little more challenging. "Let's see if you're ready to trot," he said, a playful glint in his eyes.

Willa's pulse raced at the prospect of going faster, but she trusted Jack's guidance. She braced herself as Jack gave Thunder a gentle nudge and clicked his tongue. The horse began to move faster, his powerful strides propelling them forward.

Willa whooped with joy as a rush of wind whipped through her hair and she bounced up and down with the horse's movements.

As they slowed to a stop, Willa turned to Jack, a huge grin on her face. "That was amazing," she said, feeling breathless and alive.

Jack grinned back at her, his eyes shining with pride. "You did great."

Willa felt a warmth spread through her chest at his words, a feeling that had nothing to do with the heat of the sun overhead. She looked down at Jack, her heart racing. Maybe it was time to tell him about Priya.

Jack brought out Prince, a brown quarter horse he had bought a year before. He'd learned to ride as a child at a camp. Riding horses around a ring was nothing compared to the trail ride. He had a deal with the adjoining ranches that they could use his riding trails and he could use theirs. He mounted his horse and motioned for Thunder to follow. Jack had personally trained Thunder and knew the horse would take good care of Willa.

The sun shone down on Willa's golden hair and his breath caught at the sight of her smiling face. How had he ever thought that he could forget her? This was their second chance; he had to figure out a way to show her that they could have a life here together, make her fall in love with Royal just as he had.

The sweet scent of wildflowers filled the air, and a gentle breeze rustled through the leaves of the trees, creating a symphony with the rhythmic clip-clop of their horses' hooves. Jack couldn't help but feel a sense of contentment as he rode alongside Willa. The Texas countryside was unlike any other place he had ever seen, with rolling hills and vast expanses of grassland stretching out as far as the eye could see. It was very different from the cold, gray scape of New York City. From the first time he'd seen the property, he pictured himself raising a family here. A life that didn't include crazy mayors who took out hits on people in order to get power. He was done with that life.

He turned to look at Willa, who was riding beside him. She looked so beautiful with her cheeks flushed from the exertion of riding.

"This place is stunning," she said.

"You know, there's nowhere else I'd rather be right now than here with you."

Willa smiled at him, her eyes sparkling with affection. "I feel the same way, Jack. It's like the whole world fades away when we're out here."

"That's the idea. Very different from the city. Open space, fresh air…it's a great place to raise a family."

Willa made a sound that he couldn't quite decipher. They rode on in silence for a few moments, enjoying the peacefulness of the countryside.

"Can we take a break?"

Jack found a good spot for them to dismount. He got off Prince, then helped Willa. He took the horses' reins and tied them to a tree. This was one of his favorite spots on the trail. It was near the top of the hill and there was a view of the entire ranch down below.

He put his arm around Willa and she leaned into him as he pointed out all the buildings on the ranch to her.

"Jack, you know I can't move out here, right?"

He stiffened.

"My career is in New York, or LA, or Chicago or in one of the other big cities where there are career opportunities. Royal has one local newspaper and an affiliate station. There's nothing here for me."

"I'm here, Willa."

She gave him a sad look and his heart sank. She didn't have to say it for him to read it in her face; he wasn't enough for her.

Eleven

Jack and Willa spent the afternoon shopping. If she was going to stay in Royal for a few more days, she needed some more clothes and essentials. Jack introduced her around town and he could see that she was charmed by the fact that he knew all the shop owners and they in turn knew him. Everyone went out of their way to help her find what she needed.

She'd been very clear with him on the trail ride that her career took priority. It wasn't news to him but it didn't mean he was ready to give up. Willa had only been in Royal for two nights, not enough to get a feel for the town and fall in love with it like he had.

They stopped at the RCW steakhouse for dinner. It was a restaurant owned by local Rafe Cortez-Williams. Their top cuts of beef came from the family cattle ranch and Jack rather enjoyed the old school décor. They talked about everything except the elephant in the room, their future. Jack was a problem solver and as long as Willa was committed to their relationship, he would find a way for them to be together.

"Nico knows you know about Priya."

Willa stopped midchew and Jack couldn't help but smile. *Ever the reporter.* Jack had filled Nico in on how Willa knew about Priya's death. Nico said he was okay with Jack telling Willa everything Nico had learned in prison from the driver. Now Jack and Willa could openly talk about it. He leaned forward. "Nico is okay with you finding out about the role he played. What do you want to know?"

She took a slow drink from her wineglass, then cleared her throat. "I want to know everything, Jack."

He figured as much. If there was one thing he had learned in the last couple of days, it was that there was no point in waiting to share information. If he had told Willa what he suspected about Priya's death, if he had proposed to her when he wanted to rather than waiting for the right moment, they would've had the last five years.

"You already know that I put you on George Wright because I suspected him of being dirty." He went on to detail the proof he had about the former mayor, back then only a candidate for mayor. "The night we were going to air my story, all my sources reneged. I figured they'd been intimidated. It was also the night Priya had her accident. I didn't connect the dots until five years later, when your source told you about the cab company that's a front for the Mafia."

"The cab that hit Priya was from the same company," she surmised.

He nodded

"Why didn't you tell me all this?"

"It was just a suspicion at that point. I found out that Nico was in the same prison as the driver who confessed everything, so I asked him to find out if my suspicions were right. Nico got friendly with him and found out that he'd been paid off by the Mafia to take the blame."

"If the driver confesses…"

Jack shook his head. "I've been down this road. I went and offered the guy twice what the Mafia is paying him but he won't budge. He's got a mother in a nursing home and he's afraid of what they'll do to her."

Willa sighed. "George Wright has to be punished."

Jack reached out and took her hand. "Willa, for my sake, please let this go."

"Do you remember how I became a reporter?"

He was familiar with her reasons but also knew her well enough to know that she needed to tell the story to make her point. "I was in college and my roommate was assaulted at a frat party. She did all the right things, called the campus police, reported it, got medical attention right away. But the administration didn't do anything. They actually went as far as to suggest that if a girl goes to a frat party and drinks, it's to be expected that she'll get assaulted. Tamara was a mess. She was afraid to leave our dorm room. Anytime she heard a boy's voice in the hallway, she jumped. When the police wouldn't do anything for a week, I began looking at all the social media posts from that night. It took maybe ten hours of work to find a clip of the boy handing my roommate a drink."

Every time she told the story, her eyes teared up. He gently squeezed her hand but his own insides were churning. He knew where she was going with this and he was going to have a battle on his hands.

"The police barely questioned the boy, who said he didn't even remember giving Tamara the drink. He was the son of a powerful local businessman and they were asked to let it go. So I went to the school paper and wrote a story. I had our local radio do an interview with me and Tamara. That shamed some of the people at the party to come forward and talk about how they'd seen the boy take a half-conscious Tamara into a closet. Then it became hard to ignore what he'd done."

She leaned forward. "If that boy hadn't been punished, he would've done it again and again."

"I know what you're getting at. But this is different."

"Because George Wright is a powerful man."

"Yes."

"All the more reason to make sure he's held accountable."

"Not at the expense of the safety of the people I love."

They stared at each other for a while. Jack sighed. "You know that after Priya died, my family fell apart."

He didn't have to retell the story to Willa. Her eyes acknowledged that she remembered. After Priya died, his mother had become obsessed with Jack and his brother Peter. His parents tried to control every aspect of their lives. Jack had to distance himself from them. His brother moved to California and nearly stopped talking to them. Disheartened, his parents moved back to India and they grew even farther apart.

"It took a lot for me to rebuild our relationship. I had to risk that they might overstep again and they had to trust that I wanted them in my life. Reopening the George Wright story is going to bring up old wounds. It's not worth it. My life is in a good place right now and I want to leave it."

"You don't care about punishing him?"

"He's been punished. His career is ruined, he's bankrupt. Believe me, if it looks like he's rising from the ashes, I will do something. I've made sure that no one invests in his businesses, that he's a pariah in social circles. Would I like to see him in prison? Yes. But not at the expense of my family's safety."

Willa didn't look convinced but she nodded.

"Besides, without the driver's testimony, there's no way to prove that the hit was purposeful and ordered by George Wright."

"What about the cab company connection?"

"It's circumstantial."

"Are you sure the driver won't talk? What if we can get his family into witness protection?"

Jack shook his head. "You're not getting it Willa. I don't want to pursue this. My parents are happy, my family is doing well, I'm in a good place. Priya's death was an obsession with me for too long. I don't want to go back there. The driver is in prison for the rest of his life—he can't get a worse sentence. And George Wright is ruined. We need to accept that's the end of the story, whether we like it or not."

Willa opened her mouth, then closed it. He had a bad feeling that this was not the last conversation they would have on the subject.

"Now your turn to tell me your deepest, darkest secret. Start with where you were for the two years you disappeared."

Willa nearly choked on the asparagus she'd just put in her mouth. It wasn't an unexpected question but one she didn't know how to answer. Rogerio's comment that Jack might want custody of Priya had thrown cold water on her plans to tell Jack. She couldn't tell him without understanding what he might do.

"I'm not ready to talk about it yet."

Jack's smile fell. It took him a second but he reluctantly nodded.

"Tell me what you've been up to. I would've expected by now you would've at least conned someone into a long term relationship, if not marriage." Willa's tone was teasing.

He smirked. "That was the plan but I ran into this little problem called finding the right woman." His mouth twitched and she broke eye contact to look down at her plate. The meal had been delicious.

"Your parents didn't want to set you up with some nice girl from India?"

"Oh, they did. They found quite a number of them. Apparently I'm something of a catch despite the fact that I'm a little on the old side at forty-four, but given my money and good looks, most families are willing to overlook that."

She smiled. "I'm sure they are. So what happened? Didn't like the shovel the gold diggers came with?"

He laughed. "I actually met some really nice women, some of whom were wealthier than I am."

"So?"

He shrugged. "None of them were you."

Her body warmed and she looked down again.

"Do you ever wonder where we would be if I had proposed that night?"

"We'd be married with 2.5 kids and you would want to leave the city and move to Royal to become a rancher," she said, her stomach hard.

He shrugged. "Maybe I'd have been happy in the city with you."

"But what if you weren't? What if you and I had kids and you wanted to move out here and I said no. Then what would you do?"

"That's too much of a hypothetical. Why are you asking?" The slight suspicion in his voice and the way he leaned forward put her on edge. She had to be careful.

"I'm revisiting our conversation on the trail. Just wondering how we're going to make this all work."

Jack rubbed his thumb on the inside of her wrist, sending pleasant goose bumps down her arms.

"Growing up, I never particularly liked outdoor sports. I just didn't see the appeal of spending hours sweating or freezing when you could play in a temperature-controlled environment. Then when I was in college, I began dating this girl who was an avid hiker and backpacker. She took me on my first hike, and I was amazed by the stunning views when we reached the summit, despite the fact that I was sweating like a pig. After that I took up trail running, rock climbing and skiing. I realized that sweating and freezing is what makes the sport fun and the torture is worth it for the sense of accomplishment."

He gave her a dimpled smile. *Why does that give me butterflies? Every time!*

"Why don't we first figure out whether there's something between us to make work. If there is, I think we'll both be more willing to do what's needed."

He was right. But what he didn't know was that regardless of how their personal relationship worked out, they were connected for life. There was no strapping on some skis and seeing if they enjoyed the slope. They were already invested in a ski chalet.

Twelve

As they walked out of the restaurant, they bumped into Nathan Battle, the local sheriff. Jack shook hands with him. Nathan was about Jack's height, with close-cropped dark brown hair and kind, brown eyes. He was one of the first friends Jack had made in Royal. Nathan was always fair and gracious, and played an excellent game of poker.

"Well, well, well, look who we have here," Nathan said, grinning. "The town's newest k!smet connection."

Jack grinned and introduced him to Willa. "You on duty?" Nathan was dressed in his khaki sheriff's uniform.

"Yeah, a couple of teenagers tricked one of the tourists to buy them beer. Ol' Fred wasn't too happy."

Jack turned to Willa. "That's the monthly crime spree here."

Nathan laughed. "Normally that would be true but with the Diamond Gate necklace going on display soon, we've got a lot of tourists coming into town, and people tend to get a little crazy before the holidays. I have the sweetest couple locked up."

"Why?" Willa asked. It was clear Nathan was itching to tell the story.

"The guy, Larry, is a local and he was finally ready to propose to his girlfriend, so he decides to get this big billboard made. He puts it up in front of Frankie Junior's shop thinking the guy has closed for the holidays like he always does. Except Frankie decided to stay open later this year because of all the extra tourists here to see the diamonds."

Nathan shook his head with amusement. "Now, Frankie decided to be gracious and leave the billboard cause he didn't want to mess up the proposal. But the girlfriend doesn't live here and her flight gets delayed. Frankie thinks the proposal has happened, so he removes the billboard and throws it in the dumpster. One of the out-of-towners sees the billboard and decides to rescue it. Larry sees the guy trying to take the billboard and, without thinking, tackles him."

"Can't blame the guy." Willa said.

Nathan shrugged. "I know, but I had to break it up. I go to take him in and the girlfriend says I can't take him without taking her. So they're both cooling their heels in cell 3."

Jack couldn't help but laugh. "You gotta let them go."

"Oh, I will. I'm leaving them in for a few hours so Larry learns his lesson."

"The girlfriend lives out of town?" Willa inquired.

"She's from LA. They met on vacation and fell in love. Took them a while to figure out how to make it work. It's a sweet story."

"What did they do?" Willa was listening intently and it warmed Jack's heart. He made a note to introduce her to Dev and Caitlyn, who had also found a way to make it work. It didn't escape his notice that she seemed worried about their geography. If things did work out between them, he'd never ask her to give up her career. It meant a lot to her and he recognized that she'd have to be based out of a major city. But Dallas was not that far away, and he still had connections in the media that he could use to help her out if she wanted that.

"The girl's a lawyer. She convinced her firm to let her work remotely for now. Larry's working on finding a job in LA. When you love each other, you find a way to make it work." Nathan gave them a meaningful look.

Jack and Willa looked at each other, then at Nathan and laughed. "Aren't you subtle." Jack said as he slapped his friend on the back. Nathan was happily married to his wife, Amanda, who owned a local diner. He never passed up an opportunity to remind Jack how wonderful marriage could be.

"Well, I better go release those lovebirds. Nice to meet you, Willa." He winked at Jack. "Now, you two better get going before I charge you with loitering."

They laughed and parted ways.

* * *

As Jack led Willa through the door of his ranch, she couldn't help but feel a mix of excitement and apprehension. They'd had an intense conversation at dinner, and she needed to unwind.

"How about some wine in the living room?" Jack suggested.

She smiled. "You read my mind."

The living room of the ranch was warm and inviting, with soft lighting and a wood-burning brick fireplace. Willa sank onto the plush couch, feeling a sense of relief and comfort as she curled up against the cushions.

Jack opened a bottle of red cabernet and poured them both glasses of wine. She watched him move around the room, admiring the way his muscles flexed under his shirt and the way his jeans hugged his hips. She felt a warm flush rise in her cheeks and looked away, feeling a sudden shyness.

Jack stacked some wood in the fireplace and added paper and starter sticks. Once it was lit, he came and sat next to her. Willa watched the play of the flames reflecting in his eyes.

"Is there anything more soothing than the sound of a crackling fire?" Jack asked, glancing up at her with a smile.

Willa felt a sudden warmth spread through her chest, and she smiled back at him. "Not really. It's one of my favorite things about winter."

"I remember. The contractor thought I was nuts, wanting a wood-burning fireplace in Texas. He wanted to put a fake electric fireplace for ambience."

"Can't fake a real fire."

He smiled and his dimples lit a fire deep in her belly.

They talked for hours, about everything from the best books they'd recently read to reminiscing about their favorite New York restaurants. It almost felt like she was sitting with her best friend catching up on everything they'd missed. But as the night wore on, a different kind of energy crackled between them, something charged and electric.

"I'm glad you're here," he murmured.

Willa met his gaze, her entire body warm and tingly. He was looking at her as if she was the only person in the world. She reached up and brushed her fingers across his cheek, feeling the rough stubble of his five-o'clock shadow.

"Me too," she said softly.

Jack leaned in and brushed his lips against hers, sending a shiver down her spine. "I've missed you."

"Me too."

Jack leaned in closer to her, his gaze intense. Willa's breath caught in her throat as he took her hand, his thumb tracing circles on her skin. Jack leaned in and brushed his lips against hers, electrifying her nerves. Willa's eyes fluttered closed, and she let herself sink into the feeling of his warm breath against her skin. She tilted her head to deepen the kiss, savoring the taste of him on her lips.

As Jack pulled away, Willa's eyes opened slowly, her gaze meeting his. She looked into his deep, brown eyes. Their intensity made her heart skip a beat. He took her hand, and she turned her palm up to meet his. They let their fingers intertwine. As Jack leaned in, the heat emanating from his body made hers melt. His lips trailed down her neck, sending her nerves tingling. She tilted her head back, giving him better access to that spot between her neck and shoulder that drove her crazy. His kisses were gentle at first, but soon grew more urgent.

She let out a soft sigh of pleasure, and Jack's lips curved into a smile. He moved his mouth to her earlobe, nibbling gently before running his tongue along its curves. Hot heat rushed through her body. She brought her hand up to Jack's face, trailing her fingers along his strong jawline before burying them in his hair. With a gentle tug, she brought him closer to her, and their lips met in a slow, languorous kiss.

Their mouths moved together in perfect harmony, their tongues dancing in a sensual tango that left them both breathless. Willa wrapped her arms around Jack's neck, pulling him closer as they deepened the kiss. She could feel his arousal pressing against her thigh, and she shifted slightly to bring him even closer.

Jack's hands roamed over her body, caressing her breasts through the fabric of her clothes. Willa's hands moved to Jack's shirt. She pulled it over his head and threw it aside before running her hands over his chest. The feel of his hard body under her fingers sent a rush of fire through her.

She was ready for him but Jack had other ideas. He pulled off her jeans and panties and put his mouth between her legs. He licked and sucked and drove her to the edge so many times that it was too much to bear. As their bodies finally came together, it was as though the world fell away, leaving only the two of them in a whirlwind of desire and passion.

As they lay in each other's arms and the fire burned down to embers, Willa couldn't help but feel the sting of doubt. Was she ready to fall in love with Jack all over again?

Thirteen

Willa gave herself a last look in the mirror just as Jack knocked on the door. She opened the door and smiled when she saw him. He was wearing jeans and a T-shirt while she'd spent the morning shopping for the perfect dress and the last hour getting her hair and makeup perfect.

"Hmm, if you're going to look this good, then I might have to postpone dinner." He put his arms around her waist and she playfully pushed him away.

"I am not going to keep your parents waiting."

He put a hand on his chest in mock protest, then stepped out of the room. She took a breath and followed. She'd been in Royal for almost a week. Jack's parents had come back from India earlier in the day and he wanted her to meet them. Although it wasn't her first time meeting them, she was nervous. What did they think of her? What had Jack told them about their relationship—past and present?

They walked downstairs to the foyer. Jack's parents were walking over from their apartment on the property. Willa shifted on her feet. Was now a good time to tell Jack that she had to get back to New York the next day? She missed Priya, and her boss, David, was getting impatient with her. Rogerio had already left, much to his chagrin. She'd kept David at bay by doing an interview with Misha Law, and a story on the preparations for Maggie Del Rio and Jericho Winters's wedding. But he'd called her earlier that day to say that she had to return. He was none too happy about the fact that she hadn't gotten a story on Jack. Willa didn't know how to tell Jack. They'd had a magical week together but the time had come for them to have the difficult conversation they'd been putting off.

Jack's parents, Sanjay and Maria Chowdhry, were one of the cutest couples Willa had ever met. Sanjay was six feet tall and chose to dress in the kind of track suit Willa associated with elderly bingo players in Florida. Maria on the other hand was impeccably dressed in tailored dress pants, a silk shirt and pearls. They greeted Jack with hugs first, then turned their attention to Willa. Maria gave her a hug and Sanjay shook her hand a little awkwardly.

Jack and Willa had cooked a simple dinner of chicken biryani and cucumber yogurt. "Won't your parents be sick of Indian food after being in India for a month?"

Jack shook his head. "Weirdly, they miss Indian food

as soon as they leave India. It's like they believe they won't get any Indian food until they return to India, so they come home and it's all they want."

The kitchen smelled of garam masala and cardamom. The ranch had a formal dining room but Jack preferred to serve dinner at the kitchen table. "It's a little more intimate," he'd said.

"So Willa, it is nice to see you again. Jack has not stopped talking about you for the last week," Maria remarked.

Willa couldn't help smiling at the look of chagrin on Jack's face.

Jack's mother asked her about her family and Willa relaxed into the conversation. It was easy to talk about her parents and sister. Then Maria leaned in a little closer and asked, "So have you and Jack talked about marriage yet?"

Willa's face turned bright red. Jack laughed as he served the chicken biryani. She looked at him expecting him to answer the question but he gave her a half-dimpled smile and stepped away from the table to get the pitcher of mango lassi they'd made earlier.

"Uh, well, we're just taking things one day at a time," she said, trying to keep her tone light. "We only reconnected a week ago."

"Not quite," Maria said. "You dated for months before. That time counts."

Willa shifted in her seat. "It's complicated. My life is in New York." She snuck a look at Jack, who took a seat next to her on the table.

"Has Jack told you the story of how Maria and I got

married?" Jack's father was soft-spoken and quietly introspective. He was very different from her own boisterous dad but exuded the same warmth that Jack did.

She shook her head, and Sanjay and Maria looked at each other and smiled in the secret way that couples sometimes did. Willa found herself looking at Jack, who gave her his signature dimpled smile.

"This was the 1970s in India," Maria began. "My father was the minister at a local church in Goa. Just like now, Goa was a big destination for tourists and my job was to go around to the beaches and hand out church pamphlets."

Sanjay took over the story. "I was on holiday with my parents celebrating my graduation from college. My father was so proud of me for completing my engineering degree. Now, you have to realize that my father was a very hard man. He had very high expectations, I had to bring the best marks."

"Gee, that sounds familiar." Jack smirked.

Sanjay turned to him. "This is why you are so successful. Parents have to push their children a little."

"Just as my father was a minister, Sanjay's father was a Brahmin pundit. I didn't know this of course when I approached him and gave him a brochure to come to the church."

"Before she tells this next part, Willa," Sanjay said, "you have to understand that my father came from a long line of Hindu pundits. He was taught that his was the only religion that mattered."

"So when I approached him to ask whether he'd like

to come learn about Christianity, he had a little reaction."

"She's sugarcoating it," Jack interrupted. "The first time I heard the story, my grandfather, *Dadaji,* had steam coming out of his ears and had to pray for twenty-four hours straight to calm down."

"When my father gets angry, he talks with his hands, and I stood too close to him and he accidentally hit me and I fell and hit my head."

Maria patted Sanjay on the hand. "It was his bad luck that when he fell he hit his head on the edge of a concrete sidewalk. There was so much blood. His mother became hysterical, his father was in shock."

"So Maria tears a piece of cloth off her long skirt, puts my bleeding head in her lap, and holds the cloth against my wound. That was the moment I fell in love with her."

Willa looked at Maria. "What about you? When did you fall in love with him?"

"I'd say the next day. I came home from distributing brochures and saw Sanjay sitting with my father in our living room learning about Christianity. Again, you have to remember that in those days in India, a Brahmin's son would never do something like that. He came to my house every day for a week with yellow and white flowers that he picked himself. We talked for hours and fell in love."

"That's such a sweet story," Willa remarked.

"That's not the sweet part of the story," Jack said. "Wait for it."

Now Willa was intrigued. The story unfolded as they

ate. Sanjay and Maria had clearly told the story several times, because they were perfectly choreographed in how each one told their portion. As expected, Maria and Sanjay's parents were against the marriage. As leaders of their respective religions, having their children marry outside the faith was a nonstarter. Maria and Sanjay did everything they could to convince their parents, but when they wouldn't listen, they ran away and got married.

"We took vows in a church, and went seven times around the holy fire in a Hindu temple." Maria said.

"What did your parents do?"

"Once we were married, there was nothing they could do. They both respected the religious ceremony but they disowned us."

Willa gasped. She couldn't imagine her parents shunning her for marrying someone they didn't agree with. Sanjay and Maria explained that in those days in India, social standing was very important, especially for religious leaders.

"We knew they would have no choice. It was a sacrifice we were willing to make, for love." Sanjay looked lovingly into Maria's eyes. "And fifty years later, I can tell you that it was worth it."

Willa put a hand on her chest, sure that her heart was about to burst.

"So whatever it is that is complicating your relationship, dear girl, consider whether fifty years from now, it'll be as important to you as it is today." Maria's tone was kind but Willa felt the admonition in her words.

She looked at Jack but he was studiously staring at his mango lassi.

"How was your trip to India?" Willa asked, desperate for a change of topic.

Sanjay and Maria exchanged a sad look. "It's a difficult thing, to remember the death of one's child. But it was important to Sanjay to go to Varanasi and pray for peace. Not just for Priya, but for our family too." Maria looked at Jack. "Some of us are still trying to find a way to honor and make meaning of her death."

Jack stood, walked to his mother and gave her a hug. "I'm okay, Ma. I've come to terms with Priya's death. I told you, if I ever have a daughter, I'm going to name her Priya."

The comment hit Willa like a bullet to the chest. She couldn't breathe, couldn't move, couldn't speak. Her food threatened to come up her throat.

"Excuse me, I'm not feeling that well." She pushed back her chair and ran to her room. Shutting the door behind her, she doubled over, then sank to the floor and curled into a ball. She tried to take deep breaths but her chest was so tight that all she could do was gasp.

The room was closing in on her, suffocating her. Her heart was racing. It was as if a weight was pressing down on her, making it hard to move or even think. She closed her eyes and took a deep breath, trying to calm her nerves.

What kind of person was she? All these years, she'd kept a daughter from her father, a grandchild from her grandparents. Priya could have given them that small token of comfort to help them cope with the loss of their daughter and she had denied them that. Why? Because she was selfish. If she were honest with herself, she'd kept Priya from Jack all these years because she didn't want to share her. Maybe a small part of her was punishing him. In doing that, she hadn't just denied Jack and his family but had also denied her own daughter the opportunity to know her father and grandparents. *What kind of person am I? How am I ever going to make this right?*

Jack knocked on the door. "Willa, are you okay?"

No, I am not okay.

She wanted to tell him to go away, to say that she wasn't feeling well and was going to bed. Then she could pack and leave after he went to bed. She'd leave him a Dear Jack letter, go back to New York and pretend that the last week hadn't happened.

She took a shuddering breath, then stood and opened the door.

trying to process what he'd just heard. He had a daughter. With Willa. Four and a half years ago, she'd had his baby and kept it secret from him all this time.

As soon as Willa's words sank in, Jack's blood boiled. How could she keep something like this from him? Their relationship hadn't been perfect but they had a close connection, had been able to talk about anything. Yet, she hadn't found a way to tell him that she was pregnant?

He clenched his jaw, trying to contain his anger. But it was no use. The rage was building up inside him, threatening to burst out at any moment. In the last week, he'd found a way to let go of his anger at her walking out on their relationship because they had a disagreement at work. He'd come up with a number of reasons to forgive her: the fact that she saw his actions as betrayal, that she had no idea he'd been about to propose to her. He'd even accepted that maybe she hadn't been in the same place with their relationship as he had. But keeping his child from him was inexcusable. Even if they'd just been a one-night stand, he deserved to know.

"You had my baby?" he choked out. "And you didn't tell me? Why would you do that?"

She shrank back from him. Fresh tears fell down her cheeks. His heart lurched but the rage boiling in his veins was too strong for him to feel anything but anger.

"I was scared, Jack," Willa replied, her voice shaking. "I didn't know how you would react. I didn't want to burden you with a child when we weren't even together."

"What made you think I wouldn't want a child? What right did you have to make that decision?"

He had always wanted children, had dreamed of being a father. And now he had a daughter, a beautiful little girl that he had missed out on for over four years. The thought of it made him furious, and he couldn't help but lash out at Willa. "How could you keep her from me for over four years?" he demanded, his voice rising. "Do you have any idea how much it hurts to know that I have a child out there that I didn't even know about?"

Willa flinched at his words, her face contorted with pain. Jack could see the regret in her eyes, but it was too late. The damage had been done, and he wasn't sure if he would ever be able to forgive her. His fingernails dug into his clenched fists. "I had a right to know about my child. How could you think it was okay not to tell me?"

She squeezed her eyes shut and a fresh stream of tears fell down her cheeks. "At the time, Jack, there was so much to process. I'd lost my job..."

"You quit!" They both flinched at his raised voice. He took a breath to bring his anger under control.

"I felt betrayed by you, and then I found out I was pregnant. I didn't know how I felt about it, I wasn't sure what I was going to do. A few days after I found out, I started bleeding and I thought I was going to lose the baby. The pregnancy was touch and go for a while. In that moment, all that mattered to me was keeping our baby alive."

His anger deflated, replaced by an emotion he couldn't name. *I need some air.* He stood and opened the doors to the balcony, stepping out into the night air. The heat of the day had been replaced with a cool night.

He took a long breath of the fresh air, letting the scent of wildflowers soothe him.

He didn't know how long he'd been standing there. Willa tapped him on the shoulder and silently handed him her phone. The image on the screen took his breath away. His hands trembled as he held the phone. *My little girl.* She looked like a lighter-skinned version of his sister. The same big brown eyes, the same wide smile. There was some Willa in there too. Rosy cheeks, the teeny dimple in her chin. She was perfect.

"What's her name?" he asked, his voice barely above a whisper.

"Her name is Priya."

His hands shook and he clutched the phone so tightly that the case popped off. The weight of her words pressed heavily against his chest, choking the life out of him. His emotions mixed together in a volatile cocktail.

He handed the phone back to Willa.

"I can't be here right now."

Fifteen

Willa stood alone on the balcony, watching the stars twinkle in the night sky. The cool breeze brushed against her face, but it did little to calm the raging storm inside her. Jack had walked out of the room without a look back at her. What did she expect? She had just told him that they had a child together. A child he didn't even know existed. She had kept this secret for four and a half long years, and now, everything had come crashing down around her.

Her breaths came in short gasps as she recalled the look on his face when she told him the truth. The pain, the anger, the confusion, the betrayal. She couldn't blame him for any of it. She had kept his child from him, denied him the chance to be a father.

Willa's mind raced with all the things she could have

done differently. She should have told him she was pregnant and let him decide whether or not he wanted to be a part of the child's life. In her mind she had packaged the baby with their relationship and assumed if she and Jack weren't together, then he didn't factor into the equation with Priya. How wrong she'd been. If she were honest with herself, there were many times during the years when she had thought about telling Jack. The first time Priya said "dada" because the toddlers in day care did. Then there was the time when her pre-K class drew family portraits and she asked why she didn't have a daddy.

Willa took a deep breath and wiped away her tears. She knew what she had to do. She had to find a way to make it right.

She went to Jack's bedroom door and knocked. There was no answer, so she opened it. He was sitting on the bed, lost in thought. She didn't wait for permission to enter. As she sat next to him, his body stiffened.

"I wish you had told me sooner," he said, his voice soft. He stood, walked over to a safe on the wall, punched in a code and returned holding a jewelry box. He handed it to her.

She opened it and saw a beautiful sapphire engagement ring. "I was going to propose to you. If you'd told me that you were pregnant, I would've been ecstatic. If you didn't want to be with me, didn't want to marry me, I wouldn't have forced a relationship on you. All I would've asked is to be a part of my daughter's life."

Tears wet her cheeks.

"What would you have said?"

"What?"

"If I'd gotten to ask you to marry me. What would you have said?"

Her stomach knotted. The answer was not one she liked or even wanted to admit to herself.

"I wasn't ready back then, Jack. Don't get me wrong. I loved you, with all my heart, but my sole focus was on my career. I wanted to make it as a journalist and marriage was not on my radar."

He took the ring box from her and put it back in the safe. "The ring belongs to my *nani*. When my mother left her home with my father, her mother felt guilty that she couldn't support her daughter and gave her that ring so she'd always have a connection back to her family. . My mother had planned to give it to Priya but when she found out that I had finally found the woman I wanted to marry, she handed it to me."

Was it possible for her to feel even worse than she did? "I'm sorry, Jack."

"Why didn't you tell me you were pregnant?" He'd asked the question before but she needed to answer him.

"I was angry and scared."

"Don't you think the punishment for disagreeing with a *business* decision I made was a little excessive?"

"Jack, no! This wasn't a punishment." She bit her lip. "I was afraid that if I told you, you'd take her away from me. I was at a low point in my life and Priya is all that mattered, all that kept me going. I couldn't…" Her voice cracked.

"Do you think I'm the type of guy to take a child away from her mother?"

No, he wasn't. "I couldn't take the chance."

"So why tell me now?"

"Because it's time to make things right." She handed him a folded paper. He opened it and she caught the smile that twitched on his lips.

"She loves to draw and color. Before I left New York, she wanted to make sure I had something to remember her by, so she drew me a picture of herself with her favorite stuffed animal who she calls dog."

"What's she like?"

Willa spent the next hour talking about Priya. She told him about how spunky their daughter was, how she liked to talk nonstop but had the attention span of a bird. Jack listened attentively as Willa recounted the last four and a half years of Priya's life, from how she was a tiny, underweight baby when she was born, to how she could currently put away two quarter-pound burgers when she was hungry.

"I've missed out on so much these past five years."

"I know," Willa replied, tears streaming down her face. "I'm so sorry, Jack. I shouldn't have kept her from you."

Jack silently scrolled through the pictures of Priya on Willa's phone. There were photos of them eating giant stacks of pancakes with whipped cream, one of Priya riding a pony at a petting zoo, a picture of Willa laughing as Priya kissed her on the cheek. He stared at the picture for a long time, his heart a jumble of emotions. He loved Willa, he always had. But how could he could forgive her for keeping Priya from him.

Then another thought hit him. "Why did you come to Royal?"

She looked down at her lap. "When the opportunity came, I figured it was an opening to see you. I couldn't exactly call you up out of the blue and tell you that you have a daughter."

His throat was tight. Had she planned to rekindle their relationship to soften him up for the news?

"And us? Was that planned too?"

She put a hand on her mouth. "No! Believe me, it's the last thing I wanted."

That stung. Had she even considered the fact that they could be a family together? Was the loss of her career so important to her that it trumped everything else? Had she punished him five years ago?

"How could you be with me the last week and not tell me about my daughter."

She blinked and fresh tears fell down her cheeks. "I hadn't planned for us to happen like that."

"But once we did…"

"I was waiting for the right time to tell you."

The right time? They'd spent nearly every waking moment together in the last week. Each day had been filled with long talks and each night with the kind of intimacy that he'd never shared with anyone else. And all this time, she had kept this secret from him and he had no idea. He hadn't gotten to be a successful businessman by not being able to read people. It usually took him a few minutes to know when someone was lying or bluffing. He could've written the book on how to size up situations and people in order to negotiate the best deal. Hadn't he just done that with the Del Rios and Winterses? Then how could he have missed it with Willa? How had he not known that she'd been keeping something so big from him.

"The right time?" he repeated, his voice laced with anger and hurt. "When exactly was that supposed to be? After we slept together? After I started to fall in love with you?"

Willa winced at his words. "No, Jack, it wasn't like that. I just didn't know how to tell you. I was afraid of your reaction."

Afraid of his reaction? Had he ever given her a reason to fear him?

As if reading his mind, she touched his arm. "I'm sorry, Jack. I truly am. Scared of your reaction, scared of what you would think of me, scared of how this would change everything." Willa's voice trembled. "I was afraid of losing you, of losing Priya."

Jack shook his head in disbelief. "You were afraid of losing me? You already lost me, Willa. You should have told me the truth from the beginning. You should have trusted me enough to know that I would have been there for you and our child."

He'd had blinders on when it came to Willa. Loving her had kept him from truly seeing her. Keeping Priya from him was a colossal act of selfishness. How could he ever forgive her for that? How could he ever trust her again?

"This changes things between us, doesn't it?"

"It has changed everything, Willa," Jack said softly. "I don't know how to move forward from here. How can

I trust you again? How can I be with someone who's kept such a huge secret from me?"

"I understand if you can't forgive me," Willa said, her voice trembling. "But please know that I never stopped loving you. And I regret what I did."

Jack looked at her for a long moment, his eyes searching hers. Was she telling the truth? How would he know? Clearly he didn't have the ability to be objective when it came to Willa. Finally, he sighed and ran a hand through his hair. "I need some time to think, Willa. I need to figure out if I can forgive you, if I can trust you again. But one thing I know for sure is that I will love our child, and I will always be there for her."

Willa nodded, tears streaming down her face. "Thank you, Jack. That's all I can ask for."

They both sat in silence for a few moments, the weight of their conversation heavy between them. A lump formed in his throat as he imagined all the moments he had missed with his daughter; all the things his friends talked about as being magic. Hearing her heartbeat on the sonogram, cutting the umbilical cord, holding her for the first time. Naming her.

"Why did you name her Priya?" It didn't make any sense. Willa had kept him out of his daughter's life. If the Diamond Gate story hadn't brought her to Royal, and if they hadn't rekindled their relationship, would she ever have told him? Why name their daughter after his sister? Willa had to know that if he ever found out about her child, he'd know right away she was his. If she'd planned to keep Priya from him, why give her such a meaningful name?

"I knew how much your sister meant to you. Even before she was born, I wanted our daughter to have a part of you. I knew she would one day ask me why I'd chosen the name and I planned to tell her about her father, and how much he'd loved his sister. I never wanted her to forget that she was half you."

Just like that she had pierced his heart with an arrow so sharp, he felt it tear through his chest and lodge itself firmly in his soul. They sat in silence for a few more moments, lost in their own thoughts. Jack tried to imagine what it would be like to meet his daughter. Would she embrace him in her life or resent him for having missed so much of it already?

"I want to meet her," he said finally, his voice determined. "I want to be a part of her life."

Willa nodded, a tear sliding down her cheek.

"I'll book a private jet to take us to New York first thing tomorrow morning."

"We can't do that, Jack."

Sixteen

Willa hated the look on Jack's face. Now that she'd finally told him, the sense of relief was so immense that she wished she hadn't waited so long to do it. At the same time, she couldn't help but feel a sense of dread creeping in. She had always thought that keeping this secret was for the best.But now, seeing the hurt and betrayal in his eyes, she couldn't help but feel like she had made a terrible mistake.

"Jack, I have to tell Priya about you first. If I just show up with you, I don't know how she'll react. I need to prepare her."

"What have you told her about her father?"

"Nothing. She's four and a half. Priya's still at the age where you can distract her with a toy if she asks tough questions."

He ran his fingers through his hair. Would he ever be able to forgive her? She'd always known that telling Jack would be hard, but the expression on his face and the look on his eyes were like ice picks through her heart. Jack's anger was palpable, a seething energy that radiated off him in waves. She could see it in the way his jaw clenched, in the tightness of his fists. It was a cold, bitter anger that made her shiver. And yet, there was something else there, something that she couldn't quite put her finger on. A deep, raw emotion that went beyond anger or hurt. It was a feeling that made her feel small.

"So what's the plan, then?"

She didn't have a plan. Willa had been so focused on when and how to tell Jack that she hadn't fully thought through what came after. How was she going to integrate Jack into Priya's life? Would she let him bring her to Royal? What if he wanted Priya to live here with him? Willa's life was in New York.

As the seconds ticked by, Willa felt herself starting to crack under the weight of it all. She had never felt so alone, so utterly helpless. All she could do was sit there, her heart breaking, as Jack continued to stare at her with that cold, unforgiving gaze.

"Let me go to New York and talk to Priya. Then I'll bring her here to meet you."

"Can I trust you?"

The question broke her heart. Did he really think that she wouldn't follow through on her promise? Was there so little left between them?

"I'll be back next weekend."

"I'll send my jet."

* * *

Jack didn't bother saying goodbye. She left the next morning without seeing him. He arranged for a car and a ride on his private jet for her. The only thing that kept her going was the thought of seeing Priya again. It had been nine days since she'd seen her little girl. It was Sunday, so Priya would be home from school. Willa couldn't believe only nine days had passed. It seemed like a lifetime ago. When she'd left the city, all she could think about was getting the story and her career back on track. Now her entire life had changed. Jack was going to be a part of her life. But in what capacity? Just as Priya's father or as something more? The status of their relationship was as uncertain as ever.

As Willa settled into the plush leather seat on Jack's private jet, she couldn't help but notice the opulence around her. The soft, cream-colored walls were adorned with intricate gold filigree, and the polished wooden floor gleamed in the soft light. The seats were comfortable, with soft cushions and warm blankets, and the champagne glasses on the table next to her sparkled in the dim light.

But despite the luxury that surrounded her, Willa couldn't enjoy it. Her mind was too preoccupied with thoughts of Jack. She couldn't shake the feeling that she was being swept along in a current she couldn't control, with no idea where it would take her. She closed her eyes, trying to calm her racing thoughts. She thought of Priya, of the way her daughter's face lit up when she saw her, of the life they could build together. No matter what, she had to be strong for Priya.

As the jet soared through the clouds, Willa stared out the window, lost in thought. Her life would never be the same again, but she had to keep moving forward, despite how uncertain the road ahead might be. For the sake of her daughter, and for herself.

When Willa stepped off the private jet and onto the tarmac, she couldn't shake the feeling that her life was about to spiral out of control. She thought back to the events that had led her here—the lies, the deceit and the heartache. She didn't know what the future held, but one thing was certain: she couldn't bear the thought of losing Jack or Priya.

Walking into her house, she heard the sound of Priya's laughter. Her heart swelled with joy and relief. Priya ran into her arms, wrapping her tiny arms around her mother's neck. Willa hugged her tightly, tears streaming down her face.

"Why are you cryin', Mommy?"

"I'm just so happy to see you," she said, holding on to her little girl.

"Mommy, you're givin' me a too tight hug," Priya complained, and Willa let go of her, smiling.

Willa sank into their routine like a warm, familiar couch. They ate a simple lunch of peanut butter and jelly sandwiches with a side of carrots and hummus. After a game of hide and seek, Willa packed a snack and they headed to the playground. Even the things she used to find tedious like having to peel the apples because Priya hated the skin was comforting.

At the playground, she held Priya by the legs while her adventurous daughter tried the monkey bars that were meant for the older kids. Back at home, they played a game of sidewalk hopscotch then made spaghetti and meatballs for dinner.

Willa tried to imagine Jack fitting into their lives and couldn't imagine him in their little space. Could he really cut Priya's sandwiches into little squares with no crusts? Get the tangles out of her hair? Help her brush her teeth? She wasn't sure what she was more afraid of, that he wouldn't be able to take care of Priya, or that he could. Would she be able to share Priya's affection with him?

After she put Priya to bed, she filled her sister in on what had happened with Jack. They were seated at the kitchen table, a small round with four seats. This was the house that Willa and Kylie had grown up in. The cabinets were still the same white paint they had always been, but she and Kylie had stripped the old wallpaper and painted the kitchen a cheery cream yellow. It was a far cry from Jack's gourmet kitchen but Willa had always found the space comforting.

"Willa, I think it's a mistake to take Priya to Royal. What if Jack wants to keep her there? What if she doesn't want to come back. I mean what little girl wouldn't want to live on a ranch with horses?"

Willa sighed. "I have to take that chance. You didn't see Jack's face when I told him. I was wrong to keep Priya from him and now I have to give them both a chance to get to know each other. I don't think Jack's the type of person to keep Priya from me."

"What about you and Jack?"

Willa bit her lip. Her feelings for him were real, but would he ever be able to forgive her?

"I don't know where we stand."

"If he forgives you, what do you want?"

Willa buried her face in her hands. "I don't know. My life is here. I have to focus on getting my career back on track. I'm not going to go live in a small town and write about rodeos. His life is in Royal. He's moved his parents to the ranch, has a whole community there that knows and loves him. I'd have to ask him to give that up and come back to New York. I don't want him to resent me for that."

"He wants to be part of Priya's life. How are you going to make that happen with you're here and he's in Royal?"

"I don't know. I don't know how any of this is going to work." She sighed, exhausted and totally spent.

Kylie gave her a hug. "Lets take it a day at a time for now. For starters, let's figure out how we're going to tell Priya about Jack. Then you need to sort some time off from work. You can't just take Priya for a weekend the first time she's meeting her father. You need to let them spend some time together. Maybe while you're there, you can figure out your relationship with Jack."

"I don't think he's ever going to forgive me."

"Give him time. You gave him a lot to process. By the time you go back, he'll be more rational."

He might forgive me, but can I be with him? As the night wore on, Willa found herself unable to sleep. She tossed and turned, her mind racing with thoughts of Jack. When she finally fell asleep, her dreams were haunted by visions of Jack and Priya. She knew that her life would never be the same again, but no matter what, she had to keep moving forward, for the sake of her daughter, and for herself. To do that, she had to let go of Jack.

Seventeen

Jack was completely out of his depth. He looked around at the brightly colored shelves overflowing with stuffed animals, dolls and games. He had no idea what a four-and-a-half-year-old girl might like. He'd already been in the store for an hour and all he had in his basket was a pink bath towel. It was time to call reinforcements.

While he waited for his mother to arrive, he asked the employee to watch his basket, then walked next door to Odds & Ends, Alisha Winters's antique shop.

"Jack!" Alisha came and greeted him with a hug. She was wearing jeans and a bright pink top that brought out her large, dark brown eyes. Her naturally curly black hair was loose.

"I hear you've also been hit with k!smet."

Jack had almost forgotten about that. "Technically.

Though Willa is my ex-girlfriend, so I'm not sure if that counts as a k!smet match."

Alisha smiled. "If it brought you back together, you're going to have to give k!smet some credit. So where is she? I'd love to meet the woman who managed to capture Jack Chowdhry's heart."

His stomach hardened. While she had captured his heart, he wasn't sure they had a future together.

"She's back in New York."

"Ah, that explains the long face. Are you here to buy her a present?"

He shook his head. "I was in the area and wanted to stop by and say hello, see how Tremaine is doing." Alisha was engaged to Tremaine Knowles, who ran a private investigation business. Jack had started using his company to do standard employee checks.

"Tremaine is just fine. But I am going to save you from yourself and make sure you don't leave here without a present for Willa." Before he could protest, she walked over to one of the shelves laden with trinkets.

"I just got this in and was thinking it should go to someone special." She handed him a silver jewelry box. "It's the perfect size to hold some special earrings or.... maybe a ring." Alisha winked at him. He bought the box, thanked her, and making an excuse about meeting his mother, left the store.

By the time his mother got to the children's shop, he'd put the pink towel back on the shelf, wondering if it was too girly. He'd told his parents about Priya the day Willa left. Like him, they'd been upset that they'd already missed over four years of her life but unlike him, they seemed more willing to forgive Willa. Surprisingly, his father had been the more understanding of the two, pointing out that Jack hadn't proposed to Willa, so she had no way of knowing whether he was serious about her. In an odd way, she was protecting him by making sure he didn't do something hasty like compel her to marry him and ruin both their lives. His father had a point. If Willa had told him she was pregnant, and then Jack proposed, she might not have believed that he would have proposed anyway.

He hugged his mother when she arrived. "See, this is why you need a wife. Men don't know how to do these things."

"If Willa had faith in me, I would have a wife and a daughter right now."

His mother put a hand on his arm. "*Beta*, I know you are hurting right now, but you cannot hold on to the past like that. You made mistakes and she made mistakes. Now it is time for both of you to think about Priya, not about your egos."

"How am I ever supposed to trust her again after what she's done?"

"Jack, do you remember what things were like between us after Priya died?" Jack shifted on his feet. Looking back at his behavior, he was ashamed at how he'd treated his parents. After Priya died, he had distanced himself from his family. He had rarely made time for his parents, often making excuses not to see them, even when they traveled all the way from India. The pain of losing his sister had been too much, and it was so hard for him to deal with his own pain that he hadn't been able to deal with his parents' overprotectiveness. He now knew it was their way of processing their own hurt, and he'd been unable to be there for them.

"Then one day you decide that you want us to shift to Texas, a place that we have never been. You wanted us to leave our home so we could be a family together."

At five feet four, his mother was much shorter than him, so she tapped him on the chest to get him to meet her gaze. "Your father and I trusted in you. Do you know why?" It was a rhetorical question but he answered anyway. "Why did you, after the way I treated you?"

"Because even if there was a small chance that we could be a part of your life, we wanted it. We love you so much that it was worth the sacrifice for us to have our son back."

She picked up a picture frame from a shelf and handed it to him, gesturing for him to look at it. The frame had a posed photograph of a couple with a little girl. "That is what you can have with Willa and Priya. But you need to let go of your anger and trust that you can be happy with her. Isn't it worth it to take the risk?"

He put the frame in their shopping basket and kissed his mother on the forehead.

They systematically went through the aisles and collected items. Jack had to make several trips to the checkout counter to drop off his basket and get a new one. As his mother selected dresses, his eye caught something on a shelf. He picked up the tea-set and added it to his tab.

Back at the ranch, as he unpacked his purchases, he found himself staring at the picture frame. Could he bring himself to trust Willa again?

Willa was packing up for the day when her boss, David, walked in with Rogerio following behind. Rogerio was gesturing frantically with his hands. Willa was terrible at charades and had no idea what he was trying to warn her about. She braced herself. David had not been happy about her taking next week off. He was downright livid about her failure to get dirt on Jack.

"Did I or did I not give you a chance when other networks wouldn't hire you?" David started. He was a small, wiry man with a shock of gray hair and a perpetually rumpled look to his clothes.

Willa sighed. "What's this about, David?"

"You told me you didn't get anything on Jack Chowdhry, yet I come to find out that there is something shady about the way his sister died, and you just happen to be taking personal time to go to Royal. Are you planning to sell the story to another network? Are you going back to CMG? What did they offer you?"

Willa looked at Rogerio, who made a face she couldn't read. "David, I'm going back to Royal for personal reasons. There is no story about Jack's sister. Rogerio and I heard some rumors but then didn't get much traction."

David turned to Rogerio, who looked sheepishly back at her. "I had Steve talk to some people in town. His sister's death was definitely not an accident and both Jack and Nico Law know it."

Willa's stomach turned. She hadn't told Rogerio that Jack had shared the full story with her. She didn't want it accidently getting out. Already on thin ice with Jack, she couldn't even fathom what would happen if the story got out.

"What about the story I did on k!smet and the Winters-Del Rio wedding."

"You and every other reporter that was in Royal last week. I need something exclusive. I want this story on Jack's sister."

"David, there is not enough there for a story."

"But you can get more."

"No, I can't."

David put his hands on his hips. "Fine. How's this for motivation. Jerry Kramer just quit the politics desk. You want to be an investigative journalist, that job is yours if you bring me this story."

"David…"

"Your choice, Willa. Come back with the story or plan to stay on the gossip beat for the foreseeable future." David walked out without giving her a chance to respond.

"Rogerio!" She rounded on her friend.

He put his hands together in apology. "I'm sorry. He overhead me talking on the phone to Steve and got the story out of me. I thought you were pursuing the story about Jack's sister. When did you decide to drop it?"

It was her fault for not having told him earlier. "Jack asked me not to pursue it for reasons I can't tell you."

"So what're you going to do now?"

"I'm going to go home and get Priya ready to go meet her father. When I'm done with that, I'm going to look for a new job."

Eighteen

As promised, Jack sent his private jet early Saturday morning. Willa had sat Priya down a few days ago and told her about Jack. She showed her pictures of her father. The little girl was beyond excited. She hadn't stopped asking questions about Jack and his ranch.

They boarded the plane and settled into the plush leather seats. Priya had never been on a plane before and Willa enjoyed her childish amazement. A car was waiting for them at Dallas airport when they landed. Jack had wanted to come to Dallas but Willa suggested he meet Priya at the ranch, where there wouldn't be the awkwardness of a car ride home.

Jack was waiting at the front door when they arrived. Willa watched anxiously as Jack walked over to them. She could see the love and joy on his face as he took in the sight of his daughter for the first time. Priya grabbed on to her leg and she put her arm around the little girl.

Jack slowly walked over to Priya and dropped to his knees in front of her.

"Hi, Priya. I'm your daddy," he said softly and held out his hand for her to shake. Priya studied the hand for what seemed like a very long time. Then she let go of Willa's leg and hugged Jack.

The gentleness with which Jack hugged Priya made Willa's heart melt. "Do you want to come see your room?"

Priya looked at Willa and she nodded encouragingly at her daughter. Had it only been a little over two weeks when she'd first walked through the front doors of the ranch? As they stepped through the front door, Willa gasped. The house had been decorated for Christmas. The railing of the staircase was wrapped in garlands of evergreen and twinkling lights. At every other step, a small Christmas tree glowed with sparkling ornaments. A beautiful poinsettia was the centerpiece of the foyer.

Priya took it all in with wide eyes and girlish awe. Jack led them upstairs toward the guest room that Willa had occupied just a week ago. The room had been transformed into a wonderland fit for a little princess. The walls were painted in a soft shade of pink, and there were colorful decals of flowers, butterflies and fairies dancing around the room. A fluffy white rug covered the wooden floor, creating a comfortable space for little feet to play. Priya's bed was a white, four-poster canopy bed, draped in delicate pink curtains that billowed in the gentle breeze.

In one corner of the room, there was a small play area, complete with a tiny table and chairs, a miniature kitchen set and a bookshelf filled with colorful children's books. A child-sized teepee tent sat in another corner, offering a cozy hideaway.

"This is all for me?" Priya's eyes were wide as she lapped the room, touching things, picking them up, then carefully putting them back.

"All for you," Jack said, watching her. "But you know what, I think the room is too neat. What do you say we mess it up a bit?" He walked to the bed and plopped down on it, grabbing a pillow and throwing it on the floor. He patted the bed and Priya gleefully climbed on top of it. She giggled as she jumped. "Mama, look, this bed is super bouncy."

Willa couldn't help but laugh at the sight of her daughter jumping on the bed and Jack valiantly pretending he couldn't keep his balance as he bounced with her.

"I have another surprise for you," Jack said to Priya once she had her fill of jumping on the bed.

Priya's eyes clearly conveyed her enthusiasm. Jack took her hand. As they passed by Willa standing in the doorway, Priya grabbed her mother's hand so she was between both her parents as they made their way to the kitchen.

On the table there was a little pink tea set with small round cups and saucers in pink and white. The teapot was the centerpiece of the set, with its long spout and elegant handle. It was painted with the same pink color and floral pattern as the cups and saucers. Little plates were filled with mini sandwiches and scones.

"Do you like to play tea party?" Jack asked.

Priya squealed.

She immediately took a seat at the head of the table, close to the teapot. She directed Jack and Willa to sit on either side of her. They happily obliged, sharing a smile with each other.

A warmth spread through Willa's chest. Jack had put so much thought into this first meeting with his daughter. He hadn't just bought her a bunch of toys but thought of something that would make them interact and bond.

Priya poured out the tea, which was really chocolate milk.

"Did Steve have fun cutting up these mini sandwiches," Willa asked, popping a ham and cheese one in her mouth. She suddenly realized she was starving. While she'd made sure to feed Priya breakfast and lunch, she herself hadn't eaten all day.

Jack picked up a up a cup and saucer, and holding it delicately just the way Priya had shown him a few seconds earlier, he took a sip. "Steve could not understand the concept of plain ham and cheese and peanut butter and jelly sandwiches. His first batch had arugula and garlic aioli. They're in the fridge in case you're hungry. These I made myself."

The idea of Jack cutting crusts off sandwiches made her heart warm.

They continued to pour and sip tea, chatting and laughing together. Jack was attentive, asking his daughter questions, discovering her likes and dislikes, her dreams and aspirations.

"Thanks for playing with me, Daddy," Priya said, looking up at him with her big brown eyes.

Willa's breath caught and she didn't miss the shine in Jack's eyes. It was the first time Priya had called him daddy. Jack was a natural father.

Jack's parents came for dinner. Priya was much more reserved with them, sticking close to Willa but by the end of the evening, they'd managed to win her over enough to schedule a play date with her the next day.

As Willa gave Priya a bath in the gigantic tub in the bathroom, the little girl enjoying all the little water toys Jack had bought for her, she turned to her mother. "Mama, I love it here. Can we stay forever?"

And just like that, Willa's worst fear was coming true.

Jack stood silently in the doorway, watching as Willa gently tucked their daughter into bed. Priya snuggled up to her mother, wide-eyed and eager. Willa smiled down at her, then opened the book and began reading. Her soft voice filled the room. As Jack watched, his heart swelled with love and adoration for both his daughter and the woman who held her so tenderly. He couldn't believe how much he already loved this little girl, despite only just meeting her that day. The way she looked at Willa with such trust and affection made his heart ache. If Willa had told him she was pregnant, they would be on that bed together right now, instead of him watching from the doorway.

Willa finished the story, closed the book and began to sing a lullaby. Her voice was soft and sweet, like a gentle breeze on a warm summer night. Priya's eyes grew heavy as the sound of her mother's singing filled the room. Jack could see the love and devotion in Willa's eyes as she looked down at their daughter. Jack's heart kicked. Willa had done a great job with Priya. The little girl was polite, kind and smart, and Jack could see why.

As the lullaby came to an end, Willa leaned down and placed a gentle kiss on Priya's forehead. She tucked the blankets in around her daughter, making sure she was warm and comfortable. Then she turned and saw Jack standing in the doorway. Their eyes connected and they stood for several minutes looking at each other.

Willa motioned for him to come and say good-night. He kissed Priya on the head. "I can't believe she's ours," Jack whispered, his voice thick with emotion. They stood there for a while, silently watching their daughter sleep.

Willa turned to him, tears in her eyes. "I'm sorry I kept her from you." A lump formed in his throat as he looked into Willa's eyes. How could he forgive her? But then, how could he not? She was the mother of his child, the love of his life. She had raised his daughter, all alone, into a wonderful human being. Willa had named his daughter after his sister, without him needing to ask. She had kept his sister's memory alive in the most touching way possible. He had never felt so much love and gratitude toward another person.

Priya made a little sleepy noise as she turned over and tucked herself even tighter under the covers. Jack and Willa smiled. "I've only known her for a day and I already love her more than words can express."

Willa placed a hand on his arm and without thinking, he put an arm around her. They watched Priya sleepily toss again before settling into her comfy spot on the bed. They basked in the warmth and tenderness of the moment. This all felt right to Jack, his arm around Willa, looking over their daughter, kissing her goodnight. It was what he'd wanted for a long time. A family.

He turned to Willa and she looked back up at him. He leaned in and placed a tender kiss on her lips. It didn't take long for the kiss to turn into more. Willa's arms went around his neck, their bodies pressed together. He deepened the kiss, exploring her mouth with his tongue, savoring the taste of her. She moaned softly and he knew that she was just as lost in the moment as he was.

As his hands snaked under her shirt , the feel of her skin sent fire racing deep into his belly. Only Willa was able to ignite him this way.

Suddenly, she pulled back. He looked at her, his heart racing, as she stepped away from him.

"What's wrong?" he asked, his voice a whisper.

"I can't do this," she said, her voice barely audible.

Nineteen

As she lay in bed next to Priya, Willa stared up at the ceiling, feeling the weight of Jack's absence more acutely than ever. Every time she was near him, she wanted him with a hunger that scared her. She couldn't stop thinking about Jack, the way his arms felt around her, the warmth of his embrace and the taste of his lips on hers. But, every time they were together, she felt the sharp pang of dread, knowing that it could never work between them.

She looked over at her daughter. Willa loved Priya more than anything in the world, and the thought of breaking her heart was unbearable. When she told Priya about Jack, she'd made it clear that her mommy and daddy weren't going to live together, but that she would get to spend time with both of them, just separately. She

had talked to Priya's preschool teacher and school guidance counselor before talking to her daughter. Both had
recommended that Willa be very clear about the terms
of her relationship with Jack and what Priya should expect. She was too young to understand complicated relationships and would have a better chance at adjusting
with consistency. If she and Jack got together and then
separated, it would break her daughter's heart, and that
was a risk she couldn't take. Plus, the school counselor
warned that if Priya saw her parents together and then
apart, it would make it difficult for Priya to accept Jack
or Willa with anyone else.

She also couldn't ignore the fact that she couldn't
have a career in Royal and Jack was settled here. He'd
worked hard to build a life for himself. She loved Jack
with all her heart, but she didn't want to end up resenting him if she gave up her career for him. It wouldn't
be fair to either of them if she gave up her dreams
and goals. It also wasn't fair to ask Jack to give up his
home. He had taken years to build the ranch and settle
in Royal. It was where he wanted to raise his family.
What if he gave that up for her and things didn't work
out? Given that they had to be parents together, she
couldn't afford to have things sour with Jack.

As she thought about their relationship over the past
week, she realized that she was stuck in a never-ending
cycle of heartbreak. She wanted to be with Jack and
Priya, to wake up next to them every morning, and to
build a life together. But the thought of the heartbreak
that would ensue if things didn't work out was too much
to bear. She and Jack were connected for life through

Priya. There was no longer an option for her to walk away from Jack if things got difficult.

The next morning, Willa woke to find that Priya wasn't next to her. The sun was streaming from the windows and she bolted out of bed. Her churning thoughts had kept her from sleep most of the night, and it had been early morning when exhaustion took over. She'd clearly overslept.

She leaped out of bed and checked the bathroom. No Priya. She was in her pajamas but she ran downstairs to the kitchen and stopped short. Priya was sitting at the kitchen table with Jack. He was pouring milk into her glass.

"Mama, look! Daddy made me pancakes shaped like Minnie Mouse."

Willa took a seat next to Priya, dropping a kiss on her head. She didn't dare look at Jack. After he kissed her, she'd asked him to leave. Correction, after she'd kissed him back.

"Where's Steve?"

"I gave him the week off. I figured it's best to keep the number of new people Priya has to meet to a minimum."

It was very thoughtful of him. "Besides, we had fun making pancakes together."

"Why didn't you wake me up, sweetheart," Willa asked her daughter.

"I was going to but then Daddy said to let you sleep."

Willa finally looked at Jack. "I knocked on the door and Priya opened it. You seemed to be fast asleep and she was okay with coming downstairs with me."

"Did you brush your teeth?" Willa asked Priya.

Her daughter stopped midchew and widened her eyes.

"Oops. Didn't think about the teeth." Jack said.

"It's okay. Eat your breakfast then we'll go brush teeth and get dressed." Willa smiled.

"What're we doing today, Mama?"

Willa looked at Jack, who grinned and turned to Priya. "How would you like to ride a pony?"

Priya's expression said it all. Jack had emailed Willa a list of the activities he had planned for the week. They were all a child's dream. Pony rides, a trip to the zoo and aquarium in Dallas, and movies. Priya would never want to leave, an eventuality that Willa was mentally preparing for. She and Jack had only communicated via email and text while she was in New York. He'd assured her that he had no intention of taking Priya away from her but he wanted to be a part of her life. They'd agreed to discuss the details while she was spending the week.

"Do you want to resume your riding lessons?" Jack gave her his signature dimpled smile and her heart kicked, right on cue.

She squared her shoulders. "You know what, that would be great." Willa didn't want to be left out if Jack decided to take Priya on a trail ride.

After breakfast, they walked over to the stables, and just like he had with her, Jack introduced Priya to the horses. Then he led a small pony out of the stable and helped Priya up onto its back. She clutched the reins tightly in her small hands, her eyes wide with excitement. Willa watched from a distance, feeling a sense of tenderness wash over her as she observed Jack's patience and care with their daughter. He gently helped Priya get used to the pony. Willa hadn't seen the animal the last time she was in the stables, so she assumed Jack had bought the little horse just for Priya. It was just like him.

Her mind wandered back to before Priya was born, when they had just started dating. They were taking a weekend trip to the Hamptons and had stumbled upon an antique store. Willa had pointed out a pink Hello Kitty doll and told Jack all about a similar doll she'd had as a child that had been her night terror doll. Willa used to have nightmares when she was a child and her parents had bought her a Hello Kitty doll and spun a tale about how the doll would protect her from bad dreams. Willa had believed them and slept with the doll every night. It was extra special because the doll was blue, Willa's favorite color. A few months later, she'd had a bad day at work and Jack surprised her with that blue Hello Kitty doll. He had found it online, purchased it and waited until the right moment to give it to her.

Willa had forgotten how good it felt to be around Jack, to witness the care and love that he poured into everything he did. She walked over to Jack and Priya. Jack smiled at her, and Willa smiled back. Priya was now happily riding the pony around the ring by herself.

"Want to give it a try?" Jack asked, gesturing to Thunder, who was grazing in a nearby pen.

Willa hesitated for a moment before nodding. Jack helped her on to Thunder and they spent the afternoon riding. Jack had arranged a picnic cooler with sand-wiches for lunch.

Once Priya was comfortable on the pony, Jack took them for a tame ride around the ranch, all the while holding on to the reins of Priya's pony. For a few hours, Willa almost forgot that they weren't a family, that all of it was temporary. It felt so natural to have Jack tak-ing care of her and Priya.

But it wasn't real, and she had to remember that.

Priya normally didn't nap but the sunshine, fresh air and excitement of the day tuckered her out. She couldn't even walk back to the ranch, so Jack carried her back and set her in bed.

"How about a glass of wine?"

Willa paused. Being alone with Jack was not a good idea. Not with her heart full of warm and fuzzy feel-ings for him.

"Sure."

As Jack led her toward the living room, Willa felt butterflies in her stomach. They were about to have a serious conversation that would change everything between them. Willa couldn't help but notice the way Jack moved with a confident ease. If he felt negatively about her turning him down last night, he wasn't show-ing it. He never did. Wasn't this technically a negotia-tion? If it was, Jack Chowdhry never let the other party see him sweat.

He walked over to the bar and grabbed a bottle of wine, effortlessly uncorking it with a corkscrew. He handed her a glass and she took in the scent of the rich bordeaux. Jack had great taste in wine and he knew what she liked. She took a seat on the couch, tucking her legs underneath her. She cupped the wide-mouthed glass in her hand and took a sip, savoring the rich, fruity flavor.

Jack took a seat next to her and her heart fluttered. She'd done a lot of soul-searching in the last week. The truth was that she'd let her life run on autopilot for the last few years. Between taking care of Priya, going back to work and figuring out how to make it all work, she'd been too overwhelmed to really examine her career options. But she knew what she had to do now.

Jack turned to face her, his intense gaze meeting hers. He reached out and grabbed her hand. Willa's heart thumped. She took a deep breath.

"You're great with Priya," she started.

"She's a wonderful kid. You've raised her well."

"I'm ready for you to be in her life."

Jack gave her a dimpled smile and her heart jolted. How was she going to spend a lifetime being near Jack and not being with him.

"What about you, Willa? Why can't you be in my life too?"

Her chest tightened. "It's too complicated. There's my career. You know that I can't be a serious journalist in Royal and your life is here."

"What if I moved?"

"You would do that for me? Give up everything you've built here?" She gestured around her. "You custom-built this house, moved your parents. Your entire

life is here. What would you do back in New York? You
want to go back to being a business executive?"

"I can figure it out." His words were sincere but his
smile didn't reach his eyes.

"Then there's Priya."

"Exactly."

He leaned forward and grabbed her other hand so
both her hands were now in his and he was looking at
her so earnestly that the only thing she wanted to say
to him was *yes, yes, yes!*

"Willa, I want us to be a family. I want you and I to
raise Priya together. We were together five years ago
and neither you nor I have found someone else."

"Well, I was a little busy," she said a little defen-
sively.

"I tried really hard to forget you, to move on, to
stay angry at you for leaving me. But I couldn't. You
are burrowed deep in my heart and soul. I want to be
with you. Now we have more reason than ever to find
a way to make it work. You and I are connected for life
through Priya. Why not spend it together rather than
pining for each other."

Willa sighed. He was right. Even after all these years,
the mere thought of Jack could make her pulse race. She
had tried to move on, to forget about him and find happiness elsewhere, but it was like trying to outrun a hur-
ricane. Jack had left an indelible mark on her heart, one
that no amount of time or distance could erase. Every
time she thought about their time together, her chest
tightened with a mix of pain and longing. She knew
that she would never find anyone else who could make

her feel the way Jack had, and that knowledge was both a comfort and a curse.

"What if it doesn't work?" she asked.

"What if it does?" He held her gaze, his eyes dark and intense. "Tell me honestly that you don't feel what I feel. I love you, Willa."

Her breath caught. They were words she had longed to hear from him five years ago. It was what she'd always felt for him but was too afraid to say out loud.

"Are you going to tell me you love me or leave me hanging?" His dimpled smile melted any last doubt she had. She leaned in and kissed him. As their lips touched, a wave of emotion washed over Willa. She was floating on air, like nothing else in the world mattered except for this moment.

But as the kiss ended, a pang of fear gripped her heart. What if this was all just a dream? What if it was too good to be true? She pulled away from him, searching his eyes for any sign that he was just playing with her heart. But his gaze was unwavering, filled with an intensity that made her heart race. "I love you, Willa," he whispered, his voice husky with emotion. "I've loved you for so long I can't imagine my life without you."

Tears stung her eyes and she couldn't help but let out a small sob. It was as if a weight had been lifted from her chest, as if all the pain and heartache of the past five years had finally been worth it.

"I love you too, Jack," she managed to choke out, her voice barely above a whisper. "I loved you five years ago and never stopped. I was always too scared to tell you. I didn't know if you felt the same way."

He pulled her close, holding her tightly as if he never wanted to let her go. "I've always felt this way about you, Willa. I just didn't know how to tell you. But now that I have you in my arms, I'll never let you go."

He pulled her onto his lap and she straddled him, then weaved her hands into his hair and kissed him. He returned her kiss with equal fervor. It didn't take long for him to respond to her touch. She ground against him, enjoying the way he moaned and shifted beneath her. Willa took off her top and bra, savoring the feel of his hands and mouth on her breasts. She wanted him bad and despite his protest, she stood to take off their clothes. Her hands trembled with anticipation as she tried to unbuckle his belt. He stilled her hands and took over while she peeled off her jeans and shucked her panties. He grabbed a condom from his wallet and put it on. She resumed straddling him, her slick, wet core sliding on top of his hard shaft.

"Slow down," Jack muttered, which only spurred her on.

She rubbed her core against him while he sucked and nipped on her breasts, squeezing them just the way she liked. When she was right on the edge, she lifted her body up and slid him inside her. He felt incredible and she clenched around him. He leaned her back, then put his hands between her thighs and caressed her clit with his finger. It threw her over the edge. She arched her back and gave in to her release.

Once her brain engaged again, she noted that he was still hard inside her. Had he not enjoyed it? In response, he moved inside her. "I think you need another one,' he said, his voice deep and throaty.

Yes I do. There were so many emotions she'd been bottling inside her, anxiety over telling Jack about Priya, dread over how she was going to be close to him without being with him, fear over how she was going to make it all work, and exhaustion. More than anything, she was tired from five years of loving and hating a man all at the same time.

Jack moved inside her, using his hips to move both of them in perfect rhythm. He used his finger on her core, teasing her at just the right times. She clenched so hard she wasn't sure she could even hold Jack inside her. This time her orgasm was explosive, the love that she'd felt for Jack and couldn't express bursting out of her. He held on to her as her body shuddered with pleasure.

Their bodies were slick with sweat and Willa put her head on his shoulder to catch her breath. He held her tight.

"You forgive me for not telling you about Priya five years ago?"

"You forgive me for not letting you air the Mafia story?"

She leaned back and shook her head and he did the same.

"Forgiveness is overrated," he said. "Let's just say we'll move on."

She smiled. "Just one thing, though, Willa." His voice grew serious and she stared at him. "Please don't break my trust again. Whatever it is, we'll work through it together, but I don't think I'll be able to handle you lying to me."

Willa's heart dropped. There was one more secret she was keeping from him.

Twenty

Back in New York, both Willa and Priya missed Jack. They'd spent a magical week with him, including Christmas, but had returned to the city after the new year. Willa had to return to work. Priya was ready to stay back with Jack but Willa hadn't been ready to let go of her daughter. Jack was planning to fly down midweek to spend a long weekend with them.

Willa finished typing her latest story on the fundraiser of a wealthy socialite and hit Send with the same disgust she felt every time she filed one of these frivolous stories. It was time for a change.

For now, she and Priya would live in New York. Jack had a subscription to a private jet service and he was more than happy to use it to fly them back and forth. Meanwhile, Willa had sent out her résumé and made calls, and was working her old connections for another job. She was done with NYEN. Jack had offered to make a call for her at CMG but she forbade him. She needed to know that she was being hired for her talent, not because of her boyfriend.

The desk was a mess with littered Post-its, print-outs and file folders. After sending her fluff piece, she turned her attention to collecting the papers on her desk.

David walked in without knocking. "Shouldn't you be leaving? It's going to take you at least an hour to get to Rikers Island.

"Forty-five minutes," she said shoving the papers into her messenger bag. She wanted to make sure she had all her research with her in case she needed to reference it during the interview.

"Listen, Willa, no pressure but I need to tell you something. There's a lot of interest in this story. Our ex-mayor George Wright just announced that he's running for the US Senate fifteen minutes ago."

Willa's eyes widened. "What!"

When she returned from Royal, she'd planned to drop the story about Jack's sister's murder. But then George Wright, the guy who had ordered the hit, had gotten a successful ruling from the state supreme court overturning his previous conviction. He'd beaten the legal charges against him on some technicality. All the work that Willa had put in to get him into prison, all the heartache of losing Jack had gone down the drain with one legal maneuver. The guy was not only free, but now he was using his notoriety to get back into power?

"If you can get this taxi driver to turn on him..."

He didn't need to tell her what it would mean. For one, it would put a murderer in prison, where he should have been all along. Second, it would be the story of her career. Despite making multiple calls, nothing had panned out for her in terms of a job better than the one she had. Her old connections all had the same thing to say—she'd been out of the game for too long. Right now, she was only known for her fluff stories; she'd been shoehorned into that category. She needed to break something good to get the attention she'd need to get the type of job offer she wanted.

Once she talked to Jim Ross, the taxi driver who had hit Jack's sister, she would convince Jack to let her publish the story. There was no point in having the argument with him if the driver didn't have some proof. His testimony alone wasn't enough—a man in prison already convicted of manslaughter didn't make for a believable accuser. But if he had proof—a phone call, a text message, email, or better yet, payment paper trail, then she had a story she could sell to her network, and to Jack.

David had pulled some strings to get her an interview with Jim Ross. Willa had considered talking to Nico Law while she was in Royal but decided against it. Nico was Jack's friend and she was well aware of where Jack stood on the story. She felt guilty for keeping it from him but also knew that she could better convince him once she had details. Jack was worried about his family's safety, but if she was able to get explicit proof that would put George Wright in prison, he would feel differently.

Willa took a deep breath as she walked through the sterile, fluorescent-lit corridors of Riker Island prison. Her pulse was racing and she reminded herself that she had done this before, that she had interviewed dozens of prisoners in her career as a journalist.

But this was different. This time, the stakes were personal, and they were really high. She'd reviewed every document related to his legal proceedings and talked to the prison guards. In the prison, Jim had a reputation for being difficult, uncooperative and even violent. But she had to get his story, no matter what.

As she entered the small interview room, Willa's eyes scanned the space, taking in the surroundings. It was a sparse room with gray walls and a small, rectangular table in the center. Two chairs were positioned on opposite sides of the table, and a guard stood in the corner, watching them.

Jim Ross was already seated at the table, his hands cuffed in front of him. Willa couldn't believe her eyes. He was a small, wiry man with thinning gray hair and a face that was almost boyish in its features. From the trial photos, it was obvious he had lost more than a hundred pounds. He looked up at her with a mixture of fear and defiance, his eyes darting around the room.

Willa took a seat across from him and set up her recording equipment. She hadn't been allowed to bring her phone, so it was an old-fashioned microphone recorder. Jim's eyes were on her, watching her every move. She tried to ignore him as she adjusted the microphone and hit Record.

"Mr. Ross," she said, her voice steady. "Thank you

for agreeing to speak with me today. I have some information for you that I hope will compel you to give me something in return."

Jack was filling out paperwork so he could legally marry Maggie Del Rio and Jericho Winters. Wedding preparations were in full swing. When Maggie had first asked, he'd felt a little weird as a single man talking about love and marriage but now that he had Willa and Priya, he was looking forward to it. Even though he hadn't proposed, his mother was already planning his and Willa's wedding. He had to rein her in. While they were in a good place, they still had to figure out how to make it all work.

Willa didn't want him helping her find a position, and he understood and admired her integrity, but he knew how the media world worked. Willa had been out of the limelight for too long. Her most recent stories were what people remembered. She had the talent but she'd need some help. He'd made a subtle inquiry at the CMG station in Dallas. They had a position open for a local beat reporter. It wasn't exactly what Willa wanted; she'd be doing local interest stories but it was a step better than the social beat she was on now.

He had just signed his name to the officiant paperwork when his phone rang. It was one of his former associates at CMG, Gail Flowers. Gail was an intern at CMG when he'd first started there, before he bought the network. He had personally mentored her and she was now an executive. He hadn't heard from Gail since he'd left CMG. Why would she be calling him now?

Maybe she'd heard about him inquiring about potential openings and had something for him. She certainly owed him.

"Gail, it's nice to hear from you."

They exchanged pleasantries for a few minutes before Gail got to the reason why she was calling.

"Jack, I'm calling as a courtesy because I owe you. Willa St Germaine is working on a story about your sister. Apparently, she's got something good because NYEN is advertising a special story for tonight's broadcast."

Jack nearly dropped his phone. The floor gave out from underneath him. There was no way that Willa would betray him like that. Not after what they'd been through, not after what they'd shared.

"I don't have any other details but our news desk is working on finding out."

He thanked Gail for the warning, then went to the NYEN website. Right there on the front page was the ad for their nightly broadcast. A special investigation about the death of Priya Chowdhry, sister of Jack Chowdhry.

His stomach roiled. How could Willa do this to him? She hadn't mentioned the story since they'd last talked. There had been no indication that she was still working on the story after he talked to her. Why was she doing this? Was it payback for five years ago, when he'd taken her story? He thought they'd moved on from that, but clearly they hadn't.

He took a breath and called her. It went to voice mail. He hung up and called the jet service. He needed to see her. If she really had betrayed him, he wanted to look her in the eyes and understand why.

The interview with Jim Ross had gone better than her wildest expectations. He'd been reluctant and petulant at first but then she'd given him the leverage she'd brought. Willa assumed that the only reason the taxi driver would protect George Wright was because he'd gotten a payoff. After looking carefully into his family and relationships, she'd discovered that at the time he'd hit Priya, he had a mother in a nursing home. She was in an expensive facility and Willa correctly guessed that George Wright was paying for the mother's nursing home bills. The facility his mother was in cost several thousand dollars a month on top of what insurance covered. Well over what a taxi driver could afford, especially one with only a hundred dollars in his commissary account. Jack had implied that Jim Ross was also afraid for his mother's life. What Jim didn't know was that his mother was already dead. She'd died several months ago from natural causes but he hadn't been notified.

Jim Ross was appalled to see his mother's death certificate. He'd been told that she'd been moved to an even nicer facility to thank him for his continued loyalty. Once he found out that he hadn't even been given the opportunity to attend his mother's funeral, he was more than happy to turn on George Wright. Not only was Jim Ross willing to tape an interview, he also had a recording of the phone call between him and George Wright directly making the deal when Priya died. On the recording that Jim had saved to a cloud account, George was clearly heard saying that he had asked Jim to injure Priya badly, not kill her, but now that he had, he was willing to make a deal. The evidence was damning enough but the cincher was that Jim had a paper trail of his lawyers' fees that had been paid by George Wright.

She had used the prison pay phone to immediately call David to send over Rogerio and a camera crew to tape the interview.

Once they were done taping, she finally retrieved her phone and saw that Jack had called. Something turned in the pit of her stomach. She'd been so excited to get the story, the familiar feeling of being hot on the trail of something explosive, that she'd almost forgotten about him. Then her heart sank as she saw the messages from David. They were running the story that night. While she had been interviewing Jim Ross, David had fact-checked and talked to the network. They were eager to run the story.

With a sickening feeling, Willa called David and asked if the network could wait a day.

"No way in hell," David said. "Breaking this story on the day that George Wright made his announcement to run for senate is going to pack a punch. Plus, CMG has been sniffing around. We don't want them scooping us. Get to the studio. You're on air in two hours."

Bile rose in the back of her throat as she hung up with David. This was bad. She called Jack as she left Rikers. He didn't answer. She called Steve, who told her that Jack was on his way to New York. He was probably in flight, which was why he wasn't answering. Steve didn't know why he'd suddenly decided to go to New York but Willa could guess. The network had decided to advertise the story before she'd even finished interviewing Jim Ross.

When she got to the studio, it was chaos. She had to finalize the details of the script for the teleprompter, find something to wear on screen and get her hair and makeup done. She'd called Jack several times with no luck.

She'd tried talking to the producer to postpone the story, arguing that they were not ready, but there was no stopping the runaway train.

Twenty minutes before airtime, Jack finally answered his phone. "Where are you?"

"Outside the studio."

She ran to the lobby and stopped short when she saw the look on his face.

"Jack, I need to explain."

He crossed his arms. "Explain? Please explain how you took something I told you in confidence and decided to use it to further your career."

"It's not like that."

"Then tell me how it is."

"I found proof that George Wright ordered the hit on Priya, then covered it up. Proof that's admissible in court. He announced today he was running for Senate. We can't let him go free after what he did to your sister."

"Yes, we can. When I asked you not to pursue the story, I didn't even know about our daughter. Now more than ever, the threat is too much. George has had it out for me for years. When he finds out that I have a daughter, Priya will be a target. No story is worth that risk."

"If we don't run the story, the guy will continue terrorizing people. He belongs behind bars. Surely as a former journalist, you know that I can't sit on a story like this."

"Even if it's at the expense of your family?"

"That's where we differ. It's for our family that we need to get people like George Wright put away. When our daughter is old enough to understand, I want to tell her that I was strong enough to stand up to a bully and get justice for her aunt. What I don't understand is why you don't want the same thing."

"That's not the point. I don't disagree with the fact that George Wright should be put away. I take issue with the fact that I shared what happened with Priya in confidence with you and asked you not to pursue it and you did it anyway. Is your career more important than us?"

"Are you asking me to choose between the two?"

"No. You made it very clear five years ago where you stand on that front."

They glared at each other, at an impasse. "You can't do the story, Willa."

He could not seriously be asking her that. "Excuse me?"

"Look, I'm not asking you to never do the story. Push it off for a couple of days. Let me do a threat assessment, get you and Priya some protection."

"Jack, why do I feel like we're having the same conversation we did five years ago?"

"We're not having the same conversation."

"Correct. Because this time, I'm not letting you make the decision. I go live in ten minutes."

"This wasn't your story to tell."

"It is now."

Jack stared at her. "It'll be at the expense of our relationship."

Willa met his icy stare. "So be it."

Twenty-One

"Daddy, when is Mama coming back?"

Jack looked at his little girl as she handed him a little pink teacup.

"In fourteen days, sweetheart." He had learned to tell her in days rather than weeks, and was prepared for the inevitable next question.

"Why does Mama have to be gone so long?"

"Your mama is a really awesome reporter and she is covering a big story in Brussels. Don't you like watching her on the morning news every day? It's important for her to go, to make sure the story gets told right."

"Mama is the only one who can do it right?"

He nodded, his chest tight. After Willa broke the story about how George Wright had ordered a hit on his sister, her career had taken off. Without Jack's knowledge or intervention, CMG had called Willa to cover a special United Nations story. It was a high-profile opportunity. Willa had arranged to take Priya with her but had called Jack to ask if he wanted her to stay with him instead. He had readily agreed. Willa had made it very clear that while their relationship might be over, she intended to make sure he had every opportunity to be a father to Priya.

He was still very angry with Willa for moving forward with the story even though he had to admit that she had been right to do it. George Wright had been arrested, and Jack's own legal and security consultants assured him that the case against the former mayor was pretty damning. Jack didn't know how Willa had convinced Jim Ross to turn on George, but the driver had provided evidence for a pretty compelling case.

Despite everything, Jack still couldn't let go of the fact that Willa had lied to him. Again.

She'd explained that she planned to tell him if Jim Ross decided to turn on George Wright but things had moved quickly. He accepted her explanation but didn't excuse her behavior. She should've told him from the beginning that she was still pursuing the story. So what if he disagreed? How could she keep something like that from him? *The same way she kept Priya from me.* What bothered him most was that Willa still didn't trust him.

"When Mama comes back, will she come stay here with us?"

He shook his head. "No, sweetheart, remember, you and Mama will go back to your house in New York. I will come visit you again soon or you'll come here for another visit."

"Why can't Mama come stay here? I like it here."

Somehow, *It's complicated* didn't seem like an appropriate response. How did he explain to his four-year-old daughter that her parents loved each other very much but couldn't trust each other and therefore couldn't be together.

"Your mom has a really important job, and that job is in New York."

"Then why can't you come to New York?"

Because I can't forgive your mom. Because she hasn't really forgiven me.

"My life is here in Royal. Sweetheart, your mom and I love you very much but we all can't live together. Don't worry, you'll get plenty of time with both of us."

She smiled. "Can we have hot dogs for dinner?"

"Absolutely," he said with way too much enthusiasm, glad the conversation was over for the day. He knew that it would take Priya some time to get used to their arrangement. What he didn't know was how long it would take him to get over losing Willa.

"I'm telling you, I've got to deputize a bunch of college kids just to make sure we have enough traffic police for the wedding." Sheriff Nathan Battle played a set of sevens.

Jack looked at the cards in his hand and eyed the poker table. He'd made plans to host a poker game for the guys weeks ago. Normally he looked forward to these games, a chance to drink beer and catch up with the guys, but he'd almost canceled today. He tried to gauge what Jericho had, but his face was completely neutral. This was why he liked playing with these guys. He selected an eight and put it down.

Jericho chuckled and shook his head. "You're not even paying attention, man. You just played an eight on a set of sevens."

Jack frowned and looked at his cards again. "Sorry, I guess I'm just a little distracted."

Lyle Drummond sat back in his chair and took a sip of his beer. "Would that distraction be your k!smet match?"

Lyle had k!smet to thank for his fiancée, Giselle Saito. Jack sighed and rubbed his forehead. "We broke up."

Jericho raised an eyebrow. "What? When did this happen?"

"A month ago," Jack replied.

"Is it because of that story on George Wright?"

Jack nodded at Jericho. "I told her not to pursue it. It could've put our whole family in danger but she did it anyway."

Sheriff Nathan laughed. "Oh man, you really haven't been in many serious relationships, have you?"

Jack frowned at him. Nathan leaned forward. "Listen, I've been married for a while, so take it from me that one of the worst things you can do is tell your partner they can't do something that they really want to do. It'll never work out for you. Not if you're with someone who is strong and knows her mind."

"That she definitely does."

"Listen, when Amanda and I were first married, she had this idea that she wanted to open this diner in Royal. I came up with a million reasons why she couldn't, starting with the fact that we didn't have the money to invest, it was a lot of work, and I wasn't sure if a diner could even complete with the hoity-toity restaurants we have here. But you know what I failed to take into account?"

The fact that Amanda owned the Royal diner clearly meant Nathan had lost that battle.

"What I didn't realize was that Amanda didn't need my permission. She needed my support."

"Wise words, Sheriff." Jericho slapped him on the back.

Lyle smirked. "Can you imagine Royal without Amanda's milkshakes?"

They all laughed. Jack studiously studied his cards but his chest was tight. How many times had Willa told him how important her career was to her? Not because it was a job, not because it made her wealthy, far from it, but because she truly believed that investigative journalists played an important role in making sure justice was served.

"No relationship is perfect. Just ask anyone who's been married. All I'll say is, if she's the one screwing up your poker game, you're in trouble."

Jericho laughed and gave Nathan and Lyle a high five. "Looks like I've got a pretty good hand here," he said as he laid down a pair of aces.

Sheriff Nathan raised an eyebrow. "Slow down there, cowboy. Let's see what Jack's got first."

Jack looked at his cards and sighed. "I've got nothing," he said as he laid down his cards.

Jericho grinned. "Looks like it's just you and me, Sheriff."

Sheriff Nathan chuckled. "Well, let's see if your aces can hold up against my full house." He laid down three kings and a pair of fives.

Jericho's grin faded as he looked at the cards on the table. "Damn, nice hand. You got me beat."

Jack couldn't help but laugh at his friend's victory. "Nice one, Sheriff."

Jericho shook his head. "I can't believe I fell for that. I thought for sure I had the winning hand."

Sheriff Nathan grinned. "You can't always rely on luck, Jericho." He gave Jack a hard look. "Sometimes you've got to play the odds."

Twenty-Two

Willa finished the afternoon broadcast, which would air over the morning news back at home. She wondered whether Jack watched her reports.

"You should be on the top of the world. That was amazing."

She smiled at Rogerio. When she took the job with CMG, she'd been able to bring Rogerio with her as her camera crew. "I am. The network is really happy with us." They were in Brussels covering the NATO defence ministers' meeting. The scent of fresh-baked waffles and the sound of street musicians filled the air. Willa loved the vibrant energy of the city but it did little to improve her mood.

"Then why do you look like you have the stomach flu?"

Willa's smile faded. "It's nothing," she said, shaking her head. "Just missing Priya."

"Is it Priya you're missing or someone else?"

Willa swallowed against the lump in her throat. She did miss Jack, but there was no doubt in her mind that she'd made the right decision. Journalism was more than a career for her and Jack had never understood it.

"It doesn't matter if I am missing him. I can't be with him."

"Tell me again why not."

She sighed as she and Rogerio headed back to their rental car. "He doesn't prioritize my career. To him, it's expendable. How can I spend my life with a man who doesn't value my work? There are always going to be reasons why I shouldn't do something. I want to know that the man I'm with can understand what's important and support me. Today it's about a story, tomorrow it might be about where Priya goes to school or where we live."

"So he's a control freak and you're worried he's going to take over your life."

"When you say it like that, it sounds trite."

"Steve says he's a darling with Priya."

That was something Willa already knew. Her daughter loved her father. She couldn't stop talking about how great he was.

"How's it going with Steve?"

Rogerio shrugged. "Long-distance is hard but we're trying to make it work. Did I thank you for this one-month assignment, by the way?"

"You're welcome."

"Are you going to take that job in London?"

She sighed. She'd been offered a job by a renowned international network but it was based in London. The assignment with CMG was only for a month but they'd also offered her a permanent position much closer to home. Suddenly she was exactly where she wanted to be. Her career was taking off.

"I have a lot of offers but nothing like London. These types of opportunities don't come by very often."

"But…"

"But that would mean Priya doesn't get to spend a lot of time with Jack. Dallas is a three-hour flight to New York City but London is ten to twelve. It's not a weekend trip and when she's in school, he'll only see her on holidays."

"Are you worried about her seeing Jack or you being close to him?"

She rolled her eyes and got behind the wheel to drive them back to their hotel. Willa gripped the steering wheel tightly as she maneuvered through the bustling streets of Brussels. The city's historic architecture and quaint cobblestoned streets were a beautiful sight, but navigating through the maze of cars and pedestrians was a challenge. She had to either take or decline the London job today. They'd given her until the end of the day for her answer.

She caught glimpses of the towering spires of the Cathedral of St. Michael and St. Gudula and the impressive Palace of Justice as she weaved through the city's twisting roads.

When they got to the hotel, Rogerio gave her a goodbye hug. "Just remember one thing. Sometimes being at the top of the mountain is no fun when all you can do it keep looking down at what you left behind."

She called Priya. Jack was great about making sure she got online at their arranged hour and stayed out of the way. Priya had apparently made a new friend at a play gym that Jack had taken her to but she complained that he only liked to play on the monkey bars and Priya wanted to go play on the swings. Willa listened with patience to Priya's arguments for why the swings were better.

"Priya, you know if you want to make friends, you can't just do what you want to do. Sometimes you have to play the way they want."

Priya pouted and Willa's mouth went dry. The more she thought about Jack and Priya, the more her heart ached. She had never felt so torn in her life. She wanted to be a family with them, but she couldn't let go of her dreams. The weight of the London job decision was crushing and suffocating her.

As the day wore on, Willa found herself aimlessly walking the streets of Brussels. She missed Priya, even longed for the routine of their day, making breakfast in the morning, seeing her off to school, hearing about her day.

But career opportunities like the one London was offering her didn't come by very often. She was at the top right now, she'd felt the dregs of what it was like to be at the bottom.

She knew what she had to do.

Twenty-Three

"What time is Mama coming?" Priya asked for the millionth time. Jack smiled patiently and checked the GPS on his car. He'd sent a driver to the Dallas airport to pick up Willa. "Good news, she'll be here in a minute. Why don't you go to the door to greet her?"

Priya didn't need any encouragement. By the time Jack got to the front door, she had managed to swing it open just enough to squeeze through.

Willa leaped out of the car and mother and daughter ran into each other's arms. Jack's heart swelled as he witnessed the tender moment between Willa and Priya. He couldn't help but smile as he watched Priya cling to her mother tightly, their laughter filling the air.

As they pulled away from the embrace, tears glistened in Willa's eyes as she held Priya's face in her hands. It was clear she'd missed her daughter.

Willa looked up and their eyes met. His pulse jumped at the wistful smile she gave him. How was it possible that she was even more beautiful than when he'd seen her just a month ago, when she dropped off Priya? Was it just that he'd missed her? No, it was not his imagination. Her face had a new glow, her eyes had that old sparkle she used to get when she was hot on the trail of her story. She was happier. Without him.

As he continued to stare at her, memories of their time together flooded back, reminding him of how he felt when he was with her, and what he went through when she wasn't in his life. He wanted to reach out and touch her, to tell her how much he still loved her. But he couldn't do it. She looked happy and content. Maybe she was better off without him.

"Daddy, look, Mama's back."

Priya held out her hand and he took it. For a moment, they stood there, the three of them connected in a bubble of family happiness. It pinched his heart.

Jack walked through the fields of his ranch, surrounded by tall grasses that swayed in the wind. The sun was setting behind him, casting a warm glow over the landscape. As he approached the stables, he heard the neighing sounds of the horses.

As he turned the corner, he saw Willa standing by the fence, her hair flowing in the breeze. She was wearing a long sundress, and the light fabric danced around her legs as she moved. His heart squeezed so tightly that he had trouble taking a breath.

He paused for a moment, taking in the sight of her. She was holding a carrot, and Thunder had come up to her, his nose nuzzling against her hand. Willa looked up and saw him, and a smile spread across her face. He took a deep breath to steady himself.

"Willa," he said, his voice barely above a whisper.

"Everything okay with Priya?"

He nodded. "She's having dinner with my parents." Jack had asked his parents to come babysit for the evening so he could talk to Willa. Who knew if he'd get the opportunity again? He'd heard from his former media colleagues that she'd accepted an offer in London. She was getting ready to move far away from him.

The idea of losing her made things very clear for him. He could no longer live with the emptiness he'd felt for the last five years without Willa. There was no doubt in his mind that she was the only woman for him. But he had driven her away with his stubbornness and arrogance. Over the last month, he'd replayed their arguments over and over in his head, wondering how he could have been so blind to what really mattered. He had been so convinced that he was right, so determined to get her to see things his way that he hadn't considered what was really important. Nathan had been right. Willa didn't need his permission, she needed his support, and he hadn't been there when she needed him the most.

He didn't know if she would forgive him, but he had to tell her how he felt, even if it meant risking everything.

Her smile faltered as he approached and his heart squeezed tight. He'd never been more nervous in his life. He reached into his pocket and pulled out a piece of paper, handing it to her.

"What is this?"

He smiled. "It's my new home in London. Not quite as grand as this—it's a smaller row house, but the Realtor tells me that it's quite charming and within walking distance to your new offices."

Willa stared at the picture of the house. What was Jack saying? "Jack, why….what…" She looked up from the paper and stopped short. He had dropped to his knees and was holding out a silver box with a ring nestled inside. His grandmother's ring. Her heart stopped.

He cleared his throat. "Willa, I've been a complete ass. I was so afraid to lose you that I drove you away. You were right in revealing the truth about Priya's death. George Wright deserves to be punished. I was so focused on doing what I thought was right that I forgot about what was really important. I know you have no reason to trust me, but I promise you that I will be there for you, to support you in whatever you want to do."

His eyes were shining and her chest was so tight she couldn't breathe. Was he saying what she thought he was saying? Could this really be happening?

"My home is where you are. All this…." He gestured around him. "I built this for us. When I designed the balcony in my room, I pictured watching the sunset with you. I imagined us cooking together in that kitchen, and teaching our children how to ride horses in this ring. Without you, none of this means anything. My home is wherever you are and I will follow you to the ends of the earth if you will just let me."

His voice cracked and her heart lurched.

"Willa, I have never stopped loving you, and never will. You are the only woman for me. You are the one who makes my heart sing, who brings a smile to my face even on the darkest of days. You are the light that guides me, the wind that carries me, the love that sustains me. You are the mother of my daughter, the keeper of my heart, the one I want to spend the rest of my life with. I can't live without you. Will you marry me?"

She dropped to her knees in front of him and cupped his face. He leaned forward and kissed her and she kissed him back with the ferocity of a woman who'd been waiting five years for this moment.

Jack broke the kiss. "So is this a yes?" His voice was deep and throaty and his anxiety was clearly written across his face. He deserved to suffer for a few more seconds for making her wait this long.

"That depends."

"Whatever you want, Willa, you can have. I owe you a lifetime of happiness."

"Can you return that house in London?"

"What?"

She grinned at him. "I turned down London. This last month has been hell. I was in this beautiful city doing what I love, at the top of my game, and it all felt empty. All I could think about was you."

His eyes widened. "I took a job in Dallas hoping that I could convince you to let me live here."

His face broke into a smile and his dimples made her heart flutter. How could she have thought, even for a minute, that she could live without this man?

"So that's a yes?"

Willa's heart swelled. She had finally found her missing piece, the person who made her feel complete. Her dream job hadn't given her even a fraction of the happiness that she experienced with Jack. There was no doubt in her mind that she couldn't live without him, and she didn't want to.

She nodded. "A thousand times yes."

He kissed her and they held each other tightly. The sun set, coloring the sky in shades of purple, orange and pink.

Epilogue

"Hurry up, Priya, we'll miss the flight." Willa shouted to her daughter as she threw the last few things into her bag.

Jack leaned down and kissed the back of her neck, sending goose bumps down her arms. "You know the jet won't leave without us. We're the only passengers."

Willa smiled. "I forgot. I'm used to flying coach."

"I can't believe I get you for a whole week to myself."

She smiled. They were flying to Texas for Maggie Del Rio and Jericho Winters's wedding. Jack was officiating and adorably nervous about the responsibility. Priya was excited to see her pony, whom she had named Cotton. Willa was grateful for how quickly Priya had adjusted to London. Jack had talked her into taking the job, arguing that it was much easier to move around when Priya was young. Once Priya was older and less enthusiastic about changing schools, they would move back to Royal.

They had all moved into the London home Jack had bought and he'd effortlessly integrated into the school pickup and drop-off life, allowing Willa to fly all over the world chasing down stories. It had been great for her career and she had no idea how she could've done it without Jack.

"You know we better set a wedding date. Everyone in Royal is going to ask. Especially Misha. She's over the moon that k!smet made another match." Jack picked up Willa's bag and they headed to the front door where Priya was still figuring out how to tie her shoelaces.

Jack bent down to help his daughter, who put her little arms around him in gratitude.

"Mama, do I get to be a flower maid at your wedding?" Priya asked.

Willa smiled at her. "You get to be a flower girl and a junior bridesmaid."

Jack kissed his daughter. "And your *dadi* is going to order you some very special clothes and jewelry from India." He turned to Willa. "My mother is going overboard with the wedding preparations. The longer we wait, the crazier she'll get." Willa laughed. They were going to have a traditional Hindu ceremony and a church wedding just as Jack's parents had had. Their biggest challenge was finding a two-week period where Willa was available. Jack was insistent that they were going to take a honeymoon after the one-week Indian wedding festivities.

"Tell your mother she can go nuts. I've waited more than five years to marry you and I don't care how it's done as long as I'm your wife." Willa had grown close to Jack's parents, who had been wonderfully support-ive of their engagement and move to London. They re-mained in Royal but planned to spend the summers in England, where the weather was tolerable.

She raised her face and Jack dropped a kiss on her lips. As they pulled away from the kiss, Jack looked deep into Willa's eyes and said, "I can't wait to spend the rest of my life with you, Willa. You're my soulmate, my best friend, and the love of my life."

Willa's heart pounded. Jack still gave her butterflies every time he gave her his signature dimpled smile. "I love you, Jack."

As they held each other, they knew that nothing could ever come between them again. They had faced challenges in their relationship, but their love had only grown stronger. And now, as they planned their wed-ding and looked forward to their future together, they knew that their love would continue to grow and flour-ish for many years to come.

* * * * *

New York Times and *USA TODAY* bestselling author **Barbara Dunlop** has written more than fifty novels for Harlequin, including the acclaimed Gambling Men series for Harlequin Desire. Her flirty, lighthearted stories regularly hit bestseller lists, with one of her novels made into a TV movie. Barbara is a four-time finalist for the Romance Writers of America's RITA® Award.

Books by Barbara Dunlop

Harlequin Desire

Texas Cattleman's Club: Diamonds & Dating Apps

The Texan's Secrets

High Country Hawkes

Breakaway Cowboy
From Highrise to High Country

Gambling Men

The Twin Switch
The Dating Dare
Midnight Son
Husband in Name Only

Visit the Author Profile page
at Harlequin.com for more titles.

You can also find Barbara Dunlop on Facebook, along with other Harlequin Desire authors, at Facebook.com/HarlequinDesireAuthors!

Dear Reader,

It was an honor to participate in this year's Texas Cattleman's Club series and revisit the good folks of Royal, Texas.

I love writing both ranch and city settings, and *The Texan's Secrets* was a perfect blend of downtown and country.

Nico Law and Emilia Scott are hardworking, successful tech entrepreneurs. They're completely satisfied with their professional lives but have hit some bumps keeping their personal lives private. Attraction catches them off guard, forcing them to double down on their secrets as they navigate a growing relationship.

The Texan's Secrets was great fun to write, and I hope you enjoy the read!

Barbara

THE TEXAN'S SECRETS

Barbara Dunlop

For my husband

One

For a black hat hacker, the law was irrelevant. For a white hat hacker like Emilia Scott, the law was, at times, discretionary.

"You have to break some eggs…" she muttered to herself as she hit a series of keys on her PC, attempting to break into the computer system of multinational construction company Stiner Rosch.

She had a contract with the company to test their security, so she could have used a password. But it was fun to do it the old-fashioned way. Plus, it would help her figure out how the bad guys might approach a theft. The best way to guard against a thief was to pretend to be one herself.

Once she was in, she poked around in the lines of code and the subroutines until she found a possible vulnerability. Then she tested her theory and successfully made her way into the detail of the company's customer files.

"Ha! Voila. Omelet." She screenshotted the process that could potentially allow backdoor access to billing information, then saved the documentation to her report file.

Afterward, she devised a temporary patch and uploaded it directly to the server where it would go live.

"Take that, you no-good cyber thieves." Satisfied, she sat back in her chair, removing her glasses to rub the bridge of her nose before raking her short hair from her forehead.

Next, she took a gulp of her coffee, instantly grimacing at the taste and nearly choking on its bitterness. There was cold. There was stale. And then there was vintage. "Yuck." She shuddered.

"Hey, Emilia?" her roommate, Paris Fortin, called from the bottom of the stairs.

"What's up?" Emilia called back, picking up her mug to dump the contents. Nobody was that thirsty.

Paris's bedroom was the lower floor of the small house in downtown Royal, Texas, while Emilia was spread out in the loft. The two women shared the kitchen and living room on the main floor in between.

It was Wednesday afternoon, Paris's day off from her job as assistant manager in the dining room at Chez Verte, a local French fusion restaurant. With the holidays over, she'd spent the day pulling down the decorations and packing them into the small garage.

Emilia had planned to help, but the security call from one of her biggest customers had taken priority.

"Did you read about the k!smet Surprise Me! dating event they're having in connection with their IPO launch?" Paris was making her way up the stairs as she talked.

"Who hasn't?" Emilia's social media feed, not to mention her email box, was full of advertising for the social app's promotion. The marketing department had gone wide with it.

"What do you think?" Paris stepped up to the airy loft.

"It'll probably work. The app's members are obviously engaged. There's been plenty of back-and-forth on all the social media sites."

Emilia had once worked for a rival dating app to k!smet and could appreciate the huge brand development and marketing strides the k!smet team had made over the past few months. They deserved their success.

"You going to sign up for the chance to win?" Paris moved into the room as she scrolled along her phone screen.

"Me?" Emilia chuckled at the thought of trying to be one of the first ten matches in the contest. Her look was at best mousy—no makeup, casual clothes, flat shoes and oversize glasses to give herself a wider field of vision. She was hardly top-ten material.

"Sure, you. Why not you? It'll be a hoot."

Emilia gestured to herself with spread fingertips. "Have you met me?"

Paris looked up from her phone. "You look terrific."

"I look dowdy."

"Ha!" Paris sobered when she saw that Emilia was serious. She moved close and brushed aside Emilia's short hair. "What's this? You have gorgeous eyes. Your lashes are to die for. You're beautiful, Emie."

Emilia chuckled even while she appreciated Paris's vote of confidence. "*You* are not a matchable man. So, your opinion is irrelevant. Plus, you love me."

"What's that supposed to mean?"

"It means you see me through a benevolent filter. And I'm not signing up to be humiliated."

"I do love you. But I'm not blind." Paris looked concerned now. "You do know you're pretty, right?"

"I don't care." Looks didn't matter to Emilia one way or the other. She wasn't much on having a social life, preferring to focus on her work, which was mostly on her computer screen.

"You need to get out more," Paris said with a pout.

"I was working on the balcony just this morning."

"You know that's not what I meant. Sign up. Take a flyer on this. You could win an all-expenses-paid date."

"You sign up."

"I already am. I'm totally on board for this."

Emilia was surprised by the optimism in Paris's voice. "You know the long odds of winning the free date."

Having been involved in the backend of a dating app, Emilia knew the mathematics on a perfect match.

"Sure, I know the long odds," Paris said breezily. "But k!smet is paying, and I want to go somewhere nice for a change. It's not like I'm looking for happily ever after. I'm not wearing rose-colored glasses."

"You read the rules, right? It has to be a love match to qualify. And they're using the Surprise Me! function, so you'll get…you know, something unexpected."

The k!smet Surprise Me function was famous—make that infamous—for matching together very unlikely couples.

Paris shook her head, her thick auburn hair fanning around her lovely face. "Who cares who it sets me up with? I can fake a love match, at least temporarily."

Seeing her friend's excitement, the wheels began turning inside Emilia's head. She'd hacked into the k!smet app once or twice, just to look around—professionally curious to see how their algorithms were structured. She'd discovered the Surprise Me! function in particular had some very elegant coding.

"That's actually a great idea," she said as she formulated a plan. Code was code, and she could help here. With a little judicious hacking, she could make Paris's dream of a free date come true.

She started for the stairs then, her short-term objective the kitchen and something better to drink.

"For you too." Paris called out as she followed along. "We could double-date."

"Not my thing."

"The app or the date?"

"Both. Neither." Emilia rounded the corner in the foyer and headed through the dining room. "I'm a homebody."

"No kidding. But what if I went ahead and signed you up for it anyway?"

"You can't." Emilia dumped her cold coffee into the sink.

"I know your membership number."

Emilia stopped dead. "You can't possibly know that." She hadn't even told Paris she'd applied for a k!smet account. She'd only done it for research purposes. She barely filled out the profile. It was no surprise she hadn't been asked on any dates.

"You wrote it down on your desk."

"What were you doing at my desk?"

"Seriously? Hijacking your bandwidth like I always do."

Emilia shook her head and placed her mug in the dishwasher. She didn't mind Paris sitting at her desk or saving money by using her bandwidth. She was very cautious about locking up her clients' information, even if she had slipped up with her own. Not that Paris wasn't completely trustworthy in either event.

"The IPO launch party's at the grand ballroom in the Texas Cattleman's Club," Paris noted.

"I know." k!smet was about to offer public shares on the stock market. Creator, Misha Law, had worked hard to get to that stage.

Since Misha was best friends with Emilia's close friend, Maggie Del Rio. Emilia had met Misha a few times. From what she could tell, the woman deserved all the accolades.

Paris's tone rose with increasing enthusiasm. "The contest matches also get an invitation. The TCC is big.

It's grand. It's opulent as all get-out. I've seen pictures. I'd love to see it in person."

"I'm sure you'll love it." Emilia opened the fridge.

She knew Paris would love mingling with the who's who at the k!smet IPO launch party. Paris would also love winning a free date—which Emilia now intended to ensure she won, even if it meant engaging in a few hacker shenanigans to make that happen.

Emilia spied a pitcher of a telltale pale green liquid and her interest perked up. "Margaritas?"

"Yes, they are. Have one. Or have two. Then we'll come back to your intransigence."

Emilia coughed out a laugh as she extracted the pitcher. "You won't change my mind."

"Don't sell me short." Paris retrieved two glass tumblers from a cupboard and brought them forward.

Emilia set the pitcher on the counter and went for the freezer, dropping handfuls of ice cubes into the glasses while Paris held them out.

"Did you plan dinner?" Emilia asked, thinking margaritas on an empty stomach were a bad idea, especially while Paris was trying to talk her into something.

Paris shook her head. "We can order a pizza."

"Pineapple and sausage?"

"Heathen. So long as we can add pesto and dried tomatoes."

"You don't think dried tomatoes are redundant?" Emilia closed the freezer while Paris poured the margaritas.

"No such thing as redundant vitamin C."

Emilia lifted and contemplated her drink. "You really want to do this?"

"Drink margaritas?" Paris joked.

"The free date. You really want the free date with who-knows-who?"

"I'm a gal on a budget."

"And I'm a gal who'd rather stay home."

Paris heaved a disappointed sight. "Okay. You win. I won't sign you up." She clinked her glass against Emilia's. "Here's to both of us getting what we want."

Emilia hid a calculating smile. "Here's to that, then."

Nico Law had been skeptical about coming home to Royal, Texas. His sister, Misha, hinted, then nagged every time they'd spoken on the phone—which was daily. He'd finally given in. Royal was an up-and-coming tech hub, and he'd decided his company would fit in perfectly. But he'd known it would be hard to keep a low profile in the place. But, so far, he'd succeeded, with very few Royal citizens figuring out he'd come back home. Fewer still knew he was growing a tech company right here in their midst.

His local friend Rafe Cortez-Williams understood Nico's burning desire for both freedom and privacy. So, the two men spent countless hours enjoying Rafe's vast family ranch. Horses didn't care if a man had a criminal record. And few people outside the Cortez-Williams family ventured into the hills and valleys of the cattle range.

"I'm serious," Nico said as the two men rode side by side down the gradual slope of a trail next to the river that bisected the family ranch. He'd replaced his usual nondescript beanie with a Stetson and his khakis with a pair of jeans. "You've all treated me like family. It's about time I contributed."

"It's not like we have a shortage of horses. You don't need to buy your own."

"That was just one idea. Or I could pay for a new barn or something."

Rafe laughed. "We don't need a new barn."

"An extension on the house. Wouldn't your mom like a brand-new kitchen?"

"Don't you go messing with Mom's kitchen. She loves it just the way it is."

"Then, you tell me."

"Do you really think my parents would take your money?"

"Help me out here. I'm a man with a simple lifestyle and way too many zeros in my bank balance."

Rafe laughed again. "Do some charitable works."

"You know I already do." Although his donations were anonymous, the local animal shelter and children's wing of the hospital had received significant endowments from his tech company AlgoXcell's philanthropic foundation.

"I know."

"I'm here all the time. They feed me, let me go riding and fishing."

"Maybe there's a hint right there, Nico. You should get a social life. Spend some of your money on a nice woman."

Nico frowned. "You know I can't do that."

Back in prison, Nico had grown a beard and let his hair grow long. The disguise suited him now that he was back in Royal where people had known him as a teenager. The beanie he wore was another form of camouflage, as were the beige Henley shirts that were slightly too big for his frame.

There'd been other physical changes while he was in prison. He'd gone in as a young man—a lean and wiry twenty-two. He'd filled out while he was there, since the gym was one of the best places to kill time. And it didn't hurt a guy to be physically capable while inside. It made those looking for trouble think twice about messing with you.

"You plan to be a hermit for the rest of your life?" Rafe asked.

Nico would never admit it out loud, but these past few months he'd grown tired of leading such a solitary life. He'd found himself lonely for some female companionship. He didn't mean sex. He'd had a few no-strings relationships since getting out of prison. They were fine, as far as it went.

But sometimes he really missed the intimacy of a woman's laugh, hearing her ideas and opinions, her take on the world. His friends Rafe and Jack Chowdhry were great to hang out with. But it wasn't the same as more intimate companionship.

Instead of saying any of that to Rafe, Nico made a show of scanning the river, forest and hills. "This is hardly the hermit lifestyle. Maybe I should buy myself a ranch."

"You?" Rafe was clearly incredulous. "You don't know the first thing about ranching."

"I could hire someone to do it for me. Maybe one of your brothers wants a job."

"You think Dad would let them leave? He's barely forgiven me for opening the steak house. It's way easier for you to just hang out here when you want to get away from it all."

"Then back to my original offer. How can I contribute?"

Rafe kicked his horse into a faster walk. "You can eat hearty tonight and tell my mom how much you love her cooking."

Nico followed suit, speeding up his own horse. "That goes without saying."

The sun was dipping toward the horizon, so Rafe's mother, Carmen, would be cooking up something extraordinarily delicious. Nico couldn't help hoping for her grilled peppers and empanadas.

He and Rafe had some fresh-caught trout in their cold packs. Carmen was sure to spice them up with her special blend, send them outside for Rafe's father to grill over hot coals, then serve them with avocado salsa. There was nothing better to go with a tall bottle of crisp, cold beer.

"I take it business is booming?" Rafe asked as they started across the bridge, heading for the old windmill where they'd pick up a ranch road back to the main house.

"It's hard not to make money in tech."

"See, that's yet another good reason to avoid ranching." Rafe gave a whistle. "It's more than tough to make money in ranching."

"Royal's done well all these years with ranching as a backbone."

"There's a reason why we're branching out to tech. And you and Misha have both done very well for the town."

Rafe was right about that. Nico's sister's new social app, k!smet, was about to go public and, by all indications, was about to go big.

"Stick with what you know, I say," Rafe added.

"I suppose buying my own ranch would be overkill." Nico hadn't really been serious.

He'd considered leaving his penthouse apartment for a house with a big yard. But he liked the security in the building. It meant nobody could surprise him at his front door, and his neighbors mostly kept to themselves.

Then again, there was something appealing about a rambling house, maybe on a hillside with miles and miles of a view. He could always build a fence and install a gate at the end of the driveway to protect his privacy.

Rafe brought his horse to a halt in the middle of the bridge, turning it sideways. "I know something you could do."

Nico had lost the thread of the conversation. "Could do about what?" He reined his horse to avoid getting too close.

"For my family. You can update the ranch computer systems. Matias has been fighting with their clunky programs for years on end."

"Are you saying you've had the same programs for *years*?" Nico couldn't even imagine.

"See the problem?"

"Count me in." Nico loved the idea. "I can write them an app, customize it to whatever they need. They could use it on their phones in the field to feed into a central system." The enthusiasm in his voice grew as his mind catalogued the possibilities. "Is Matias at home? Can I talk to him tonight?"

Emilia worked her way through the k!smet code, its data fields and subroutines. The more she explored the Surprise Me! function, the more impressed she was with whoever had written it.

Because she was friends with Misha she knew something about k!smet's origins and aims. But the one time the Surprise Me! function had come up in a conversation, Misha had turned oddly vague about it. Emilia hadn't thought anything about it at the time, but now she was becoming curious. It felt different from the rest of the app. Misha was a good coder, but this was great coding. Interesting.

Paris had left to work the dinner shift several hours ago, and dating day, or "D-Night" as they'd jokingly dubbed it, for the k!smet promotion event was coming up fast. Emilia intended to do everything in her power to make sure Paris got her free date. Given the randomness of the Surprise Me! function, Emilia figured nothing would be compromised if she nudged the algorithm in her friend's direction.

She worked her way into the membership data records and tracked down Paris's membership. She planned to hide a piece of code behind the profile and use it as a Trojan horse to manipulate the broader system.

From what she'd seen of the past, well-publicized Surprise Me! matches, she couldn't trust its unpredictability to make anything resembling a love match for Paris. So, Emilia was going to do it the old-fashioned way and choose the most likely man from those who'd signed up for the event. After all, she knew Paris better than anyone.

She scanned her way through Paris's profile, smiling to herself at her friend's whimsical answers to the get-to-know-you questions. Paris had a gift for description and wry wit, and it left Emilia feeling lacking.

The read inspired her to track down her own profile and spruce it up. She might not be using it, or plan to use it in the foreseeable future, but it was embarrassingly meager at the moment. The field for her childhood was completely blank, and her career description consisted of a single line. And her photo. Good grief, she'd completely forgotten about her photo. It looked like a mugshot.

Impulsively, she decided to do something about that right away.

She hopped up from her chair, stripped off her clothes and headed into the shower. Her hair might be short, but it was lightweight and glossy brown when it was freshly washed and blow-dried.

After the shower, she applied some makeup, then headed downstairs to raid Paris's closet for something bright and trendy since her own clothes were all earth tones and casual.

She settled on a cobalt blue chiffon blouse with lace cap sleeves and a bright scatter of rhinestones decorating the scalloped vee neckline. It was ridiculously out of sync with her olive cargo pants, but she was only planning a headshot, so nobody would ever know.

She pulled down her cream-colored window shades and dragged a lush, potted tree fern in front of them to create a backdrop. She tested a selfie and decided it needed…something.

Glancing around the room, she spied a pair of red wooden candle holders that had sat on her mantle since she moved in. They were fake antiques, painted to look faded and aged. But they'd add a touch of panache and a splash of color.

She dragged an end table next to the fern, chased up some short, white candles for the holders, then arranged the fern fronds around the setting.

She tried another photo and liked it. She took several shots, most of them comical, until she came up with a half smile that seemed to have put a slightly secretive glow in her eyes. It was much better than the mugshot, and she uploaded it to the system.

When the downstairs door slammed shut, Emilia realized how much time had passed. Caught up in her own profile, she hadn't even started setting Paris up for success.

"Emilia? You up?" Paris called out.

"Yes." Remembering the purloined blouse, she

quickly stripped it off and hung it in her closet, tugging a T-shirt over her head.

Hopefully, Paris would take a shower before bed, and Emilia could covertly put the blouse back where it belonged. Paris wouldn't mind loaning it out for the photo, but Emilia didn't want to own up to her moment of vanity.

"Still working?" Paris asked as she came to the top of the stairs.

"Just finished." Emilia sat down at her desk and shut off her screen.

"What a night." Paris flopped down on the love seat tucked into the corner of the loft.

"Busy?"

"And how." Paris cocked her head to one side. "Why'd you move the plant?"

Emilia had forgotten about the photo setup. "More sunlight."

Paris's gaze narrowed. "You're going to leave it sticking out in the middle of the room like that?"

"Just for a couple of days." Emilia squelched her guilt. She hated lying to Paris, even about something innocuous.

"Hope it helps. We had this couple in the restaurant celebrating their fiftieth anniversary. They had a huge table, over forty people there to celebrate."

"Fifty years?" Emilia couldn't even imagine staying with one person for that long.

Paris nodded.

"Did they look happy?"

Paris chuckled at Emilia's doubtful expression.

"Don't be so skeptical. Yes, they looked happy. They were over the moon. They had seven great-grandchildren."

"That's got to be rare." Abandoned when she was young, Emilia didn't remember her own parents. As a foster child, she hadn't seen a whole lot of happy marriages.

"Rare, maybe. But far from impossible. You have to have a little faith, girl."

"I have faith," Emilia said staunchly. "In myself, my career and my independence."

"I don't want independence."

"You want *dependence*?"

"I want happily ever after with someone who adores me. I mean, eventually. After I have some fun along the way. I'm too young to settle down yet."

Emilia tried hard to hide her skepticism. "I wish you nothing but good luck with your long-term plan."

"I could even meet Mr. Right at k!smet's D-Night. It's coming up fast."

"D-Night is definitely coming up fast," Emilia acknowledged.

Luckily, Paris was working again tomorrow night. Emilia promised herself she wouldn't get distracted this time. She was determined to pick out a great guy for her friend and increase the odds of Paris's happily ever after.

"As in *happily ever after*?" Nico asked incredulously. His sister, Misha, quickly backtracked. "I'm not suggesting you use k!smet for real. I mean—" She fought a smile. "I've known you way too long to think that."

"We're talking about data collection, pure and simple," Maggie Del Rio added. "The marketing team wants to do a deep dive into the Surprise Me! function and the IPO event."

The three were sitting on the deck of his penthouse apartment overlooking downtown Royal. Unseasonably warm for January, it was coming up on five, and the rush hour traffic hummed below them.

"We'll make you a fake profile," Misha continued, making it obvious the two women had been plotting together for a while on this. "We can call you Nick."

"Nick?" Nico wasn't crazy about the idea of going undercover on k!smet.

To learn anything meaningful, he'd have to go out on a date or dates. He'd been careful to keep his presence in Royal under wraps. And unlike the no-strings dates he sometimes went on in Dallas, the women of k!smet were looking for a relationship. They'd try to get to know him. And that was the last thing he needed.

"It's not like either of us can do it," Maggie said reasonably. "Everyone in town knows who we are."

"Plus, you're both attached," Nico pointed out.

It was obviously impossible for either of them to take on the task.

"We need to work out the real-world kinks," Misha said. "Nobody knows the Surprise Me! function better than you do."

"After all the scandal and build-up to the IPO launch, it *has* to be a success," Maggie said.

"And we both know theoretical and real-world are two completely different things," Misha added.

Nico couldn't argue with that. Part of beta testing was seeing how an app behaved on a larger scale when real and inherently unpredictable people got involved. It was never what you expected.

"You don't think people would recognize me?" Even if he did agree in principle with the plan, there were definitely some real-world problems on his end.

Misha waved off the concern. "Nobody in Royal has seen your face in six years."

Nico's hand went to his thick beard. As disguises went, it had proven very effective. He didn't go out much, but he could walk the streets of downtown or pick up groceries without being recognized, even though he'd grown up here.

"I know *I'm* curious to see what he looks like under there," Maggie added.

Because he loved Misha dearly, he considered humoring her. "*If*, and I'm only saying if. If I did agree."

Both women instantly beamed.

"Don't get ahead of yourselves," he warned. Although he knew he couldn't realistically turn them down, at least not without a very compelling reason.

"Sure," Misha said. But her expression told him she was certain she'd won.

Which she had. She was right about this, and he never argued with his sister when she was right. Not that he argued much the rest of the time either. He adored her, and he'd do anything for her.

"How would it work?" he asked.

Maggie sat up straighter. "You'd lose the beard, get rid of the beanie and, for goodness sake, cut your hair."

"I've grown fond of the beanie." The slouchy brown knit hat drew attention. It kept people from looking too closely at his face. Plus, it kept his head comfy warm. It was to the point that he felt a little naked without it.

"It's all gotta go, bro," Misha said on a laugh.

"What if it's completely obviously me under there?" he asked, worried that half the town would recognize him as soon as he got rid of the disguise.

"We won't know until we check," Maggie said reasonably. She rose from her chair.

"What are you doing?" he asked with suspicion.

"Getting a pair of scissors to cut your hair. You must have some kicking around the kitchen."

"What? You? Now?" A vague sense of alarm shot through him. "I haven't said yes yet."

"Sure, you have," Misha said, then looked to Maggie. "What do you think? Haskap's downtown, or should we take him into Dallas for new clothes?"

"Haskap's has plenty to choose from."

Nico heaved a sigh of capitulation. "And...you're talking wardrobe too?"

"Absolutely," Misha said. "Now, go with Maggie. Get her your best scissors."

"I have a beard kit in the bathroom," he admitted.

"Perfect," Maggie said. "I'll leave it longer on the top and clip the sides short. Get your hair wet. Take off your shirt and put a towel around your shoulders."

"The things I do..." Nico muttered as he heaved himself from the chair.

"Nick." Misha tried on the name for size. "I like the sound of that." She pushed up her sleeves, obviously getting ready for business.

Maggie tied back her long hair and positioned a bar stool in the middle of the kitchen while Nico hunted down his beard kit.

A couple of hours later, all three of them stared into the mirror at "Nick."

"You have a great chin," Maggie said in awe.

"Strong," Misha agreed. "Really square. I don't remember it looking like that."

Nico tilted his head sideways to take in another angle. "I was twenty-two when I grew the beard."

"You look—" Misha paused.

"Rugged," Maggie finished.

"Not like a computer nerd at all."

Nico cracked a smile. "Computer nerd?" Although he supposed that's exactly what he was.

"You looked soft and fuzzy with the beard, beanie and all that hair," Misha said.

"Now you look angular," Maggie added. "Hard-edged, like you mean business."

"I've always meant business." Nico stepped back, uncomfortable with their intense scrutiny, especially since he was standing there shirtless.

"Matching him's not going to be a problem," Maggie said as Nico dragged a T-shirt over his head.

"We'll be fighting them off with sticks."

"It's an algorithm," Nico pointed out with an eye roll. "And since we know who wrote it we have complete control of my matches."

"Oh, no, we won't," Misha said with a shake of her head. "We're going to let the system do its work and see what happens."

"Next, he'll need a profile," Maggie said.

"I'm on it," Misha answered. "Who knows Nick better than his loving sister?"

"I can write my own profile," Nico said.

"You have more important things to do."

Nico raised his brow.

"Go clothes shopping with Maggie. She has an excellent sense of style."

His sister's enthusiasm was starting to entertain Nico. "So, this Nick, he's a style guy?"

"And how," Maggie said. "He has excellent taste in clothes, and a very high credit card limit."

"Women like that," Misha added.

"We don't care if they like me," he pointed out. "I just need a few dates to gather data." The last thing Nico needed was pressure to actually impress a woman. He hadn't tried to do that in many, many years.

Two

Driving down the gravel ranch road in her compact sedan, Emilia promised herself she hadn't cheated Paris. In fact, she'd matched her friend with a terrific guy. He was Chase McMillian of the McMillian Ranch. The family were long-time members of the Texas Cattleman's Club, which was a huge credential in Royal.

Chase came from a ranching family, but he'd made his own fortune as an architect and builder. His profile was smart and funny—just like Paris's. But it was the video clip that had sold Emilia. Chase came across as open and genuine. She saw intelligence and kindness behind his blue eyes. The two were out on their k!smet-sponsored date right now.

But for all that, as she pulled up to a huge ranch house with its sprawling front porch, Emilia couldn't shake the feeling she'd scooped up the best guy for herself.

While hacking for Paris, Emilia had come across the profile of a member calling himself JustSayYes. His warm eyes had all but leaped out at her. He wore a half smile that said he had depth, if not outright secrets. His anonymity, his job as a programmer, plus his hobby of horseback riding had intrigued her.

In a moment of impulse, she'd hacked her own profile and forced the match between them. And now, here she was, about to discover if she'd shortchanged her friend, or conversely made a colossal mistake by setting herself up with JustSayYes.

She shut off the car engine just as the front door of the ranch house swung open.

She couldn't fight her own smile as JustSayYes emerged into the sunlight. She'd have known his russet hair, chiseled chin and deep hazel eyes anywhere, especially when he smiled back. Her heart took a funny lurch.

"Sorry, Paris," she muttered as she closed the driver's door behind her.

He trotted down the short staircase and came her way with an easy stride.

"Emilia," he said, holding out his broad hand. The lilt of his deep voice made her think he'd had doubts she'd show up.

"We did say five o'clock."

"And you're right on time." His hand closed over hers. The touch was gentle, like he was holding himself back, careful not to hurt her. It was a comforting shake that ended too soon for her liking.

"Chronically punctual," she admitted.

"That's an admirable quality."

"Your friends don't mind us invading their space?" Emilia took in the expanse of neatly trimmed lawn, shrubs and shade trees that seemed at odds with the cattle fencing beyond. It was an impressive home and a bigger than average ranch, judging by the length of the private road from the highway.

"They don't mind at all. The Cortez-Williams family is as open and friendly as they come. Don't be surprised if there's a full-blown family barbecue waiting for us when we get back."

"Really?" She couldn't tell if he was joking and hoped he was. A big boisterous family was a lot for an introvert like her to take on.

"Not your thing?" he asked, correctly assessing her expression.

"I've spent a lot of years coding in my basement. I'm not all that well socialized."

He laughed, obviously assuming she was joking.

She wasn't. Not really. She didn't code in a basement anymore. She loved hanging out with Paris and Maggie, but she still spent plenty of time alone interacting with her screen instead of real people.

"I don't even know your name yet," she said, changing the subject.

He paused for a split second before answering. "Nick. My name's Nick." He held out his hand again.

This time he was slower in shaking hers. His warm

palm sent a wash of awareness up her arm to her shoulder and deep into her chest. On first blush, he was one impressive and sexy man.

She silently apologized to Paris once again.

"Nice to meet you, Nick." She took her time letting go. "So, why the anonymity?"

He released his grip, and she reluctantly did the same.

"It was my first time on a dating service. I was slightly intimidated."

Emilia couldn't imagine him being intimidated by anything. "What did you think would happen if you used your real name?"

"I guess I wanted the chance to back out."

"But you didn't."

"No, I didn't." A beat went past. "And I'm glad."

"Nice of you to say." She knew he was being polite since they'd known each other all of five minutes. But politeness was another positive attribute.

"Are you ready to ride?" he asked.

"As ready as I'll ever be." She'd been horseback riding a few times since moving to Royal, but she was very much a beginner.

"Rafe said he'll give you a gentle horse."

"Rafe?" She fell into step beside Nick.

"He's my good friend, a member of the Cortez-Williams family."

"Rafe Cortez-Williams?" The name surprised her, and Royal suddenly seemed like a very small town. "The owner of RCW Steakhouse?"

"Yes."

"What a coincidence. My roommate works in the restaurant industry."

"You don't say."

"She's been at Chez Verte for about a year now. She met Rafe—saw him at an industry function of some kind."

Another beat went by before Nick responded. "He's a good guy."

Nick fell oddly quiet then as they made their way down a pathway to the back of the house and beyond where they came to a barn. It was long and low, with butter-yellow walls and a peaked green roof. A huge set of doors were open in the center.

They stepped inside the hollow-feeling interior, and Nick, looking pensive, pointed to a bench. "Take a seat, and I'll go find Rafe."

Emilia was surprised at being left behind. She was curious to see the rest of the barn and would have liked to tag along.

"I'll just be a couple of minutes," he said.

"Sure. Okay." Feeling slightly uncomfortable at his apparent turn in mood, Emilia perched on the wooden bench.

Things had started off so positively, and now he'd all but ditched her to talk to his friend in private. Was he going to ask Rafe to make an excuse to get him out of the date?

Pessimistic scenarios built up in her mind while the minutes ticked past.

She was about to slip out of the barn and head for home when the two men appeared around a corner. She studied Nick's expression as they approached, trying to gauge his level of regret.

"Emilia," the other man opened with a broad smile. "I'm Rafe." He looked at home on the ranch, tall and lean with an undeniably handsome bronze complexion.

She realized she'd seen him from a distance one night while dining at his steak house.

She stood and accepted his handshake. "Nice to meet you, Rafe. I've enjoyed your restaurant."

"Thanks. Nick says you've ridden a few times?"

Emilia slid her gaze to Nick, but his expression was neutral, and she couldn't guess his mood. "We don't have to go too far." She tried to offer him an out.

"We can always turn back if you get tired," he said levelly.

"I've saddled Belle-Blue for her," Rafe said to Nick.

Nick nodded thoughtfully. "I thought we'd take the river trail to the shelter." To Emilia, he said, "It's wide and level with beautiful vistas."

"If you're sure about this." She wished he'd smile. If he smiled like he had on the porch, she'd feel like he really wanted to go on this ride.

His brows drew together instead, looking puzzled.

"Good choice," Rafe said heartily. "Let's get you two going."

Riding side by side along the river, Nico worried Emilia wasn't enjoying herself.

He'd pointed out the sights as they rode, the old windmill, a herd of horses galloping through a field and a distant waterfall in the hills surrounding the ranch.

Her answers were polite but generic. There was a tension in her manner he hadn't seen earlier.

"Ready for a break?" he asked, knowing the shelter was around the next bend.

"I am if you are."

"I'm ready." He'd brought along a bottle of wine, and there was a charcuterie box tucked in his saddlebags courtesy of Rafe's mother.

It had been an unexpected hitch in the plan, discovering Emilia's roommate was directly acquainted with Rafe. The connection was too close for comfort.

Nico hadn't told Rafe he was incognito for this date. But Rafe knew now, so Nico's secret was safe for the time being.

They rode to the shelter—an octagonal log building with a peaked roof and half walls all around. Benches and picnic tables sat on the concrete floor around a circular stone fireplace under a chimney in the middle.

Nico dismounted and clipped a lead rope to Dancer's bridle.

"Want some help getting down?" he asked Emilia as he tied the lead rope to a hitching rail.

She shifted in her saddle and looked to the ground. "Maybe come watch me, just in case."

"You got it." He quickly strode over to assist.

She braced herself on the saddle horn and kicked the opposite foot from the stirrup.

"Oh," she groaned as she swung her leg over Belle-Blue's back.

"Takes you by surprise," he said sympathetically.

As she started to drop, he braced his hands around

her hips, slowing her decent. Her hips were warm, slim, flexing slightly under his touch. He inhaled deeply, catching a whiff of a citrus scent.

"I didn't even feel it while I was riding."

With her feet on solid ground, he forced himself to let her go. He'd rather have turned her in his arms, gazed into her beautiful eyes and either kissed her or asked her if something was bothering her.

He wanted the kiss. But, more than that, he wanted to know what was going on inside her head.

"Okay?" he asked, ready to support her if her legs were wobbly.

"Good." She turned. "It's a little like getting your sea legs."

"Did it happen the other times you went riding?" He knew he should step back and give her space, but he didn't want to move. He liked being close to her.

"I think the other rides were shorter. Or maybe—" She seemed to cut herself off.

"Maybe, what?"

"Nothing." She tucked her rich brown hair behind her ears.

He didn't want to let it go. There was something going on with her. "Come on. Give."

"Fine. Okay. I happen to be feeling a little tense right now."

The answer took him by surprise. "Out here?" He gestured to the serenity around them. "Why?"

"Because…you. That's why."

"Me?" He took a half step back, worried he was crowding her. "What did I do?"

"You seem…" She gestured to him, up and down. "I don't know. Uncertain."

"Uncertain of what?"

The answer made no sense. Was she referring to his riding? He might not be the best rider in the world. He was nothing compared to Rafe. But he was at least competent.

"Of me. Of this. I get the feeling you'd rather have canceled this thing altogether."

"Our *date*?" He was truly baffled now. "Why would I want to cancel our date?" That was the last thing he wanted to do.

He hadn't learned much about her yet, but he liked what he had, and if the sizzle of attraction running through him was any indication, their kisses—assuming they got to any kisses—were going to be spectacular.

She was quiet for a long minute.

He waited.

"You got very quiet back there."

"Back where?" He thought he'd done fine holding up his end of the conversation. If anyone had turned quiet, it was her.

"While we were walking to the barn. You went from joking around to thinking deeply. Like you were contemplating—I don't know—how to escape or something."

As soon as she said it, he knew what she meant. It was right after she'd told him that her roommate had met Rafe, the moment when his cover was in danger of being blown. But she had it backward.

"It wasn't you," he said.

She skeptically arched her brow. "It was you?"

"Yes. I apologize. I got distracted for a moment."

"By?" she challenged.

"Your beauty and your grace."

"Nice try, cowboy." But she was fighting a smile.

"A work thing," he told her honestly.

"You were figuring out a problem?"

"Something like that."

She tilted her head, gaze narrowing. "Let me get this straight. You're coding inside your head instead of interacting with your date? You're really not helping the computer nerd stereotype."

He laughed, appreciating her joke. Then he held up his hands in surrender. "Guilty as charged."

He clipped a lead rope on Belle-Blue, led her away and tied her up next to Dancer. The ropes were long enough that they could stand and graze.

"What were you coding?" she asked as they made their way into the shelter.

"Now who's perpetuating the stereotype?"

"You've got me professionally curious."

It was an easy answer. "Rafe asked me to develop an app for his family's ranch."

"A custom app?"

The sun was heading for the western horizon, leaving a chill in the air. So, Nico peeled off a few sheets of newspaper from a kindling box near the fireplace. "Their software is hopelessly out of date."

"They can't just buy something shrink-wrapped off the shelf?"

"They could. But his parents aren't tech savvy. They

feel good about having something custom designed that eliminates the extraneous fields and processes they'd have with something generic."

"It seems needlessly expensive."

"It's not costing them anything." He realized how that sounded and wanted to be clear he wasn't bragging about his altruism. "They've been very, very good to me over the years."

"So, this is a volunteer gig?"

He crumpled the paper and tossed it into the open fireplace.

"Interesting," she said, but he couldn't gauge the tone of her voice.

He set some kindling on top of the newspaper and lit a corner.

As the slivers of wood caught flame, he turned so he could see Emilia's face while he asked the follow-up question. "Interesting how?"

"It's been a while since I coded for free." She paused. "I mean, if you don't count doing things recreationally or for friends."

"Want to sit?" he asked, gesturing to a bench near the fire.

She took him up on the invitation.

He sat down on the opposite end. The wooden seat was solid and comfortable beneath them, hand hewn then sanded to a smooth gloss with a sloped back and armrests on either end.

"Recreationally and for friends is exactly what I'm doing for Rafe's family."

"I've never created an entire app for a friend."

"You should try it. It's satisfying."

"I suppose," she said with a nod. "If I knew someone who needed something like that." She held her hands out toward the fire. "This is nice."

"It sure takes the edge off when the weather turns," he agreed. "Thirsty?"

"Sure."

He rose and tossed a couple of larger sticks of wood on the fire. "I've got water and a bottle of wine."

She smiled and looked around them. "Wine in the wilderness."

"If you're up for it."

"Sounds good."

He was happy to hear her say that. "Red okay for you? It's a Pinot Noir, light and crisp."

"That's fine by me."

Leaving Emilia by the fire, Nico dug into his saddlebags for the wine, two clear acrylic, stemless glasses and the charcuterie box.

"It's picnic style," he said as he set everything out on the closest table.

"It looks great." She stepped up to help, peeling back the cover of the plastic box while he popped the cork on the wine.

"I didn't even realize I was hungry," she said as they took in the selection of slice meats, cheese, fruit and crackers.

"We have Rafe's mom to thank."

"Nice of her. They do sound like good people."

As they settled on the picnic table bench, the fire

crackling beside them, Nico pivoted to face her. He raised his glass. "To first dates."

"First dates," she answered and leaned to click her glass to his before taking a sip.

Her eyes lit up. "Yum."

"One of my favorites."

Their gazes caught and held. He felt an inexplicable connection with her, and an odd warmth seeped from his limbs to his core.

One of the horses whinnied and shook its head.

Emilia glanced their way. "Do they mind waiting on us?"

"No. Like us, they're happy to take a rest and have a snack. We'll go down to the river later and let them drink." As he spoke, he realized he'd left the water bottles back in the saddlebags. "Did you want some water?"

She grinned. "From the river?"

"I filled bottles at the house for the humans."

"I'm fine with this right now." She set down her glass and selected a small wedge of cheese, paring it with a cracker.

Nico did the same, adding a sausage round to his.

"There's something about the fresh air," she said. "It makes everything taste better." She ate the cracker, then put together a second combination.

Having used the ranch as a refuge, Nico agreed that everything was better out here. "Do you spend a lot of time outdoors?" He wondered if she'd grown up in a camping or fishing family.

But she shook her head. "I'm a hothouse flower."

He hadn't expected that. "Why did you say yes to horseback riding?"

"You seemed enthusiastic about the idea."

"We could have done something else—dinner, dancing."

"I also thought it sounded like fun." She took in his expression. "And it was fun. Is fun. I was curious about you, and this is telling me something."

"Telling you what? That I'm too self-centered to figure out what a woman wants out of a date?" He honestly felt that way in the moment.

But she grinned and chuckled. "I'm having a perfectly fine time."

"Wow. Fine. Music to a guy's ears." The statement came out sounding more peevish than he'd meant.

"Oh, get over yourself," she said good-naturedly and took another sip of her wine. "If I'd wanted a fancy dinner, I'd have said so. And the sun's about to set. Isn't that why we're here?"

He looked over his shoulder and saw that the light cloud cover was cooperating, and the horizon was turning pink and golden.

"It's your chance to redeem yourself," she said as she rose to her feet.

Standing side by side with Nick on the riverbank, Emilia stared in awe at the magnificent sunset. The small balcony of her bedroom faced east and was blocked by taller houses around it, so she rarely had the chance to sit still and simply drink in the sight.

The golden ball slipped between two mountain

peaks, leaving nothing but a wash of pink, purple and gold sweeping across the sky.

"Wow," she said under her breath.

Nick slipped his hand into hers. "Agreed."

"Do you watch this often?" She liked the connection of his hand around hers. It felt natural, oddly comforting.

"Not often enough."

"Can you imagine building a house here?" she asked, fantasizing. "Right here, with a sweeping front porch so you could watch this every night?"

He chuckled low. "That's an idea."

"My view faces east."

"My deck faces north. It's a nice view of downtown, but it's a stretch to see the sunset most of the year."

"I suppose it wouldn't be the same inside a house. Not like this. Not with the wind in your hair, hearing the birds, smelling the pine and wheatgrass."

He nudged his shoulder against hers and squeezed her hand. "So much for being a hothouse flower. I think you're secretly a wild rose."

Her heart skipped—not because he'd given her a compliment, but because it came close to the truth, although not in the way he was thinking. She had an untamed streak, something deep inside her that liked to shake things up. She was trying to tamp it down, spending her time consulting instead of hacking. But she still loved the thrill of going rogue.

"What about you?" she asked.

"What about me?" He turned to face her.

"Wild or tame?"

He gazed into her eyes, rose-colored light on the planes of his face. "I wish I could say tame."

"Why?"

"It's safer than wild."

Her heartbeat deepened and her skin warmed with an undeniable sexual attraction.

He took a step forward. "If I was tame—" he slowly lifted a hand to her cheek, sliding his fingers into her hair "—I'd behave myself right now."

She inhaled deeply, liking where this was going. She swayed forward, anticipating the touch of his lips against hers.

"Where's the fun in that?" she whispered, tipping her chin to a better angle.

He gave another low chuckle and brought his mouth to hers.

The kiss started soft but then firmed, generating its own sensual current. Her lips parted. So did his. They explored each other's contours, sending a wave of awareness through Emilia, warming her from the roots of her hair to the tips of her toes.

She looped her arms around his neck, took another half step forward to press herself to his body, loving the feel of his heat, the firm muscle of his thighs, his stomach and his chest. Her breasts turned heavy, sending tingles into and along her spine.

His arm curled around the small of her back, holding her close, while his hand slipped to the back of her neck, tangling in her hairline.

He gasped in a breath, then kissed her again and again.

The sunset had faded, and twilight surrounded them when they finally parted.

It took her a moment to catch her breath. "Wow. That was wild."

He grinned as he eased back. "It seems neither of us is the tame type."

"I guess not." Although she'd never come close to reacting that way to any other man. The combustion between them rocked her to her toes. "I guess it's a real date now."

"Good to know you're on board." He planted a quick kiss on her lips, leaving a final sizzle in its wake. "More wine?"

She looked to the sky, disappointed that the beauty had faded. "It does look like the show's over."

"Good thing there'll be another one tomorrow."

For a moment, she thought he was alluding to a second date. But the idea disappeared as quickly as it had formed. It was a casual observation, nothing more. She'd be foolish to assume the kiss had rocked his world the way it rocked hers.

"I'm up for more wine," she said briskly and turned back to the shelter.

The air had grown cooler with the sunset, and she welcomed the warmth of the fire. Considering the walls were mostly open, the ceiling seemed surprisingly efficient at trapping the heat. She couldn't help but admire the structure's design.

Nick tossed on a couple more logs, while Emilia settled down to finish her glass of wine.

"We can ride back in the dark?" she asked.

"Bright moon tonight. And the horses know the way. Their eyesight is much better than ours."

"That's comforting."

"You think I'd put you in danger?" He didn't seem affronted, merely curious.

To the contrary, she felt confident in him. Confident enough to joke about the situation. She put an ominous tone in her voice. "It occurs to me that I'm out in the woods, at night, with a stranger."

"Who was vetted and approved by the exclusive k!smet application," he countered easily.

She could have told him she knew exactly how comprehensive the application vetting process was, and that she had complete confidence in anyone who'd made it through. But then she'd have to admit she'd been cruising the company's computer code. And he might ask questions about who she really was.

For the moment, she was simply Emilia, an ordinary computer programmer on a date with a handsome and compelling man. He had no idea she was the slightly infamous hacker, Emilia Scott. And since some people equated hacking with crime and theft, it wasn't something she had planned to share up front.

"You do have their stamp of approval," she agreed.

"So do you." He turned contemplative. "Strange thing, that Surprise Me! function."

Her guilt kicked in just a little bit. "Strange how?"

"You have to wonder what prompts people to use it." He seemed to be watching her closely as he posed the question.

"You used it," she pointed out, wondering now why he'd chosen to do it.

"I was curious," he said.

She gave a careless shrug. "I imagine that's the same reason for plenty of people." She was happy to let him think that was the reason for her. "From what I've read, the majority of online dating users grow jaded after a few months if they don't meet their match. Surprise Me! is a way to shake things up."

"Have you used other dating services?" he asked.

"No."

"What brought you to k!smet?"

She hadn't used her last name, and it seemed Nick had missed her press conference a few months back, he didn't know about her connection to k!smet's rival application HitMeUp and her own inadvertent role in cyber sabotage against k!smet. She'd turned whistle-blower on that one and immediately canceled her contract with HitMeUp, appalled to discover the company was engaged in such unethical business practices. She wanted nothing more to do with them.

"The notoriety, I suppose," she said. "That and the exclusivity. It's smart for the company to vet its members. It gives everyone involved confidence and comfort."

He twisted his nearly empty wineglass. "Were you disappointed?"

"In you?" The question puzzled her. Sure, they might have had a rocky start when they first left the ranch, but things had gone smoothly at the shelter. Plus, that kiss…

He smiled, and it was clear she'd misunderstood his meaning. "I meant in previous matches with k!smet."

"I didn't have any previous matches with k!smet. I only finished my profile a few days ago."

"And you went straight to Surprise Me!?" He was clearly taken aback by that.

She borrowed Paris's reason as an excuse, giving a slightly self-conscious laugh. "I was after the free date. Plus, an invite to the IPO launch party. I hear the decked-out TTC ballroom is a sight to behold."

Nick's grin widened. "Ah, so this is purely mercenary."

"Completely," she said with a straight face.

"I don't believe you."

"Why not? Who wouldn't want an expenses-paid date and an invitation to a great party?"

"You're an introvert."

It was true. She was. But that wasn't on her bio. "Why do you say that?"

"Because you're a coder. And coders are invariably introverts. It takes far too much alone time. Extroverts would reach out and find themselves some company before they finished writing their first module."

"Some introverts like parties," she challenged.

"Not many. Mostly, we end up huddled in a quiet corner with another introvert."

She couldn't disagree with that. "The best conversations happen when you're huddled in a quiet corner."

He raised his glass in a mock toast. "I'm not about to argue." He polished off his wine, then a contemplative look came over his face. "I wonder what it was."

"What what was?" She followed suit, lifting her glass to finish it.

"I wonder why Surprise Me! tossed us together."

Emilia choked on her final sip of wine, wheezing then coughing.

Nick hopped up and came to her. "Are you alright?"

"Went down wrong," she managed.

"I'll get you some water."

While Nick retrieved the water bottles from his saddlebags, Emilia squelched her guilt. She wasn't about to admit to Nick that it was his compelling gaze, secretive half smile and her own hacking skills that had thrown them together. The Surprise Me! function's algorithm had nothing to do with the match.

Three

"You see?" Misha said to Nico from across the table as she glanced around the bustling RCW Steakhouse. "Nobody's paying the slightest bit of attention to us."

Nico's back was to most in the room, but he believed his sister was right. He continued to be amazed that he wasn't being recognized without his beard and with his hair cut short. He knew his face had changed quite a bit since he was twenty-two. It was leaner, the planes and angles sharper. His chin had squared out, and his features were heavier now.

Still, he kept expecting someone to point and shout his name and remind the world he was an ex-convict.

They paused the conversation as a waitress brought their cocktails, thanking her before she left the table.

Misha had ordered an old fashioned, while Nico had gone for a straight bourbon.

"So, how was your first Surprise Me! date?" Misha asked after they took their first sips.

"I didn't learn much about the function itself." That had been a failure on Nico's part. Distracted by Emilia, he hadn't remembered to bring the conversation back to Surprise Me! while they rode back to the barn. It wasn't until after a long goodbye kiss in front of her car that he'd remembered his data-gathering mission. "I asked some questions, but she gave vague answers."

Misha pulled a face. "But did it seem like a promising match? Did you like her?"

"Sure." Nico had no intention of admitting just how much he'd like Emilia, never mind his intense, almost electric sexual attraction to her. Their kisses had all but buckled his knees. "She seemed nice."

Misha sighed. "Nice. Okay. Not exactly a ringing endorsement. But I don't know how much more we could have expected on a first date. I mean, Maggie and Jericho had fireworks pretty early on. But I suppose their situation was an anomaly."

"I thought I'd ask her out again," Nico said.

"Really?" Misha seemed surprised by that. "You don't think someone new will provide more data?"

"Maybe." He pretended to consider the idea, but he'd already made up his mind to see Emilia again. If nothing else, he needed another kiss and another long embrace. Plus, he'd take as much as she was willing to give. "Since our Surprise Me! date was tied to the IPO launch promotion, I thought it would look odd if I didn't take her to the party."

The statement seemed to give Misha pause. "That's a good idea. Yeah. You should do that. You can always date a few more people afterward, right?"

The idea of dating other women didn't appeal to him at all. But he couldn't exactly argue. "Right."

She clearly saw the hesitation in his expression. "You can't back out on me now, Nico," she warned.

"I'm not backing out on you." He opened the menu to hide his expression. The idea of dating someone else left him feeling disloyal to Emilia—which was preposterous since they'd only just met. Still…a guy didn't kiss a woman like that and simply move on to the next date as if it meant nothing. "Are you having a steak?"

"The halibut, I think."

"You haven't even opened your menu."

"Some of us get out more often than others," she said teasingly. "I've been here quite a few times. The halibut is to die for."

"I'm in the mood for a T-bone, baked potato, all the trimmings."

"You're Rafe's kind of guy."

As if on cue, Rafe strode up to their table. Misha hopped to her feet to give him a hug, while Nico rose to shake his hand.

"I'm surprised to see you here," Rafe said to Nico. He knew more than anyone Nico's reluctance to be recognized.

Nico had been convinced by Misha to test his new

look somewhere public. "It seems my non-disguise works just as well as my disguise."

"Well, sit down and enjoy," Rafe said. "I've asked the sommelier to bring you a bottle of Chateau Madeleine. It's new on the list, and I think you'll like it."

"Misha says she's going with the halibut," Nico said, thinking red wine might not be the best choice.

"I can switch to a filet," Misha offered good-naturedly.

"I can have the chef make you a surf and turf," Rafe offered. "But the Chateau Madeleine is light enough to go with anything."

"I'd love surf and turf," Misha said.

"Nico?" Rafe asked.

"Whatever's going," Nico answered, knowing Rafe's chef, JJ Yeoh, wouldn't steer him wrong.

Rafe removed the leather-bound menus from the table. "How did it go with Emilia?"

"She enjoyed the picnic. Thank your mom again for me."

"Will do."

"Emilia?" Misha asked, looking worried.

"His Surprise Me! date," Rafe answered. "Didn't he tell you about it?"

"Her name was Emilia?" Misha glanced from Nico to Rafe and back again.

Nico tried to figure out where his sister was going with this.

"What was her last name?" Misha slowly asked.

"I don't know. I wanted to stay anonymous, so I didn't ask for details from her. I mean, if she gives me hers, then I have to give her mine, and I'd rather not make up a fake last name." A variation on his first name felt dishonest enough. If he made up a last name, he'd feel like a total fraud.

"What does she look like?"

Nico and Rafe glanced at each other.

"Pretty," Nico said. "Slender."

"Shortish," Rafe added. "Hot. But don't tell Gina I said that."

"Hair color? Length?"

"Dark hair," Nico said. "Short. She wore glasses."

"Sexy librarian look," Rafe said.

Nico sent Rafe a look of censure, even though it was completely true.

"Just observing," Rafe said.

"Emilia Scott," Misha said.

Nico couldn't believe he'd heard right, and he shot his sister an expression of disbelief.

"That sounds like Emilia Scott," Misha repeated.

"*The* Emilia Scott?" he asked incredulously.

Misha nodded.

"*Hacker*, Emilia Scott?" he further clarified. He'd admired the woman's work over the years.

Misha kept on nodding. "We talked about her in that press conference on the hack."

Nico had missed the press conference.

Emilia Scott was a legend in the programming world, but her social media persona was carefully cultivated for privacy. There were only distant off-angle photos of her floating around cyberspace.

"Hang on." He rapidly regrouped. "You're saying Emilia Scott lives in Royal?"

"You must have heard she was involved with Hit-MeUp."

"I heard something about that." He hadn't paid any particular attention, having been more focused on the company itself at the time than on the specific players. "But she could have worked on that from anywhere."

"She's not anywhere. She's here. She's good friends with Maggie. She rented an office next to Maggie's art studio when she first came to Royal, before she found a house."

"Good friends with Maggie?" Nico's voice trailed off in bewilderment while he digested the information. "How am I supposed to stay incognito when everybody around here knows everybody else?"

"We couldn't have guessed you'd match with Emilia," Misha defended herself.

Nico saw her point. But it didn't help. His risk of discovery had just taken a huge leap.

"Don't worry," she continued placatingly. "It's fine. I'll talk to Maggie, and we'll keep it quiet. Nobody else knows about any of this."

"Rafe knows. And Emilia's roommate has met him." Nico felt like the walls were truly closing in.

"Dude, you know I can keep a secret." Rafe sounded affronted.

"Will it be a problem?" Misha asked Rafe.

"Not at all," Rafe said. "I met the roommate once. Nico's getting fussed about nothing."

"I'm not fussed." Nico wasn't fussed. He was facing the reality of the situation and wondering if he'd made a mistake agreeing to this venture in the first place.

Then Emilia's kiss flashed through his mind.

Okay, not a mistake.

If only for the kiss, he was glad he'd done the matchmaking. But he was tangled in deception now.

"This doesn't really change anything," Misha said reasonably. "I mean, she's playing along, using the anonymity to keep her own identity a secret. As far as she's concerned, you don't know her either."

Nico would admit his sister had a point. And the fact that he'd liked Emilia didn't change his promise to investigate k!smet incognito. If Emilia was keeping her identity under wraps, there was no reason to think he'd have to own up to his own past.

The plan was still short-term. After next week's IPO launch party, he'd move on to another woman, another Surprise Me! match and more data.

"We can contain this," Misha promised. "I'll call Maggie right after dinner."

"It sounds like nothing more than a hiccup," Rafe said. "So, for tonight, please enjoy. I promise you'll love the wine. And JJ will send out some appetizers. Any requests?"

"Surprise me," Misha said with a playful smile.

Rafe looked to Nico for his opinion.

"Go ahead and surprise me too. Surprise Me! is obviously the story of my life these days."

Misha and Rafe both grinned with shared amusement.

Emilia was alone, but her sappy smile still embarrassed her as she read the text from Nick.

He'd invited her on a second date—a second date

after only twenty-four hours. She wasn't an expert at this online dating game, but she couldn't help but feel flattered by the fast turnaround.

Sure, she was attending the k!smet party anyway. But it would be much more fun to go with Nick. They were going to waltz into the posh event like a couple. She couldn't help thinking Paris would be excited about that.

She texted back a yes as she crossed to her closet, wondering if she had anything fancier than a standard black cocktail dress lurking in the back. As a fiercely independent woman, she knew she shouldn't fuss over dressing up for a man. But this was one incredibly handsome man, and she was one ordinary-looking woman. She'd need some help to hold up her end of being a couple.

Her phone pinged with a new text, and she glanced down.

It was a happy face emoji from Nick, which made her smile all over again. It struck her as both sincere and concise. She liked that in a person.

Then, to her surprise, he followed it up with a question about his cattle ranching app—comparing two different approaches to data design.

Her interest perked up. She needed more context and asked for it.

A second later, her phone rang, and Nick's name came up on the screen.

Her heart rate jumped a little bit as she answered. "Hi, Nick."

"I hope you don't mind me bothering you like this."

"No. Not at all." She was irrationally happy to hear his voice.

"Am I interrupting anything important?"

Her gaze shifted to her closet. There was zero chance she'd admit to acting like a teenager and planning her wardrobe for their second date. "Nothing important."

She plunked down on the bed. "What are you trying to do?"

"Dynamically link tombstone data with both health and geolocation without cluttering up a screen the size of a phone."

Emilia was confused. It was a decision, not a problem. "Is this a database question or look and feel?"

"Both."

"So, what are you asking?" If she had a suspicious nature, she'd have thought he was making up an excuse to call her. Which was kind of sweet and gave her a warm glow.

"If you have a few minutes, I can show you," he said.

Emilia hesitated. She fiercely guarded her privacy and wondered if he was angling to come over to her house. That seemed too intimate for someone she'd only just met. Plus, she'd have done a deep cleaning if she was expecting company. "Uh…"

"I'm at Workspace Plus on Thermal Avenue. Are you anywhere close?"

Close? She was very close, only ten blocks away. "That's not too far from me."

"I rent an office on the third floor. Suite 309. You take a right as you get off the elevator."

"Sure," she said, energized by the thought of seeing him again so soon.

They ended the call, and she ran a comb through her

hair. She changed from her yoga pants to a pair of khakis and pulled a forest green bulky knit sweater over her faded T-shirt. Then she stepped into a pair of flats and crossed the strap of a small purse across her torso for the walk.

It was a chilly evening. But there were plenty of families and office workers on the sidewalk between the tree-lined boulevard and the neighborhood shops, likely out for an early dinner or making their way home from work.

Before long she came to the double glass doors of the Workspace Plus coworking space and entered the spacious foyer. An elevator took her to the third floor of the building where she found Nick's office with the door propped partway open.

She entered a large, generic but comfortable-looking reception area. It was subtle toned, with four taupe armchairs around a polished maple coffee table. There was an empty reception desk against the back wall. A hallway opened next to the desk, but she couldn't see all the way to the end. The space was bigger than she'd expected. She'd always thought most coworking spaces were small cubicles or common meeting rooms that rented out by the hour.

"Hello?" she called out.

Nick quickly emerged from the hallway in a steel blue dress shirt and a pair of charcoal pants. "That was fast."

"I was close enough to walk, so I didn't have to hunt for a parking spot."

He crossed the room with smooth strides, drew her

gently into his arms and gave her a quick and surprisingly natural-feeling kiss. "I'm glad you could make it."

"This is nice," she said looking around at the potted plants and a wall of windows overlooking the street. "Is it all yours?"

"It's leased, of course. And I do most of my work from home, but I prefer to meet clients here."

Emilia almost never met her clients in person. She worked for firms all around the country and overseas, making her a fan of video chats.

"Do you employ staff?" For some reason, she'd assumed he ran a one-person operation like her.

"A few," he said. "The administrator works here daily. But most everyone else works from home like me. It seems more efficient—work-life balance and all." He toed a wedge from beneath the door to the public hallway and let it swing shut. "My office is down this way." He pointed across the reception area to the interior hallway.

She went first, seeing five open doors, two on each side and one at the end. The end door seemed to lead into a boardroom.

"Second on the right," he said.

His office was as impressive as the reception area. About half was taken up by a U-shaped desk with an array of six monitors and plenty of open desktop space. She was envious of that alone. But the rest of the office was equally well-appointed. It had the same muted tones, lush plants and wall of windows as the reception area. A four-person meeting table sat in one corner. In the other was a sofa and two armchairs around a square, glass-topped coffee table.

"Thirsty?" he asked, opening a small fridge beneath a sink and counter.

"Sure. Whatever you've got," she answered, moving to the big desk. "If this was me, I'd sure work here all the time."

"I've got a setup almost exactly like it at home. Soft drink? Beer? Spritzer?"

"I have monitor envy."

He chuckled at that.

"A spritzer is an option?" she asked, liking the sound of something refreshing.

"It looks like it is. I haven't checked in here for a while. Key lime lemonade or blueberry pomegranate. I assume there's some wine in these things as well."

"Is that even a choice?" she asked, turning to face him.

He lifted a brow in puzzlement.

She kept a straight face as she teased him. "I mean, isn't it obvious?"

"Sure," he answered without missing a beat. "Blueberry pomegranate it is." He twisted off the cap and held the bottle her way.

"Gutsy," she said.

"Was I right?"

She moved closer and took the bottle. "I'd have gone with either."

"Me too." He opened a key lime lemonade for himself and shut the fridge door.

"What are we working on?" she asked, feeling unexpectedly relaxed as she took a sip. The beverage was tart and flavorful.

"Second monitor from the left," he said, making his way to the desk.

She took in a mocked-up screen design.

"Have a seat," he offered, gesturing to the padded swivel chair.

She sat. "It looks very straightforward."

"That's exactly what I'm going for—a technical ranch management system for the nontechnical rancher. The cattle are each registered with a multifaceted number. I'm picturing a single drop-down menu expanding to health, feed, geography, history and finance."

"For every cow?"

"There'll be a chip in their ear tag, easy scanning with a handheld device. That's not my original idea. It's all over the place these days."

A cute, animated calf appeared on the screen and plaintively mooed. Then a cow appeared and nuzzled the calf.

Emilia twisted her head to look back at Nick. "Seriously?

He was bent over the chair, his arm across the back. "Rafe's mom is whimsical."

"And you're doing all of this for one ranch?" She was both amazed and impressed by his diligence.

"It might have some commercial value in the future, especially if it's blockchain verified. But, for now, yes. It's specifically for the Cortez-Williams family."

His smile warmed his dark eyes, drawing her in, making her realize how very close he was and that his arms were all but hugging her. He'd kissed her when she first arrived, and that had been nice. But their passionate kisses at the ranch had been well beyond nice.

She wanted one of those now.

Nick seemed to read her mind.

He leaned slowly forward, giving her plenty of time to pull away.

She didn't, and their lips met once again, hotter this time, moving instantly into a deep and passionate kiss.

Keeping the kiss going, he turned the chair until she faced him. She stood, and he drew her into his arms, wrapping her close, smoothing his hands along her back, while his kisses began to roam.

She tipped back her head as he kissed her neck. He pushed her sweater aside and kissed his way to the tip of her shoulder. She gripped his arms, hanging on tight as her legs turned wobbly.

He returned to her mouth and found the hem of her sweater, reaching underneath to the flimsy fabric of her T-shirt. His hands felt warm, strong and purposeful as they circled toward her breasts.

She started an exploration of her own—across his shoulders, his chest, his washboard abs. She pulled up the hem of his shirt to expose his skin, and he groaned as her fingertips made contact.

Overheating and impatient, she stripped off her bulky sweater, tossing it aside.

His expression was intense with passion, his breathing deep and steady.

She reached for the buttons on his shirt, and he kissed her again. His hands slipped under her T-shirt, cupping her breast, bringing a moan to her lips while she awkwardly undid his buttons.

He stripped off his shirt, while she tugged her T-shirt over her head, releasing her bra and adding it to the pile of their clothes on the desktop. Seconds later, they were skin to skin, their kisses going wilder and deeper.

Want and desire coursed its way through Emilia, until she thought she might explode from need. It had been far too long since she'd been held in a man's strong arms. And Nick was as hot and sexy as they came.

She popped open the button on his pants and drew down the zipper.

He drew back to look at her. "You sure?" he asked, eyes smoldering.

"I'm sure," she answered in an unnaturally husky voice.

He helped her with his clothes, then made short work of hers.

For a moment they simply gazed at each other. Dressed, he was a handsome man by any benchmark. Naked, he was magnificent. His chest was broad, his abs flat and defined. A tan line delineated his hips. And below…below he made her suck in a gasp.

He gently removed her glasses, slightly blurring her view.

"You're beautiful," he whispered as he wrapped her back up in his arms. "Absolutely beautiful."

She decided to believe him, though it was a stretch. But he made her feel it.

He kissed her softly and deeply, while his hands began to explore.

She matched him touch for touch, caress for caress, until they were both gasping with need.

He scooped her into his arms. It was totally unnecessary, but also totally sexy, and he carried her to the sofa.

He'd pulled a condom from somewhere, and they lay down together, arms and legs entwined, their touches growing more intimate and their passion rising higher and higher.

Just when she thought she couldn't stand another second, he moved between her legs and slowly, firmly, inexorably eased inside.

She called out his name, thrusting her head back and her hips forward, struggling to get closer and closer still.

Then his rhythm started. He laved her neck with kisses, moving to her breasts, sending shards of desire rocketing to her core.

She rode the wave as it went on and on. She never wanted it to stop.

Then something shifted. His body tensed. His breath hissed. And his thrusts came faster and faster.

She cried out and clung tightly to him, as he captured her mouth in a kiss that matched the fireworks of their bodies.

He slowed while she struggled to catch her breath. Gasping, her chest rising and falling against him.

"I'm too heavy," he said and shifted to one side.

"It's fine," she said breathlessly.

"I feel like I'm crushing your chest." He moved a little move, bringing them side to side, holding her with both his arms and legs so she couldn't slip off the sofa, their racing hearts thudding against one another.

She rested her head against his shoulder and waited for reality to return.

After a few minutes their breathing stabilized, and their heart rates fell back to normal.

"Looks like," he whispered as he smoothed back her hair, "the Surprise Me! function got this part exactly right."

She smiled, liking his lightheartedness. "Score one for Surprise Me!"

Nico could have lain on the sofa all night holding the naked Emilia in his arms.

Her toned form fit perfectly spooned against him. Her hair smelled enticingly of citrus. It was soft against his chin. Her breasts were perfect, and he had to fight to keep from cupping them in his palm all over again.

Instead, he rested his hand against her smooth stomach. He kissed her temple and adjusted his thighs more intimately around hers. Then he sighed and wondered exactly how long she'd be willing to lie here with him.

"I sure wish I could reach my spritzer," she said on a note of regret.

He took that to mean she was ready to move.

"I'll get it for you." He gently disentangled himself, sat up and rose from the sofa.

She followed him back to the desk and slipped into her panties.

He tracked her in his soft vision rather than staring, sorry to see her put on her bra and pull her T-shirt over her head.

It was cool in the office. And he really didn't expect her to sit around naked sipping her drink. Still, he felt like something precious had been taken away.

He dressed alongside her, and they settled back on the sofa.

"Hungry?" he asked. He was both thirsty and starving.

She nodded. "Are there snacks in that fridge?"

He retrieved his phone. "I was going to order something. There's a great Thai place next door."

"I'd go for Thai."

"What do you like?" He pulled up the app.

"Surprise Me!" she joked, and her smile lit something warm and bright deep inside his chest.

"You got it."

"Though I'm not sure spritzers are the right beverage for Thai food."

He agreed with her on that. "There's beer in my fridge," he offered. "And probably some wine in the boardroom. But I don't know if there's much of a selection in stock."

"Can I check it out?" She came to her feet.

"Absolutely. Pick whatever you like. And grab a couple of glasses from the shelf," he called as she headed to the hallway.

He ordered satay, shrimp wraps, curry and noodles. Then he added marinated beef and plain rice to make sure they didn't run short.

As he confirmed and paid, Emilia came back, a bottle in one hand, two glasses in the other, and a corkscrew tucked into the pocket of her khakis.

"I don't recognize the label," she said. "But it's a merlot."

"I don't buy the wine, but our administrator, Sandy, has excellent taste."

"Thank you, Sandy," Emilia said cheerfully, setting the wine and the glasses on the meeting table. She peeled off the foil top and twisted in the corkscrew.

"Food is on the way," he said.

"We can do some more work while we let this breathe," she offered.

A shot of guilt kicked in as he moved her way. "I... have a confession."

She stilled, looking worried. "You're married? Engaged? Have a girlfriend?"

"No, *no*," he quickly answered with a definitive shake of his head. "Nothing like that."

She blew out a breath. "Scared me there for a second."

"I didn't mean to scare you."

"You really shouldn't start a sentence that way, you know."

"You're right." She made a very valid point. "Okay. Here's the thing. I got you here tonight under false pretenses."

"You mean you didn't need my help with an interface a first-year technology student could build?" Even with a smirk, she was beautiful.

He gave her a sheepish grin. "That obvious?"

"I was hoping."

"Hoping?" He wasn't sure he'd heard her right.

"That it was a ruse because you wanted to see me again."

"It was a ruse because I wanted to see you again," he confirmed and moved in a little closer. "And I didn't want to wait until the k!smet party."

"Impatient?"

"Yes." And it was unusual for him. In fact, everything about this situation was unusual for him.

Making love with Emilia had been off the charts fantastic. But it wasn't enough. He wanted more. For starters, he was more than curious now about the always-elusive hacker Emilia Scott. What he knew of her from public sources was impressive. And now, what he knew of her in person was amazing.

Her smile widened, a question in her eyes as she lifted the bottle, clearly offering to pour.

"Please do. So, from Boston you said." He reminded her of one of the few personal information exchanges they'd had while riding. He'd told her then that he grew up in Royal but had moved away for a few years.

She nodded now. "North End mostly."

"Do you have any brothers or sisters?"

"None that I know about." She edged one of the glasses his way and sat down.

"You suspect you might have secret siblings?" It was yet another intriguing element to her.

"I was put into state custody when I was four years old."

Orphaned himself as a child, his heart went out to her. "Something happened to your parents?"

"Maybe." The expression on her face said it all as she took a sip.

He fought an urge to draw her into his arms and comfort her.

"What I do know," she continued, "is I was found in a park. Nobody claimed me, and nobody saw who left me there."

The story was worse than he'd expected. "So, you don't know anything about your family?"

"Nothing about them at all."

"Were you adopted?" He was holding out hope for a happy ending here.

"Foster care. Seven homes, thirteen years until I aged out."

His heart went heavy, his chest tight. "I'm so sorry to hear that."

"What matters is I made it through."

"Childhood should be much more than making it through." Though he'd lost his parents, he and Misha had their grandmother. She was stern, from an older school of thought. But she was loving and fair.

"We don't get to pick," Emilia said wistfully.

"We don't," he agreed.

"Some homes were good, some sucked. I got used to the feeling of being physically unmoored. But wherever I went, house to house, school to school, there was always the internet and social media. I joined Coders Plus as a teenager."

"I know Coders Plus."

They were a great, free online teaching service.

Through his company AlgoXcell, they'd asked him to volunteer as an instructor, to make a series of video workshops for their students. He'd reluctantly told them no, knowing the videos would draw unwanted attention. But he'd often wondered if he should have stepped up.

"My online friends followed me wherever I went," she said.

He took a first taste of his wine. "This is good."

"I like it," she said.

"It sounds like you made the best of your situation." Nick couldn't help but be impressed by that.

"I like to think I did. And here I am now."

"Successful."

"Successful enough. I like my job, my friends—live and in person now." She grinned at her own joke.

He smiled too. "I was raised by my grandmother."

Her expression turned apprehensive. "Where were your parents?"

"There was a—" He almost said car accident but checked himself in time. Emilia knew Misha and might have heard the real story about their parents. He didn't want her putting two and two together. "They both died in an accident."

"That's rough."

"For sure. But I had Grandma. That's more than you had."

Her expression turned contemplative, and she sipped her wine. "Do you ever wonder about an app that could do that?"

"How do you mean?".

"Go deep into the internet, identify us and scrape up whatever breadcrumbs might be out there about our lives?"

"That seems pretty invasive. Nico imagined people would rather present their best selves on a dating app.

"You an orphan, me abandoned. The possibilities boggle the mind."

"Surprise Me! is a fun feature, not military quality AI spyware."

"How can we know for sure?"

He could almost see the wheels turning inside her head. He supposed he shouldn't be completely surprised that she'd go there. After all, she must have seen some sophisticated and nefarious things during her hacking career.

"In our case, I was anonymous," he reminded her. "Plenty of people start out that way."

"They *think* they are. For example, you set up your profile from here, right? Or from home? And you provided a photo. Based on that alone, bad actors could do facial recognition, access your geolocation information and take it from there."

"k!smet is not a bad actor."

It was ironic that Emilia would allude to other people's nefarious actions, since he now knew she'd been involved with HitMeUp's attempted sabotage of k!smet.

"I know. But from what I saw, the Surprise Me! function was—" She seemed to stop herself mid-thought.

"Was what?" he prompted, curious to gather helpful data for Misha.

"You're right." She took a hearty drink while Nico's phone pinged to announce the food order's arrival. "It's nothing but a fun feature to shake things up."

Four

At home later that night, Emilia worked her way back into the Surprise Me! code, considering the possibilities of AI and deep social media dives to the online dating world.

She heard the front door close and knew Paris had arrived home from work. She backed out of the app, carefully erasing her tracks, and headed downstairs, both nervous and excited to share some girl talk.

"Hey, Emie." Paris dropped her shoulder bag on a chair in the front foyer.

"Good shift?"

"It was long. The cash didn't balance, and we had to hunt down the error. Why do people even use cash these days?"

"Anonymity."

Paris kicked off her high-heeled shoes and hung her jacket on a hook. "They make an online reservation, use a map app to find us, post pictures of their dinner on social media then use cash to maintain their privacy?"

Emilia smiled at the irony. "In that case, I really don't know."

"How was your night? Are you thirsty?"

"Sure. I'd go for soda and lime." After two glasses of wine with Nick, Emilia knew she should hydrate.

"Splash of vodka or anything?" Paris went for the liquor cabinet.

"Not for me." Emilia retrieved a lime and the bottle of soda water from the fridge.

They filled two tall glasses over ice with Paris adding a slug of vodka to hers.

"Catch any bad guys tonight?" Paris asked as she flopped down on the sofa and curled her feet beneath her.

The kitchen and living area was an open rectangle with windows overlooking a small backyard, dark now except for the porch light of the house up the bank behind them. Their furniture was comfortably soft with magazines and books strewn around on the tabletops. Paris loved to wander around barefoot, so a huge, patterned rug covered the hardwood floor.

Emilia settled into an armchair. "Not tonight."

"Too bad."

"I thwart them more than catch them. And I get paid by the hour not the bounty."

Paris smiled. "As you should. I've decided we should eliminate tips."

"Oh?"

"It's an archaic system. Pay everyone a good wage, I say. Charge the prices you need to charge."

"Did something happen tonight?"

"Nothing that doesn't happen every night. Some of the hardest working waitstaff can get stiffed. But I've been thinking about it for a while now."

"Is it an actual possibility? Can you talk to your boss?"

Paris gave a short laugh. Then she took a drink. "Not a chance. The whole industry would have to change. I'm just fantasizing."

"Start a movement."

"Maybe I will. But not until tomorrow." Paris tipped her head back on the sofa.

"Nick asked me for another date," Emilia said into the silence.

Paris's head bobbed back up. "Say, what?"

"He texted, invited me to the IPO launch party."

"But you were going to that already." Paris frowned. "All ten matched couples were invited."

"The point is, he asked me to go with him to the party, so it's a second date." Plus, tonight he ordered us Thai food and bought a really great bottle of merlot. Well, I suppose his company technically bought the merlot."

Paris sat up straight. "Wait. Slow down. Back up. *Tonight?*"

Emilia grinned over the rim of her glass as she nodded. "He called. After he texted and I said yes to going to the party, he called."

"And invited you…where?"

"To his office. He wanted to talk about an app he's developing."

"His office?" Paris wrinkled her nose. "What is wrong with this guy?"

"Nothing. At least not that I can tell so far."

"He invited you over to talk work. I'm guessing he didn't pay you."

"No, but—"

"He ordered Thai food? He didn't take you out for a steak or some boeuf bourguignon, maybe a bouillabaisse?"

"It wasn't that kind of a night. And the Thai food was terrific."

Paris shook her head. "Emilia, Emilia, Emilia."

"We had sex."

"Wait…*what*?" Paris's voice rose an octave with each word.

"Right there on his office sofa. And it was amazing."

"Talk about burying the lede."

"It just sort of happened."

Paris leaned forward. "Details, please."

"He's hot."

"Like, athlete hot or nerd hot?"

"Does it matter?"

"Only if it matters to you."

"Both, I guess. He's—" Emilia tried to put a word to it "—intuitive, perceptive, really clever, also athletic. He engages my brain while looking like a cover model." She gestured to herself. "And it's me, plain ol' me."

Paris seemed taken aback. "What do you mean, *plain ol' you*? You're not plain, and you're not old."

Emilia appreciated her friend's staunch support. "I'm not exactly cover-model material either."

Paris took a beat. "You do know you're pretty, right? I wasn't just saying that the other day."

"Whatever." Emilia had never aspired to pretty. She was content with ordinary.

There was absolutely nothing wrong with ordinary. In fact, she liked it. She could go out for a drink with friends and not have to fend off random men trying to chat her up.

She'd seen what happened to Paris when her friend dressed up and went for a night out. With her long legs, narrow waist, shapely bust, and the way her deep green eyes were brought out by her rich auburn hair, she attracted more attention than she wanted.

Paris was adroit at fending it off, but it looked like a whole lot of work to Emilia. *No thanks* to that, for sure.

"I don't get it," Paris said, seeming puzzled now. "I mean, I know you downplay your looks all the time, because… Well, I'm really not sure exactly why you do that. But your eyes are wide, that mixed color of hazel is fantastic. Your brows are perfect. I wish I had your nose."

Emilia's hand automatically moved to her nose. "It's just a nose."

"It's perfectly straight and exactly the right size. Man, even your lips are balanced. And you don't need lipstick, because they're full and dark all on their own. Don't get me started on how you can wear anything off the rack and look terrific."

Emilia was getting amused now. "Do you think you might be just a little biased?"

"Biased?"

"Rose-colored glasses, because you're my friend, and you love me."

"I'm not biased. I'm jealous."

Emilia went speechless. In what universe could Paris possibly be jealous of Emilia's looks? She gestured her friend up and down. "But you—"

"But me what?"

"You're *gorgeous*."

"No." Paris shook her head. "Not naturally. I've learned to do a lot with makeup and a blow-dryer. And I pay a fortune for these highlights." She shook a lock of her hair. Then she turned her head to profile. "Look at my nose. Plus, my arms and legs are too long, and my bust is out of proportion to my hips. It takes me forever to find dresses and slacks."

Emilia burst out laughing. "There's nothing whatsoever wrong with your nose."

"It's crooked."

Emilia peered closely and critically. "It's not crooked."

"Right here." Paris pointed to a slight flaw at the bridge.

"You call *that* crooked?"

"What would you call it?"

"Incredibly vain if that's what's bothering you."

Paris waved a dismissive hand. "Chase McMillian didn't seem overly impressed."

"You said you two had fun."

Paris had come back from her k!smet date—a hot-air balloon ride followed by dinner at an exclusive lakeside resort south of town. By her account, it had been a picture-perfect romantic evening.

"I did. I thought he did too. But he hasn't called."

"It's only been a couple of days."

"Nick called you. He enticed you to his office. Where's his office, by the way?"

"He rents a space in Workspace Plus. I hadn't been there before. It's really nice. Back to Chase."

Paris polished off her drink. "I don't want to talk about him."

"Did he kiss you goodnight?" Emilia pressed.

"Yes."

"How was it?"

"Short. Too short, like he didn't want to commit."

"Or like he was being a gentleman." Emilia couldn't help remembering Nick's kisses. There was absolutely nothing gentlemanly about them. There was nothing gentlemanly about anything else he'd done either. His moves had been flat-out hot and sexy.

Paris groaned like she was in pain and rolled to her feet.

"What?" Emilia asked.

"Your obvious memories of bliss. You're killing me here. I need another drink."

"He'll call," Emilia said with conviction as Paris headed for the kitchen.

At the desk in his home office, Nico stared at his phone, ridiculously tempted to call Emilia.

He knew he should wait. There were only a couple more days until the IPO launch party, and he'd see her then. But he was impatient. He couldn't get the woman out of his mind.

The lovemaking was one thing. He'd do that again in a heartbeat. He'd also take a kiss or a hug. In fact, he'd be happy just to watch her smile from across a room.

He pictured her smile, then her laugh, then thought about her incredible strength of character. He and Misha had had it tough losing their parents. But their struggles paled in comparison to Emilia's. She seemed to have grabbed every little opportunity in her life and made the most of it.

Take the Coders Plus organization. It sounded like she'd worked her way through most of their workshops and lessons, and that had got him thinking.

He'd shied away from making a teaching video for them when they asked. And he still didn't want to bring that kind of attention to himself. But being featured in the video was only one part of the equation. Somebody had to develop the workshop.

He could do that part. He'd like to do that part. And Emilia might be interested in helping him. It was a worthy cause, and she obviously respected the organization. And how many budding Emilia Scotts were out there right now who couldn't afford expensive tuition?

The more he thought about it, the better he liked the idea.

Giving in to his impulse, he tapped her number.

"Hi, Nick." Her voice was breezy when she answered.

"Are you working?"

"Lunch break."

"Oh? Where?" Maybe he could meet her somewhere.

"At my desk." There was a smile in her voice. "Why? Where do you usually eat?"

"At my desk," he admitted. "Sometimes I move to the table." It depended on how intensely he was coding. He often had to keep his mind focused on the sequence. In some cases, if he walked away, he had to reread a whole bunch of lines of code to get back into the groove.

"Nothing like productivity," she said with a chuckle.

"I wanted to run something past you."

"Okay."

"Could we meet?"

"Are you afraid to ask me over the phone?"

"I'm not afraid." Not in the least. How he felt right now was lonely. Which was unusual and embarrassing. He was a very independent man.

"Nick?" she prompted.

"It'll take me a few minutes to explain my idea."

"The Cortez-Williams app?"

"No. This is something different. I think you'll like it."

"Okay. Sure. When?"

"What works for you?"

"I'm on a break right now."

"Good. Perfect. My office?"

There was a pause. "Is this a booty call?"

"No," he quickly assured her. "That's not it." He heard her soft chuckle and regrouped. "I mean, unless you want it to—" He left a pregnant beat. "I'm joking. There are other people in the office right now."

"I know you're joking."

He liked their give-and-take. "I was thinking coffee, maybe a muffin."

"What kind of muffin?"

"That matters?"

"A woman wants to know what she's in for."

"What kind of muffin do you want?"

She paused, then answered with a tease in her voice. "Surprise me."

He liked that the phrase was becoming their inside joke. "Will do. See you soon."

"I'll leave here in just a few minutes."

Nico pocketed his phone and rushed out of his apartment. He had a stop to make and intended to arrive at Workspace Plus before Emilia.

There was a popular gourmet bakery on the way, and he wanted to meet her expectations for a surprise muffin. It couldn't be a simple blueberry or banana nut.

He got stopped by traffic lights, and the bakery lineup was longer than he'd expected. Luckily, his office came with an underground parking space, so he made up some time there. When the elevator doors opened at the Workspace Plus lobby level, Emilia was standing there in front of him.

"Nice timing," he said, as she and a few other people got into the elevator.

As they rode, he leaned down to whisper in her ear. "Greek yogurt blackberry muffins with streusel topping."

"Tasty," she whispered back.

The elevator doors opened on the third floor, and Nico froze, coming face-to-face with his sister, Misha.

"Ni—" she started, then thankfully spotted Emilia.

"Emilia," she said instead, doing an impressively smooth pivot. "Imagine meeting you here."

"Hey, Misha. Nice to see you." Emilia stepped off the elevator.

"Great to see you too." Misha gave a nod, her gaze skipping to Nico and back again.

"How's the IPO launch coming?" Emilia asked while the elevator closed behind them and whooshed away to the upper floors.

"We're pretty much all set to go there. Publicity has been positive."

"This is Nick," Emilia introduced him. "Nick, this is my friend Misha Law."

"I've heard of you," Nico said, keeping his tone cool and even.

"I bet she's heard of you too," Emilia said, causing both Nico and Misha to look worriedly her way. "You're in her k!smet database. Nick and I were matched up through Surprise Me!" Emilia continued. "But maybe you know that already."

"I did know that," Misha answered. "I saw you two had your date already."

"A sunset horseback ride," Emilia answered. "It was quite beautiful. Now we're—" She looked to Nick for the answer.

"Collaborating. And we won't keep you." The longer the conversation went on, the more likely they were to accidentally give something away.

"I'll leave you to it," Misha said easily, pressing the elevator call button. To Emilia she added, "See you at Natalie's."

"It's going to be fun."

"Can't wait."

Then the doors slid open, and Misha stepped inside.

Nico breathed a sigh of relief as they headed for his office door.

Since he'd sent Sandy on errands for the rest of the afternoon, he knew the door would be locked. He swiped the key. "Who's Natalie?"

"Bridesmaid dresses at Natalie Valentine's bridal shop. Our final fittings."

He paused. "A wedding?" He only knew of one upcoming wedding where his sister was involved.

"Maggie Del Rio. You must have heard about it. The feud? The necklace? The scandal?"

"I heard. Are you saying you're a bridesmaid?" He couldn't believe Misha had skipped over that important fact.

"Guilty as charged. I'm not keen on silk and chiffon, but Maggie has terrific taste, so I'm sure our dresses will be classy."

"Not my area of expertise." He opened the door. "Sandy had some errands," he said to explain the empty reception area. The truth was, Nico had sent her out to keep her from blurting out his real name in front of Emilia.

"So, what's this all about?" Emilia asked as she walked inside. "We're collaborating on something?"

"I hope so. If you're willing. You were talking about Coders Plus the other day."

"Uh-huh."

He led the way to his office. "You admire the organization."

"I sure do."

"I admire it too, and I thought we might be able to contribute."

"Contribute how?" Her gaze paused on the sofa for a moment before she turned to sit at the meeting table.

He hoped she was having fond memories. His were certainly fond, beyond fond, mind-blowing if he was honest.

He ordered himself to exercise some self-discipline and shook the memories away as he took the chair cornerwise to hers. "Deliver a workshop," he answered her question.

"On what?"

"Anything. It could be introductory or something more sophisticated. I hate being in front of the camera, but you—"

Her expression faltered, and she went still.

"What?" He'd hoped she'd like the idea.

"You want me to go in front of the camera."

That was exactly what he'd had in mind. She'd be fantastic. She was beautiful, articulate, animated. Plus, she'd inspire more girls to get involved in the industry.

But he could see the idea unnerved her. "Not necessarily. Not that I don't think you'd be great. You really would be great."

She gave a self-conscious laugh. "Well, I *would* attract a crowd."

"I bet you would."

She pressed her lips together and folded her hands on the table. "Nick."

He waited. "Emilia."

"I'm…" She seemed to be carrying on a debate inside her head. "Have you ever heard of Emilia Scott?"

So *that* was where she was going. He was happy, honored that she was willing to share with him.

"Yes, I have."

"You know she's a hacker."

"Top ten in the world."

She frowned. "I'm not sure how they did the metrics on that."

"Somebody thought you were very good."

"Sure, but—" She obviously caught the meaning of his words. "You know?"

"I know."

"Why didn't you *say* something?"

He gave a shrug. The main reason was because he was carrying on his own deception. But he wasn't anywhere near ready to admit to that. Being a famous hacker was completely different than being an ex-convict. If he shared his truth, he'd lose her, and he wasn't ready for that.

"I figured you'd tell me when you were ready," he answered the question honestly, then tried to move the conversation along. "So, what do you think? Are you ready to give back to the students?"

She bit down on her bottom lip, obviously contemplating the question.

He didn't mean to pressure her. "I know you keep a low profile." He rattled his way into the bakery bag, slowing down the conversation by setting a muffin on a napkin in front of her. He took the other for himself.

"I do." She gazed at the muffin. "That thing is huge."

"Do your best." He pulled back the wrapper and split his in half.

By contrast, she tore off a bite-size chunk of the glazed top. "To a degree," she continued. "I mean, it's not like I'm a covert operative. But I'm careful to keep my geolocation off the radar."

"That's easy enough to do. Are you at all comfortable in front of a camera?"

"I don't know. I usually interact with the world as an avatar."

"Where?" He was curious now. "You hang out in a cyber world?"

"Sometimes," she admitted sheepishly. "Firsthand testing is the best way to understand new technologies."

"I have to agree with you on that." He felt a jolt of guilt over the firsthand test of the Surprise Me! function he was undertaking right now. He paused for a bite of the muffin and to regroup. "We could do a test, mock up a segment of a workshop and have you try it on for size on camera. If you don't like the way it turns out, we'll delete it."

"On a local drive only? No cloud or online service."

"Absolutely." He didn't blame her for being wary of an unedited video clip getting out into the wild. "I have an air-gapped computer if you'd like."

She rolled her eyes at that. "We don't have to go overboard. We're not plotting a government sting operation."

"That sounds like a yes to me."

"Sure. Okay. I'll give it a try." She looked thoughtful as she ate another bite of the muffin. "I would have liked to see more woman-led workshops when I was using the service."

"You're a great role model."

"I don't know if I'd go that far."

"Don't sell yourself short. You came up in this business at a time when it was especially tough for girls, and things haven't changed nearly enough. Need a coffee before we start?"

Emilia accepted a glass of champagne from a silver tray and sat back in a plush diamond-tufted chair in Natalie Valentine's bridal shop.

Maggie was busy changing in the large, velvet-curtained cubical behind the mirrored dais.

"Well, this is very civilized," Misha noted, setting her long-stemmed flute down on the low white table next to a fruit and cheese tray.

"Is it always like this?" Emilia asked, helping herself to a plump green grape. "I've never been a bridesmaid before."

"You're going to have a great time. Maggie's the belle of the ball, of course. But some of the VIP treatment rubs off on us."

"So far, it has." Emilia took a sip of the champagne, letting it froth crisp and sweet on her tongue. There was a delightful decadence in enjoying champagne at two o'clock in the afternoon.

Then the heavy curtain slid opened, and Maggie stepped out onto the dais beaming with a wide smile.

Emilia and Misha gasped in unison.

The classic white satin dress was the epitome of simplicity and elegance. Unfussy, like Maggie herself, it was extraordinarily beautiful, especially on Maggie's tall, svelte frame.

Strapless, with a sweetheart neckline, the asymmetrical ruched bodice highlighted her slender waist. Sparkling crystal beading adorned a wisp of a tulle bolero wrap that brought attention to her slim shoulders, while the soft fabric flowed over her hips in a shimmering floor-length skirt.

Maggie swirled her long, dark hair onto the top of her head. "Hair part up, part down, maybe some braids with a few flowers. I was thinking of going simple on the jewelry—diamond studs and a little diamond pendant." Her dark eyes shone while she spoke. "And take a look at this." She turned to show them the dress's low-cut, lace-up back of satin ribbons.

"Fantastic," Misha said breathlessly.

"It's perfect," Emilia echoed.

"Fits like a glove," Natalie said. "Now, stay right there." She disappeared into the back, returning with two cobalt blue dresses draped over her arm.

"You went with the blue," Misha said, coming to her feet. "Great choice."

"It's called Lapis Iceberg," Natalie said. "I can't wait to see all three of you together."

Leaving her champagne behind, Emilia took her dress into a changing room. Natalie had taken extensive measurements and, as expected, it fit her perfectly.

Like Maggie's dress, it was strapless satin, with a sweetheart neckline and a similar ruched bodice gathering at one side of her waist. The skirt was shorter than Maggie's, knee-length, and the dress came with a matching sheer shawl.

Emilia pulled back the curtain and left the changing room just as Misha emerged from hers.

"What should we do with these?" Misha asked, holding out the shawl.

Natalie stepped forward. "You have lots of options. But I'd suggest—" She looked critically at Misha and then at Emilia. "How about this."

She took Misha's shawl and looped it loosely around one of her shoulders, tying a square knot on the other shoulder, letting the ends flow down the front.

Misha turned to the mirror. "I like it."

"And for Emilia." Natalie came her way. "Turn around."

Emilia turned.

Natalie draped the center of the scarf loosely across her chest, then fastened it in an open loop knot in the middle of her back.

"Unless you want them the same," she said to Maggie.

"No. I love these." Maggie circled them both. "It gives just enough contrast between the dresses."

"How do they feel?" Natalie asked, taking a closer look at each of them. "I don't see any obvious need for alterations."

"Mine fits perfectly," Emilia said.

"I'm good," Misha said.

"Stand altogether, and let's see." Natalie went for her camera and took several shots of them posing, then more casually talking and laughing as they admired each other's dresses.

"Champagne and snacks after you're changed out of them," Natalie announced.

"The last thing we need is an accident," Maggie said, taking a last long look at herself in the three-way mirror.

Emilia shuddered at the thought of spilling something on the gorgeous dress.

"We're shipping them to your family's house?" Natalie asked Maggie.

"Please," Maggie answered. "I thought we'd all dress there together," she said to Emilia and Misha.

"Of course," Misha said.

"That seems like half the fun," Emilia said. "And let us know what else we can do."

Maggie shook her head. "The wedding planner has it well in hand. Wait until you see everything. The flowers will be beautiful, and the cake is going to be delicious. Also, Ashley is bringing a few people to my parents' place from the Saint Tropez Salon the morning of the rehearsal dinner for manicures, trying out different hairstyles and makeup, even massages if we want them."

"Can we come for the whole weekend?" Misha joked.

"I'm down for that," Emilia agreed. She quite liked the sound of a pampered girls' day with friends. It was another thing she'd never done.

"Come as early as you like. My parents have plenty of room," Maggie answered. "Stay over after the rehearsal dinner if you want."

"We're joking," Misha said.

"Think about it," Maggie offered.

She headed for the dressing room while Emilia tried to imagine how being a pampered bridesmaid with two wonderful girlfriends had become part of her unassuming life.

Five

"You're doing great on camera," Nico said encouragingly as Emilia tripped up on a sentence for the second time in a row. He didn't want her to get rattled over the little mistake.

"Should we restructure the sentence?" Taylor Atkins asked from behind the camera. "Do the words consistency and concurrency have to be so close together?"

"It's a darn good thing we're not live on this," Emilia said with obvious frustration, pushing up the sleeves of her block-colored Henley shirt. It topped a pair of faded button-fly jeans and maroon sneakers.

Since they wanted to appeal to teenagers, they'd agreed she'd opt for a young, casual look and a breezy delivery style, which she was pulling off like a pro.

"That's why we planned a full rehearsal day," Nico said.

"We sure need it." She blew out a breath and rotated her shoulders.

They'd set up a temporary studio in a private room of the Glass House restaurant at the posh Bellamy resort. The space overlooked the grounds and magnificent gardens. He'd rented it for three days to give them a fresh, upbeat backdrop.

After reviewing the current list of Coders Plus workshops, Nico and Emilia had decided to focus on database development rather than straight-up coding. They'd come up with the cheeky title: Putting It In and Getting It Out—Relational Database Modeling.

Nico was sure it was going to be a hit. Who wouldn't want to watch Emilia and listen to anything she said?

"You're just getting tired," he pointed out.

"I'm fine," she responded tartly.

"How about we review the game tape and start fresh tomorrow?" he suggested.

Emilia pulled a face, still looking frustrated, but she didn't argue.

"You need me to hang around for that?" Taylor asked. It had been a long day for him too.

"We'll be fine," Nico answered. "Just point me to the video files."

"They're in the current directory under today's date."

"I can keep going," Emilia offered.

"It's not an endurance contest," Nico said. He wanted the project to be fun, not grueling.

"Then, can we order something to drink?"

Taylor grinned as he packed up his camera.

"Whatever you like," Nico answered. "I'm sure they'll bring us something in here, or we can sit in the dining room if you'd rather."

It was coming up on five o'clock. The lunch rush would be over, and dinner wouldn't be underway yet. Nico was sure they could easily get a table.

"Here's fine," she said, settling at the table that held the laptop. She brought up the file directory.

"See you tomorrow," Taylor called on his way to the door.

"Can we start earlier?" Nico asked him. "Emilia and I have a thing later in the evening."

"Nine? Ten?" Taylor asked.

Nico looked to Emilia.

"Nine's fine for me," she said. "I'm sure I can use the extra time."

"Nine it is," Taylor said and pushed the door open in front of him.

Nico moved up behind Emilia's chair, resting his hands on the back, squelching an urge to rest them on her shoulders. Their previous lovemaking had been amazing. But they hadn't talked about it afterward. They hadn't extended the intimacy in any meaningful way again.

He wasn't sure what she expected now.

"Hungry?" he asked. "Or just thirsty?"

"Thirsty."

"A cocktail? Wine? A soft drink?"

She looked up at him over her shoulder. "Honestly, I was thinking water."

He was struck anew by her beauty and by his intense desire for her. But he kept his voice light. "Anyone ever tell you you're a very affordable date?"

"Do you usually video record your dates?"

"Oh, man, there is a very sexy joke in there."

She made a face.

"Joke," he repeated with emphasis. "Definitely a joke."

Her eyes softened, then deepened as their gazes held, and his pulse took an erratic jump.

It seemed natural to lean in. He moved slowly and steadily in case he was misreading, and her sultry expression didn't mean what he thought it meant.

But she didn't move, except to tilt her head to meet his lips.

One of his hands tightened on the chair back. With the other, he cupped her cheek to his palm, deepening the kiss. Then he shifted in front of her and drew her gently to her feet. To his delight, she stepped into his embrace and wrapped her arms around him.

His desire escalated to passion. He slipped his fingers beneath the hem of her shirt, skimming the warm skin of her back, imaging his hands roaming farther, higher, touching her soft breasts all over again.

She pulled back with a gasp, her eyes wide, lips dark pink and swollen. "There are a lot of windows in here."

She was right. There were people in the gardens outside, and the door leading from the restaurant to the glass room was unlocked for anyone to wander in.

"Your place?" he asked, hoping she'd want to take this somewhere private.

"Paris is there. Yours?"

He wished. Oh, how he wished he dared take her home to his bed.

"Just painted," he lied. "Enamel. The fumes need a few days to clear." He hoped she chalked up the strain in his voice to disappointment, not guilt.

"Here?" she suggested. "A room?"

He didn't know why he hadn't thought of it himself. They were at a resort. Resorts had guest rooms. The Bellamy had incredibly elegant guest rooms. He couldn't think of a better place for a romantic interlude.

"Here," he agreed and took her hand. Reviewing the video could easily wait until later—holding Emilia in his arms could not.

She gently stroked his bicep with her free hand as they walked to the lobby. It was a romantic touch, a sexy touch, a touch that had him increasing his pace until he was all but jogging to the front desk.

He tossed down his credit card and asked for their best room.

"Are you trying to impress me?" Emilia whispered in his ear, amusement in her voice.

"Is it working?" he returned, while the clerk checked her computer.

"It's wasted."

He glanced at her in puzzlement.

She nudged him with her hip. "I was impressed already. You could have booked an economy room with a parking lot view."

"The Bellamy doesn't have economy rooms."

The clerks overheard his last remark and smiled.

"He's right about that. Every one of our rooms is luxuriously appointed with state-of-the-art technology to meet all your needs. I think you'll love the Gold Oak Suite." She slid two key cards across the desk to Nico.

"I can't wait," Emilia responded with a smile.

The subtle sultry lilt in her voice had him impatient all over again.

They took the elevator to the top floor and found a set of double doors at the end of the hallway. The doors opened into a huge suite with a massive bow window overlooking the park and the hills beyond.

As the door swung shut behind them, he dropped the key on a side table and took Emilia into his arms once again. His entire body seemed to sigh in bliss as she molded herself against him.

Their kisses intensified, desire rising between them. He peeled off her shirt, then stripped off his own.

When she tossed her bra, he kept going, and soon they were naked.

Part of him wanted to stand there and simply drink in her beauty. But he had to touch her. He had to touch her everywhere.

As his hands explored, hers did too. A sheen of sweat formed on his skin as his racing heart sent anticipation coursing through him. He cupped her breasts, then kneaded her thighs, slipping his hands in between.

As their bodies grew slick and their caresses more intimate, he steered her gently backward, into the bedroom and to the bed. There they tumbled together on the thick white comforter.

He touched her face, looked deeply into her beautiful eyes, then kissed her reverently on her heated lips while he stroked his hand from her neck to the back of her knee, canting her leg, settling closer, to feel the sweetness of her soft body form around his.

Her hands slipped down his back, lower still, impatiently pulling him to her.

He reached for a condom before pushing inside, watching the glow in her eyes, kissing her smile as she wrapped her legs around him.

"This," she hissed, then kissed him deeply. "Is—" She kissed him again, arching her back, welcoming him, sending shafts of desire careening the length of his body.

"I know," he managed, sliding her arm beneath her back, arching her further, thrusting harder, letting the haze of passion obliterate every thought but her— Emilia, Emilia, Emilia.

Time stopped as their passion spiraled higher. He held on tight, never wanting to stop. How could he give this up?

Then she called out his name, and his body convulsed, fireworks going off behind his eyes as ecstasy cascaded through him, over him, all around him.

Making his way back to earth, he rolled to his back, holding her on top, struggling to pull in enough oxygen to satisfy his straining lungs.

He could feel her heartbeat and hear her labored breath.

He didn't know what to say. He didn't have the words to express what had happened to him. There was sex, and there was sex. But he'd sure never felt this blinding passion that defied gravity. It wasn't something a man could put into words.

It was Emilia who broke the silence. "I'm sure hungry now."

Across the table from Nick in the Glass House restaurant, Emilia was determined to keep it light. She didn't want to give him the wrong impression—that she was about to get all expectant and eager because they'd made love a second time.

They had a physical attraction, a very strong physical attraction, sure, but it was no big deal. They were both adults. Their passionate lovemaking didn't mean anything more than the obvious—they desired each other, and they were good together in bed. Okay, great together in bed. In fact, she'd go so far as to say outstanding together in bed.

But they were still just an early computer dating match, and she wasn't about to make it anything more than that.

She helped herself to a breadstick. "I've been thinking about it, and we should beef up the key field analysis before tackling the queries sections."

He blinked. "Huh?"

"I don't think we've been clear enough about the function of the key fields in the relationship. If students aren't clear on that, they'll get lost when we start talking about queries, especially when we get to multiple tables." She took a bite of the tender, warm bread.

"Queries?" He looked amused.

"These are delicious." She waggled the stick. "Herb and parmesan, I think."

A waitress appeared and set two martinis in front of them. "Have you had a chance to look at the menu?"

"Not yet," Nick answered.

"Take your time," she said cheerfully. "I'll just let you know, in addition to the menu, our appetizer special tonight is a crab avocado cocktail with lemon truffle vinaigrette. For the main, we have pan-roasted halibut with pesto on a bed of porcini mushroom, goat cheese risotto. And if you're looking for a special dessert, the chef has made a dark Belgium chocolate brownie with salted caramel ice cream and praline garnish."

"The brownie, definitely," Emilia said, loving the sound of the sweet dessert.

"Something to go with that?" Nick asked her with an amused smile.

"I'll give you a few more minutes," the waitress said before she left.

"Did I mention I liked chocolate?" Emilia asked him as she opened the menu.

"I'm usually a savory guy." He opened his menu.

"Then you should try the breadsticks." It was true that she was feeling particularly hungry at the moment, but the breadsticks really were to die for.

She worked her way down the menu, not really in the mood for anything fancy. A filet mignon might be okay. But she was more in a carb-loading mood.

Then she spotted it. "Beer batter fish and chips." That sounded perfect. "Do you suppose they'd give me sweet potato fries with that?"

"I expect they'll give you anything you ask for. You don't want to try something more exciting? The chardonnay braised beef or the Scottish salmon?"

"Fish and chips for me," she said, setting down the menu.

"Alright, then." He closed his own menu and took a sip of his martini.

She did the same, finding it crisp and tart, just the way she liked it.

"So, the key fields," she said. "What do you think?"

"I think you should teach whatever and however you want to teach. Seriously, Emilia, you're fantastic on camera—relaxed, natural, relatable."

"I keep stumbling on my sentences."

He gave a shrug. "That's just practice. It's only been one day. Are you sure you haven't done any teaching before this?"

She shook her head. "I barely graduated high school. What about you?"

He looked surprised by the question. "Me? Teaching? No."

"What about college? Did you go?"

"I went for a couple of years." He settled his fingertips on the stem of his glass and focused there. "Then I discovered how much I could learn on my own that was more practical from an employability perspective."

"Where?"

He took a drink. "Same as you, online classes and workshops. They don't give you a degree, but they do give you abilities."

"I meant which college."

"UT Dallas. It was ranked the best value, and I didn't have a lot of money back then."

"When I left foster care, I didn't have any money at all." She sipped her martini, remembering waitressing until late at night at the Pineview Café, dragging herself out of bed early in the dank basement suite she'd rented on the cheap, then jolting her brain with caffeine to focus on her learning.

"You definitely pulled yourself up by the bootstraps." There was admiration in his voice.

"I have watched a lot of teachers over the years," she said. "Maybe I subconsciously worked out what I thought was good and bad about the way they approached subjects."

"You're a very clear communicator."

"So are you." It was one of the things she admired about him. "You're very poised. Like, all the time. You know, you should give it a try too." She picked up her phone and hit the video app, pointing it his way. "Do me a quick demo."

Through the lens, his expression shifted, going hard, a steely, determined look coming up in his eyes. And a split second later, his hand blocked the lens. He lifted the phone from her hand. "Don't." His reaction startled her. It seemed so out of character from what she knew of him.

"You can't be all that camera shy."

His expression smoothed back to normal. "I am."

"It was only for fun."

"I'll stay behind the scenes."

She wanted to probe his strong reaction, but the waitress returned to their table. "Are you ready to order?"

Nick looked Emilia's way, clearly waiting for her to go first. "The fish and chips. Can I substitute sweet potato fries?"

"Certainly."

The waitress turned her attention to Nick.

"She also wants the brownie," he said. Then he lifted his brow Emilia's way, a teasing note in his voice. "Two spoons?"

"You want me to share?" she asked with mock concern.

"I can double the order," the waitress offered.

"Sure," Nick answered. "And I'll take the New York strip."

"Can I bring you any appetizers?"

"I'm good with the breadsticks," Emilia answered.

"I'm with her," Nick said.

As the waitress walked away, Emilia picked up the conversation. "I don't know why I have to be the only one out of my comfort zone."

"I thought we were both pretty far into our comfort zones." The mischievous smirk on his face told her he was referring to their lovemaking.

"I mean in front of the camera."

"We should have ordered some wine." He twisted in his chair to look around for their waitress. "Do you prefer a white with your fish?"

"Fish and chips isn't exactly fish."

"It's not?"

"From a wine perspective. When you batter them

up and smother them with tartar sauce, you don't need a delicate wine."

"So, a robust Cabernet Sauvignon? I could go for that." He raised a discrete finger to get the waitress's attention.

"We're not going to talk about it, are we?" Emilia challenged.

"The wine?"

"You, getting in front of the camera."

"We should go with our strengths, and you're really good at it."

The waitress arrived, and the two began conferring on the choice of wine.

Emilia blew out a sigh and gave up trying to get answers out of Nick. Taking a bite of her breadstick and a hearty swig of her martini, she instead settled in to enjoy what looked to be a fabulous meal.

Who wanted to argue in a place like this?

"No argument from you, Emie," Paris insisted while Emilia stared into the mirror. "The invitation said formal, and *this* is the one."

"Did it say ball gown?" It was the third of Paris's dresses Emilia had tried on tonight and the fanciest of them all.

"This isn't a ball gown."

Emilia swayed, and the full-length, layered chiffon skirt rustled around her legs. It sure looked and felt like a ball gown.

"It's an evening dress," Paris finished.

"It's gown-like," Emilia insisted, although she'd admit she was no expert.

"You cannot wear a cocktail dress to the party tonight. And do you still have your contact lenses?"

"Somewhere." Emilia hadn't worn them in months.

"Put them in. That way you won't hide your eye makeup."

"Are you insulting my glasses?"

"No." Paris took a couple of steps back to survey Emilia. She grinned. "I'm just getting into this Cinderella thing."

"I'm not Cinderella," Emilia insisted, although she felt transformed in the plum-colored dress. The V-neck of the bodice and the drop sleeve were made of sheer netting with beautiful lace appliqué. A jeweled belt showed off her waist and matched the strappy silver rhinestone heels Paris had lent her.

It was one of the most dramatic outfits she'd ever put on.

"Into the bathroom. We'll put a little mousse in your hair."

"What's wrong with my hair?"

"Trust me."

"I don't know." Emilia wasn't sure she wanted to feel even less like herself. "What about you? Shouldn't you get dressed?"

"It'll take me fifteen minutes, tops. Everything's ready."

"Did you hear from Chase?" Emilia tried for a distraction as Paris ushered her toward the bathroom.

"Yes."

"You *did*? Why didn't you say something?"

"He called this afternoon. He asked if I was coming to the party. As if I wouldn't be."

"Did he offer to pick you up?"

Paris turned on the taps and ran her hands under warm water. "He said he'd meet me there."

Emilia wasn't sure what to say. She didn't want to offer sympathy, but she didn't want to be falsely cheerful either. Paris would see right through that.

Paris ran her wet fingers through Emilia's hair, dampening it. "He doesn't want to pick me up? Okay. Then I'm going to dress to the nines and knock his socks off."

"So, you should be getting yourself ready instead of worrying about me."

"You're the one with a hot date."

"He's not a hot—"

"Oh, yes he is." Paris smoothed some mousse into Emilia's hair, then went at it with a brush and a blow dryer.

"Okay. Maybe a little hot," Emilia admitted.

She'd spent the day working with Nick on the video workshop. Taylor had been with them, so she'd kept her hands to herself. She'd admit that she was looking forward to dancing with Nick tonight.

"There," Paris said with satisfaction, surveying her work.

Emilia turned to the mirror. Her hair was parted at the side and waved in sections over her head, giving it volume and sophistication. Paris had tucked the rest behind the opposite ear and somehow turned it slightly under at the neck. It looked like something from a fashion runway.

"What do you think?" Paris asked.

"It's…not exactly me, is it?" But Emilia liked it.

"You need something dramatic on your ears. And I seriously want you to put in your contacts. I'm going to swoop your eyeliner, and I want him to see your gorgeous eyes."

"Swoop my eyeliner?"

"If not tonight, Emie, seriously, when?"

The only answer Emilia had for that was never. But she didn't say it out loud.

"Contacts." Paris said the word like an order as she marched out of the bathroom. "I'll find you some earrings."

It took Emilia a few minutes to get her contacts in. Then a few more minutes to get used to wearing them again.

"Here we go." Paris returned carrying a pair of long drop crystal earrings.

"Those aren't mine."

"No kidding. Try them."

Emilia slipped them into her ears. They felt heavy, and they sparkled and swayed as she moved.

"They look really good," Paris said as she dragged a chair into the bathroom and set it down in the middle of the floor. "Sit."

"You are *so* bossy."

"We don't have a lot of time here."

"That what I keep saying. Go get ready already."

"I'm not worried about me. The worst that can happen is I'll be fashionably late. You have to be ready for Nick."

Emilia agreed on that. "I don't want to keep him waiting."

"Compulsively punctual," Paris muttered. "So, close your eyes and let me get to work."

Emilia sat still while Paris fussed over her makeup. Finally, after what seemed like an inordinately long time, Paris gave her permission to look in the mirror.

Emilia stood, then stared at herself.

"What do you think?" Paris asked, peering around her shoulder.

"That's me?" Her eyes looked too big, her lashes thick and cheekbones defined. Her lips were full and dark with a sheen she'd have never put on herself. Even her eyebrows looked smooth and shaped. And she had to admit, the earrings were an excellent choice.

"That's you," Paris said with soft satisfaction.

"It doesn't look like me."

Paris grinned at that.

Emilia turned her head to get a different angle. "It feels like false advertising."

"Don't be silly. It's all you."

"With the help of a skilled professional."

"I'll take the compliment. You have five minutes to spare. Do you need a jacket?"

Emilia gave a helpless shrug. "I don't have anything remotely suitable."

"You can't exactly toss a hoodie over that, can you?"

"I'm sure it'll be warm in the ballroom."

"Go," Paris said on the laugh. "Just go."

With a last look in the mirror, Emilia headed for the stairs, walking carefully on the unfamiliarly high heels, afraid she might trip. She didn't even want to think about how hard it might be to dance in these things.

"Thank you!" she called back over her shoulder.

"See you there," Paris called back.

Emilia made it out the front door just as a black sedan pulled up.

Nick hopped out of the back seat and came her way. Halfway across the sidewalk, he saw her and stopped in his tracks. "Emilia?"

She took in his nicely cut tux. "Nick?"

"You look fabulous."

"So do you."

The man could fill out a tux like nobody's business. It showed off his height and the breadth of his shoulders. The black suit and vest set off the white shirt. He'd gone with a straight tie, glossy black that looked both urbane and masculine at the same time.

He started walking again, coming briskly up the stairs to offer his arm.

Given the shoes, she was happy to take it.

"You have a driver?" she asked.

"They're serving cocktails."

"Good planning then."

They made their way slowly down the stairs.

"My roommate did all this," she said.

"My sis—" He cleared his throat. "My tailor did all this."

"It's not a rental?"

He pulled a face. "Please. If I must go black tie, it's at least going to fit properly."

"Indeed, it does." She smoothed his lapel.

He opened the car door and paused to gaze at her. Then he gently brushed her cheek with his thumb. "I want to kiss you, but I don't want to muss you up."

"Be gentle," she suggested, wanting a kiss herself.

He brushed his lips briefly and tenderly against hers. "To second dates," he whispered.

"To second dates," she whispered back.

Six

As they walked into the grandeur of the Texas Cattleman's Club ballroom, surrounded by wafting music and the din of lively chatter, Nico expected Emilia to attract attention. She was stunningly gorgeous in her dramatic gown. He loved her day-to-day sexy librarian look, but the contacts showed off her beautiful eyes, and he was already having fantasies about her strappy, high-heeled shoes.

In every way, he was elated to be her date. And he wouldn't have traded the evening for anything. Still, he couldn't shake the worry that while people were staring at her they might too easily recognize him.

"Will you look at all that." She slowed her steps, gazing at the arched beams of the high ceiling. Decorative lights had been strung along the beams and up the pillars, giving a soft glow to the polished walls and reflecting off the rich wood floor.

There was a bar in every corner and a colorful hors d'oeuvres buffet offset to one side of the big room. The bandstand at the far end held a chamber ensemble playing background music for the beautifully dressed people who were chatting in pairs and groups. He knew everyone who was anyone in Royal had accepted Misha's invitation, and happiness bloomed inside him for his sister and her success.

A waitress came their way carrying a tray of craft cocktails. He knew they'd been designed specially for the occasion by the Silver Saddle tapas bar. She offered them amber-and-gold-layered drinks in tall, footed goblets with crushed ice and a thin lime round.

"Want to try one?" he asked Emilia.

"I'm game if you are," she answered cheerfully.

He took two of the drinks and thanked the waitress.

"Might take the edge off," Emilia said as she put the drink to her lips.

"Are you nervous?" He was, but for reasons he couldn't explain to her. He took a quick glance around to see if anyone seemed to recognize him.

It didn't seem like it. He blew out a breath of relief. So far, so good.

"This isn't exactly my comfort zone." She took an experimental sip, then turned her lips in and smacked them. "Yum. That's really good."

He tried the drink himself. It was very good, not too sweet, with an undertone of citrus against what he was guessing was tequila and maybe an herbal liqueur. "You might want to take it slowly," he advised.

"Feels like it's got a kick," she agreed but took another sip.

The band played a flourish, attracting everyone's attention as Misha took the stage.

His sister looked both elegant and professional in a gold, drop-sleeved gown with just enough sequins to glitter as she walked confidently to the microphone.

Applause came up, and she beamed at the audience.

"Welcome," she said heartily, looking impressively poised and comfortable on the stage. It was a side of her that Nico didn't often see, and his chest expanded with pride.

"Welcome to k!smet, investors and future investors. And a special warm welcome to our ten matched couples from the Surprise Me! event. Thank you for taking a chance on our fun and innovative function. Your participation helped make this launch both thrilling and successful. I'll be tracking down and talking to each and every one of you during the course of the evening for a private chat." She looked to the side of the stage. "As will our media host, Kaitlin Gander, and the video crew. I hope hashtag k!smetlaunchparty will be trending tonight, so keep those social media posts going out and amplify your friends!"

The crowd sent up a cheer, clearly enthusiastic about sharing their experience far and wide.

Nico wasn't enthusiastic at all. He took a wary look around for cell phone cameras that might be trained his way. He was having second thoughts about risking his identity here, along with the sinking feeling that the night could easily end badly.

"In case you haven't heard," Misha continued, "k!smet stock is up twenty-three percent since opening this morning. I'll have some more business announcements later in the evening. But, for now, enjoy the hors d'oeuvres and special cocktails created by our friends at Silver Saddle."

Another cheer went up, this one clearly in support of the cocktails.

"And the dancing," Misha added above the din. "Enjoy the music of local band Orian's Angle."

She gave everyone a wave as she backed away from the podium, and the band started in on a catchy popular song with a strong dance rhythm.

"She's great," Emilia said, applauding along with the rest of the room.

"Yes, she is." Nico pretended he'd barely met Misha. "Very poised."

"Very successful," Emilia said. "It's impressive how she's weathered all the storms that came her way."

"Storms?" Nico asked, keeping up the ruse.

Emilia cringed. "You do know what happened with me over k!smet, right?"

"What happened with you?"

"It truly wasn't on purpose."

He knew she was talking about the HitMeUp sabotage, but he didn't want to appear too knowledgeable about the inner workings of k!smet.

"I was involved with HitMeUp for a little while."

"I thought you said this was your first dating app."

"I consulted for them." She paused. "While they were busy sabotaging k!smet. It was all over the news."

"I do remember something about that," he admitted. "How did you get involved with a dishonest outfit?" He was honestly curious about that part.

He knew she'd been exonerated. Back then, he'd thought Emilia was smart enough to avoid getting caught, and maybe she had had a hand in it. Now, though, he'd put his money on her innocence.

"My sin?" She paused then, as if she was parsing her words.

He felt a moment's hesitation. Was she about to confess?

"I wasn't looking closely enough at my client. I completely missed what they were up to." She gave a chopped laugh. "Embarrassing, I know. But that's the truth."

"So, you weren't personally a saboteur?"

She pulled a face. "Seriously? You think I'd need to pull something like that?"

He made sure his teasing tone was obvious. "You do have a bit of a reputation as a rebel."

"I'm a white hat," she said with mock indignation. "I rid the world of thieves and brigands."

"Brigands?"

"Robbers, outlaws."

"I know what brigands are. Are you fighting pirates?"

"Digital pirates, yes." She gave a toasting gesture and took a drink.

"Okay, then. Pirates it is. If it makes it more exciting for you."

"You're darn right. And it does. They digitally roam the world looking for the weak and the vulnerable to steal their treasure."

"You've made your case." It was a more apt metaphor than he'd realized.

"It would be more fun if there were sailing ships, costumes and swordplay, I suppose," she allowed.

He grinned with amusement at her sardonic tone.

"Oh, look." She gestured with her near empty glass. "There's Paris with Chase McMillian. And they're interviewing with the video crew. Let's go check it out."

"You go." Nico scrambled for an excuse to avoid being recorded. "There are a couple of people I want to track down."

Emilia's brow narrowed in bafflement. "They'll want to interview us too."

"They can do it later. Let me take your glass." He reached out his hand.

"But—" She absently handed it over, perplexity clear on her expression.

"I'll find you again. Don't worry," he assured her.

"You're really not coming with me?"

"I promised a couple of people I'd catch up…" He let his voice trail off.

"You can't talk to them later?"

He hated that he had to dig himself deeper and deeper. "They said they can't stay very long. Go ahead." He nodded across the room. "Visit with Paris. You can tell me what questions they're asking so I'm prepared."

Thankfully, she nodded to that, because he was running out of reasons to leave her alone. And he felt like a heel for doing it. But he couldn't stand in front of the camera and answer probing questions. They'd put his face and voice all over social media. The name "Nick" wasn't much of a disguise, and a whole lot of people in this town knew Nico Law was Misha's brother.

He'd be recognized by someone for sure.

"I'll find you," he promised as he moved away and left her standing alone. Then he wove his way through the crowd, looking for an exit to a hallway or a patio where he could lie low for a while.

Emilia watched Nick disappear into the crowd without a backward glance.

Her lighthearted Cinderella-at-the-ball feelings evaporated as she wondered why he wouldn't want to introduce her to his friends. He hadn't even suggested she come with him.

Her self-pity moment was interrupted by another waitress with a tray of cocktails.

The woman gave Emilia a friendly smile and helpfully pointed to the glasses on her tray. "The tall one is called a River Fizz, and the blue one is an Ocean's Fifty."

The River Fizz looked refreshing to Emilia, and her last Silver Saddle cocktail had been tasty, so she took one. Then she squared her shoulders, determinedly shook off her dejection and headed for Paris and Chase, who were laughing as they spoke with Kaitlin Gander. Maybe Paris's joy would improve her mood.

"I'd call this our second date," Chase was saying in a smooth baritone as Emilia approached.

Paris grinned at her and gave a little wave, looking like she was in high spirits.

Emilia made a mock gasp, gesturing to Paris's outfit. She'd worn a vibrant forest green off-the-shoulder gown, dripping with sequins and accented with a wide sash at the waist. Her lustrous hair was in a messy updo, and her earrings were dangling gold starbursts.

She was tall in her high heels, but Chase was taller still, and they made a striking couple with his black tux and bow tie. For a cowboy, he sure cleaned up nice, and his blue eyes gleamed a little when he met Paris's gaze, making Emilia think their second date was going very well.

Abandoned or not, Emilia was happy for her friend.

"I think that will do it," Kaitlin said to Paris and Chase, handing her microphone to a member of the crew. "Great interview, you two. Thanks for doing it."

"It was fun," Paris said.

"Thanks, guys," Chase said to the crew members.

"And now I'm ready for a drink," Paris said to Chase as she moved Emilia's way. "Are those any good?"

"I don't know yet." Emilia took an experimental sip.

"Chase? This is my roommate, Emilia."

Chase ambled up with a broad smile. "I've heard all about you, Emilia."

"Good, I hope," Emilia joked.

"Absolutely."

Emilia offered Paris a sip of the drink. "I like it."

"Well, there was that one story about your banana cake," Chase said.

Paris nudged Chase with her elbow. "Hey."

"You told him about the banana cake?"

Paris gave a sheepish grin as she lifted Emilia's drink from her hand. "It's funny. You come off looking—"

"Like a dork," Emilia interjected.

"Endearing. This *is* good." Paris held the drink up to show Chase. "I'll take one of these, please."

"It's called a River Fizz," Emilia offered, reclaiming her drink.

"I thought it was a sweet story," Chase said to Emilia.

She frowned and muttered into her glass, "A dozen bananas later."

"It speaks to your tenacity. Most people would have given up after the first three cakes."

"It was Paris's birthday."

"One word," Paris said, stifling a laugh. "Bakery."

"No, no." Chase jumped in on Emilia's side. "Only a quitter would have gone to a bakery."

"The cream cheese icing was to die for," Paris said.

"I'm sorry I missed it," Chase said. "I'll be right back with the drinks."

"I can't believe you told him that," Emilia muttered with a shake of her head.

"Chill. It wasn't the first thing I told him about you. And it wasn't the only thing I told him. I also told him you were brilliant, hardworking and creative." Paris glanced around. "Where's Nick?"

"He went to look for friends."

"Friends?" Paris looked appalled. "He ditched you to find his friends?"

"I don't know if he ditched me or not," Emilia admitted. "I said I wanted to come talk to you and he just... decided to find his friends."

"You think it was me?"

"No." Emilia regretted the way she'd put that. "He's never even met you. But it was a little weird."

She replayed their conversation in her mind. The only other thing going on was the interview. But that couldn't have been a surprise. All the Surprise Me! contestants knew there would be social media coverage of their dates at the launch party.

Chase returned. "One River Fizz." He handed Paris her drink.

He'd gone with a beer for himself. "Paris says you're a computer genius."

"Paris is exaggerating," Emilia said.

"She's very humble," Paris said.

Emilia gave an eye roll as she took another drink. The River Fizz was going down easy.

"You run your own company?" Chase asked.

"Just me. A sole proprietorship." Emilia didn't want to overstate the situation.

"With clients all over the world," Paris put in.

"That part is true," Emilia agreed. "It's one of the big benefits of a tech career. You can mostly do it from anywhere."

"And you chose Royal."

"It's an up-and-coming tech hub. Just look around at all this. Misha's helped to put it on the map."

"Chase's family is part of old Royal," Paris said.

"We're not snobs about it." He paused. "But we do value our roots. This isn't called the Texas Cattleman's Club for nothing."

"Nick, my date—" Emilia took a quick glance around, beginning to wonder if he really had ditched her. She didn't see him anywhere right now. "He's working on an app for one of the local ranches."

"That's interesting. We use technology on the ranch now, everybody does. But it's mostly standard programs. Do you know which ranch?"

Emilia almost blurted it out, but then realized it might be confidential. "I can't really say."

"Fair enough."

A tall, burly man came up behind Chase and clapped him hard on the shoulder. "Hey, bro. How's it going?"

"Sammy?" Chase asked, a big grin splitting his face. "When did you get home?"

The two men heartily embraced then separated, both still grinning.

"Paris, Emilia," Chase said. "This is my little brother Sammy. Sammy, Paris is my date, and Emilia is her roommate."

"Somebody's dating you?" Sammy asked Chase, pulling a face. "I'm so sorry, ma'am." He reached a big hand out to shake Paris's. Then he turned to Emilia, the friendly gaze in his blue eyes softening his craggy face. "Emilia, is it?" He offered his hand to her. "Are you anyone's date?"

"Down, Sammy," Chase said. "She's here with someone."

"I am," Emilia said as Sammy gently shook her hand. He was clearly aware of his strength and power and careful with it.

"I don't see anyone with her," he joked.

"He's around here somewhere," Emilia said, keeping her smile in place. "It's nice to meet you, Sammy."

Sammy took a step back and looked to Paris. "So, you're dating my brother."

"We matched on the k!smet app," Paris said easily, looping her arm into Chase's.

Chase looked happy about her move. "Second date," he said.

Sammy looked from one to the other. "How's it going so far?"

"Good," Paris said.

"None of your business," Chase said overtop of her.

Paris's expression faltered for a split second at what could have been interpreted as Chase's lack of enthusiasm.

Emilia caught it and, apparently, so did Sammy. He immediately turned to Emilia. "Care to take a spin around the dance floor?" The invitation was clearly intended to end the embarrassing moment and give the couple some space.

"Love to," Emilia said and took Sammy's arm.

The tune was quick and catchy, and Sammy was surprisingly graceful for his size.

"Have you been away?" Emilia asked, picking up from Chase's greeting.

"I'm a rodeo clown."

She drew back from the light hold of his arms. "Seriously?"

"Bullfighter mostly. But, yes, I dress up in bright colors and run around the rodeo ring entertaining the audience."

"That's fascinating," she said. She'd seen a few live rodeos since moving to Texas. She knew what bullfighters did, and she was in awe of their bravery.

"What about you?" he asked.

"Nothing near so exciting. I write computer code."

He pulled a face. "That does sound dreary." The man had good comedic timing.

"Doesn't it?"

"Lots of money in that?" he asked matter-of-factly.

"Enough. What about bullfighting?"

"Depends on the circuit. I do okay. Plus, my family owns land, so I always have a free place to stay when I'm in town."

He gave her a spin, and she laughed, relaxed by the two drinks and enjoying his easy company.

"I wouldn't take on Sammy McMillian if I was you," Misha told Nico in a dire tone. "He stares down bulls for a living."

Nico's jaw was clenched, his feet planted apart as he watched Emilia laughing and dancing with the rancher. "What's she doing dancing with him?"

"Maybe he asked her."

"I'd ask her. I could have asked her."

Emilia hadn't said anything about wanting to dance.

She'd said she wanted to talk to Paris. So, where was Paris?

"So, why are you standing on the sidelines?" Misha asked.

Before Nico could answer, a willowy forty-something woman stopped and touched Misha lightly on the arm. "Wonderful party, Ms. Law. Congratulations. Such a successful, successful launch."

"Please, call me Misha. And thank you so much," Misha responded.

"I'm Cecily Trunk, over from Plano. My husband and I invested this morning. Not a huge amount. But we have a midsize retirement portfolio, and you've already strengthened it for us."

"I'm so glad to hear that," Misha said. "I hope you enjoy the party."

"We will. We *are*. I won't take up too much of your time. I know it's a busy night for you." The woman left with a wave and a happy smile.

"That has to feel good," Nico said.

"It feels great! I hope all kinds of people do well in the venture."

He nodded, but his attention was pulled back to the dance floor.

"You can't possibly be jealous of Sammy." Misha folded her arms across her chest, her tone admonishing.

"Who's jealous?" Just because a guy didn't want his date dancing with another man, didn't make him jealous.

"You've been on *two* dates with Emilia."

"I'm well aware of that." And while it might be

strictly true, Nico had spent plenty of additional time with Emilia over the past few days. They'd progressed a whole lot further than your average two dates, that was for sure.

"You should take another run at Surprise Me! in the morning and see who comes up next," Misha suggested.

Nico looked to see if she was serious.

Her gaze narrowed with what looked like confusion. "That's the plan…right?"

He didn't answer right away.

"Nico?" she pushed.

"Sure," he said, working to keep the reluctance out of his voice. "Sure. Why not?" That was the plan. Despite how he felt now, that had been the plan all along. "But you better keep Kaitlin Gander away from me tonight, or my cover's going to be blown before I can do anything more."

Misha gave a considered nod. "I'll tell her not to bother you."

Despite his sister's assurance, Nico felt like the walls were closing in. "Emilia is expecting us to be interviewed."

"I'll take care of that too."

The band switched to a slow song.

Out on the dance floor, Sammy leaned in and said something in Emilia's ear.

Her gaze darted to the four corners of the room. After a second, she gave a little shrug, smiled, and he took her in his arms.

Nico had had enough. He started forward.

"Nico?" Misha called from behind, a warning tone in her voice.

But he kept going, his vision tunneling down to Emilia as he made his way across the dance floor.

"Excuse me?" He tapped Sammy on the shoulder.

Sammy stopped and turned, his expression incredulous. "You're cutting in?"

"You're dancing with my date," Nico said.

"So what?" One of Sammy's hands was still on her shoulder.

"So, it's your second dance." Nico hardened his look. "And she's with me."

"Nick," Emilia interrupted, sounding anxious.

Sammy gazed curiously at Nico. He seemed to be trying to place him, and Nico realized he might have blown his cover all by himself. He and Sammy hadn't been friends in high school, since Nico was a few years older. Still, they'd crossed paths from time to time.

But Sammy raised his palms. "Hey, man. No offense. I'm not looking to cause trouble in the middle of a party."

Nico wasn't looking to cause trouble either, especially not at Misha's big event.

Sammy backed off, turning to walk away, and Nico switched his attention to Emilia.

She looked annoyed.

"Dance?" he asked, hoping to blow past the uncomfortable situation.

"Are you kidding?" She turned to leave the dance floor.

He quickly followed, coming up beside her. "Hey."

"*What* was that?" she asked.

"If you want to dance, we can dance."

"You left me," she accused.

"I had—" He realized his excuse for leaving her was lame. He countered instead. "You said you wanted to talk to Paris."

"I did talk to Paris. And Chase introduced me to his brother. And his brother politely asked me to dance."

They cleared the dance floor, but she kept walking fast.

"Twice?" He tried to go on offense again.

She gave him a hard look. "Is that a crime?"

"Did he know you were here with a date?" Nico realized the conversation was going off the rails, and it was his fault. He also realized he was admitting his jealousy by so doggedly pursuing the situation.

An open door to a patio loomed up in front of them. It seemed like a really good idea to get some air. He gestured to it, inviting her outside.

"*Yes*, I told him about you," she said tartly. "I also looked for you. I didn't find you. Was I supposed to just stand there while—" She clamped her mouth shut.

"While what?"

The cool air on the patio surrounded them, and the music faded as they kept walking toward the edge. His frustration abated now that they were alone together.

"While what?" he asked again, softer this time.

"We were dealing with an uncomfortable moment."

"With Sammy?" Nico tensed again.

"No. With Paris and Chance." She slowed as they came to a raised garden. "Sammy asked them a question, and they gave slightly conflicting answers. Paris looked embarrassed, and I thought it was best to give them some space."

"So, you danced with Sammy." Nico liked the sound of that much better.

She hadn't found the rugged, powerful Sammy irresistibly attractive. She was trying to be a good friend.

"So, I danced with Sammy. What choice did I have? Since my date abandoned me to hang with his pals." She sounded half annoyed, half joking now.

He wished he could tell her he hadn't been hanging with his pals. He wished he could tell her he'd been avoiding the cameras. But then he'd have to tell her why.

"I think we just had a fight," he pointed out instead. "Well, an argument, really." He didn't want to blow it out of proportion, and he hoped she didn't either.

She nodded. "I guess we did."

"Our first argument."

"Yes."

"And I still want to kiss you." He desperately wanted to draw her into his arms, apologize for being a boor and kiss her like there was no tomorrow.

She didn't turn into his arms. Instead she rubbed her bare shoulders as she gazed off into the lighted, manicured grounds.

He shrugged out of his jacket and draped it around her.

"So," he said.

"So," she returned.

"I think that means I like you." He caught what looked like her reluctant smile.

"Well, I'm a likable person."

"I mean I like you a lot, Emilia." He gently turned to face her, touching his hand to her shoulder.

When she didn't resist, he ducked to catch her gaze.

"This wasn't supposed to happen," she said, but she didn't look away.

"What wasn't supposed to happen?" He thought he knew, but he wanted to hear her say it out loud.

"I did it on a lark, for a free date. Paris really wanted—" She shook her head, looking regretful. "This…liking you…being attracted to you… It wasn't supposed to happen."

Joy rose within him as he lightly brushed her cheek with his thumb. He could hardly keep the delight out of his voice. "But it did."

She seemed to search his eyes while he stared thoughtfully into hers. He didn't know what he was going to tell Misha. But he sure as heck wasn't using the Surprise Me! function to make another match tomorrow. He wasn't dating another woman while he was with Emilia.

He kissed her.

She kissed him back, and he engulfed her in his arms.

He'd have to tell her the truth about himself, sometime, someday. But not now. Now, he simply wanted to hold her tight and pretend this could last forever.

Seven

As the sun pushed the darkness from her bedroom, Emilia awoke. She was in her own bed but cozily spooned in Nick's arms.

She lay still for a moment, reflecting on the fact that she'd never spent an entire night with a man and wondering if she should feel awkward. She didn't feel awkward. She only felt happy.

"Awake?" his low voice sounded in her ear.

"Yes."

He stretched out his legs. "Good. I can safely move. There's not a lot of room in here, but I didn't want to disturb your sleep."

He was right about that. The bed alcove in her loft was narrow, only fitting a standard double bed. Since she'd never had company, there'd always been plenty of room.

She stretched out while he sat up.

"What are the options for coffee around here?"

"There's a coffee maker downstairs in the kitchen. But Paris might be home."

"Do you not want Paris to know I stayed?" He frowned at that.

Emilia sat. "Oh, no. It's not me. I thought that you might—" She shrugged.

"Be self-conscious about spending the night?"

"I wanted to warn you, just in case."

"I'm not remotely self-conscious." He swung out of bed. "Can I bring you a cup?"

"Sure. Uh, coffee's in the top cupboard beside the fridge. The grinder can be finicky—" She pulled back her covers. "I should do it myself."

"No, no. Stay right there." He buttoned his slacks under his open white shirt, then leaned down and kissed her. "I'll figure it out."

"You sure?" It seemed wrong to let him play host when they were in her home.

"Positive." He headed for the stairs.

Emilia laid back, relaxing into her pillow, feeling satiated and content, if a little bit restless now that she was alone.

She heard the lilt of Paris's voice downstairs followed by the deep intonation of Nick's. Rising, she stepped into a pair of fleece shorts and pulled a loose, long-sleeved T-shirt over her head. She padded barefoot down to the kitchen.

"You must be Nick." It was Chase's voice.

Emilia couldn't stop an ironic smile as she came through the archway from the front hall. She supposed if anyone wanted to be self-conscious, they could all be self-conscious together.

"My brother Sammy said he met you last night," Chase added.

"I was out of line," Nick said, impressing Emilia with his humility.

"He didn't say anything about that," Chase said.

"Emilia," Paris called out as she spotted her. "There you are. Coffee's almost ready."

"I hope you made a full pot," Emilia said.

Paris wore a colorful silk bathrobe over the tank top and shorts she normally slept in.

Nick had buttoned his shirt, while Chase was also dressed in his tux slacks and dress shirt.

"Anyone want to make a bagel run?" Paris asked. "There's a bakery down the block."

"I'll go," Chase offered.

A phone rang, and Nick pulled his from his pants pocket to look.

Emilia tried not to be nosy, but her eyes betrayed her, glancing at the screen. It said Misha. *Misha?*

Nick's gaze met hers for a split second. Then he accepted the call, putting it to his ear.

"Misha. Good morning. I'm surprised to hear from you. Is this about last night? I'm here with Emilia."

"Any bagel requests?" Chase asked, rolling up the sleeves of his shirt.

"Blueberry for me," Paris said as she poured the coffee.

"Emilia was worried about that," Nick said, moving farther away from them and into the living room.

"I'll take mine with me." Chase snagged the first full cup of coffee.

Emilia told herself to stop eavesdropping.

So, Misha was calling Nick. It wasn't all that strange. He was part of the k!smet promotion after all. It made sense that she'd have his number.

Still, she could have called Emilia if she had questions about their match.

"Emilia?" Chase interrupted her thoughts. "Do you have a bagel preference?"

"Everything if they've got it. Otherwise, anything."

Chase glanced at Nick's back. "I guess Nick will take what he gets."

"I'm sure it'll be fine." She hadn't gotten the sense he was choosy about what he ate. Then again, she really didn't know that much about him.

"Back soon." Chase gave Paris a quick kiss goodbye.

"So…" Paris opened with as soon as they were alone, a gleam in her eyes as she lifted a cup of coffee with both hands. "Have a good date?"

"I did." Emilia gave her attention to Paris. "We had a good time."

"Clearly." Paris sent a pointed look Nick's way.

"Well, you too," Emilia noted, claiming one of the remaining cups of coffee for herself.

"Bit of a stumble there when he sounded so unenthusiastic about me."

Emilia nodded. "I hoped you two would work that out."

"Chase said Sammy's the family gossip."

"So, he was playing it close to the vest?" Emilia guessed.

"Yes. Apparently, any remotely serious relationship in his family is met with questions about an engagement ring, wedding venues and how many children are planned." She chuckled. "But he assured me in many, many ways that he thought our relationship was off to a very good start."

Emilia smiled, happy for Paris. "That's fantastic."

"Misha wants to talk to you." Nick returned to the kitchen, holding out his phone.

Emilia studied his expression, feeling like she was missing something here. "Everything okay?"

"Go ahead." He touched the phone to her hand.

She took it, setting down her cup. "Hi, Misha."

"Good morning," Misha said brightly. "Good date?"

"It was." Emilia moved into the hall, leaving Paris and Nick's low voices behind.

"Maggie will be very happy to hear that. But you missed your interview last night." Misha sounded disappointed.

"I looked for Kaitlin and the crew but couldn't find them."

"That's what Nick just said."

"Do you want us to do one this morning?" Emilia had felt guilty about that last night, and she felt even worse now for not holding up her end of the deal.

"I told Nick Kaitlin says she got plenty of footage, but if she needs more, I'll hit you guys up for it, okay?"

"Of course."

"I wanted to ask you what shoes you're wearing for the wedding? Can you send me a picture? I've got a few choices, so I can coordinate to whatever you have."

"I hadn't thought about it yet." Emilia realized she should have been paying more attention to the wedding details. She didn't have much in the way of dressy shoes. She might have to buy something. "I don't have a whole lot to choose from."

"I was thinking gray or silver, or maybe something with a few rhinestones."

Emilia tried to picture her closet. She had a pair of black pumps. Her gray shoes weren't very fancy.

"What size are you?" Misha asked.

"Seven, maybe seven and a half."

"Great. Then I've probably got something you can borrow. Can you swing by next week?"

Emilia hesitated. She occasionally borrowed Paris's shoes. But she and Misha weren't exactly close friends. Maggie was what bound them together.

"I'll text you my address," Misha continued. "Maybe after work on Monday?"

"Whatever works for you. I'm flexible. It doesn't have to be after office hours." A huge perk of working for herself was that Emilia could set her own schedule.

"Even better." Misha sounded happy. "Say two o'clock?"

"Sure. I can do that."

"Great. See you then! Bye, Emilia."

"Bye." Emilia ended the call.

"All done?" Nick appeared from behind her.

"All done." She handed back his phone. "Do you know why she called *you*?"

"It was about missing Kaitlin last night," he said easily. "Chase is back with the bagels."

"I'm curious why she didn't just call *me*." They stepped back into the kitchen.

"Maybe it's because I talked to her last night."

"You did? When?"

"While you were busy dancing with Sammy. She knows I invested in k!smet right out of the gate."

Emilia was surprised to hear that. Although, when she thought about it, it did make sense. Nick seemed to be running a successful software company. Why wouldn't he want to invest in what was looking more and more like a highly lucrative app?

"Everything bagel for Emilia," Chase said, setting them out on small plates. "Got a serrated knife?"

"Drawer at the far end," Paris answered as she put on another pot of coffee. "Cream cheese in the fridge."

"We also have blueberry, plain and asiago," Chase said as he hunted for the knife.

"So, she was schmoozing you," Emilia said to Nick.

"She's a smart businesswoman."

"You've got that right." It occurred to Emilia that she might want to get in on the k!smet action. It would be the first time she invested in a company instead of consulting for one. But who didn't appreciate passive income?

It was too bad that, unlike Nick, she hadn't thought of it on Friday morning when k!smet was first listed on the market.

* * *

Nico found his sister in a meeting room at k!smet HQ, walking in as some others filed out, leaving Misha alone at the oblong table.

She looked up with a guilty grin. "Sounds like I almost blew your cover with my phone call."

"Emilia saw your name come up on the screen, so I had to roll with it."

"Oops." Misha came to her feet, tucking her tablet under her arm. "I thought I recovered well about missing the interview."

"Yes. I also told her you were schmoozing me because I was an investor."

"You are an investor."

"I let her think I'd invested as soon as you opened the stock to the public." He moved with her toward the door that led to the hallway.

"Smart," she said with a considered nod. "I'm guessing you two didn't just happen to meet up somewhere for breakfast?"

He gave her a warning look as he opened the door.

"Purely a professional interest," she said airily. "You're both adults."

"That's right."

"But will the details be included in your written field test report?" She was smirking now.

"Not a chance. And there won't be a written field test report."

Her brows knit together in confusion. "I'm quite sure you agreed to submit a written report."

He knew he hadn't signed up for that kind of extra work. And he knew his sister. She was trying to corner him into something he hadn't agreed to.

He redirected the conversation. "Chase was there too. He spent the night with Emilia's roommate, Paris."

The interest in Misha's voice rose as she turned into her office space. *"Really."*

Nico waited until they'd passed by her admin assistant and entered the inner office. "Yes, he was."

"Both couples after the launch party? Nico, is there some secret, next-level coding in Surprise Me! that you didn't tell me about?"

Nico cracked a smile. "Emilia posed that same question. I wish I was that smart."

"You're plenty smart."

"Well, there's no next-level algorithm pushing logical matches and making them look random." He sat in one of the guest chairs while Misha settled behind the desk.

"Would you tell me if there was?" she asked. "Because I heard reports that another couple checked into a hotel after the party. Three out of ten is a whole lot more than random."

"Are you spying on the Surprise Me! couples?" Nico's thoughts went to his own privacy.

"Please. Royal's a small enough town. And the event was trending during the party. People see things. People tell me things."

The admin assistant appeared in the open doorway. "You have a message from Maggie Del Rio. She tried your cell while you were in the budget meeting."

"Is it urgent?"

"Something about the wedding."

"That might be urgent." Misha picked up her phone as her assistant walked away. "Did you see the share price today?" she asked Nico while the call rang through.

He shook his head.

She smiled and jabbed toward the ceiling with her thumb. "Hey, Maggie. What's up?" Misha paused, then her smile disappeared. "No way."

Nico came alert.

"Was there much damage?" She paused to listen.

He raised his brow in Misha's direction, hoping she'd let him know if Maggie was in trouble.

"Nothing you can do about a fire."

"A *fire*?" Nico mouthed on a whisper.

"Hang on. Nico's sitting here. A fire in the bakery kitchen," Misha said. "The one making Maggie's wedding cake."

"Anyone hurt?"

Misha shook her head. "You might have to look further afield," she said to Maggie. Then she grinned. "Yes, it would be."

Nico eased back. Clearly, it wasn't a life-and-death emergency.

"Definitely overkill," Misha said. "But I can't think of anyone local."

"JJ," Nico said, the idea jumping into his head.

Misha looked up. "What?"

"Not what, who. JJ Yeoh is Rafe's head chef over at RCW Steakhouse. His mom does specialty dessert catering."

"Could she do a wedding cake?"

"Maybe," Nico said. "She uses RCW's kitchen in their off hours."

Misha went back to the phone. "Nico has a line on someone local. You want us to reach out?" She listened again. "No. It's no trouble at all. Don't you worry about it. You have plenty to do." She paused. "I will." She paused again. "Okay. Bye."

"I'll call Rafe." Nico took out his phone.

"Maggie's shooting us the cake details in case JJ's mom can do it. But you usually book these things weeks if not months in advance."

"I'll tell JJ it's an emergency," he said and tapped Rafe's cell number and waited a few rings.

"Hey, Nico," Rafe answered, the clatter and voices of the restaurant kitchen a backdrop behind him. "What's up? You going riding with Emilia again?"

"No. At least not yet." Nico didn't want to say never on that. "I have a favor to ask."

"Ask away." The clatter faded as Rafe obviously left the kitchen.

"It's not for you specifically."

"Who?"

"JJ's mom."

"Are you throwing a party?"

"It's for Maggie's wedding. Her cake supplier fell through at the last minute."

Rafe whistled under his breath.

"Do you think Mrs. Yeoh could bake a wedding cake for Saturday?"

Misha's text pinged his phone, and Nico gave it a

read. "She calls it a southern hazelnut praline cake. I'm reading here. Vanilla cake with puff pastry layers, hazelnut liqueur, praline buttercream and dark chocolate shavings. There's a picture too—four tiers, classic white flowers with gold leaf and cupcakes, many, many cupcakes."

"Hey, JJ," Rafe called out.

Nico heard JJ's muted response.

"Nico needs an emergency wedding cake for Saturday. Think your mom would do it?" There was a pause. "I'm putting you both on speaker."

"Depends," JJ's voice joined the conversation. "Can you make it worth her while?"

Rafe chuckled.

"Absolutely," Nico said without hesitation. "Tell her to name her price." He caught Misha's grin and shrugged his shoulders. It was a wedding after all.

"Nico's got a picture and description," Rafe said.

"Send them over," JJ said.

"Thanks, man," Nico said with appreciation.

"No worries. I'm sure she'll do it. She's a sucker for romance. She won't gouge you either."

"I'm serious," Nico said. "Tell her to charge a premium for rush service."

"I will. But she won't."

"Coming at you," Nico said and sent the text.

"I'll call you after I talk to her," JJ responded and signed off.

"You're a good man," Misha said as he set down his phone.

"I'm not doing anything. It's Mrs. Yeoh that's a good woman."

"You think she'll say yes?"

"JJ thinks she will. He's going to call me back."

"Good." Misha nodded with satisfaction. "I feel like a worthy bridesmaid today." She paused. "With an outstanding team behind me. You have some very good friends."

Nico agreed. Implausible as it might have seemed at one time in his life. "Not bad for an ex-con."

Misha frowned. "You're not an ex-con."

"That's exactly what I am."

"We all know it wasn't your fault."

He shook his head in disagreement. "No. A few people know it wasn't my fault. The rest, well, all they know is what was said in court."

She looked thoughtful for a long moment. "Do you ever want to tell the truth? Let everybody know what really happened that night?"

Nico felt a surge of unease. "No. And you can't either."

"I won't."

"I'm serious, Misha. I will never, ever, *ever* mess up Dylan's life. I did my time, and it's over now."

"It's not over," she said softly. "You're practically in hiding."

"I'm not in hiding." But even as he protested, he knew it came too close to the truth. "I'm fine. It was worth it."

Misha looked unconvinced.

"It was the eve of his wedding, and his fiancée was five months pregnant."

Dylan had been drinking that night, and the other guy in the fight—a complete and utter jerk—more than had it coming. Plus, the fall and resulting head injury had been accidental.

"I know your rationale," Misha said. "But it should have been a night in jail or a few months' probation at most."

"But that's not the way it went." His voice came out harsher than he'd intended as he came to his feet. He tried not to dwell on the past but, every once in a while, it chafed Nico to recall how power and money had swayed the justice system and saddled him with a ridiculously harsh sentence.

"I'm saying it wasn't fair." She was right about that.

He moderated his tone. "And I'm saying it's in the past."

None of it, not the past or the present, was in any way Misha's fault. She'd stood by him when few others had, and he'd always be grateful for her love. He'd do anything for her, anytime, anywhere. "I'm also saying don't worry about it. I'd do it the same way all over again."

His friend Dylan and his wife had three little girls down in Austin now. He was an outstanding father with a wonderful family. When Nico found himself resenting the justice system, he thought about Dylan's life, and it eased the sting.

"You're a good man," she repeated.

"Saint Nico of wedding cake procurement," he joked.

She smiled. "It's not nothing."

"I just happened to think of the right person."

"Let me know when you hear back? I can't wait to give Maggie the good news."

"I'll call right away. You should get back to work. The shareholders are counting on you to make a profit."

She grinned. "Get out of here."

"Yes, ma'am. Love you, sis."

"I love you too."

"They absolutely loved the idea," Nick said to Emilia as they waited for their pizzas and drinks at Central Snacks, a take-out eatery on the town square, while taking a lunch break from filming.

"I thought we were going to edit the video before we showed anything to them." Emilia was unnerved by the idea of anyone getting the raw footage. Her delivery was improving, but she still stumbled on the odd sentence and had to redo parts of the workshop.

"I sent a few clips as samples." He took in her expression. "Don't worry. They were great. You looked very poised and very smart."

The young woman from the kiosk slid their pizza slices and soft drinks across the counter.

"So long as I don't look like an übergeek."

"You could never look like a geek. Can you carry the drinks?" Nick balanced the two oversize slices on their paper plates.

Central Snacks bordered on a small grassy area with picnic tables and shade trees, and they headed that way.

"I'm short, nerdy, wear glasses and talk about SQL and syntax. It's the very definition of a geek."

"You're not short." His grin gave away the fact that he was teasing her.

She rolled her eyes.

"And, like I said, I only sent the good clips."

They came to a vacant table and sat down.

"I better not find myself on the internet messing up the phrase 'compliant with multifaceted commitment capability.'"

He smiled, obviously remembering. "You did struggle with that one."

"I have trouble enunciating alliteration with multi-syllabic words." She paused, her eyes glittering with amusement. "I can't believe I just spit that out right the first time."

"I can. You're way too hard on yourself. You're human. Deal with it." He took a bite of his thick Chicago-style pizza.

"I don't like being human," she groused but couldn't keep the grin from her face. She knew she could be a perfectionist.

She took a bite. "Mmm." The crust was tender, the peperoni flavorful and the thick layer of cheese just the right amount of gooey.

"Meet your high standards?" he asked.

"Close to perfection."

"High praise. They deliver too."

"I'll have to remember that. Paris and I order from Trilby's downtown. It's good too, different, more conventional."

"You need to be hungry to do justice to Central Snacks." He took another big bite, chewed and swallowed. "Coders Plus is also excited about your name recognition."

Emilia took a drink of her cola. "I wish they wouldn't make a big deal about it being me. They should let the workshop content stand on its own."

"It will stand on its own. But you know how these things go. Branding is its own element, and notoriety drives traffic. Even if they downplayed that it was you, word would get out and cause a sensation." He paused. "You know, that might even be better—the news organically going viral. I'm going to suggest it to them."

"Don't oversell my reputation. It's not going to be a hackers' workshop. There'll never be one of those by me."

Emilia would never put her methods out in the world for anyone and everyone to see. Hacking responsibly was one thing. As she did...most of the time, with one notable recent exception. But she sure wouldn't give random strangers the knowledge and power to mess around in organizations' systems.

She sent a quick glance Nick's way, recalling again how she'd hacked her way into meeting him. It had seemed like a lark at the time. But now that she was getting to know him, getting to like him, hoping their relationship went somewhere from here, she was feeling guilty about how it had started.

"Not willing to give away your best tricks?" he asked.

"Not about to let that kind of knowledge loose in the world. Most people aren't trustworthy."

He frowned. "Most?"

She modified her answer. "Many."

"I'm curious," he said, looking thoughtful now. "What do you suppose makes a person untrustworthy?"

The question puzzled her because the answers were so obvious. "Ethics, values, conscience, behavior. If, for example, a greedy person lacks ethics, they might steal."

"Too bad you can't tell just by looking."

"People hide their true nature, especially if they're up to no good."

"They lie." He looked even more thoughtful.

"They might."

"About who they are."

"Or what they're planning." She took another bite of her cooling pizza.

"Or about what they've done."

She swallowed. "Past action is one of the best predictors of future behavior. So, sure. Why wouldn't you lie about robbing a bank if you planned to rob another one?"

"Do you think people are inherently good or bad?"

"You're getting awfully philosophical here."

It took him a moment to respond. "You make an interesting point about not trusting people."

"I trust plenty of people." She thought about the answer, then moderated it. "I trust some people. But I've seen some of the underhanded things people try online. Maybe that makes me fear the worst."

"Has it made you a cynic?"

"It's made me a realist. Clients hire me to look after their security. And, believe me, you have to plug every single little loophole in your system. Because if you don't, sure as heck, a bunch of people will exploit it for their own selfish gain."

"That sounds cynical. I mean, there are millions of people who won't exploit it."

"True. But I have to worry about the ones who will. So does everyone else in network security. So, there's no way I'm taking my hard-earned knowledge and accidentally teaching it to the bad guys."

She took a drink and a final bite of her pizza, too full to finish the entire thing.

"Do you think people can change?" he asked.

"Go from being a black hat hacker to being a white hat hacker? Maybe a few. But the moral makeup that led them to black hat hacking in the first place is hard to alter. If presented with the same circumstances again—" She gave a shrug. She'd never trust her tools and knowledge to someone who'd proven devious once. It was way too much of a risk.

Finished his pizza, he downed his soft drink. "What about the opposite?"

"Opposite of what?"

"Someone with a strong moral makeup who did something wrong one time and felt guilty about it."

She couldn't help comparing the question to her own situation. If not for her cheating the Surprise Me! function, Nick wouldn't be sitting here right now. She wished she dared come clean about that, but she wasn't brave enough to take the risk.

"It depends," she said.

"On what?" He seemed to study her as she framed her answer.

"Mostly on if anyone got hurt."

"What if hurting someone was accidental?"

There was something odd about his expression, and for a second she wondered if he knew she'd hacked into k!smet and forced their match. But he didn't look annoyed or even critical of her. It had to be something else.

She pondered the question.

If she took the position that accidental harm didn't matter, she'd be letting herself completely off the hook. She wasn't sure she should do that.

"Whoever took the unethical action should have foreseen the consequences. If they ignored them, then I'd say they should be held accountable." She was prepared to face the consequences of her hacking. At least she would be someday.

"You're a purist."

"I wouldn't call it that." Although she did try to hold herself to reasonable standards.

"Are you done here?" he asked abruptly, gathering up his plate, cup and paper napkin. "We should get back."

"Do you disagree with me?" She gathered up her trash. If he had a different perspective, she'd like to hear it.

He came to his feet. "Not necessarily."

"What does that mean? Take a stand, Nick."

He gazed into the distance. "It means sometimes situations get out of control and all you can do is ride out your mistake and make the best of it." He paused. "So people don't get hurt even further."

"Are you thinking of a specific situation?"

"No."

"Okay." She didn't have anything concrete to go on, but she couldn't shake the feeling something more was going on under the surface.

Eight

Nico took a back door into the kitchen at RCW Steak-house. He'd detoured on his way home to thank JJ for arranging Maggie's wedding cake. Maggie had been vastly relieved by the arrangement, and Misha was delighted to have taken a problem off the shoulders of the bride.

They were into the dinner rush, and JJ stood in his chef's uniform and hat in front of the long gas grill in the center of the big kitchen. The sizzle of steaks and sautéing vegetables combined with the clatter of pans and dishes as the kitchen staff efficiently moved around the kitchen preparing meals.

A spicy aroma was enticing to Nico, even though he'd had a huge slice of pizza just a few hours before.

"JJ?" Nico moved a little closer to the stove, careful to stay out of the way of the working staff members.

Waitstaff bustled in and out with meals and baskets of fragrant sourdough bread.

JJ smiled a greeting. "Hi, Nico."

"I wanted to thank you and your mom for agreeing to do the cake," Nico said.

JJ wiped his hands on a towel and gave an instruction to another chef before coming around the end of the stove.

He indicated a hallway off the kitchen, and the two men moved out of the way.

"Not a problem," JJ said. "She's excited to do it. I gave her Misha's contact information so they could talk directly."

"Misha's trying to keep Maggie out of the fray for these last few days. It sounds like there's plenty for a bride to worry about leading up to a big wedding."

The few stories Misha had told had Nico considering the merits of eloping. Not that he had any plans to get married. Not anytime soon anyway. He blinked away an unexpected vision of Emilia in a white dress.

"It sounds like the social event of the season," JJ said.

"The guest list is long." Nico had heard details on that as well.

"You're going?" JJ asked.

Nico nodded.

"Maggie sent my mom an invitation yesterday."

Nico was impressed by Maggie's gracious courtesy. "That's nice. Fitting."

"She asked me to be her plus one."

"Then, I guess I'll see you there."

JJ looked slightly uncertain. "Will it be excessively formal?"

"No more than any other wedding. A jacket and tie should be enough. At least, that's what I'm wearing." Nico didn't have an official role, so a tux sure wasn't necessary. And given how many people there could potentially recognize him, the more he blended with the crowd, the better.

"I can do a jacket and tie," JJ said with a relieved nod of his head.

A door opened at the end of the short hallway, and Rafe emerged from his office.

"I thought I heard your voice out here," he said to Nico.

"I better get back to it," JJ said with a nod to his boss.

"Thanks again," Nico called as JJ headed back to the kitchen.

"What's up?" Rafe asked.

"I wanted to thank JJ in person. It sounds like the wedding cake is well in hand."

"Mrs. Yeoh is the best. Trust me, the cake will be both spectacular and delicious."

"What more could a bride ask for?"

"How did it go at the party with Emilia?"

"Good." Nico automatically gave the polite answer. Then he considered that it was Rafe who was asking and decided to confess his growing discomfort. "It was mostly good. We did have an argument at one point."

"Uh-oh."

"The argument wasn't the problem."

"Want to come inside?" Rafe gestured to his open office door.

"Sure." Nico took him up on the invitation and followed him in.

Contrasting with the more traditional dusky tones of the dining room, Rafe's office was light and airy with cream-colored walls. His desk was honey oak with clean lines and a low-back chair faced by two light brown leather armchairs.

A bank of windows overlooked a lush greenbelt. It had grown dim outdoors. The sun hadn't set, but black clouds had rolled up the valley over the past couple of hours, and the first drops of rain now splattered against the windows.

Rafe bypassed the six-person meeting table, snagging a decanter of whiskey before sitting in one of four armchairs in the small conversation group around a low square table.

Nico joined him while Rafe poured the amber whiskey into two heavy cut crystal glasses.

"So what exactly was the problem?" Rafe asked, settling back with his drink as the rain fell harder outside.

"We made up after," Nico said, taking a sip and letting the warmth spread down his throat.

"Tragedy, that," Rafe joked.

"This whole thing, it was supposed to be a casual date." Nico framed his concern. "The plan was for a no-strings, Surprise Me! date with a woman who, let's face it, I expected to be—" he searched for the right words "—offbeat, quirky, unsuitable. k!smet is supposed to make the good matches. Surprise Me! shakes things up. I should know. I wrote the code. It wasn't supposed to find me—"

"The perfect woman?"

"She's not perfect." But even as he protested, Nico realized he was selling Emilia short. He was hard-pressed to think of anything about her that wasn't top-notch. "Not perfect for me anyway."

"I don't get it," Rafe said. "So, she's great. What's the problem?"

"We've had two dates. Plus, we're collaborating on a video project. We've slept together—more than once." It sounded even more perfect as he listed things off. So, he got to the crux of the matter. "She doesn't know who I really am."

Rafe frowned. "You mean she doesn't know about your prison sentence?"

Nico shook his head. "And that's not all."

"Does she know you own AlgoXcell?"

"Not the name of the company. She only knows I develop software." Nico paused. "And she doesn't know about Misha. She still thinks my name is Nick—no last name." Thinking about that, he realized it was miraculous the question hadn't come up.

Rafe sat back. "When are you going to tell her the truth?"

"That's the thing. I hadn't planned on telling her at all, so I don't have a go-forward plan for this." Nico downed half his drink and rose to pace across the office. He'd expected to be on to the next date by now, rerunning Surprise Me! To find a new match and gather more real-world data.

"You can stick with plan A and cut it off."

Cutting things off with Emilia was the last thing Nico wanted to do.

"I can see you don't like that idea," Rafe said, sounding amused.

"Even if I did—" which Nico did *not* "—she's one of Maggie's bridesmaids."

Rafe whistled low, and thunder rumbled in the distance as if to punctuate the problem.

Nico sat glumly down as a bright flash of lightning reflected off the facets of his crystal glass.

"So then tell her who you are and take it from there."

"Tell her I'm an ex-con who lied to her?" Nico could imagine exactly how that would go. "She has a thing about ethics and mistakes, and she's not big on second chances."

"It's either plan A or plan B. There is no plan C where you stay with her and don't tell her. But you know that."

Nico did know that. But he wanted a plan C. He badly wanted an option where Emilia learned who he was without walking away. "There has to be a solution."

Rafe counted on his fingers. "A, you tell her who you are. B, you don't. The chips are going to fall where they fall."

"I want the chips to fall where I want them to fall."

"So, plan A, subsection one? That's going to be dastardly hard to pull off."

"But not impossible?" Nico asked hopefully.

"I don't know, Nico. I get what you want here. But

if you don't want to hurt her, your best bet might be to walk away and leave it all as a happy memory."

Nico hated that Rafe might be right.

Just then lightning lit up the sky, and a split second later thunder vibrated the room.

Both men looked to the window where the rain was pouring down.

"That looks serious," Rafe said.

"I hope Aspen Street doesn't flood again."

"Are you driving your pickup?"

Nico nodded. It had been a toss-up between his sedan and the pickup truck this morning. Thankfully, he'd gone with the three-quarter ton. It had significantly more clearance if the storm drains overflowed.

The lights in the room dimmed, then went dark. Silence rose as the ventilation system powered down. A split second later, lightning lit everything up, and thunder vibrated above them.

Rafe turned on his flashlight app while Nico rose to peer out the window.

"See anything out there?" Rafe asked.

"Power's out in every direction." Nico couldn't see so much as a distant light down the valley.

The office door opened, and JJ appeared carrying an industrial-size flashlight. "Everything okay in here?" he asked.

"We're fine," Rafe answered. "What's happening in the dining room?"

"We're adding extra candles to the tables. We're comping drinks and offering any menu item we can grill over the gas."

"Good." Rafe came to his feet.

"Some parties are ready to leave," JJ said. "Not many have cash."

"Don't worry about it," Rafe said. "Until the power is back, send them home with a discounted bill and our accounting email address. If a few don't pay up, we'll live with it."

"How can I help?" Nico asked.

"Can you escort people to their cars?" JJ asked Nico.

"Not a problem."

"I'll set you up with a flashlight and a high-vis vest."

Although the blackout was an inconvenience to Rafe's customers and everyone else in Royal, Nico would take the temporary distraction from Emilia. He didn't like any of the options reality offered for their relationship, but time was forcing him to settle on something.

Candlelight flickering in the dark room behind her, Emilia watched the lightning storm from her window. She'd turned an armchair to give herself a better view and poured a glass of chardonnay before the fridge had a chance to warm up.

Paris was out with Chase, and Emilia would be shocked to see her before morning. Who wouldn't want to snuggle up with a hot guy on a pitch-dark stormy night?

The image sent her thoughts to Nick and where he might be right now. She imagined him here with her and smiled around her sip of wine. Her bed might be compact, but they'd fit fairly comfortably in it last time, their limbs tangled together under her thick comforter.

She picked up her phone, tempted to call him and see if he'd join her. But she hesitated, her thumb hovering over his name.

How could she ask him to drive on the flooding roads? According to social media, conditions were deteriorating fast. The citizens of Royal were being advised to shelter in place for the next few hours.

She set down her phone and settled more deeply into the soft armchair as lightning bolts reflected off the wet street below and thunder rattled the windowpanes. The rain grew harder still, fat drops falling thick and fast, sheeting their way down the glass.

It was too early to go to sleep, so she decided on reading a book. Her corner bookcase was full of mysteries, adventures and biographies—most of which she hadn't read in years.

She took the brightest candle to check out the shelves. She didn't want anything frightening. Not that she was afraid of storms. But blackouts were a little bit unnerving, especially when the old house creaked and groaned around her.

A biography seemed best. She located the glossy hardcover bio of a famous comedienne and decided it was a good bet.

Book under her arm and candle in hand, she returned to the chair and spread a knitted afghan across her legs. As she opened the first pages, the house rumbled again. Then it creaked louder, odd-sounding groans coming from the lower floors.

She told herself to chill. She was in a loft in downtown Royal, not in a horror movie. The aliens were not about to emerge from pods in Paris's bedroom. Emilia focused on the birth and bucolic early childhood of the comedienne.

A sudden loud metallic bang had her sitting up straight, her skin going cold then hot.

There was no way that was the house settling.

She sat frozen, waiting, listening intently.

Something clunked. It clunked again, then again, continuing rhythmically.

She forced herself to her feet, turning on her phone flashlight and walking shakily to the top of the stairs.

The rhythmic clunking continued.

"Paris?" she tried, but her voice came out low and raspy. "Paris?" she tried louder.

She hovered at the top of the stairs for a full five minutes before she convinced herself to go investigate. She'd seen enough horror movies to know it was a bad idea for the young woman to check out the strange noise all alone, but she didn't have any better ideas. She couldn't just stand here all night and be afraid.

She took the stairs one at a time, pausing after each one to listen. The noise remained the same, neither speeding up nor slowing down, and there were no more sudden bangs.

She made it to the main floor and looked in the kitchen and living room. Lightning flashed and lit the room. Nothing looked out of place. The sound was behind her now, in the stairwell leading down to Paris's room on the lower floor.

Emilia lit two more candles, setting them on the side

table in the foyer so she'd have some light to come back to.

She took a deep breath and started down the stairs.

Halfway there, she spotted the problem. At first, she breathed a sigh of relief. But then she picked up her pace, realizing the seriousness of the problem. The wood floor of the landing was under six inches of water.

Shocked and worried, Emilia stepped gingerly into the cold water. It came up to her midcalf, soaking her socks and the bottom of her yoga pants. Gritting her teeth, she rounded a corner and shone her light around the room.

Water was gushing under the back door, filling the room at a frightening rate. A chair had been caught in the current and tipped over. It was banging back against a wooden table leg.

At least it wasn't killer aliens.

Then again, the water might be worse. Given the slope of the backyard and the rate of the downpour, the flood was only going to get deeper.

Realizing her phone was in her hand, Emilia pressed Paris's contact.

It rang and went to voice mail, and Emilia cursed under her breath.

As the water crept up her legs, she brought up their landlord's number and called.

This time, she got an out-of-service message. She shouldn't have been surprised that the circuits were overloaded.

Refocusing the flashlight beam, she went for Paris's electronics first, taking her laptop and tablet upstairs to safety. It was awkward and slow going since she needed one hand for the flashlight. She could only carry so much at a time.

She made several more trips with some of Paris's designer clothes, then rescued her jewelry box.

Realizing the flood was getting out of hand, she tried Paris again. Having no luck, she retried the landlord. Beginning to feel frantic, she dialed 911 but was put on hold. Having second thoughts about the urgency of her situation, she hung up. There were likely people with medical and other emergencies that needed emergency services more than she did.

She pulled up her recent call list and saw Nick's name. Experiencing an unaccountable feeling of relief at the thought of talking to him, she placed the call.

It rang through.

"Emilia?" he answered.

"Nick? Oh, thank goodness." She tried not to sound needy and relieved, but she was.

"What's wrong?"

"We're flooding," she said. "Paris is out, and her room is just filling up with water."

"Where are you?"

"In her room. I got her tablet and computer, her jewelry and some of her clothes, but—"

"How deep in the water?"

She looked down at the blackness. "It's over my knees now and rising."

"You're standing in it?"

"Yes."

"Get out. Go upstairs. Don't worry about saving her things. I'm on my way."

"I don't think you should drive," Emilia said. "They're telling people to stay off the roads."

"I'm coming to you."

"Nick—" She stopped talking. She didn't even know what she wanted him to say or do. She just didn't want to feel so completely alone.

"I'm in my truck," he said. "I have plenty of clearance. I'm on my way. Go *upstairs*."

"Okay," she agreed, knowing she couldn't do much more down here. The water seemed to be rising faster by the minute.

As she started for the stairs, her phone light began to fade. "Oh, no."

"Oh, no, what?" Nick asked sharply.

She cracked her knee against something and stumbled in slow motion. She gasped and flailed her arms, dropping her phone and plunging the room into darkness as she fell into the water.

Panic rose in her throat before subsiding just as quickly.

Even sitting down her head was well above water. The stairway was over to her right. The dresser was straight in front of her, and as her eyes adjusted, she could see the faint flicker of the candles she'd lit in the main floor foyer. She pulled herself to her feet and walked forward.

Nico sped through the blacked-out streets of Royal, ploughing through rivulets and splashing through deep puddles that had settled on the pavement around the overflowing storm drains. As he drove, he redialed Emilia's phone over and over. He couldn't shake a dreadful image of her down and hurt, the water rising around her.

Traffic lights were out, so he barely slowed down for the intersections. He passed a few emergency vehicles and several others who, like him, had high clearance, four-wheel drive vehicles designed for rural ranch roads.

Emilia's house was in the lower part of downtown, and the flooding was deeper there. He was driving through a shallow canal by the time he made it to her house.

He parked on the street and rushed through inches of water to the stairs. The terrain sloped away, leaving the backyard as the low spot. With his flashlight he could see the flow of water rounding the corner of the house and draining to the back.

"Emilia?" he called out as he mounted the front stairs. He rattled the doorknob, but it was locked.

"Emilia?" he called louder, stepping back to kick his way in.

But the door swung open, revealing Emilia. She was wet and disheveled, the glow of candlelight flickering behind her. But she was clearly fine. She was standing there in front of him safe and sound.

He stepped forward, pulled her into his embrace, lifting her feet off the ground and holding her there, waiting for the dreadful image to leave his mind.

"You're okay," he whispered hoarsely.

"I dropped my phone," she said against his neck.

He couldn't bring himself to let her go.

"It's in the water," she added.

"We'll get you a new one."

She gave a little laugh. "We'll have to, I think. I seriously doubt it's salvageable."

"I thought you were hurt," he said, setting her slowly down and loosening his hug.

"I banged my knee. I think it's bruised."

"Does it hurt?"

"Only a little."

"I guess we can live with a bruise," he said and gave her a gentle kiss on the forehead.

"Can you try to get through to Paris?" Emilia disentangled herself and stepped back. "She's with Chase somewhere. I tried and tried to call her earlier."

"Hopefully they're high and dry. Do you know her number?"

Emilia scrunched up her expression for a second. "I haven't memorized it, no."

He knew there was nothing Paris could do right now in any case. "Why don't you show me the damage?"

"Downstairs is a disaster. Water is pouring in under the back door."

"Everything's draining to the back."

"It's an ugly mess." They used his flashlight app as she led the way down the stairs.

Nico was shocked as he looked around at the flotilla of Paris's belongings. "Has this ever happened before?"

"Never as far as I know. We've only lived here for six months."

"You're renters, right?" He was fairly sure on that.

"Yes."

"At least you won't get stuck with the repairs." From what he could see, they were going to be extensive. "Is there anything else I can save from here?"

Emilia frowned as she looked around the sopping room. "The rest of her clothes in her closet, maybe. At least the ones that are still above water. She has some expensive outfits. But the bed, the dresser, the desk. It's all going to be ruined."

"Do you expect her home tonight?"

"Not anymore. Wherever they are, I'm sure they'll stay put."

"Maybe. But Chase is a rancher at heart. He probably drives a capable vehicle."

"We could try emailing her. I know her address. Then again, she might not want to find out about all this until tomorrow."

He agreed. "There's nothing she can do tonight except worry."

They waded across the room and gathered armloads of Paris's clothes and stacked them in the living room. Afterward, they headed to the relative sanctuary of the top floor.

Emilia was soaking wet and starting to shiver.

"You need to get out of these wet things." He tugged her sweater over her head.

"It looks like it's ruined," she noted, frowning at the misshapen knit.

"Worry about that later." He stripped off her T-shirt and wet bra.

She sat down in an armchair and he draped an afghan around her shoulders. She held it close while he worked her out of the rest of her clothes.

"We should get into bed," he said.

"You're propositioning me?" She sounded incredulous through her chattering teeth.

"Only to warm you up," he answered dryly, then urged her to standing and sent her in the right direction.

"I thought you were telling me disasters turned you on," she said over her shoulder.

"I'm telling you your goose bumps and teeth chattering do not."

She gave a short laugh at that as he helped her under the covers.

He pulled off his boots and his own wet clothes, then climbed in beside her, pulling her icy body against his warmth.

"How can you possibly be so warm?" she asked with a quaver in her voice.

"You've been wet longer than me."

"Still." She pressed tight against him. "This feels so good."

"It does," he agreed. Now that the danger was over and she was warming in his arms, he was getting turned on. How could he not?

He made sure there were no gaps in the covers, then rubbed up and down her arm to promote the circulation.

"So, where were you?" she asked, her voice sounding normal again. "When I called."

"On my way home from RCW. I helped Rafe safely clear the customers."

"I can't even imagine the impact of the blackout,

never mind the flood." Concern came into her voice. "What about your place?"

"Don't worry about me." He kissed the back of her neck.

"You haven't been home to check. What if there's a flood at your place?"

"There's not."

"Are you psychic?"

"No. I'm on the upper floor of a concrete building."

"How high?"

"Eighth."

She turned her head, looking surprised in the dim candlelight. "So, you're right in the downtown core?"

"I am."

"I didn't know that."

She didn't know that because he hadn't told her anything about where he lived. He was afraid to give away any personal details.

"Which building?" she asked.

He didn't want to say. He didn't want to lie, but he didn't want to give away his address either.

"Nick?" she asked, searching his expression.

"Are you warming up?" he asked, hoping to distract her. "Getting hungry or thirsty?"

She stilled, going alert. "You don't want to tell me where you live?"

"It's near Whitmore and Green. Nothing exciting— a tall, concrete thing a few blocks from the library."

"Well, that was vague."

"How was it vague?"

"You didn't give me the address."

"Are you mailing me a letter?" He kissed her nearest cheek, working his way over to her lips, partly to distract her, but mostly because he wanted to kiss her.

But she wouldn't let it go. "It's like you're living a mysterious life."

"My place is not mysterious. It's boring, utilitarian and uninviting. Plus, it still smells of paint."

"Can I see it?"

"Sure." He'd make sure to delay her visit for as long as humanly possible. "But I warn you, I'm not much of a decorator or entertainer for that matter. The place is a bit embarrassing."

"Compared to my place?" she asked, gesturing around the compact room.

"I like your place. It's charming." He turned her in his arms, dropping his voice to a whisper. "Charming, beautiful and very, very sexy when you warm up."

"Flattery?" she asked with an arched brow.

"Honesty." He gathered her close and slanted his mouth to hers, kissing her with both desire and gratitude. He was still thankful she was safe.

"Really?" she asked when his hands began to wander. "In the midst of a disaster?"

"It's only a minor disaster," he said. "The house can be fixed. Possessions can be replaced. You're safe. We're safe. Besides—" he kissed her again, more deeply this time "—what else are we going to do?"

She laughed at the question. "Smooth talker."

"I hope so. I was afraid back there when your phone went dead and I was still five minutes away. You scared me, Emilia. I am so glad to have you safe in my arms."

"I can tell," she said on a note of humor, pressing meaningfully against him.

"You're going to tease me?" he asked in mock offense. "I'm baring my soul, and you're going to tease me?"

"I was only bruised."

"I know."

"And cold and wet."

"Are you warm now?" He slipped his hand to her breast.

"Oh, yeah," she said breathlessly, squirming a little.

He gave a low chuckle. "Good."

She kissed him deeply then, and her hands went on an exploration of their own, building a private storm of passion between them.

Nine

The citizens of Royal cleaned up after the storm with the efficiency of a town founded by ranchers, with their abundance of heavy equipment helping the effort. A day later, the water had drained off and most of the debris had already been shoveled or swept away.

With Paris's bedroom out of commission, Chase had invited her to stay at his family's big ranch house twenty minutes outside the city. He'd graciously extended the offer to Emilia too, but her suite was undamaged, and the kitchen was still functional, so she opted to stay in the house rather than impose on strangers.

Located on higher ground, the TCC clubhouse had been spared any flooding, and a joint Del Rio–Winters press conference about the heirloom necklace was going ahead as planned. Reporters from both legacy and on-

line media had crowded into the main meeting room.
There was interest in the artifact itself and in the mul-
tigenerational family feud from all across the state of
Texas and beyond.

"Will we get a close-up look at the necklace?" Emilia
asked Misha in a low tone.

The two bridesmaids were attending the event as
moral support for Maggie. Although the feud between
the two families was officially over, there was still some
tension in the air, made more acute by the presence of
local and national press.

The reporters and cameras were clustered close to
the velvet ropes that cordoned off the family members
and kept people back from the Del Rio heirloom necklace. It sat in a position of prominence in a glass display case, carefully watched over by a security guard.

Patriarch Fernando Del Rio III had given a short
speech, and it was now Joseph Winters's turn to talk
about the necklace being loaned for display at the Museum of Fine Arts in Houston.

The Winters family members—current matriarch
Camille, and children Jericho, Trey, Alisha, Marcus
and Tiffany—fanned out on the left-hand side of the
podium. While Del Rio matriarch Gail stood next to her
husband along with Maggie and her brother, Preston.

"I think we can go up and take a look after the
speeches are over," Misha said.

"Even from here, it's gorgeous." Emilia stood on her
toes for a better look at the gemstones that sparkled
under the lights against black velvet.

The infamous and beautiful gemstone necklace had

been stolen years ago by Eliza Winters. She left fiancé Fernando Del Rio for Teddy Winters and ignited the family feud. Now it was proving a symbol of the reconciliation.

It was made mostly of diamonds but interspersed with rubies and emeralds, making it even more magnificent, not to mention unique. Emilia tried to imagine having such a priceless heirloom connected to her family. She didn't have so much as a photo of her parents, never mind anything of value passed down through the generations.

"Has it been appraised, do you think?" Emilia wondered out loud. She couldn't even begin to guess at the worth of the gemstones, never mind the value of the provenance behind them.

"They must have done it for insurance at least," Misha answered. "What do you think? Tens of thousands? Hundreds?"

"It makes me want to go jewelry shopping and start my own dynasty," Emilia said with a grin, thinking she'd have to start from scratch.

While Misha chuckled at the joke, Emilia imagined a baby in her arms. The picture gave her a warm glow. After all, if she had a baby of her own, for the first time in her life there'd be someone else in the world with her genealogy.

Disconcertingly, she imagined Nick standing beside her.

Maybe that wasn't such a surprise. After all, he'd charged in to rescue her from danger during the flood. That probably made him look like good father material.

Realistically, she hadn't been in any actual danger. She'd been anxious, more worried about the house than her own safety. Still. He had rushed to her side, given her moral support and helped her get dry and warm. She felt a flush rise in her cheeks when she remembered exactly how warm he'd made her feel.

They'd slept in her small bed again that night. He'd gone out for coffee and croissants in the morning and waited for Paris to come home to see the damage. There was something noble about his insistence on staying by Emilia's side for the aftermath.

And that's where her feelings grew complicated. She felt guilty for holding back the truth from him, and she knew she had to come clean. She had to tell him she'd cheated the Surprise Me! function by hacking into the algorithm. She had to tell him she wasn't his real match, and their being together was all based on a lie.

Part of her wished he wasn't so noble.

The crowd broke into applause, startling her, and she realized the speeches were over.

"Well, that's a satisfying ending to generations of anger and grief," Misha said.

"Absolutely," Emilia agreed, even though she'd missed most of Joseph Winters's speech.

"Maggie looks relieved."

Jericho had moved to Maggie's side, put an arm around her and whispered something in her ear. She smiled, and he planted a light kiss on her temple.

"He's one of the good ones," Misha said. "Almost as good as Trey."

Misha's boyfriend, Trey, was sending her an intimate smile across the room.

Emilia's thoughts turned back to her own romantic life.

"What do you think about Nick?" she asked Misha.

Misha seemed taken aback by the question. "In what way?"

"I don't know. In the usual way. Does he strike you as a good guy?"

"Uh…sure. He does. Why?" For some reason, Misha looked uncomfortable with the line of questioning.

"We've gone out a few times." Emilia rephrased her point. "Well, two official dates. But we're also doing an online tech workshop for Coders Plus, so we're spending a lot of time together working on that."

"Wait, what?" Misha seemed unexpectedly shocked by the news.

"I'm doing the workshop delivery on camera. Nick is helping to script it. I get the feeling he's camera shy."

"He didn't say anything to me about doing a workshop."

It was Emilia's turn to be confused. Why would Nick have told Misha about the workshop?

"Are k!smet investors supposed to be exclusive?" Emilia asked. It was the only plausible reason she could come up with for Misha's strange reaction to the project.

"No. That's not—"

"*Hey*, you *two*." A grinning Maggie appeared and put an arm around each of them. "I'm so glad you're both here."

"Wouldn't miss it," Misha answered with a bright smile.

"Me neither," Emilia echoed.

Maggie looked to Emilia. "I hear your first floor flooded out. I hope it wasn't too bad."

"My roommate, Paris, got it the worst. It's her room that's on the lower floor."

"Was it really bad?" Maggie asked, looking concerned.

"A couple of feet of water. We couldn't rescue much of her stuff. She's staying with Chase's family for a while."

"I didn't know it was that bad," Misha put in.

"Bad enough." Emilia guessed the cleanup and repairs would take a week or more.

"What about you?" Maggie asked.

"My place is fine. I have the high ground in the house."

"You're living in a flooded house?"

"Sure. The cleanup crews are noisy, and they had to shut off the heat and water for a while yesterday, but—"

"You can't stay there while it's under repair," Maggie said with conviction. "Come over to my parents' place."

Emilia was taken aback by the generosity of the invitation. "I couldn't do that. I barely know them. I couldn't impose."

"It's not an imposition. They've got tons of room. We were going to make a girls' weekend of it anyway. I'll just move there a couple of days early and keep you company. It'll do Jericho good to miss me for a few nights." She waggled her brow. "Before the honeymoon."

Emilia had to admit she was tempted by the offer. The repair crew had warned her they'd have to turn off the heat and water a few more times before they finished. She hadn't looked forward to that.

Maggie read her expression. "It's settled then. We'll pick up your stuff when this thing is over."

Misha spoke up. "Emilia was just asking me about Nick."

There was an odd note in her voice that Emilia couldn't identify.

An equally odd expression crossed Maggie's face. "Asking what about Nick?"

"She's been seeing a lot of him since the matchup," Misha said.

"You like him?" Maggie asked.

"Sure, I like him." Emilia wouldn't be spending so much time with him if she didn't.

"Is it turning into something more?" Maggie asked.

Emilia wasn't sure how to answer that. They hadn't known each other very long, but her feelings for him were growing. There was no denying it.

"You don't really know him all that well, do you?" Misha asked.

"We've packed a lot into a couple of dates and a few days." Emilia had seen Nick in a wide range of situations: on at date, in bed, at work, coming to her rescue.

"They've been working together," Misha said.

Maggie arched a brow. "Working?"

"We're doing an online database development workshop."

"Nico's going on camera?" Maggie sounded astonished.

Emilia wondered why Maggie would use a nickname for Nick.

"Emilia's going on camera," Misha said. "*Nick* is behind the scenes."

"Oh. Right. Of course. That's makes more sense."

"He struck you as camera shy too?" Emilia asked Maggie, wondering if there was something about him that gave off that vibe.

"I told her that he ducked the interview at the IPO launch party," Misha put in.

"He didn't duck it," Emilia corrected. "We tried to find the camera crew a couple of times."

"Oh," Misha responded. "Okay, sure. My mistake."

Maggie spoke up again. "You might want to take things slow with him."

"Who says I'm taking them fast?" Emilia asked. The conversation was getting very strange.

"Good," Maggie said. "That's good to hear. The thing with men is, they don't always reveal themselves early on."

Misha nodded her agreement. "They hold things back. Sometimes they have good reasons, but still…"

Both women were watching Emilia intently.

"Are you worried about something in particular?" Emilia wondered if she'd missed something about Nick that her friends could see.

"No, no." They spoke quickly and overtop of each other.

"We like him," Maggie added.

"He's fundamentally a good guy," Misha said.

"Fundamentally?" Emilia asked, wondering if she should do some online sleuthing into Nick. So far, she'd been purposefully respecting his privacy, not wanting to use her unique skills to take a deep dive. But now she realized she'd never even learned his last name, or the name of his company for that matter.

Misha must know both since he was a k!smet investor.

Emilia opened her mouth to ask, but then realized how embarrassing the question would be. Who slept with a man without knowing his last name?

Even worse, it was probably too late to ask Nick himself.

"What exactly are you doing with Emilia?" Misha asked as Nico opened his apartment door to greet her.

He didn't understand the question. "In what way?"

Surely, she wasn't asking about his sex life.

"In every way." She breezed past him.

"None of your business." He shut the door behind her.

"You know she's a friend."

"And? How does that mean you get to invade our privacy?"

"You're stringing her along, and—"

"I am not stringing her along." He took offense at the accusation and headed back into his home office to finish an urgent email. "Where are you getting your information?"

"From Emilia."

Nico whirled around. "What did she say?"

"It sounds like you two have been joined at the hip."

He thought back to the last time they were together. "Her house was flooding. She needed help. What was I supposed to do?"

Misha's lips pursed, and she canted her head to one side. "You were with her in the flood?"

Nico realized his mistake. He silently cursed and sat down to type the email. "What is it you were asking about?"

"The workshop. She said the two of you are filming a tech workshop?"

"Coders Plus has been asking me for a while." He typed the answer to the last question from his client.

"And now you're doing it with Emilia? *Nico*," Misha admonished.

"Can you give me a second?" The Australian client needed an answer before trading opened on their stock market.

She stopped talking, and he heard her walk to a chair and sit down.

He typed while she inhaled a long-suffering breath.

"I'm almost done," he said.

"I'm not complaining."

He smiled grimly. "Of course, you're not."

She waited a few moments longer. "Take your time."

"It's work," he said.

"I know."

He added a quick disclaimer and an invitation to follow up with any questions, signed off and hit send.

Then he swiveled the chair to face his sister. "Did you come all the way over here to ask about Emilia?"

"I want to know what you have planned with her."

He answered with a shrug. He honestly didn't know what he had planned. He hadn't expected to like her this much.

"Two dates is one thing," Misha said.

"I know. But she was great in the workshop. And with her hacker cachet, students are going to sign up in droves."

"And you were her knight in shining armor in the flood?"

"She called me." Sure, she'd told him later that she tried a bunch of other people first. Still, she had reached out to him when she was in trouble. He liked that.

"And that's not a warning sign?"

"That she thinks I'm a capable man?"

"That's she's falling for you."

Nico digested Misha's words.

Was Emilia falling for him? He was sure as heck falling for her. Which left him in a tricky position with hard choices to make.

"Your previous criminal record notwithstanding," Misha said, "I know you're a good guy. And I know you know the right thing to do in this situation."

She was right. He did. He didn't like it, but he did know what it was.

"I'm procrastinating," he admitted.

She looked sympathetic as she nodded.

"I have to be ready for her to walk away." He paused. "I'm not ready for that, at least not yet."

He missed Emilia. It had been less than two days since he saw her, and he already missed her. He wanted to spend as much time as he possibly could with her while she still liked him, while she still looked at him with fondness and admiration.

For the first time in his life, he questioned his decision to protect Dylan that night.

"Don't wait too long," Misha said.

"I won't."

"A couple of dates is one thing."

"I know, I know. You just said that." He was exasperated with the situation, not Misha.

If the Surprise Me! match had gone according to plan, Nico would be on his second or third matchup by now. But he couldn't imagine dating anyone but Emilia.

He gave a chopped laugh. "Guess I didn't turn out to be much good at collecting data for k!smet."

Misha looked sympathetic now. "I don't know about that. This is kind of interesting."

"The Surprise Me! function isn't supposed to work this way," he said.

"What way is that?"

"You know, Emilia talked about the possibility of secret artificial intelligence embedded in a dating app algorithm that did a deep dive on social media and found compatibilities that weren't apparent on the surface." He chuckled to himself again. "Imagine that? A funny, fascinating, beautiful woman who also analyzes technology with that level of depth?"

"Does Surprise Me! work that way?" Misha asked.

He shook his head. "I wish I was smart enough to code something that sophisticated. It takes a genius level to even contemplate it with any level of technical complexity."

"You're not a genius? I'm disappointed in you, brother."

"Not that much of a genius."

"Genius enough." She nodded toward the computer screens behind him. "Take a look at the k!smet share price."

He turned to the graph on the right-hand screen. The price had shot up right before the daily stock market close.

"Nice," he said.

"You're genius enough for me," she repeated, rising to give him an affectionate hug around the neck.

"That's more you than me," he said, hugging her back. "k!smet is mostly your work, your vision, your execution."

"But look at how much fun people had with Surprise Me! That's all you, bro."

"Fun," Nico repeated with an edge of sarcasm. At the moment, it didn't feel like much fun at all.

"Would you rather not have met her?" Misha asked.

Nico shook his head. "I'd rather not be an ex-convict."

"Too late for that. She's staying at Maggie's, by the way."

He pulled back to look at Misha. "She is?"

"Until the wedding. Because of the flood. The repairs are noisy, and they had to turn off the water and the furnace."

Guilt and regret hit Nico.

If he wasn't lying to her, if he wasn't hiding who he was, he could have invited her here. He'd love to have her stay here with him just as long as she wanted.

The workshop editing had taken hours and hours, but Emilia was happy with the final product. Coders Plus had done a prelaunch marketing blitz and garnered a solid number of registrations.

They uploaded the workshop in Nick's office and sat back in satisfaction as it went live.

"Well, that's that," she said and rose from her chair.

"I have a feeling it's only the start," he said, nodding to the screen.

They had creator access to the workshop, so they could watch any activity on it.

"Why?" she said, following the direction of his gaze.

The registration numbers were climbing by ones, and then by tens.

She sat back down. "What is happening?

"My guess? People are reading the syllabus and signing up."

"That fast? Seriously?"

"We just hit one hundred."

"Who *are* all these people?"

"You have fans." He wrapped an arm around her shoulders, chuckling low and planting a kiss on her temple. "I'm a fan."

"I hope they're not disappointed." A moment ago

she'd been happy with the workshop, but now she felt a surge of trepidation.

She was having second thoughts. Had she made the concepts clear enough? Would people be able to learn from her style of teaching? Students were encouraged to leave reviews after completing Coders Plus courses. Was she tough enough to hear their criticisms?

She'd always taken risks as a hacker. But her hacking efforts were private. If she messed something up, nobody ever found out. But this, this was about as public as she could get.

"They're not going to be disappointed," Nick spoke low in her ear.

"I'm having second thoughts."

He gave her a squeeze. "Success gives you second thoughts?"

"This isn't success."

"Sure, it is."

"Students finding the workshop valuable will be success. This is just curiosity."

"You hungry?"

"Not really." She was too nervous now to even think about anything else.

He reached for his phone. "I'm going to order something. Did you like the Thai food?"

"It was fine," she answered absently before realizing she was insulting the restaurant. "It was good."

The numbers on the registration field kept climbing.

"I'm feeding you," he said, then stilled. "That's two hundred. You're definitely going to need your strength."

She reached for the mouse and shrank the window. "I have to stop watching. This is freaking me out."

He flashed a lascivious grin and leaned close again. "I have another suggestion."

"I need to get going."

He drew back in what looked like surprise and disappointment. "Where?"

"To Maggie's. I'm staying there until the wedding."

"I know."

"You know? How can you know?"

Discomfort flickered in his expression. "Misha mentioned it."

"You talked to Misha…again?" Emilia felt a ripple of jealousy.

"About the investment," he said, but something in his voice didn't ring true.

Emilia rolled her chair back and stood, unease building in her chest. "Is there something I should know?"

"About what?" His voice was even, but there was a look of guilt in his eyes.

"About you and Misha. Is something happening between the two of you?"

"No. *No!* That's ridiculous. Misha is with Trey Winters."

"That's a lot of protesting you're doing, Nick." Emilia knew Misha was dating Trey. She also thought Misha was trustworthy. But something was going on here, and she'd be foolish to ignore the signs.

"I'm not protesting." He paused and seemed to regroup. "Okay, I am protesting. But I'm protesting because you've got it all wrong."

"Okay," she challenged. "So, tell me what's right."

"I'm an investor," he said. "I'm a big investor, and she wants to keep in touch."

The explanation made sense on its face. But if the rising share price was anything to go by, Misha had a lot of big investors. Was she keeping in such close touch with all of them? And why did Nick look so guilty?

"You're lying about something," Emilia said with conviction, hoping to bluff him into telling her what was really going on.

"Not about that," he said.

She was surprised he'd as much as admitted his dishonesty.

"About what then?"

His expression softened. "I'm not lying. Sure, I'm not sharing every single thing about myself just yet. But are you?"

His question hit home.

There was still the matter of her hacking the algorithm to get matched with him in the first place. She hadn't told him that yet.

Should she?

Would she?

After all, what were the minor details of his investment life compared to that big of an omission?

"What?" he prompted. "I can see the wheels turning inside your head."

"They're not turning."

He rose and moved closer, gazing softly into her eyes. Then he brushed her chin with a featherlight touch. "Seriously?"

She wanted to confess. She wanted to throw herself in his arms and tell him everything.

She swallowed.

"Whatever it is…" His voice trailed off.

Trepidation heightened her senses, but she forced it down, squared her shoulders and braced herself. "You know I'm a hacker."

"The whole world knows you're a hacker." His gaze narrowed. "Are you saying you've had black hat moments? Did you hack into a bank or something?"

"No. I didn't hack into a bank." Her crime was something far more personal.

"Break into national security?"

"No."

"Are you going to make me keep guessing?"

"I broke into k!smet," she blurted out.

He took a step backward, looking aghast. "You actually *did* it? *You* were the saboteur?"

She instantly realized her mistake. "No. Not the Hit-MeUp sabotage. I had nothing to do with that."

His gaze had hardened then, like she'd suddenly become an untrustworthy stranger. "What did you do?"

"It was the Surprise Me! contest. I hacked the algorithm." She swallowed hard, her stomach roiling, regretting that she'd even brought it up. "I forced a match between you and me."

He stood frozen for a long moment while sweat broke out on her brow.

He finally blinked.

"You…" He seemed to be wrapping his head around it. "Matched us?"

She nodded. "Yes."

"Why?"

She closed her eyes, then opened them again, wishing she had a better reason. "Paris wanted to go on a free date and to the k!smet party at the TCC."

Nick gave his head a little shake. "What?"

"I wanted Paris to be happy, so I hacked in, then I saw you. I almost matched you with Paris."

A ghost of a smile formed on his face. "But you kept me for yourself."

"I did." She hadn't been proud of it at the time. "But Chase seems really great."

Nick nodded, his smile growing wider. "Chase seems really great for Paris."

"I'm sorry," Emilia said. It hadn't been her finest moment.

"I'm not." He gently framed her face with his hands. "I'd have been sorry if you'd matched me with Paris."

The knot untangled in Emilia's stomach. "You don't like Paris?"

"I like Paris just fine. But I like you better. I like you differently." His gaze was warm and intimate.

"So, you're not mad that I cheated?"

"Embarrassed, maybe."

That didn't make sense. "Embarrassed?"

"Embarrassed for k!smet and Surprise Me! that they were so hackable."

She couldn't help but scoff. "It's hardly high security. I mean, I doubt they expected sophisticated cyberattacks."

"Still…" he said thoughtfully. "It's probably something they should look at. There's personal data on the system."

"You won't tell them, will you?" Even as she protested, Emilia realized Misha deserved to know how her system might be at risk. She gave her head a shake. "I mean, of course you have to tell them. I'd be happy to show Misha what I did so she can plug the hole. I'll even fix it myself."

"I can keep your name out of it," he offered.

"How would you do that?"

He gave a shrug. "I'll tell her I got a tip."

"You don't have to lie for me."

"I don't have to tell her where the tip came from. She won't ask."

"She won't?" That struck Emilia as odd. If someone came to her with information on her coding, she'd sure ask for the source.

"She won't."

"How can you be sure?"

"I'm smart that way."

She rolled her eyes and shook her head. "Not half full of yourself, are you?"

He gestured to the keyboard. "Will you show me what you did?"

"You want me to back break in again?"

"We won't do any harm. Plus, I'm an—"

"—investor," she finished for him.

"A big one."

"You're really rather proud of that, aren't you?" She sat down at the keyboard.

"I really am," he agreed as she started to type.

Ten

"I know it was a missed opportunity," Nico said to Rafe as he lifted the saddle from the spirited bay gelding he'd ridden late into the afternoon.

Dancer shifted his feet and shook his head and mane, clearly happy to be done with the saddle.

"I think the word you're looking for is *mistake*," Rafe responded, hefting his own saddle and carrying it over to the racks lining a wall of an alcove in the barn.

"Semantics." Although Nico didn't disagree with Rafe's assessment. "I'm saying I realize I probably should have said something when the moment presented itself."

"No kidding," Rafe responded with incredulity. "It was the perfect chance to get out from under the deception. She confessed something to you, so you should have—"

"Told her I was an ex-con?" Nico briskly shook out the saddle blanket. That was where his conviction faltered. "She tells me she fudged an online dating match, and I come back with what? No problem, Emilia. By the way, I went to prison for assault?"

"You'd have to tell her the whole story." Rafe's tone moderated. "You had your friend's back. You sacrificed yourself for his family."

"You're assuming she'd stick around long enough to hear the whole story." Nico wasn't at all sure he'd have a chance to explain the extenuating circumstances.

The bald truth would frighten her, and she'd likely bolt before he could say much of anything at all. And he wouldn't blame her. Fear of him would be a perfectly natural reaction, and leaving a perfectly reasonable course of action.

No smart woman would stick with a guy who had been judged violent in court, and who'd lied to her all this time about his criminal record. No. If he told her, *when* he told her, he had to be prepared for the relationship to end right then and there.

"I keep thinking just a couple more days," he said half to himself. "I'll just see her a few more times." He went for a curry comb to clean Dancer's coat.

"See her or make love with her?" Rafe asked as he began brushing his own horse with long strokes.

"Either. Both. I don't know." Nico only knew he wasn't ready to let her go.

"What if she finds out on her own?" Rafe asked.

Nico paused over that. The possibility wasn't far-fetched. There were a hundred scenarios where it could happen.

At first, he'd worried constantly about being recognized while he was with her. But, so far, it hadn't happened. So, he'd grown more complacent, focusing on Emilia instead of the strangers around them every place they went.

"I know that could make it worse," he admitted.

"It would absolutely make it worse. The only hope you have is if you tell her yourself."

"I will." Nico would.

"What about the wedding?" Rafe asked.

"Tell her at the *wedding*?" Nico couldn't think of a less appropriate place to tell Emilia the truth about his history.

Rafe gave an impatient frown. "What if you're outed by someone at the wedding?"

Nico rocked back on his heels.

It was a bigger possibility than Nico had considered. Maggie and Rafe knew, but he completely trusted them to keep his secret. But everyone who was anyone in Royal would attend the Del Rio–Winters wedding. Someone would likely recognize him. Plus, Emilia was sure to get a lot of attention as a bridesmaid. People would stare at her and see him beside her.

Nico might not be famous in this town, but he was notorious. There were dozens of people who might recognize him at the wedding and give away his secret.

"The words *now or never* come to mind," Rafe said.

Nico stilled, resting his hand against Dancer's warm back. "Shoot."

"Go," Rafe said. "Do it right now. I'll finish up here."

Nico started combing again. He had no intention of leaving Rafe with the work of putting away the horses, even if a vague sense of panic was building up in his chest because he knew his friend was right.

"Go," Rafe repeated.

Nico stepped back from the horse. "Are you sure?"

Rafe waved off his concern. "I've got this."

"Okay." Nico gave a nod, knowing he'd been a fool to let it go on this long. He started for the barn door. "Okay."

He leaped into his SUV and roared down the gravel road. He maxed out his speed as he swerved onto the highway, small stones bouncing off the pavement behind him. It was miles back into town, but traffic was light and he gambled on a lack of strict speed enforcement on this stretch of highway.

It wasn't until the lights of Royal came into view that he slowed down, taking his place in a moving line of traffic that marched into the outskirts of the city. He began composing speeches in his mind, imagining how they'd sound, picturing Emilia's shock and disappointment, then discarding his ideas and starting all over again.

In the Del Rio driveway, he glided to a stop in front of their mansion, gazing at the front door and shifting the vehicle into park. This, right now, was his last chance to back out and roll the dice instead. The closer the moment came, the less he wanted to blow up their relationship tonight.

After all, he desperately reasoned, he could sit at the back of the church. He could hover at the edges of the crowd during the reception and simply wait for it to be over. Emilia would sit at the head table during the dinner. He wouldn't be with her for the formal parts of the event. Nobody would notice one innocuous guest at a corner table with strangers.

All he had to do was make it through the wedding and reception. Then he could wait days or even weeks before coming clean. She'd know him better by then, maybe like him better and trust him more.

He reached for the gear shift.

"Nick?"

A shadow came up beside the driver's window.

"Is that you?" It was Emilia's voice, Emilia's smile flashing his way. "What are you doing here?" She gestured for him to roll down his window.

He did.

"Hi," she said. Then she gestured behind herself. "I saw you drive up. We're all over there on the patio."

"I don't want to disturb you," he said, avoiding eye contact.

"What are you doing here?"

He hesitated. Not a single one of his rehearsed speeches worked in this instance. "I was looking for you," he said.

"Well, you found me."

"You probably have to get back." He glanced hopefully in the rearview mirror. Maybe Maggie would be out there waving Emilia back to the party. But he only saw the fringe of a landscaped garden and a lighted pathway.

"It's fine," she said. "What's up?"

He looked into her eyes for the first time. "I missed you," he said honestly.

She leaned a little closer. "You're very sweet."

He wasn't sweet. He was a liar. And he had to man up about this. "Can you get away for a little while?"

She gave a sultry smile. "How long did you have in mind?"

He wanted to tell her it wasn't for a tryst. But then she'd asked questions, and he didn't want that.

"Not long," he said instead.

"You're not much of a sweet talker," she joked. But she walked around to the passenger side, texting as she went.

She opened the door and hopped inside.

"Your place?" she asked as she fastened her seat belt.

He started to say no. Taking her to his place was an unacceptable risk. There were way too many things there that could give away his identity before he had a chance to explain.

But giving up his secret was the whole point here. If he took her home, he couldn't back out. Once she was inside his apartment, he'd have no choice but to come clean.

"Yes," he said and moved the SUV forward.

"Great," she said with a big grin. "I've been dying to see where you live."

* * *

Emilia had held herself back on the drive to Nick's building, then while crossing the lobby, and all the way to the eighth floor, even though they were alone in the elevator.

But as soon as they crossed the threshold into his suite, she practically threw herself into his arms. She'd missed him desperately. She craved his touch, his scent and the taste of his kisses. It felt like weeks rather than days since they'd made love.

"Whoa," he said between kisses while she went for the buttons of his shirt. "Hang—"

She stripped off her bulky earth-toned sweater and the T-shirt beneath in one fell swoop, revealing her lacy bra in the dim pot lights in his foyer.

"I missed you too," she whispered, coming up on her toes to kiss his mouth.

He mumbled around her lips. "There's something I have to—"

"Sh," she ordered. "Talk later." Having made it through his buttons, she pulled his shirt from his shoulders and pressed herself satisfyingly against his bare skin.

"But—"

"What is *wrong* with you?" she asked on a laugh. "I'm tearing off your clothes."

"You are," he agreed, looking both amused and bemused now.

"So, get with the program already." She peeled off her bra.

His eyes fixed on her breasts and darkened. "Yes, ma'am."

"That's more like it."

He cupped her breast in his warm palm, and she moaned with pleasure. Then he kissed her neck, once and again, lower, working his way to the tip of her shoulder. He slipped an arm around the small of her back and drew her closer still.

"I want to go on record here," he whispered as he kissed the shell of her ear.

"You *are* on record," she said. Then she popped the top button of his jeans. Her knuckle grazed the front of his fly, and he sucked in a tight breath.

"Fine," he growled. "Fine."

"Good," she answered.

They stripped off the rest of their clothes, tossing them to the cool hardwood floor.

He lifted her, and she wrapped her legs around his waist.

He took a few steps until her back came up against a smooth wall.

She wanted to savor the sensations, but she didn't want to wait. She shifted against him, encouraging completion.

"No," he said gruffly.

"No?" What was he talking about?

"Not here." He held her firmly against his chest and headed down a dark hallway.

She closed her eyes, feeling the strength of his broad hands, the brush of his thighs, the cool puff of his breath and the steady beat of his heart.

Too soon he was lowering her, breaking their contact, setting her on cool, smooth sheets. Before she could miss him, he'd reached for a condom then was there beside her, pulling her back into his arms, exploring the depths of her mouth and starting caresses that made her squirm and beg for more.

The room felt big, though she couldn't see the corners. The air was fresh against her heated skin. The moon shone through a big window, faint stars twinkling around it, creating a cocoon of sensuality around them.

She absorbed the magic of his kisses, ran her fingertips over his taut chest, feeling, exploring, moving lower to his washboard stomach. When she went lower still, he gasped and rolled her onto her back.

"Emilia," he rasped, gazing into her eyes. "I am falling so hard for you."

She smiled because his words warmed her through to her core.

He smiled back and eased into her.

She tipped her head, arched her back, closed her eyes and gave herself over to the sensations of his body.

His rhythm started slowly, growing steadily harder, faster and deeper.

The moon, the stars and the world disappeared as her existence shrank to Nick. Nick's mouth, his hands, his legs and hips all working together in perfect symmetry.

Their lovemaking went on and on, taking her to heights she never knew existed until it burst to a crescendo. She gasped for breath, her heart pounding hard as she desperately sucked in extra oxygen.

Then she floated back to earth, her energy spent, her bones all but melted. She didn't think she could move.

"Emilia?" Nick's voice sounded a long way off.

She tried to answer, but it seemed like too much effort.

"You're wonderful," he whispered, settling her against his slick body, pulling a sheet over them both. "You're absolutely wonderful."

She managed a smile, even as the lethargy of sleep crept over her.

In what seemed like seconds later, she blinked her eyes open.

She was wrapped warm and tight in Nick's arms.

His breathing was deep and even.

The pink of dawn was just starting to brighten the sky.

She knew nobody would judge her. But she'd prefer to be back at Maggie's before morning. It was going to be a very full day. The wedding rehearsal was tonight, and Emilia didn't want anything to distract from the bride.

She slipped carefully and cautiously from Nick's arms, gazing down at his handsome profile as she backed away from the bed, knowing she'd miss him between now and the wedding.

He hadn't officially asked her to be his date at the wedding, but he'd said he was attending. She hoped they'd dance. They'd better dance. A man didn't make such amazing love to a woman, tell her he was falling for her and then not even dance with her.

She smiled at the memory.

Nick was falling for her.

Well, she was falling for him too. She was falling very fast and very hard.

She crept out of the bedroom, dressed in the foyer and took a quick look around the living room in the dim dawn light, liking it very much. Then she let herself silently out of the apartment.

Nico awoke with a start, instantly realizing Emilia was no longer in his arms.

He sat up and looked around the empty room.

The en suite bathroom door was open, the light off.

He swung his legs off the bed, listening hard as he headed for the kitchen, hoping to find her there figuring out the buttons on his coffee maker.

But the kitchen was empty. Her clothes were gone. There wasn't a single trace of Emilia left in his apartment. If not for her lingering scent on his pillow, he might have dreamed the whole thing.

It had momentarily been a dream, he corrected himself, freezing with his hand on the coffee maker. Now it was turning into a nightmare.

She'd left early, snuck out before saying good morning or even goodbye. There were precious few reasons for her to have done that. The most glaring of which was that she'd seen something with his real name on it. If she had, it was a very short step to a search engine and his very public record of being in prison.

He looked around the kitchen, then retraced his steps.

There were envelopes on a table in the foyer with his name on them. Dozens of letters in the basket where he tossed the mail before sorting. There were count-less printouts and reports in his office, and the door stood wide open.

It was impossible to know where she'd looked. He didn't have any idea what she'd seen. He pictured her staring at the state corrections website, reading his name and his charges and conviction.

He went for his phone, opened his recent calls and touched her name.

If she picked up, he'd simply say good morning, carry on a normal conversation, gauge her mood, see if she'd give something away.

If she didn't answer… Well, if she didn't answer, she was likely dodging his calls.

He held his breath through the rings, dreading the moment it went to voice mail. When it did, he didn't bother with a message. Instead, he sat down on the bed. He curled his fist into the pillow and tried to come up with a next move.

The phone rang in his hand.

He flipped his wrist to check the screen, hoping, ex-pecting, praying for it to be Emilia.

It was an unknown number.

His first instinct was to decline the call. But it might be a client.

He accepted. "Nico Law."

"Nico, hi. It's Jericho Winters."

Nico was shocked to hear from the groom. Even though his sister and Maggie were best friends, the two men were barely acquaintances. Was it to do with the wedding or Emilia? "Is something wrong?"

"No, no. The wedding's right on track. Misha asked me to call."

Nico's heart sank further. If it wasn't the wedding, it had to be Emilia. She must have talked to Misha.

Jericho was calling to uninvite him to the wedding. Nico didn't blame them for that. The last thing he wanted to do was mar the ceremony or the reception.

"She thought you might be able to pick up the cake," Jericho continued.

The words didn't compute inside Nico's head. "The what?"

"The wedding cake. Mrs. Yeoh's van broke down and won't be repaired until Monday. Misha said your car had plenty of room."

Relief overwhelmed Nico's confusion. Things hadn't blown up with Emilia, at least not yet. "Yes," he told Jericho in an instant. "Yes, it does."

"Could you pick the cake up early in the morning at the RCW kitchen and take it to the Cattleman's club?"

"Absolutely. No problem at all."

"That would be a huge help."

"Sure. Uh…" Nico wasn't fishing for bad news, but he was fishing for news. "How's the bride doing?"

"Great. Harried and busy, but that's no surprise."

"And the bridesmaids?" Nico felt ridiculous pressing, but he was desperate to know what was going on with Emilia.

"They're having a great time in the pool house," Jericho said absently. "Massages and pedicures or some such. I think they're serving mimosas."

"Sounds great." Nico told himself that bridesmaid

duties were a plausible excuse for Emilia blowing off his call, but he didn't quite believe himself. More likely, she was angry with him but putting on a good show for Maggie's sake.

"Thanks for helping out," Jericho said cheerfully. "I'll see you tomorrow."

"Not a problem. Goodbye."

Nico tossed his phone on the bed and groaned.

He couldn't drop by the Del Rio mansion in search of a bridesmaid today of all days. And he couldn't keep calling her like some kind of stalker.

It would be thirty-six hours before he saw her in person. Surely, she'd call before then. Surely, if she wasn't so angry that she never wanted to see him again, she'd reach out and call before the wedding.

Emilia had intended to call Nick, but the busy pre-wedding day had gotten away from her. As part of the bridal party, she'd been pampered all morning. The rehearsal had taken up the afternoon. Afterward, the formal dinner at the mansion had lasted well into the night with speeches and celebration.

Before now, she hadn't known how the other half lived. She'd discovered they lived very, very well.

They'd been treated to a fancy ladies' brunch on the wedding morning, with several of Maggie's female relatives and close friends attending. The mood had been buoyant since the Del Rio–Winters feud was completely in the past, with Winters family members Camille, Alisha and Tiffany as honored guests at the brunch.

As part of their preparation for the ceremony, Maggie, Misha and Emilia had each bathed in rose-petal baths, then headed to the pool house for their hair and makeup.

Ashley from the Saint Tropez Salon was working Maggie's hair into a cascade of braids and curls around a twisting crystal vine headpiece. Emilia wasn't sure she'd ever seen anything so beautifully luxurious.

The short, perky Lisle had pulled Misha's wavy auburn hair to one side with a jeweled clip. While a friendly woman named Adeline had somehow shaped Emilia's short hair into a froth of softness, letting it frame her face while drawing a few strands back from her temples into French braids that met in a clip at the back of her head.

Emilia had worn her contacts for the wedding day, and her professionally made-up eyes looked unusually large and round. Adeline had used a glossy terra-cotta lipstick shade and done something wonderful with her cheekbones.

"Wow," she said now as she gazed in the mirror.

"I love it," Adeline said with a smile.

"You look wonderful," Misha said from her nearby chair.

"We all do," Emilia agreed. "Especially you, Maggie."

"You don't have to flatter me," Maggie said with a laugh. "I feel fantastic."

"You look amazing," Misha chimed in.

"Seriously," Emilia added enthusiastically. "Maggie, Jericho is going to be stunned when he sees you."

"That's what we're striving for," Ashley said with

a beaming smile. She was clearly pleased with how Maggie looked.

"Not too stunned, I hope," Maggie said with a mock frown. "He's got vows to recite."

"I'm sure he'll find a way to spit them out," Misha said, tilting her head sideways as she surveyed herself in the mirror.

The photographer came in through an open doorway. "Okay if I take some action shots?" she asked.

"Shoot away," Maggie said, turning in a swivel chair to smile at the camera as she came to her feet.

Emilia wished they were dressed in something more formal than satin robes. She doubted she'd ever look this fancy again, and she would have liked to get a copy of one of the photos. It never hurt to have a flattering headshot hanging around.

Natalie bustled in then. "Are you all ready?"

"Time to get dressed?" Maggie asked, looking suddenly nervous.

"It's time," Natalie said.

Maggie grasped the back of her chair. "It suddenly seems so real."

"Is that bad?" Misha asked, looking at Maggie with concern.

"She's a bride." Natalie stepped forward and took Maggie's hands in hers. "Last minute nerves are normal."

"Is everything okay?" Emilia asked, moving closer to Maggie for support, wondering if her hesitation was serious. Could they have all missed something about the relationship? Was there a problem?

But Maggie smiled bravely. "Everything's fine."

"It's not too late to back out," Emilia offered.

Six shocked expressions turned her way.

"It's not," she repeated. "If Maggie's not sure."

Pledging your life to another person was an enormous commitment.

"I don't want to back out," Maggie said. "I'm sorry if I seemed upset."

"Don't be sorry," Natalie said, giving Maggie's hands a squeeze.

"I don't know what that was," Maggie continued. "It just…all of a sudden…came over me."

"Stage fright," Ashely suggested. "I've seen that happen before. You're having a really big wedding."

"You should have eaten more at brunch," Misha suggested. "Are you hungry?"

"I couldn't eat a thing."

"Thirsty then," Natalie said. "Your dress is upstairs in your bedroom. We'll stop for something to drink on the way."

"I'm sure thirsty," Misha said.

"The bridesmaid dresses are in the front guest room on the second floor," Natalie told Misha and Emilia. "It won't take you two as long to get dressed, so you don't need to rush."

"Can we hang around?" Ashley asked. "We'd love to see you all in your outfits."

"Sure," Maggie said, seeming like she was fully recovered. "Help yourself to something to drink. There's plenty of space to sit down in the great room."

"We'll pack up here first," Ashley said as Natalie ushered Maggie out the door.

"Thirsty?" Misha asked Emilia.

"Hydrating is probably a good idea."

The two women headed across the pool deck into the back door of the mansion, picking up some sparkling water in the kitchen before making their way to the spacious guest room that held their dresses.

"How are things with you and Nick?" Misha asked as she closed the door behind them.

"There's…" Emilia girded herself. "There's something we need to talk about."

Nick might be willing to keep her name out of the k!smet security flaw discovery, but Emilia wanted to come clean.

"Is something wrong?" Misha's hand went to the back of an armchair in the corner of the room.

"Yes. There is. Things with the two of us aren't exactly what they seem. Maybe he even said something to you?"

Misha sat down, her tone going hushed. "Said something about what?"

Emilia took the chair cornerwise to Misha. It might not be the perfect time to come clean, but she couldn't quash the feeling she'd betrayed her friend.

Emilia gathered her courage. "I hacked k!smet."

Misha drew back, looking startled and confused. "What?"

"I did it. I hacked in."

"While you were working for HitMeUp?"

"No." Emilia quickly shook her head. "Nothing like

that. Then again, maybe this is worse. I hacked in for the Surprise Me! contest. I matched Paris with Chase and me with Nick."

Misha blinked rapidly. It took her a few seconds to speak. "You matched yourself with Nick?"

"Paris wanted to win an all-expenses-paid date and go to your party at the TCC. I'm really sorry."

"Nick *knows* this?"

Emilia nodded. "I told him."

A funny smile came up on Misha's face. "What did he say? What did he do? What happened after?"

"You're not mad?" Emilia was taken aback by Misha's reaction.

Misha waved a dismissive hand. "No, I'm not mad. I'm curious about what Nick said."

"That's the weird part."

Misha waited, looking expectant.

"He wasn't mad. In fact, things are better than ever. He finally took me to his place."

Misha's eyes went wide.

The two women stared at each other for a moment.

"And…" Misha prompted.

Emilia hesitated but realized there was no reason to be shy. She and Nick hadn't done anything wrong. In fact, it had all felt very, very right.

"After everything, we made wild passionate love at his place," she blurted out.

"So…" Misha seemed to search for the right words. "You…know?"

Emilia knew alright. She knew Nick was one of the

most amazing men she'd ever met. She grinned and nodded.

A knock sounded on the door, and Natalie opened it. "How are things coming in here?" She looked surprised to see Misha and Emilia sitting in the corner.

Misha quickly jumped up. "Oops. We got to talking."

"There's still time," Natalie said, sounding calm even as she efficiently stripped the garment bag from one of the dresses.

Misha and Emilia dressed quickly and were soon standing in front of the full-length mirror, admiring their dresses and the delicate diamond earrings that had been bridesmaid gifts from Maggie earlier in the day.

"Perfect," Natalie said with satisfaction. "Now all we need is a bride."

"I can't wait to see her," Misha said excitedly.

In the hall outside the guest room, Maggie stood at the top of the stairs, one hand on the rail and the other against her chest.

She looked upset again.

Emilia rushed forward, more worried than ever. "What is it?"

Maggie removed the hand from her chest, and Emilia's eyes all but bugged out.

The historic necklace glimmered against Maggie's pale skin, a cascade of diamonds, emeralds and rubies in perfect symmetry.

"What on earth?" Misha rasped.

"They want me to wear it," Maggie said with a catch in her voice. "Both Mom and Camille—to bring it full circle before it goes to the museum, they said." Maggie drew in a shuddering breath. "They want to solidify and honor the new bond between us all."

"Oh, Maggie." Emilia was choking up herself.

"That's wonderful," Misha said on a whisper. "Jericho will be overwhelmed."

Maggie nodded. Then she sniffed. "I can't cry. I'll ruin my makeup."

"Don't you dare cry," Misha warned. "You'll get us all going. And none of us are allowed to shed a tear before the pictures."

"Maggie, honey?" Gail called from the bottom of the stairs. "The flowers are here."

"The final piece," Natalie said to Maggie. "You are a stunning bride."

Maggie touched the necklace again. "I feel like I need a security guard."

"In another hour, you'll have Jericho," Misha said, linking her arm with Maggie's. "Let's get you to the church."

Eleven

Nico kept a low profile during the wedding ceremony, sitting in a pew at the back of the big church. The congregation was abuzz with news that Maggie was wearing the Del Rio heirloom necklace, but he couldn't see that level of detail from where he sat.

The ceremony was touching, and a lump formed in his chest when he listened to the vows. It was clear Maggie and Jericho were meant for each other and would have a long, happy life together. He knew now he wanted that with Emilia. He also knew it would likely never happen.

Once the church had cleared, he took his time traveling to the Cattleman's Club for the reception. It would hurt like hell to see anger and distance in Emilia's eyes. And though he still held out a faint hope that there was another explanation for her silence, he knew deep down it was over for them.

At dinner, he sat with a friendly group of strangers far away from the bridal party. Then he listened to the toasts, which were engaging, if a bit long.

When the guests began to circulate, he made his way to the nearest bar to order a cocktail. It was tempting to slip out a side door and call it a night. But Emilia was tantalizingly close, and he couldn't bring himself to stop hoping for a miracle just yet. So, he stayed.

"*There* you are." Sounding harried, Misha grasped his arm and pulled him from the short lineup.

"Shouldn't you be with the bride?" he asked as he fell into step with her.

She steered him to the edge of the big hall. "Why didn't you *tell* me?"

He was baffled by the anxious question. "Tell you what?"

Exasperation came through in Misha's tone. "About Emilia."

Nico stilled, bracing himself for the worst. "What about her?"

"That you told her who you were."

There was a simple answer to that, a tragically simple answer. "Because I didn't."

Misha looked confused. "You took her to your place."

"I did. But I didn't—" He drew a bracing breath. "It was late, and we didn't talk much."

"You made love."

"It wasn't the first time."

A beat went by.

"I didn't know things had gone that far."

"Well, they did."

Misha moved in close. "She knows who you are, Nico. She told me she knew."

Nico nodded grimly. It was exactly as he'd feared. Emilia had seen something that morning that had given him away. She'd learned the truth and now she was ghosting him. He didn't blame her.

He didn't want to put Misha in the middle of it, but he had to ask. "Does she seem really angry?"

"She didn't seem angry at all." Misha paused for a moment in thought. "Unless she lied. But why would she lie?"

Nico tried to keep the misery from his voice. "She's been ghosting me."

"Really?" Misha frowned with confusion and concern.

"She's never going to trust me, never going to give me a chance after this. I blew it big time, didn't I?"

"You really liked her," Misha said softly, compassion coming through in her expression.

"I really did." He'd more than liked her. Preposterous as it sounded so soon after they'd met, he'd begun to think she was the one—the one and only woman for him.

"You should talk to her," Misha said.

"And say what?"

"I don't know. I don't know what all happened between the two of you. Apologize for not being up front. She might forgive you."

"Why would she forgive me?" He didn't deserve her forgiveness.

He'd kept a vital piece of information from her while letting their relationship bloom. He'd made love to her over and over again under false pretenses. It was a huge betrayal of her trust.

"Shouldn't you at least try?"

Nico knew his sister was right He'd hurt Emilia. He'd taken what should have been a magical time being a bridesmaid and complicated it with his selfishness. For that alone, he should tell her he was sorry.

He scanned the room, looking for her distinctive bridesmaid dress. "Where is she?"

He didn't wait for an answer. Instead, he began striding toward the head table, hoping Emilia hadn't moved too far away from there.

He wove through the crowd, scanned conversation groups, checked every corner of the empty dance floor. When he finally spotted her, his steps slowed. He found himself delaying the moment of reckoning.

She was chatting with Maggie's brother, Preston, and his fiancée, Tiffany.

Nico reflexively noted there was a good chance one of them would recognize him. Not that it mattered now. Not that much of anything mattered now that he was losing Emilia.

Even through his dread, he couldn't help noting how incredibly beautiful she looked as he came up beside her. She was smiling right now, laughing at something Tiffany had said. And here he was about to shatter the moment.

"Excuse me," he said.

Emilia looked his way, surprise on her face.

"There you are." She didn't look angry as she turned. Then again, she was far too poised to let her emotions show in front of others.

"Nico?" Tiffany asked from behind Emilia. "Is that you?"

Emilia's smile faded and her brow furrowed, and the last hope left him.

"It's me," he said to Tiffany. "Can I speak with you for a minute?" he asked Emilia, taking a sideways step to move to a quieter spot.

"You look…different," Tiffany said.

"Nice to see you," he told her pleasantly. "Please?" he asked Emilia.

"Okay," she answered with a nod, looking uncertain.

Fighting an urge to take her hand, he wove their way through the crowd until they came to a quiet alcove. There, he stopped and turned to face her, squaring his shoulders and bracing himself.

"Nick, what is—"

"Please, just let me talk." He had to say his piece.

"But—"

"Please," he implored.

She compressed her lips. "Okay. Go ahead."

"I'm sorry," he said. "More sorry than you can even imagine. Believe me, if I could start over again, I would. I didn't mean for any of it to happen this way." He regrouped, ordering himself to take responsibility for his own actions. "I mean, obviously, the whole thing was under my control. I lied to you. Yes, it was an omission, but that's just another name for a lie."

Her lips were pursed now, her gaze narrowed. It was hard to tell her anger from confusion.

"I know there's no future for us, and I'm as sorry as I can be about that." He wanted to reach out and touch her. He wanted to kiss her. He was desperate to pull her into his arms. He curled his hands to keep them still.

"I'll stay out of your life," he said instead. "And I'll give you and Misha space. You deserve the break to be clean." He paused. "Not that it makes any difference to you, but I'm through pretending. Starting tonight, I'll walk with my head held high. I don't regret what I did. I only regret that it hurt you."

She looked very hurt right now. She also looked very vulnerable.

He couldn't stand to see what he'd done.

"Goodbye, Emilia. I wish it could have been different." He took a step back.

"Nick—" she called out.

But he was already turning away, walking fast, increasing his strides, heading for the exit.

Emilia watched Nick walk away, her heart sinking and a ball of lead forming in her stomach.

What had just happened? Why was he apologizing? Was it his odd way of ending their relationship?

She took a step to go after him, thinking maybe they could salvage something. But she stopped herself. He'd made it plain. The breakup had been strangely worded. But it was clear that whatever they'd had was done now.

Her eyes stung with unshed tears, and she swallowed a huge lump of sorrow.

"Emilia?" Misha appeared beside her.

Emilia couldn't speak.

"I don't blame you if you blame me," Misha said.

Emilia's confusion multiplied. She blinked hard to keep the tears at bay. The last thing she'd do was make a scene at Maggie's wedding reception.

"It was my idea," Misha said, sounding hugely regretful. "I convinced my brother to go undercover. We were only after information on how the Surprise Me! function was working. He was gathering data. We never thought—"

"Who's your brother?" Emilia managed, although her voice came out sounding strangled.

Misha drew back in obvious astonishment. Then she reached for Emilia's hand. "It's Nico. He didn't tell you that part?"

"Nico?" The pieces fell into place inside Emilia's head. "Nick is *Nico*? Nick is your brother, Nico Law?" And he was *undercover*?

Now Misha looked stricken. "I thought you knew."

"How would I know?"

"You said you knew. You said he took you home to his place."

"What does his place have to do with it?" Emilia's heart squeezed at the memory of their glorious lovemaking. "He didn't tell me his real name. He sure didn't tell me he was your brother."

Misha looked horrified. "Oh, no."

Emilia was more confused than ever. "Why wouldn't

you *say* something?" She withdrew her hand from Misha's.

"We thought you would go on a date or two, nothing more."

"It was more," Emilia said with a hollow laugh. "It was a whole lot more."

It was obvious now why Nick had walked away. It had been a game to him. His part in the relationship had been a sham all along.

That's why he'd apologized. He sounded like he genuinely regretted the ruse. But he'd also made it clear he wasn't feeling what Emilia felt.

He wasn't falling in love with her. But she was falling in love with him. She had fallen in love with him.

She fought back a sob of pain.

"You have to talk to him," Misha said anxiously. She looked around. "Where did he go?"

Emilia couldn't imagine saying anything to Nick right now. She couldn't imagine saying anything to him ever again.

She wanted to go home. She wanted to leave just as soon as she could possibly get away. As soon as they cut the cake and had the first dance, she was out of here.

She was going back to her place. She didn't care if construction went on downstairs twenty-four seven. She was going to bury her head under her pillow and hide there for days or weeks, however long it took to nurse her broken heart.

"We need to find him." Misha tried to tug Emilia into a walk.

Emilia dug in her heels. "I have nothing to say to him."

Misha let go of Emilia's arm. "There's something he needs to say to you."

"He already apologized."

"Something more."

Emilia shook her head. "There is nothing more. It was a ruse."

"It was data gathering."

"Fine. Whatever. It got out of hand on my side."

"I don't think you know how Nico—"

Emilia glared at Misha. She was annoyed more than angry with her friend. After all, Emilia was the one who'd manipulated the Surprise Me! function to put her and Nick together in the first place. Misha hadn't purposely orchestrated the match. And it sure wasn't Misha's fault that Emilia had tumbled into bed with Nick and lost her heart.

"Please just listen to him," Misha said imploringly. "There's something important he thinks you already know."

"What is it?"

If it was that important, Misha could just spit it out and be done with it.

But Misha shook her head. "It's not my story to tell. It might not change anything. It might make things worse. But it's the truth."

"The *truth*? *Now* we're talking about the truth?" Emilia might not be completely innocent in the whole debacle, but at least she'd come clean about her hacking.

Nick or Nico hadn't said a word about his own duplicity.

"If I find him, will you listen?" Misha asked.

"No." Emilia didn't think she could face Nick again. Her emotions were too raw, and she was too close to tears. She might humiliate herself even further.

"Please. I wouldn't ask you if I didn't think it was the right thing."

"For your brother?" Emilia was still wrapping her head around that one.

Misha was Nick's sister. Her loyalties had to lie with him.

"For him, yes. But for you too. I care about you too, Emilia. Please believe me that I do."

There was no doubting the sincerity in Misha's eyes.

"We talked about him." Emilia thought back to their conversations.

"I know."

Both Misha and Maggie had seemed hesitant about Nick. They'd advised Emilia to take things slow.

It hit her then. "Maggie? Maggie knows too?"

Misha nodded. "We talked about telling you, but we couldn't decide what was right. We were on the outside, and it was up to him, but…" Her voice trailed off for a moment. "I really thought he'd told you the other night."

"Honored guests." The hearty voice of the MC came over the sound system. "Please gather around for the first dance."

Music swelled in a tune Emilia recognized as one of Maggie's favorites.

"We have to go," Emilia said, taking an anxious step

toward the dance floor, feeling a surge of guilt for neglecting the bride.

She had responsibilities here tonight. Her personal feelings would have to wait.

Nico had tried to make his way to the exit. But he'd run into his longtime friend Jack Chowdhry, who was understandably buoyed at seeing Maggie wearing the heirloom necklace as the two feuding families symbolically cemented their bonds. It was thanks in large part to Jack's diplomatic skills that the feud was completely over. He deserved to savor the celebration.

Nico put on an upbeat front while he fought the sinking feeling in the pit of his stomach and the hollowness around his heart. Losing Emilia was his own fault, which made it even worse.

Afterward, several acquaintances stopped him along the way and were surprisingly friendly and supportive of his presence both in Royal and at the wedding. Under any other circumstances, he would have been thrilled with the acceptance. But none of that mattered tonight. He began to wonder why it had ever mattered.

Within sight of the exit, he ran into Rafe. It was impossible to keep up the cheerful front when Rafe's first question was about Emilia.

After a halting start, Nico was forced to admit he hadn't told her the truth—that she'd figured it out on her own and, yes, the worst had happened. When Rafe had clasped him on the shoulder, Nico appreciated the gesture, but he was hanging on to his emotions by a thread.

And he felt like a hamster on a wheel here trying to escape. He didn't know how much longer he could take it.

He finally saw a clear path and walked fast.

"Nico!" It was Misha's voice behind him.

He ignored her and kept walking.

"Nico," she called again. Then her hand landed on his arm.

He clenched his jaw and stopped.

"Wait," she said, coming around to face him.

"Good night, Misha. I love you, but you have to leave me alone."

"She *doesn't* know."

The emphatic words made no sense to him. "Seriously, good night," he said and started walking.

Misha kept up, walking fast and talking in a staccato rhythm. "I got it wrong. She doesn't know. I mean she didn't know who you were. She knows now. But that's *all* she knows."

Nico stopped short of the exit. "What are you even talking about?"

"She knows you lied about being Nick instead of Nico Law. I gave that away a few minutes ago."

"She already knew." He gestured to the crowded ballroom. "We just talked about it. We broke up over it."

Misha shook her head. "She didn't."

Nico thought back over the conversation.

Emilia hadn't said much, but he could tell by her expression that she was upset with him.

"Thing is, she doesn't know why," Misha said. "You have to tell her why so she can understand."

Nico wasn't buying that logic. "You think telling her

I'm a criminal will makes things *better*?" The conversation was becoming absurd.

Misha put her hands on her hips. "Do you love her?"

Nico drew back at the frank question.

"Do you?" she demanded.

"I..." He did. Heaven help him, he did love her.

Misha gave him a little shove toward the ballroom. "Go. For goodness' sake, tell her the whole truth. Don't be a coward about it."

Nico squared his shoulders. "I'm not a coward."

He had flaws, plenty of them. But cowardice? No way.

"Well, you're acting like one. Fight, Nico. Fight for the woman you love."

He started to refuse but then clamped his mouth shut.

A flash of triumph came up in Misha's eyes.

He recognized the expression.

She knew she'd won. She knew that taunt would get through to him. It had worked his entire life.

"Fine," he said, accepting the challenge his sister had thrown out. "I'll tell her. And when she walks away, you'll know you were wrong."

"If she walks away, I'll admit I was wrong."

Nico was satisfied with the bargain. He walked back into the crowd, searching for Emilia. He knew he'd been manipulated by Misha. But she did have a point.

It was bolder and braver to put all his cards on the table. Plus, a tiny part of him held out hope it would work. He tried to squelch the flare of optimism, since he was most likely going to get his chest ripped open even further.

Emilia was on the dance floor, in the arms of some man Nico didn't recognize.

Jealousy ricocheted through him as he stared at her beauty, her grace, her smile as she chatted with the stranger. Nico imagined what she was saying, something inconsequential or something weighty, maybe something outrageous or funny.

There was nothing he liked better than a conversational parry with Emilia. It entertained him, kept him on his toes and enlightened him all at the same time. He absolutely hated the thought of giving it up.

Finally, the song ended.

He was quick to approach her, worried someone else would ask her to dance.

He came up beside her. "Emilia?"

She turned, and the smile on her face dimmed as she saw him.

"Can we talk?" he asked.

There was a strain in her voice. "No."

"I have something I need to tell you."

"Not now." Her gaze flicked to Maggie and Jericho.

"It's important."

"They're about to cut the cake."

"Please? I'll be quick." Judging by the chill in her voice, the conversation was going to be over and done with very fast. And then she'd walk away, and their relationship would absolutely be over.

"Over there?" he asked, pointing to the quietest edge of the dance floor.

She compressed her lips and shook her head, but she did start walking.

He was quick to follow.

When she came to a clear spot near a wall, she turned. "You have two minutes. And that's only because of Misha."

Nico wanted to ease in, wanted to set the context, but there wasn't time. "I got caught up in something when I was twenty-two, and I went to prison."

Her eyes rounded in obvious shock. "Prison?"

"It was a fight, in a bar. A guy got hurt, and I was blamed, convicted of assault."

"And did you do it?"

Nico hesitated. Very few people knew the truth, because if the truth got out Dylan could be in trouble, and Nico's sacrifice would be for nothing.

"You did do it," Emilia stated matter-of-factly. "Well, thanks for sharing."

"I didn't," he hissed. Then he moved closer. "I took the fall for someone else. He was my best friend, and it was just before his wedding to his pregnant wife. I thought it would be a slap on the wrist. The sentence was a shock to us all."

Emilia's expression had lost some of its hardness. "How long was the sentence?"

"Three years in state prison. Dylan wanted to step up, but I wouldn't let him. By then, he had a new baby and a new wife." Nico didn't like looking back at that time, remembering the pain it had caused for them all. "I was single."

"So, you went to *prison*?"

"I did. I'm an ex-con. It's why I keep such a low profile here in Royal." He glanced around them now, remembering the positive reactions he'd gotten tonight. "But I'm through with that. I'm through hiding. People can think what they want about my past. I'm focused on the future."

He knew the odds were long, but he was clinging to the hope that his future could include Emilia.

She was searching his expression now. "Why didn't you tell me?"

He was baldly honest. "I was afraid you'd walk away."

"Because you defended a friend? Because you sacrificed three years of your life to protect the father of a little baby?" Her voice rose as she continued speaking. "What part of that makes you look bad?"

"An assault conviction makes me look dangerous. I thought you'd be afraid of me."

"You just said you didn't assault anyone."

"And you believe me? Just like that? Without any proof?" He was blown away by the thought that she'd have that kind of faith in him.

"Are you lying?"

"No."

"Because, hey, it's not like you haven't lied to me before." There was a teasing light in her eyes now.

"I'm not lying." He dared move closer, lowering his voice to a more intimate level. "I swear to you, Emilia, my only lie was of omission, about who I am, and I regretted that right after our first date."

"I can't believe you wouldn't trust me with the truth." A challenge came into her tone. "I confessed. I told you I hacked Surprise Me!"

A hitch of guilt hit his gut. "Can I tell you something else? It was another omission, but just a little one." He made a tiny space between his thumb and index finger.

She arched a brow. "Seriously? There's more?"

"I wrote the code for Surprise Me!"

To his relief, she grinned at that. "I hacked your app?"

"You hacked my app."

"Well, that's embarrassing. For you, I mean."

"Yes, it is," he agreed. He obviously hadn't paid enough attention to security. "But I blocked the vulnerability. You won't get away with it again."

Her expression softened and her lips parted.

He subconsciously closed the space between them, hoping against hope for a kiss.

"I don't want to hack it again," she whispered.

"No?"

"No."

"Dare I ask why?"

"Fishing for a compliment?"

He chuckled low. "Absolutely."

"I already matched with the best guy on all of k!smet."

"Oh, man. I was hoping you'd say that." He leaned in and kissed her.

To his absolute joy, she kissed him back. Then she stepped closer, and he wrapped his arms around her, unbelievably relieved to hold her once again.

"I love you," he whispered as they parted. "I love you so much, Emilia."

Her hug tightened. "I love you too, Nick, Nico." She laughed. "I'm going to have to get used to that."

"Call me anything you want."

She drew back and rested her hands on his shoulders, a grin lighting her face. "Misha is your sister?"

"She is. What I told you about my parents dying in an accident is true. My grandmother raised us, me and Misha."

"I can't believe she doesn't talk about you. I mean, before the matchmaking thing. We've known each other for a while."

"My low profile," he said. "Very few people knew I was back in Royal. Almost nobody knows I'm CEO of AlgoXcell."

"You're CEO of AlgoXcell?"

"Yes."

Her gaze narrowed. "I didn't see that name at your office. I would have recognized it."

"Like I said, low profile. At least it was in the past. I'm changing all that starting now."

"Why do I feel like I have plenty more to learn about you?"

"I hope I have plenty more to learn about you too." He couldn't wait to get started.

Twelve

Applause rang through the Texas Cattleman's Club's dining room as the formal dedication ceremony of the Del Rio heirloom necklace, being streamed from the Museum of Fine Arts in Houston, came to a close. Notable TTC members from far and wide were attending the lavish Royal event.

Maggie was in Houston, along with many members of the Del Rio and Winters families. A photo of her wedding to Jericho was part of the display, as was a small reproduction of the painting of Fernando Del Rio the first's mother wearing the jewels. There was a short story of the family lore, the feud and the reconciliation to let visitors understand the provenance of the piece.

As the applause died down and conversation came

up, Nico's hand closed over Emilia's. Her heart warmed at the gesture.

It was the beginning of a new era for him, with his enthusiastic acceptance by the people of Royal as they started their lives together as a couple. It was also a new era for the Del Rio and Winters families, joined now by Maggie and Jericho's marriage and also by Tiffany Winters's pregnancy with Preston Del Rio. It was a new era for Royal itself and even the Texas Cattleman's Club.

The k!smet app had helped put Royal on the map as a tech hub. Nico's role in the Surprise Me! function's creation was now broadly known. And attention had come to the ranching app he'd developed for the Cortez-Williams family. Orders were pouring in for it from Texas and beyond.

Nico had donated the profits to the Cattleman's Club's benevolent arm. In return, they'd appointed him to a brand-new board position: director of technology. At first, he'd refused the honor, since he hadn't intended his donation as a quid pro quo. But the who's who of Royal had convinced him they needed his talent and expertise to usher the organization into the future.

Spurred on by the momentum to modernize, the Cattleman's Club had elected its youngest and first-ever female president, Luisa Cortez-Williams, one of the most revered ranchers in the valley whose extended family had ranched in the Royal area for multi generations.

Emilia leaned toward Nico, understanding that after so much time on his own, big gatherings weren't his favorite activity. "How are you holding up?"

"I'm fine," he said with a smile. "With you here, I'm good."

It was all quite the change to his status in Royal—a revered and respected businessman instead of a recluse trying to hide his past. Only a few people knew the real story of how he'd protected his friend, but the rest seemed content to let bygones be bygones. It was understood by hardworking Texas cattlemen that disagreements sometimes led to fisticuffs. It didn't mean a man had a character flaw.

"You?" Nico asked in return.

"I'm fantastic," she said.

"Nervous about tomorrow?" he asked.

"A little. You?"

They had agreed to do a live Q and A on their Coders Plus workshop. Now that Nico had gone public as the founder of AlgoXcell, his cachet in the coding world was equal to Emilia's stature as a hacker. The Coders Plus marketing team was over the moon with the opportunities their participation brought to the organization.

"Not nervous," he said. "Curious, I think. I can't wait to see what the students ask us."

Emilia gave a nod to that. She liked the way he was thinking. She should forget about herself, forget about feeling self-conscious on camera and think about the students. Like she'd had so many years ago, they had a thirst to learn. She'd do her level best to help them with that.

"You're smart," she said to Nico.

He chuckled. "You're smarter."

"Ha!"

"You hacked my code, remember?"

"Only because you didn't focus on making it un-hackable."

"Believe me, I've learned my lesson. Plus, with you on the team now, our security testing protocol is un-beatable."

"Until some black hat hacker out there gets smarter than us."

"Never happen," he said.

"It'll definitely happen."

"Then we'll deal with it. We'll get smarter." He softly stroked her cheek with the back of his fingers. "To-gether, my love, we're unbeatable."

"Hey, Emilia?" Paris raised her voice from two seats down at their table.

Emilia looked her way.

There was laughter in her tone. "If Nico can bear to be parted from you, dessert bar?"

"Absolutely." Emilia set her linen napkin on the table and rose.

Nico was quick to reach over and pull back her chair.

"Want anything?" Paris asked Chase.

"Sure," he said. "Bring me whatever looks good."

Emilia rested her hands on Nico's shoulders. "You?" she asked him.

He turned his head to look up at her, love and imp-ishness shining in his eyes. "Surprise me."

* * * * *

HARLEQUIN

Dear Readers,

From the 1982 launch of *Silhouette Desire* to this month's final lineup, readers have turned to *Harlequin Desire*, where our sexy and successful alpha heroes have had hearts of gold, and our strong, independent heroines have been their equals. Now, after thousands of romances that have made us laugh, cry and swoon, Harlequin Desire's story is coming to an end.

We thank you, readers, for coming back to Desire month after month. For choosing your favorite authors and asking for more of their novels. If you're a fan of Brenda Jackson, you can look for her upcoming Harlequin books in the *Canary Street Press* imprint and in *Harlequin Special Edition*. If it's Maisey Yates's Western romances you crave, her books will also be available in *Harlequin Special Edition*. You can find backlist and new releases from all of Desire's talented authors by visiting their author pages on Harlequin.com.

And, if like most romance readers I know, you're always wanting more great reads, we'd like to introduce *Afterglow Books by Harlequin*, which launches at the end of January 2024 with stories from some of your favorite Desire authors as well as exciting new voices. These sexy, sizzling romances follow characters from all walks of life as they chase their dreams and discover that love is only the beginning. In early 2024, *Afterglow Books by Harlequin* will be available at a retailer near you.

Our readers and authors are at the heart of what we do, and we so appreciate your decades of support for Desire. We hope you'll join us as we begin a new chapter with *Afterglow Books by Harlequin*.

Sincerely,

Stacy Boyd
Senior Editor
Harlequin Desire